ACHILLES
ONCE AGAIN VISITS THE
REPUBLIC OF KOREA

Michael Klauke

Foreword by Craig Dworkin

COUNSELOR
BOOKS LLC

ISBN-13: 978-1699385678

ISBN-10: 169938567X

Counselor Books
counselorbooks.com

Contents

Foreword

Craig Dworkin

"Search for assistance and give victory to the Trojan horse.
I can buy mine for anyone."

—MICHAEL KLAUKE

There are some hundred translations of the Iliad into English (including versions by familiar, if unexpected names: Thomas Hobbes, William Cowper, William Cullen Bryant, Robert Graves). The tradition begins with a rendition "translated out of the French" by Arthur Hall in 1581, which opens: "I thée beseech, O Goddesse milde, the hatefull hate to plaine, / Wherby *Achilles* was so wroong, and grewe in suche disdaine."[1] For most of the centuries since the text was first written down, educated readers would have been schooled in Greek and had little need of vernacular versions; those that appeared—like the current one by Michael Klauke—say more about the culture of their particular historical moment than they do about Homer's heroic era. Highwater marks include George Chapman's 1611 version, which occasioned John Keats's famous sonnet "On First Looking into Chapman's Homer," an encomium to a book that allowed the Romantic poet to breathe the pure serene of the Aegean ether for the first time, and to imagine himself an imperial conquistador, when he "heard Chapman speak out loud and bold."[2] Keats, one might note, is enthralled with a two-hundred-year-old relic of the Elizabethan age, pointedly passing over Alexander Pope's stately version from the start of the eighteenth century. Pope balances and inverts, taking his time; his first book opens with the invocation "The Wrath of *Peleus'* Son, the direful Spring / Of all the *Grecian* Woes, O Goddess, sing!"[3] Chapman, in contrast, cuts to the chase, compacting: "Achilles' bane full wrath resound, O Goddesse, that imposd / Infinite sorrowes on the Greekes."[4] The parallel to Keats's ode would find a reader today enamored of James Morrice's 1809 Fleet Street translation in favor of those by Richard Lattimore (1951), Robert Fitzgerald (1963), or Robert Fagles (1990)—millions of paperback copies of which have been printed as part of the staple of required undergraduate college courses.[5] Surpassing the temerity of Stanley Lombardo's colloquial, even slangy, rendition (1997), Christopher Logue's *War Music*, published in serial installments over almost four decades, starting in 1959, sets one point by which to triangulate Michael Klauke's *Achilles Once Again Visits the Republic of Korea: An Unconventional Translation of Homer's* Iliad.[6] As far as possible from Lattimore, who hewed to a meticulous, word-for-word attention to the original, Logue—who never learned Greek—offers fragments of emphatic, insistently visual language, replete with confrontational anachronisms. He aims for the essence of the story's lessons rather than its specific language. Eschewing any apostrophe to the Muse, the first book of Logue's version, for instance, opens: "Picture the east Aegean sea by night. / And on a beach aslant its shimmering / Upwards of 50,000 men / Asleep like spoons beside their lethal Fleet."[7]

To set a second star by which to compass Klauke's project, consider David Melnick's *Men in Aïda*, which also presents an unconventional translation of the first books of the Iliad. Undertaking the inverse of Klauke's method, Melnick records a homophonic echo of the text, transcribing the Ancient Greek as if he were hearing English. Homer's opening invocation—"μῆνιν ἄειδε θεὰ Πηληϊάδεω Ἀχιλῆος /οὐλομένην, ἣ μυρί' Ἀχαιοῖς ἄλγε' ἔθηκε"—transliterates to something like <Menin aeide, thea, Peleiadeo Achileos oulomenen, he muri' Achaiois alge' etheke>, which Melnick renders as "Men in Aïda, they appeal, eh? A day, O Achilles! / Allow men in, emery Achaians. All gay ethic, eh?"[8] The verses that follow do indeed evince a gay period ethic: campy, pre-AIDS (the echo of the title's *AIDA* will shade from its opera-queen connotations within just a few years of publication), and leveraging the *homo-* in *homophonic* and the euphemism of "Greek love" to create a San Francisco bath-house orgy of exuberant, outrageous, linguistic play.[9] Thanks to the particles of Ancient Greek, such as the rhetorical markers γε and μεν (indicating intensive or restrictive senses, akin to *indeed* or *at a minimum*, and *on the one hand*, respectively), Melnick's book is filled with *gay men*. Such linguistic units are not themselves always translated directly, and part of the force of Melnick's project is to promote the implicit linguistic *structures* of the Greek language to the status of literary words. In the process, and for all the promiscuous sex of the narrative that ensues, Melnick is scrupulously faithful to the phoneme. Which is not to imply that his sounding of the Greek is rigid; in fact, part of the virtuosity of *Men in Aïda* lies in the variable palpation of subtle pressures put on phonemes and the faintest traces of aspiration and voicing that engrail and granulate the facture of the spoken language (for both Greek and English). But Melnick's auditory acuity and lexical ingenuity proceed with an extraordinary indifference to Homer's denotations.

If Melnick translates without regard to the semantics of the Greek words, Klauke's poetics—conversely—pursues a logic of pure denotation. As Klauke translates word-for-word between languages, using an online machine translation program, sound and connotation drop away as one definitional equivalent follows another. The results are paratactic, skewed, and intriguing. A stanza from BOOK V, for instance, reads:

I think the mineral bar is an excellent player.
Eye coker. Someone is headlining. So much
Blue Eastern boiling point give a pulley to someone's roots.
He and she are cutting.
The impossible falls to the ground. It is said.
Passing power with you.

Decontextualized enunciations, such as the first line above, invite readers
to imagine the circumstances under which they might be spoken, in a sort of
Wittgensteinian game of investigating language games.[10] The first statement here,
for example, is perfectly straightforward and grammatically correct, but what
exactly is a "mineral bar"? A counter made of granite, perhaps? Or a saloon offering
mineral water? Or maybe it's a limit-case standard by which to evaluate minerals,
like a point on the Mohs Hardness Scale. In any case, one would have to recon-
cile how such a thing could be an "excellent player," and whether that concluding
appositive refers to sports, music, machinery, social interactions, or something else
entirely. The abstracted generalizations of other lines elicit similarly imaginative
reconstructions: what might be a specific example of "passing power" or of a couple engaging in "cutting"? The possible answers are many, and all indeterminate.
Variations on this mode pair abstractions with specifics, as when "the impossible
falls to the ground." Yet other phrases are satisfying in and of themselves, possessing
the diminished reference and impacted sonic facture of early Language poetry; "eye
coker," for instance, could easily have come from an early poem by Bruce Andrews.
The phrase, in any case, undertakes a suggestive range with great economy, offering a
formal allegory of its own status. Simultaneously suspending conventional meaning
while also asking for an attentive reading—one focused on both sound and the visual
distribution of the letter *e* through a line balancing the descender of the *y* and the
ascender of the *k*—the phrase evokes the idiom *to cock an eye*, which paradoxically
denotes both a casual glance and rapt attention, knowingness and inscience.[11] The
incongruities of other passages are alternately poetic ("a skeleton with pipes of sorrow," to take an example from the stanza that follows) or humorous in their absurd
and surreal juxtapositions: "She protected your abdominal mind horse. / Da Nang
put a banana in his chest" (to restrict myself to an example from the same stanza).
    The irreverence with which Klauke renders a foundational, high-literary
work of the Western tradition—as well as the means by which he generates a con-
ventionally inadequate and inept translation of a classic text ("it is not my great
translation," the text itself confesses in BOOK II)—suggests a third precedent by
which to situate his unconventional edition. Amplifying the style of early internet
language in its incidental, clumsily automated, and vernacular forms, *soi-disant*
Flarf poetry emerged in the first years of the twenty-first century as the poetic

refraction of the linguistic detritus and ephemeral phrases proliferating in the age of spam, chat rooms, listservs, and internet searches.[12] Originally devised as a way to troll the commercialized poetry of the internet enterprise Poetry.com, the self-consciously "bad" and offensive verse produced to test the limits of acceptable poetry united a small coterie of writers. Following a methodology pioneered by Drew Gardener, who had used search-engine results to generate raw material that could then be subsequently crafted, "Google-sculpting" became one of the hallmarks of the short-lived subgenre. The collage of snippet previews offered by the search-results interface of companies like Google suggested both a form and an affordance: a model for the poem and a means of generating its language. In addition to this technique, Flarf poets not only shared an anti-aesthetic stance, and a tone of oddly caustic bathos, simultaneously both absurdist and condescending, but they also shared a lexicon of favored search terms (*deer, squid, popsicle, war, et cetera*). Michael Magee aggregated several of these keywords into his pastiche "Mainstream Poetry," which hangs its language on the mannequin of Amiri Baraka's "Black Art":

> Poems are, like, total bullshit unless they are
> squid or popsicles or deer piled
> on elk in the trunk of David Hasselhoff's
> Cutlass Sierra. Or black ladies dying
> of men leaving nickel hearts
> beating them down. MAINSTREAM poems
> and they are USEFUL — Great if you like
> having a Popsicle stuck in "I love George Bush," like,
> the popsicle squid goes "gong" when all the other
> dishes run out of toilet paper [....][13]

The absurd travesty of Klauke's revision of the Iliad bears an obvious resemblance to works like "Mainstream Poetry," but even more than any stylistic similarities, the tools of composition suggest a point of comparison. Working from a .txt file of Samuel Butler's 1898 Iliad, "translated into English Prose for the Use of Those Who Cannot Read the Original," and hosted by an early internet archive, Klauke used Google Translate to render the text in Korean, and then—specifying that the source text was still English, even though the Google AI would have otherwise recognized it as Korean—he used the engine to translate the result to Japanese before translating it again back into English. "Two e mama talks to Google and Google with geeks," as we read in BOOK XVII (with the suggestive proximity of *Greek* and *geek* in what sounds like a pastiche of the dozens). One should note that Google Translate does not include any version of Ancient Greek, even Attic, among its hundreds of languages, and so a machine translation of Homer would have to come always already translated to begin with. Giving a sense of the poles of Klauke's project, the passage from BOOK V quoted above, for instance, is the yield from his serial processing of the following paragraph by Butler:

> With this he hurled his spear, and Minerva guided it on to Pandarus's nose near the eye. It went crashing in among his white teeth; the bronze point cut through the root of his tongue, coming out under his chin, and his glistening armour rang rattling round him as he fell heavily to the ground. The horses started aside for fear, and he was reft of life and strength.[14]

Gary Sullivan defined "flarfy" as the willingness "to be wrong, awkward, stumbling, semi-coherent, fucked-up, un-P.C. To take unexpected turns; to be jarring. Doing what one is 'not supposed to do.'"[15] The attitude and style that result from such a deskilled aesthetic are evident even in the brief stanza quoted above, but the technical poetics implicit in the final formulation are in full accord with the position as well. Sullivan's final summation of violation — "doing what one is 'not supposed to do'"—points to a key tension in the use of Google products (a search engine, in the case of Flarf, and a translation engine in the case of *Achilles Once Again Visits the Republic of Korea*).[16] On the one hand, as I have suggested, these writers take advantage of the tools' affordances. With the present work, one doubts that Klauke would have translated Homer from English and back to English to begin with, precessing through multiple languages, much less willfully misidentifying one of them, without the implicit invitations of the translation-engine interface and its ability to accept cut-and-pasted text. At the same time, the project also emerges from a willingness to use the engine in ways that are surely not intended by the Google developers and engineers. Although automated tools metaphorically connote efficiency, uniform repetition, and economy—and while their utility might imply a single logical telos, with form following function—machines not only inevitably malfunction, but they encourage their own misuse.

Launched in 2006, Google Translate has grown from a curiosity to an application increasingly relied upon by both casual and commercial Web users; it fields hundreds of millions of queries in over one-hundred languages. Originally a discrete resource, it has now been integrated seamlessly and invisibly into other tools in the Google ecosystem to automatically render certain content in the user's preferred language. Although masked in the black box of proprietary secrecy, Google Translate operates in part through cumulative comparisons of input against tagged texts, previous user requests, and volunteered suggestions, calculating with statistically based wagers on any text that has no exact match in its vast databases. Since 2016, certain language pairs (including English and Korean) also use Neural Machine Translation algorithms, handling entire sentences and phrases rather than discrete words. The procedure, in short, has shifted from metaphrase (or μετάφρασις, the Greek translation of *translation*) to paraphrase. Self-organizing and learning over time, the engine adapts to data as it is used. Because of this new approach and other updates, projects like Klauke's, undertaken today, would be less surreal, humorous, and linguistically interesting than they once were. In other words, revisions to Google's algorithms are only "improvements" for certain kinds of tasks but they are detriments to poetry. Indeed, between the time of its composition and the time of its publication here, Klauke's experiment has become unrepeatable; one might read its uniterable style not so much as story of epic warfare in Ancient Greece as the time-capsule record of a brief moment in the history of twenty-first-century digital technology: a glimpse through the narrow window of the accelerated evolution of the internet.

Because Google Translate bases its results on comparisons between exact phrases, it relies heavily on texts that have been translated into numerous languages: the Bible, official documents issued by the United Nations and the European Union, and popular genre novels such as murder mysteries.[17] Its results are thus a projection of the cultural colonization of missionary proselytizing, national conflict, multinational corporate conglomerates, and narrative suspense. As anyone who has used it knows, the tool can appear miraculous in its effortless omniscience, but it can also veer from the mark (ἁμαρτάνειν [*hamartanein: to miss the mark*], as Homer would have recognized), with syntax, tense, and pronouns presenting particular stumbling blocks to its idiomatic accuracy. Only this year has the engine been adjusted to begin to counter gender bias in its results.[18]

Again, what might prove a fatal flaw for commercial or banausic applications is the very point from which the poetic misuse of the machine is leveraged. In terms of syntax, Homeric Greek is far more flexible than English. The opening sentence of the Iliad, for instance, is ordered object, verb, subject, possessives of the object; the second line reiterates "wrath" (as a morpheme in "οὐλομένην") and shifts the verb to the end for emphases: wrath sing goddess of son-of-Peleus of Achilles / ruinous[-wrath] it innumerable on Achaens pains laid. Personal pronouns, in Homeric Greek, themselves "indifferent to gender," inflect the text with interpretive style, since the nominative case designates what can speak and be spoken to—or what can be implored to ἄειδε, to put it poetically.[19] "In the Iliad they include only human beings, gods, and horses."[20] But the connotation of personality can be extended by the bard to compass objects that may serve as antecedents to personal pronouns, acknowledging a sense of awe (unlike the bards of medieval European epics, Homer does not personify weapons, save for the sacred spear of Achilles).[21] Verb tense and temporal markers shift repeatedly, sometime mid-speech. The Homeric epic, in short, is especially ill-suited to the Google translation treatment, even if Klauke had worked from the original. That, however, would not have been an option. Low demand aside, the lack of inclusion of Old Ionic can be read as an effect of the technical ways in which Google Translate operates and the statistical algorithms on which it relies. Not only is the corpus of Ancient Greek in multiple translations relatively small, and therefore insufficient for effective statistical analysis, but the formal base of Unicode mapping blocked out by modern Greek and unavailable to ancient dialects, together with the difficulty of accurate Optical Character Recognition of diacritics, such as rough breathing marks, exacerbate the difficulty of orthographic uniformity. Establishing the data to analyze, even if they were numerous enough, would be difficult to automate.[22]

The adaptive learning at the heart of Google Translate relies on recursivity, and the loop between computer programs and Homer is nicely recursive in its own way, sweeping Google Translate itself within the horizon of its own self-consuming circuit. In computing, a "Trojan Horse" denotes a type of virus. First used in the 1970s, the term was popularized by Ken Thompson, Bell Labs designer of Unix, and codified by MIT-trained hacker Dan Edwards: "a malicious, security-breaking program that is disguised as something benign, such as a directory lister, archiver, game or (in one notorious 1990 case on the Mac) a program to find and destroy viruses."[23] Although the story of the "Δούρειος ἵππος [Trojan Horse]" is best known from the later elaboration in Virgil's *Aeneid*, which dilates the mention of the ruse in the Odyssey, the Iliad conceals the kernel of the story beneath its narrative—a *mise-en-abîme* trojan horse of the Trojan Horse itself, discernable to canny readers alert to the lexical clues and already aware of how the war will end.[24] Users of Google Translate might do well to be just as vigilant. Thompson demonstrates the insidiousness of the Trojan Horse program in order to make the point that "you can't trust code that you did not totally create yourself."[25] Pitching from the level of compilable code to the level of the networked interfaces that now host and coordinate computer programs, one might apply Thompson's warning to the platforms of the internet in the age of Web 2.0 and its semantic extensions. Indeed, like all of the popular social-media sites, "products" such as Google Translate are themselves trojan horses. Although they ostensibly provide a service, the search results and translations of Google tools are in fact pixelated versions of the lashed and sanded lumber of a hollow equine statue concealing their real intent: to gather and commercialize user data (including the input text users submit for translation). More product than consumer, users are googled as much as they google, openly ushering its trojan horse behind otherwise impenetrably defended firewalls. Furthermore, once the born-digital text of Klauke's *Achilles* has been scanned and entered into the database of Google Books, it will complete the cannibalizing circuit and become a corroborating part of the very data from which it was written.

Sing, Google, of the wrath of semantics. Even, and especially, within the machine-readable Web.

1   *Ten Books of Homers Iliades, translated out of French, By Arthur Hall Esquire* (London: Ralph Newberie, 1581): [1].

2   John Keats: *The Complete Poems* (London: Penguin, 1983): 72.

3   *The Iliad of Homer, Translated by Mr. Pope* (London: Bernard Lintott, 1715): [1].

4   Geo. Chapman: *The whole works of Homer; prince of poetts: in his Iliads, and Odysses, translated according to the Greeke* (London: Nathaniell Butter, 1616).

5   Homer: *The Iliad of Homer translated into English Blank Verse by James Morrice* (London: John White, 1809); *The Iliad*, trans. Richard Lattimore (Chicago: University of Chicago Press, 1951); trans. Robert Fitzgerald (Garden City: Doubleday, 1963); trans. Robert Fagles (New York: Penguin, 1990).

6   Homer: *Iliad*, trans. Stanley Lombardo (Indianapolis: Hackett Publishing, 1997).

7   Christopher Logue: *War Music: An Account of Books 1–4 and 16–19 of Homer's Iliad* (Chicago: University of Chicago Press, 1997): 5.

8   David Melnick: *Men in Aida: Book One* (Berkeley: Tuumba Press, 1983): 1.

9   The local context is announced from the start of Melnick's project by "emery," which not only suggests the manicured grooming of an emery board but also evokes the East Bay town of Emeryville. One might compare the intersection of militaristic and erotic masculine soldiery in Melnick's translation with Rob Halpern's *Music for Porn* (New York: Nightboat Books, 2012).

10 One might note, in passing, that much of the poetic quality of Wittgenstein's own writing in English—the sense of conceptual frisson that arises from phrases that do not sound quite transparently natural—follows from the fact that his translators were not themselves fluent when they undertook the task.

11 See *Notes and Queries: Medium of Intercommunication for Literary Men, Artists, Antiquaries, Genealogists, Etc.* IX (14 April, 1860): 289; Eric Partridge: *A Dictionary of Slang and Unconventional English*, ed. Paul Beale (Oxon: Routledge, 2006): 234; *Oxford English Dictionary*, ed. John Simson and E. S. C. Weiner (Oxford: Oxford University Press, 1991): at *cock*.

12 The name seems to derive from the title of a Gary Sullivan poem, "Flarf Balonacy Swingle," which adapted the word from an online police blotter quoting a defendant's description of marijuana as "flarfy" [see Guatam Naik: "Search for a New Poetics Yields This: 'Kitty Goes Postal / Wants Pizza'," *The Wall Street Journal* (25 May, 2010)].

13 Michael Magee: "Mainstream Poetry: After Baraka," *Combo* 12 (Spring 2003): 31; Compare:

Poems are bullshit unless they are
teeth or trees or lemons piled
on a step. Or black ladies dying
of men leaving nickel hearts
beating them down. Fuck poems
and they are useful, wd they shoot
come at you, love what you are,
breathe like wrestlers, or shudder
strangely after pissing [....]

[Amiri Baraka: *Selected Poetry of Amiri Baraka / LeRoi Jones* (New York: Morrow, 1979): 105].

14 *Cf.* Samuel Butler: *The Iliad of Homer* (New York: E. P. Dutton & Co., 1923): 73.

15 Qtd. Dan Hoy: "The Virtual Dependency of the Post-Avant and the Problematics of Flarf: What Happens When Poets Spend Too Much Time Fucking Around on the Internet," *Jacket* 29 (April, 2006).

16 In the case of Flarf, a certain navel-gazing handwringing emerged over the use of a corporate tool, as if there were some modern writerly existence not implicated in, and complicit with, Capital—or as if the tools of other writers, availing themselves of proprietary word-processing programs, Remington typewriters, Pelikan inks (or any other writing instruments) were not the products of exploitive corporations [see, for example, Hoy, *op. cit.*.]. These critics seemed to forget that their sanctimonious denouncements were themselves aired over privatized, commercial networks of protocol, articulated by the switches and routers of multinational silicon valley conglomerates, powered by publicly traded utilities.

17 See Saanya Jain: "'Solving' Translation: Women's Labor on the Page," *The College Hill Independent* (8 February, 2019).

18 See James Kuczmarski: "Reducing Gender Bias in Google Translate," https://blog.google (6 December 2018).

19 George Melville Bolling: "The Personal Pronouns of the Iliad," *Language* 22: 4 (October–December 1946): 341; *cf.* Bolling: "Personal Pronouns in Reflexive Situations in the Iliad," *Language* 23: 1 (January–March 1947): 23–33.

20 Bolling, "The Personal Pronouns," 341.

21 *Ibidem*, 342.

22 Google Translate does offer Latin, which perhaps benefits from a narrower dialect variance than Ancient Greek but is included thanks to the mass of bureaucratic government translation from Italian and other diplomatic languages generated by the Vatican, where it survives as a living language. One might compare the repeated rejections of Ἀρχαία ἑλληνική as a Wikipedia language [see the discussion and documentation at https://meta.wikimedia.org/wiki/Requests_for_new_languages/Wikipedia_Ancient_Greek].

23 See Paul A. Karger and Roger R. Schell: "Multics Security Evaluation: Vulnerability Analysis," *ESD-TR-74-193*, Vol. II (June, 1974): 60; Ken Thompson: "Reflections on Trusting Trust," *Communications of the Association for Computing Machinery* 27: 8 (August, 1984): 761–3; *New Hacker's Dictionary*, ed. Eric Raymond after Guy L. Steele (Cambridge: MIT, 1991).

24 See George Fredric Franco: "The Trojan Horse at the Close of the 'Iliad'," *The Classical Journal* 101: 2 (December–January 2005–6): 121–23; the entire poem, one might recall, ends on the word "ἱπποδάμοιο" [of horses]. Klauke's translation, ironically, includes "Trojan horse" over 170 times, despite the absence of the phrase in Homer.

25 *Op. cit.*, 763.

Introduction

Michael Klauke

This book is a rare (if not unique) example of a text that was translated from English into English.

The idea came about one day when I was experimenting with Google Translate. It occurred to me that it might be possible to run an existing English text through several iterations and then back to English in a way that would produce a humorous and perhaps oddly compelling "translation" of the original. After many tries, I stumbled across a pattern that produced what were, to my mind, both extremely funny and interesting results. Armed with that particular algorithm, I began experimenting with excerpts from a number of well-known works of literature to see what I could come up with.

The pattern I discovered involved my copying a segment of text that was in English, pasting it into Google Translate, and translating it into Korean. Next I copied and pasted the resultant Korean translation into the source section of the program and then directed the program to translate that into Japanese. However, at this point I changed the process in a way that made it a bit less straightforward. I asked the program to translate English into Japanese, even though it was in fact translating Korean into Japanese. The Japanese translation it came up with was then copied and pasted into the program and translated into English.

I'm sure the absurdities that made their way into the final English version were due to the "confusion" the program encountered on being told it was translating English into Japanese, when it was actually translating Korean into Japanese. In other words the results only came about because I managed to find a way to trick the program. In hindsight this seems like an appropriately digital equivalent of what the Greeks did with the Trojan Horse—getting a desired result by disguising something as something else. It also shows that a sophisticated program can be fairly easily deceived, or at least made to do something it wasn't designed to do.

The reason I wound up using Korean and Japanese is due to the hit-and-miss method I employed to come up with the process. I thought the results might be a little more surreal if I used languages that employ a different alphabet than English. After many tries with different combinations, including Hebrew, Russian, Chinese, etc., I finally settled on the English-Korean-Japanese-English path as yielding the most interesting phrases or wording.

I ran excerpts from a number of famous works through this process, and once I started using it on Homer's Iliad, I became driven by the idea that I should take the entire text of this timeless classic and turn it into a work of absurd literature with tenuous connections to the original source. I was also inspired to take on the project because of all the poetic "accidents" that made their way into the results. Each new paragraph that was translated yielded sentences and phrases that I was confident have never been written before, in any language.

What finally resulted was not really a translation or another version of the original but something that seemed like the text had been run through a blender, coming out the other side clipped, truncated, and turned on its head. I found it fascinating that although I was working with a prose version of the story, the program changed it into a much more figurative style, reminiscent of the original epic poem. Many of the character names remained intact at times but then in other instances were altered in bizarre ways. Somehow Jesus and Barack Obama both managed to make their way into the story. New words came into being, and often a word appeared randomly written in all caps.

As for the plot itself, it became unmoored in the opening paragraph and quite frankly never reappeared. With that in mind, perhaps the best way to appreciate this book is to dip into it at random places. Since there is no real linear plot, there is no reason to read it from beginning to end, as almost every paragraph or stanza can seem like a small found poem that could exist independently.

The following brief excerpt and its subsequent translation give a good example of the transformation that took place.

ORIGINAL TEXT:
Silver-footed Thetis answered, "My son, be not disquieted about this
matter. I will find means to protect him from the swarms of noisome
flies that prey on the bodies of men who have been killed in battle.
He may lie for a whole year, and his flesh shall still be as sound
as ever, or even sounder. Call, therefore, the Achaean heroes in assembly;
unsay your anger against Agamemnon; arm at once, and fight with might
and main."

TRANSLATED TEXT:
Telacey Blue replied, "My child, it depends.
Problem. What you want to protect is that you want.
I stroke a human body.
When lying to you within a year, his body is still noisy.
Someday, or even challenge. Achaean is on Facebook.
Retaliate with Aga-man. I crawl on the pearl at the top.
Also the main."

A couple of months after I finished this translation of the Iliad, in the fall of 2018, I tried the same protocol on a new text and discovered that Google had made adjustments or updates to the program, because it no longer produced the same kind of results. I even tried redoing a few of the older translations to see if it would duplicate them, and the results were quite different. The new results were somewhat repetitious and rather dull—all of which means that the exact process is lost forever.

The reader might want to know how much editing I did with the final text that was produced by the translation program, and the answer is: very little. I thought it was important to present the final version with as few changes as possible, to keep it true to the random aspect of the project. I did standardize and clean up the punctuation in places where it interfered with the flow of the text (like missing periods or commas, or misplaced quotation marks, for example), but the words and the word order were not changed at all. I can state that the final version is 99 percent exactly as the translation program gave it to me.

One reason for undertaking this project was the hope that it would yield results that were absurd enough to be humorous, although not so far afield that readers would totally lose connection with the original source. But as I got deeper into it, translating this text began to feel like being an explorer, but of a never-before-seen language. It was as if the program was creating uncharted terrain in front of me and I had to find my way through it. As I read the results, I found myself literally thinking in ways that I had never thought before.

The unusually evocative aspects of the text run through every paragraph. Some lines are downright silly or surreal: "Chest, get off at the grassland without it, Megi Sue ripped barbecue" [Book XV]; or "Even if my mother enters Jove's mouth, I do not like heavy stairs" [Book XVI]. There are a great many lines that read very much like conventional poetry: "From the morning to the morning, I will shed a day" [Book I]; "Our wicked road is a solitary road" [Book X]. And then there is the occasional bit of gibberish: "Hulxon Juff e food biphon omnibus" [Book XIV].

Some lines somehow call to mind more contemporary events, like this one that seemed to eerily bring up images of the 9/11 terrorist attacks: "Madness in the Middle East will you truly fly an airplane?" [Book XXIII]. And there are even numerous passages that read like peculiar maxims, such as "Do not forget headcaution if you are troubled with your head" [Book IV], or "Take your vitality and be awesome as a solo lover and a witch" [Book IX]. The text offers an amazing array of pleasures and discoveries. It is filled with both humor and a strange beauty all its own.

I hope you will enjoy your own experience of exploring this unique text, and I'll leave you with a quote from Book XIII: "The Universe and the Universe and the Universe, it is hidden in your hand."

"You struggled and threw out words"

— BOOK XVI

Book I

Goddess, O, I separate Achilles tendon of Peleus.
Countless soldiers in Achaids. Many forgiveness lives.
A lot of lovers who greeted by Hades.
Jordan's listening,
Your nutritionist Atreus's child and great assets are first,
It is different.

So, do you think that it is in the temple? You,
A child of Jove and Leto. I bet a reverse Han,
Atreus's sons,
Mr. Chryses worker. Then Chryses has become Hansen.
You take care of the big daughter.
Body length: It also invites the circle of Apollon.
Who is reliable?
Two of the two lumps Atreus.

"The sons of Atreus." All other Achinese people will house the Shinto.
"People who live in the Olympic Games put the Preasis in the jar.
There is nothing in your house. It takes the inner shell into the pull-in body.
She asked Jolo's son Apollo."

Then it is not a cry.
Invite the colonel. Also,
He has a grudge. "Non."
You are above us
Already. You and your financial affairs are beneficial to you.
Yes. I pooled her. She lives in us despite Argos.
We encourage you to wear the bed.
Sofa; there are more.
You.

I will hand it that nice again. Not even one person.
Ask the Apollo to the crying sea front.
Lovely one Leto is a dignity. "It will be my end."
Chryse and bold Cilla protected with Tenedos,

You map Smint to pain thou. I know your personality,
Your Happy B Saw So Son So So Bryan Towerwarser,
Reach out.
Danaans.

Glyph sucks air. You are
Citric acid.
Shoulders, shoulders, shoulders, shoulders, waist,
That's it. That is,
Everyone wishes to give you flowers.
Crowd. Please be glad to see No Sand and Sunny Edge.
But I dislike it to all and all.
Absence of a child who died only one day.

On 9th we will dedicate arrows to you,
It will not get hot.
You have killed yourself by everyone.
They. Well then, you are blowing a rose.

I said, "Son of Atreus. We will move on to Kochi immediately.
Since we were defeated,
Only one time ahead of schedule. You will get it originally.
Dream of the dream (Don Dong Da).
Apollo can not speak much.
We do not offer herachrome (hecatomb), and
I hate salt of positive chlorine.
All of us are nearby."

His son Calchas, the most wise,
Do you know current and future things? That
Are you anywhere (Achaeans). Is Indian a day (Ilius)?
Phoebus Apollo praises that. When
Tell all truth and intent of sin.

"Asian countries I love in heaven, I will go to you on a stomach.
Apollo River, Iowa. Considering before, United Alliance.
I can wait progressively your words and actions.
I,
Ackine is welfare. A normal person can not say no.
Miki Surface Ryu.
Well then. That's you.
Please."

The Achilles heel replied, "I,
If you get into the sky, you
Do not forget to give something to us.
To walk on your own face only.
Well, it is a person who knows Argeman John Jean.
Achaeans."

Talk to you Omiya. "I am fortunate for 'Shinto silver'
On his or her body, wearing his clothes, someone Agamemnon.
To go well,
Cover her. To you,
I will support other people. Let's appeal Danain from regurgitation.
Agamanon gave her a girl without a monetary body.
My father, Chryse, borrows a bold hecatomb. That is,
Please."

Agamemnon broke up. Someone's heart,
I made a big deal of fuss in Cali Proposition (Calchas) with a big fuss.
"A bad line viewer, you will not have another one.
However, there are bad examples. If it's you,
You are the Top Good Pass Doddler. Now it is a bowler.
Between Da Nang, and I suffer from Apoloro.
Mommy to weigh the cheese. I set it up.
My heart knows her. I like her more.
My side job is terrible for her figure,
Function, understanding, and personality. I will go to you.
In my case, for you.
I am not an ARGIVES co-symbol devoted to helping me.
One. Usability you, my deposit is.
I bought it."

The Achilles heel replied, "A favorite man, Alews's noble child.
On in lute you, do the people of Acacia do another sharing? We are.
You can not protect one. We are instant people in town—
That's it. We can give you the power.
Image. Please give a woman to you.
We need four out of three attitudes to push our Troy town against the children."

Agaman Neu. "Achilles, look, I'm impressed.
It is pastry past you, it is not a confection.
Me. Do you know?
Who is recruiting that girl? The Alesians will try to go this time.

To exchange my desire for a process, I try to conscious myself.
The delicious water of Azelsu Nanly Leez has that part.
Ogoker. But that is our positive right. That,
Currently, I carry the ship to the sea and make her a victory.
Obviously; Hectam recruiting Chryseis.
Also, more Gotoda our most important person this Accord,
Or Idomeneus, or you, yourself, the son of Peleus,
To sacrifice us,
God."

Achilleas sounds bigger. "You are lawless and true.
And the desire for gain. Will you get Achaeans?
Did you get involved? I'm here.
Pastor Troy is wrong with me.
You are short of my height.
Secondary word of Phthia: Here is Wie Dash here.
Space, acid, and win in. We are waiting for you, unfortunate circumstances!
We will take your enjoyment from the Trojan horse.
Your strange horn and Menelaus. I deny you.
I,
Associate me with Achaids. Achaens commits suicide of buzzer,
I like you when Troy's life.
You can ask for a better part of the cold. When to share,
It is worth your effort. And I can do it over again.
My back can be obtained by me.
Thanks. I returned to Phthia this time. You
Come home with you, I am with you.
You have gold bullion."

Agaman answered, "You give me the faith to you.
Nega. I have helped anyone.
Jove, a hero of a transformationist. Here, yeah.
It is perhaps to move you. Idolung,
Are you pardoned? Na Yo Won Heaven No? I go home.
Your abs and arteries are to maintain Myrmidons. Nadok.
To you, degree of degree. Liar: Phoebus Apollo
Put Chryseis between my father and me,
But I am with you.
You love you
Compare with fellow friends."

Wear another person sideways, and
Please protect the son of Atleus and confirm the division.
Do not forget your heart.
That Cali, Mineralba falls in heaven (Lord blessed her).
She always loves you with Jiruha, and she son of Peleus,
Confused people.
I saw her. Achilles is a playrada.
Her eyes made her mineral birdie adul al. "Why?
Looking at the self of Agamenon,
The son of Atleus? Tell me. You should pay that person.
It is rude for me."

And Mineralba said, "I am composed of heaven.
Maintain you as a caliper. The master admires you, everyone is Hearn bone.
We play cricket even though we attack attack by this word. He is a rail.
Negative one trade woman. Please wait for you.
You can receive a gift.
Turn on current desires. Also,
To obey."

"The goddess," replied Alexis.
"You are a command. It is the best sound now.
That is a pure husband."

Do you know?
The mineral bar is punished. Next is the next one again.
The other god is Olympos, and to the house of Joe who is not the place of Beaufort.

But the son of Peleus initiated the son of Alease again.
But my husband. "Drinker,
You can not go out with another host from you.
We tell you.
I value yourself.
Who is your motif? You dislike yourself three times.
You are a king and a king. Previous page.
You should still continue treatment. You are not.
Pulse Seco, my soul.
We will recruit parent stems.
Mountain-Road a fumbling arrangement of leaves and shells of ax,
The reprint house and the guards corps of Akha (Achacs) are not yet collapsed yet.
Follow the command of heaven—Do you silence to be cautious?
From you,

Who is your person?
Allergy prophylaxis.
Please do not forget your feelings even for a moment,
Achaeans."

So Peleus's son—bestedded the throne.
The son of Atreus,
They are different things. The next uprose movement is a tongue Nester,
How to use Pirans
Even more sweet. Men of Tarnana Autonomous Generation from Pylos.
I come back from my side, and this time is the third time.
The acts of all truth and sin are as follows: —

"The truth is," Big fears Achaean is a befallen.
"I like Plymouth and Trojans are insult.
Between the two,
It is very restful. I have lots of Niagara.
Indonesia. A friend I met with.
If there are people bigger than that, you refuse.
I got Pirithous and Dryas.
Egyptian, Euradius, New Polyphemus, Theceus,
Son of filthy fellow Aegeus. The wisest person.
At this point,
Mountain yaman has the highest priority.
Your Philos came there and ropeda.
Please do your best with me. I live now.
I can hear it
By them. That is really dangerous.
Method. There is something you need.
I am energizing the people of Ackae.
Between you and other people,
Jove's Rowa Kel gets honored with Agamemnon.
You can afford in love with you, for your mother. No
More people went down this river. Son Atreus,
Please check your calipers. Along with Achilles.
You want an Akahan for you to fight."

Agaman answered, "Teacher, you do not know this fact.
This person energizes us. This week,
You, all of you, anyone, anyone.
Divine forgery,
Then where is defense permitted at all times?"

Achilles is a rejection. "I played beef.
I will exercise you all in one day. I command another person.
It is another kind of seed. I,
Your heart—I do not have a boyfriend with this guy.
It was given to the sedans. Everything
I was helpless and fell down from my belly. Troublesome.
Boyle / Giustic; negative, my window is your peer."

You are like butter.
Deployment of the Achaean. The child of Peleus is raku.
Menoetius and his son and his wife and abdomen,
I added Agamemnon and selected 20 passengers.
Nom. Hensenburg and Hessen welcome
Believe. And Rate Leece confronted.

When it is right, I headed to the sea on top. But,
The sons of Atlas were doing legitimate investigation. That's Pata.
Please throw yourself in the ocean more. Later, he offered hecatombs.
Yado and Chlorine in Badaiga and its smoke,
Tears strike along with the smell of sacrifice.

Well then, I will do the same. But Agaman
To you, Chelsea McDonald,
Megan and squalth Talthybius and Eurybates. I said, "Gala."
Tears of Peleus's son Achilles; "Catch Bride's Siaz by hand.
She is a date wailer here. You have no grace.
I'm squeezing her more strongly."

I broke up with more survival, more distant parts.
Please do not forget.
Myrmidons belly. You know yourself.
Please make yourself a distraction. You.
Both of us are sincere, and are being shunned.
However, we are welcoming, with the myth of the Meininger
Man. "Nearby multi gas. I will not tolerate internal combustion.
You are cheering for the butsys. Love, Patroclus, she deto.
I gave them that woman and said, the witness of the worshiped gods.
Philippine human body, and Agamann Norton,
It is necessary to save incandescence from ruin.
The stare you looked at. Agamanon is secreted.
Alexander,
You have a warranty."

Patroclus is its great. Let's date Briseis.
She tells her to beat her.
That forgot the girl. Swing,
It goes away together in the ocean of Hoorge.
To infinite waste of things. Please help with you.
I heard a mother behind him, "Mother." You knew fate.
"Kill in a little season; pretty warm, kind, pathetic job (Jove).
It was true. Yes. Agamenon, son
Atreus, in love with me without hurting me."

If you listen boldly, anyone can do it.
Father is father. Straight line,
She is a guide dog.
By that, I hurt my ear,
"His son is twitching? Are you nearby? Expectation Ji Mara.
Agavehall with us."

Achilles can get a drop. "You are useless.
Do you already know well? We will apply for Tebec United.
Take the victory and hit the previous article. Ackines Sons
Position comrade positively, love Chryseis.
Agedmen's meed; But Chryses, Apollo clergy is a bat.
You take care of the big daughter.
Weight: You can have other holes of Upon Pon.
It is reliable to find Achaeans and all
Your son's son."

Achaeans accused Johngrad.
Invite the colonel. Also,
He has a grudge. I'm fine.
Apoloro who loved too much chased him. Swing,
God opposes each other, people good night.
Alternate, crazy.
Achaeans. A line maker with knowledge filled with mind advertised it.
Please do not forget us to be the oracle of Apollo.
Atreus is gaining, and more and more.
Well then, one day. Achaeans are now aiming for girls.
Tell the god to Chryse, and the sacrifice;
Please do not disturb your daughter.
Achaeans water you.

"My lover knows me.
You play a single play, please.
Jove. At the Father's house,
Are you confused?
Juno, Neptune, Pallas Minerva,
High level. I will make you a minor measure.
Old Fu is a new club,
Aegaeon, finally escape. Other
Saturn's son, spiritual light was placed from another god.
You tell.
There is nothing useless for you.
A lover's lover.
I will give you the ocean repayment.
Agaman Stanction
The Achaeans's highest."

Thetis says, "My son Via is about to drop the item to the yard.
Or wet you. Can you receive your spam for free?
Each other's grief, traitor. Ah, Nana,
The longest longevity and friends.
To dislike it. Originally
The wolf's eyes are in this. If,
Please listen to our prayers.
Achaens will go with you with you.
Jove, Oceanus, Ethiopia inward facing, Acetic acid,
Other Shinto shrines came near. Roger Golf.
You; I, I."

I made her well on this day.
That is not it. Meanwhile Hillary arrived in Chryse along with the core of Haig.
Do not forget your recruitment.
You are in appellate status. Who will garage the forest?
Please do not forget to attack somewhere.
Her lie. I made a feldshoron you inherited.
His hawsers. In order to protect the coast, we finished landing the monster.
Receive Apollo; Chryseis is carrying her,
The ransdens to transport her in her hands. "Chris," I was told.
"So, you should pray again.
Sacrifice Apollo to miss Danaans.
Arguments encourages to receive sorrow."

I dedicated it to her.
You made Haye Kam all yours second.
God. Did you think that you would wipe your hands?
Aie, Chris borrows the victim and shouts loudly.
Solder.
"Inka. Protect Chryse and bold Cilla and hit Tenedos with your power.
To energize
Achaeans, this time, listen, protect these two people.
Front line disease of Danaans."

Glyph sucks air. Hamburger
Bori — multicolored, fry and go back to you.
I killed the victim so much. When you try it,
Strongly set the basic body from the layer of the strata.
Place it on the dish, in addition Chryses is a desperation for trees. And
The young man stands up in Igarashi.
I disturb you. Happy G Tao.
I will eat the meat on the inside.
When paying its attraction, its benefits are saved,
Get ready to leave them at the end.
Everyone refused all people.
Nobody is here.
Missing—to eat and regain water,
Everyone is that drink.

All day longing is hard work.
You can enjoy it.
Kisou; But, you have left the hospital.
Cosmic ray track cable,
Child in the morning, the wall of the ring of the rose, the spaceship again.
It opposes the Achaean host. Apollon is entering process.
Anyone can ask. Momentum,
It is not a high price going out with the wind,
She is making noise about her behavior. They
At the Achair's Plaza,
She knows her strong Sodog.
Her road and fate of fate and ballot camera.

But that is disappointing. Still.
At the prestigious general meeting, and before the fight, Merge, Ghost, God, Ah,
Shoot.
It is an obstacle to your heart and war.

Now 12th Itun Pos (Olympus),
And Jove spreads India to you. Tethys discards the child.
Search her. You remained in the sea.
Heaven above the wolf.
Saturn's son mixed up and fitted to Good Great Lively Lively Line. She is ours.
Among them,
She takes her nose.

"Jove you.
You have a dreamlike dream.
Please give it. Please dismiss the Agamenon cow.
Hell with her. John Olympic Juin in Good.
Search for assistance and give victory to the Trojan horse.
I can buy mine for anyone."

Job is silent.
The twentieth. Inclination,
Your head she showed, and ignore it.
You are not anyone.

So,
She was with her and she did.
Her journaling consecutive theory; the next girl is always my pre-existing disease
Prevention.
Other gods will not help Trojans. Once again
I know she was. I,
Son and take-away opening. I believe in you.
You have God. I can not refute.
Listening to my words, stepping on, I can not do what I say.
Inner head.

Appeal to the angel's son,
The vast Olympus is crazy with mercy head.

When planning contradictory, they are healthy.
The house, goddess stop Olympus's clearance in the meantime.
Depth of the sea. The temple exploded.
It was not decadent. Who are they?
But all people start this garbage. There, he,
But he and his grandfather's daughter (Merman's daughter).
Does Estrus (Thetis) tell her?
For you. She cried, "New star story.

Have you received your counseling now? You always solve the problem.
Naito disease secret, and that's still so.
One maddy in your chest."

"Juno," reported the exploitation of the newborn.
"Do all the advice. I will put you inside of me.
I am doing it. You are here waiting for you.
Everyone, God or human, everyone wants more.
Disorder the problem."

"Two of Saturn," Talking Ya?
"Me? Match and question? Nothing. I can take your path on all days.
Daughter of the loved one Tetes (Thetis),
You are perfect.
I want this to be remembered. You will receive me.
Offer Nürburgring to you.
The Achaean's back."

"Oh," Jove said, "You certainly will not.
Out. I know about you.
More, and you will go more enthusiastically. You know this story in reality.
I am not happy. Hold your shoulder and dedicate to you.
Please connect me to the first place.
For you, for you."

Enono will be her wealth herbs without grass.
It is opaque. However, principals of heaven and earth will refrain from holding:
First-come, first-Served.
Jove's trade worker Vulcan. In this game start game.
Please enter Juno. I was told, "Please wait.
2 packs are discarded and nondeterministic and heavenly Purgeda
Fischer. We solicit late and we,
I enjoyed it at our meeting. I will solve my mother's help.
I dislike you and other people more.
Father Jove, please kill her.
Orange Saint, please abandon us all to our place.
You have a tough person.
It is not a good breast awareness with us."

Two couples and two husbands
It is my mother's hand. "I love you, cheerful supporters."
It's the best. I love you. You are very grateful.

Give a treble. I am Spar Jad, I will doll.
It is completely different from Jove. To recap at the very beginning,
I want you. He makes me speak.
Text section. From the morning till the morning, I will shed a day.
It falls on the island of Lemnos. And, I,
It was born in that.
Me.

She laughed at her, and her son fell down.
Owned. Balcon (Balkan) has moved out with a mixing bowl (mix bowl) falling out.
The man who is there, and then,
Everyone is the truth.
Sky.

The sun settles in the sun,
Everyone helped everyone. Apollo,
I hear mute,
They react with each other. However, the shining of the sun,
I am afraid to protect you.
He deals with excellent skills. Ultra Jove,
The beauty of panting is always a valid fact. Over
That is disastrous.
They have a seat.

Book II

Now the other innocent gods and other gods will not dry.
But Jove can not do it. Given the collapse Achilles and thinking about the way,
People of Achaeans have many people. Last,
It is a sense of value for you that will make your dreams come true.
Please give me a word to you. "A dream to attach, Barroga.
Agun's Eucharist Argamion,
I will chase you now. I will receive an immediate red carpenter.
Do not forget to take away weapons. There is no case where it was placed further.
Nova: Please sacrifice your temper.
Troy."

Tell your feelings.
The Achaeans's belly. Atreus's son,
Tears are comfortable in that part. I pulled your tree hair.
Neleus's son Nestor and his hair, Agamemnon this,
That is: —

"You are Jagon, the son of Atreus, his cheerful person.
I am also interested in you. Heard
I am Jove and I'm Meshinger Londa.
Let's think of you and you. You are pursuing it.
You are calling Troy. That place,
I will split the anomaly more and proceed. The Lord is dead.
Beyond her heart, Via puts that Trojan horse
Jupiter. Please do not forget
You."

My mind will move on to the next. And surely things thought.
Do not take the Eucharist. By the time,
Invite the Pream. However, the heart was forgotten even a little.
Jove shows that Danaans is having other serious problems.
Troy. Fresh message
He said,
You have a useless outpatient. You are.
He warmly applauds him, he is guarding the Park.

Shoulder; It is not a waste of his father.
Achinese's abs has appeared.

Spacious Olympus direction.
Agamanon was relieved.
It is useless if there is an entire white paper at home.
People dream. But you called it.
Elders and mistakes from the belly of King Nestor of Pylos.
You have a benefit.

My buddy said,
"That face and person is a spell of Nestor." This
End in hair. "You are a child of Gola, a child of Atreus. One,
They are taught,
Please stop it. Kill me only once,
Jove, think about taking a child with him.
You. Akka straight up a parlor.
Use Troy. We will not divide it into more strange things. Juno,
Trojan horse taught me
Jove's hand. Know. That dream is resolved
About me. We are reasonable that your descendants will decrease. But,
I hope you will satisfy my desires,
I am angry with them and I will take you. Does someone see you?
You and you are wearing film."

At that time, all the genitals including Pylos yellow crown in Nestor
And, "My friend said that.
People of Arkaiveth (Argails), Ackine and others,
I love my dream.
It has nothing to do with anyone. But I am real.
We are Middle. We know people.
Weapon."

In India, other people are accepted.
The word of Agamann of tea is in love with pure things.
People are challenging him in the soul league.
In the second half,
The flower seems to be stuck with mine note. A lot.
Learn
Coast of wide crystal shape, seeing them San Bunsson, Meg,
Try the future of Jove. People who came back.
Mitchenlan's, and the earth is the root of a man's brassie.

People were found. Even if 9 people are not mouth,
Throwing sogan to you,
I love you.
Agaman Onee Water Macdonald. Code
Valentine, Jove is indebted to Mercury.
Argus, guide and guardian's slayer. Mr. Murakuri will be Ferrerros.
Atelus Pelops.
Atleus was with you.
Reduce the burden of Agamemnon in your turn.
As expected by all Argos and Old Dodds, I will reply next.
Argives.

"Inner," I said. "Spirit, seed of fire, hands of heaven,
It is irrelevant to me. A sorry job asked you.
Appeal to the child to the town of Priam,
You will be like Argos.
I will excuse a lot of people. A yacht magazine could not be done.
We sacrifice a number of people and admire a lot of people.
Tension. You will not speak.
My husband is once mid-grade and forgiveness is late.
Exponentially; not yet. Make
The Akae (Achaeans) and Trojan horse unleashes a solemn Andal.
Their numbers are Mama Trail Horses.
We are ten companies. Let's think about more.
We went home.
We have many things.
I can not have my account bet. Is there.
It does not move in a foreign body.
Kill Ilius's Bruges Wansian. Jove's ninth section is between;
I hate our Baba. There is no more noise.
We love you.
We are at the end now. You,
We will fight. We will sail the earth.
Mala to date Troy."

This is,
You are not negotiating insurance for Agaman. People express.
And the rocky part of Ikari Sea (Icaria Sea) and South,
The wind is tired from the sky clouds. Or
The wind turns muddy and gives voices and voices.
A loud noise is shaking.

There is dust behind. No one is difficult.
Together between the sea lorocos. No one got it.
First breast. Please tell us your opinions and impressions: Create your own review.
You and Welkin are pleased. Truly.
Da first.

You are Arguments,
No lucky name. Juno said to Minerva, "Ayas, a daughter of assistance,
Jove, unwearable, Argives pulled out of the house on the ground.
It turned the Prayum and Trojan horse into the light of the future.
You can have herren. Because,
Troy, collapsed from the assembly? The organizer is Javaloro.
They have a process and someone did
Ocean."

Minerva is enthusiastic about her. She is
The highest rank of the Olympics,
Achaeans. There are enthusiastic friends there.
Chaos. Please prepare your hand. I regretted.
And Mian. She spoke it closer. "Telesis, Kochi and his son
Laertes, are you your Barro Ayal?
Do you drink beer? Play a premium.
Trojan horse, many people know Helsin.
Leave the Achaean house from Tsai. Purifier,
You step by step,
Dedicate you to the sea."

Her voice is a girl's voice.
GROOIN MONDOUG GOOD GOOD START. Boyfriend, Man of Ithaca,
I will be pleased, openly waiting there.
Direct from Agamemnon and they, uncertain forces.
Staff. Long-lasting for the people of Loagaga this day.

It refused it.
The teacher said, "This flight is private, and
I will help you recruit people and also to your articles. You do not deny it.
The warm heart of Agamunkun. Let's beat us.
To disagree, I visit Ackine. We did not have us all.
At that time, I am angry.
Hachiwo to us. Ikrago of the pride of the king.
Jove is with them."

But there is not such a thing.
Where were you?
Peace, peace, and better human language. You ask.
"He is not a soldier. You have no contradiction. We have nobody.
Wang Yela. More acquaintance first son,
Who are you?
A large house of one household you."

Let's memorize it.
What is association?
Actions on the coast of supporting heaven are all.
The sea is sunlin.

In your place,
But Thersites steps on the tongue who can not unwill enemies.
A lot of words, and dishonest things; Mitchell's Ryugaku,
Do not forget everything, winding around him.
I will do Achaons well. Everything was lost.
Troy—instantaneously the feet of the feet one year, one else's clause,
It is rumbling in the scolding struggle. Comment,
It took a head over it. Achilles and Ray Trisies,
Please do not forget.
Controversy. But you are not.
Faculty of fight against Agaman. Achaeans is angry with Ganpogo.
That person gets hurt while unaware of the child of Atreus.

I was told, "Agamemnon." Are you doing better now?
"Your embryo is handled as Kiyo at any time.
We choose to choose you. Do you want to protect even more?
Gold, Trojans do not hurt your body.
Where is the other Acca India? Or a girl's permission.
Do you play Hidden Go? You, Acka Life Master,
It is midfetal. Ohitul abuse,
You are deprived of our house and leave Troya's friends here.
Do you know who we are?
You do not. Achilles female is the best man.
West Bank of the Jordan River. I think the fundamental strength.
That Okires shows warm and original signs. Boys and girls, boys,
Atreus, you should not keep silent."

So, Thersites, however, Rate Leasys immediately placed the book there.
It is safe. "Please check your tongue, Thersites," be be, "and babble

Maddy again. Make it with the prince.
You. Whether there are living things with children in the past.
Atleus. Have them make fun of me.
I commute a violent commute at home. We progress the situation here.
Achaeans is a good successor type.
Danaans did something with Agamemnon.
Does he insult other phases? I will talk about you. You choose.
You will hear it again.
Another thing about Telemachus is adultery.
You are Digimon Gekko, not your house.
To you, this is a backlight."

And fold the shoulder blade and shoulder blades.
He fell. Graduated from Golden's kingdom Ipi.
Recruit people lined up behind.
I smoke tears from my eyes. People fainted.
But one forgot him.
"Rate Leeds has upgraded many good days to peaceful parliament with peace
Of Mind.
Argives, please do not say anything.
With prating over colleague's mouth. I will make a round trip.
He."

I will talk later. Well then, you sing Mineral verbs.
Exemplified representations and familiar exist.
Think of equal facts. Other,
All sex and ethics, just like that.

"Agamenon (Agamemnon), Ackine (Achaes) are everyone
Human race. You waste every single person.
Argos, you are prepositioning in advance.
Troy, and they set the gravity
At home. I missed it.
One person dislikes harassing, not alone.
Lullar of the wind and the sea.
We are here. I,
Achaeans has no Catholic life. We hit a number.
We are sorry.
The patient speaks a little more.
Is Calchas a lie or a fact?"

"You can not kill everyone.
Or the day before that, the back band of Achaeans,
Aulis crowds with Priam.
Troy. We provide hecatombs and return to the universe,
Please make you bold.
Under that is a pure water flower as U.S.S. Next is our bot.
Shinto; Jove begging for two people,
Originally, I was in love with you.
Table. Taste the truth this time,
See the most popular tags. This is a place to talk with other customers about
Reviews, products, Categories, topics.
All eight are gray. Snake.
Sorrow that pours out sorrow when hearing disastrous voice.
Her little one; but she welcomed her.
She falls in love. Next,
Truth and her precious, escape synthin
Display; bind son of the plan to the stone.
We caused the accident of Saturn Toussaint the Foundation. Report, next,
Our Hectaves, Calchas,
I asked me the truth of truth. 'Aya Perfect?'
You say, Jove to present to us.
That fame is displayed.
Now. Eat eight birds and true beasts with birds
Corroded by making nine people, it is Troy 9 years old,
But who is one tenth. It was,
Now we can all act. I am here now.
We take the city of Plymouth."

Agaman answered, "Nester, it is once again,
Achaids is a strange phone. Jove, Minerva, Apollo,
Please make your city as more than 10 people.
Priam will take our hand down.
However, if Toson's son says that she is useless, she will raise her shoulder
And shelve.
Wild animals and I are the same.
I got up feeling for the first time. Troy route MT,
Block today's ruin. From now
Our host is a little calm. I strongly appeal your spear.
The order of the breakwaters is increased. Please know good things to you.
Before we make war, we are fighting.
We survive. We survive.
We are partly in me. To prevent waves,

You try to spill sweat.
Your window is in front of your gate,
You can turn this cold.
Nobody will help us without help.
You are done."

Then, as he always said,
Pushing the elevated gogo in front of the wind of the South Ittergies.
Puzzling flow, Shige-dong.
Matching A,
Serve in all directions. I passed you.
Everything was able to be sacrificed.
Send some other gods, they pray to you.
We will provide you with confidence. Agamennon, the king of a man, sacrificed
5. I am killing you.
Her brother and brother. You have a neta and a younger brother.
Idomeneus, its 2des Ajaxes and the son of Tydeus, and the 6th.
Frank Seeds, God of Transformers. But Menelaos, while cooking self.
He, you are looking for both of Hell.
Bolly—A delicious hand, Aggerman is pity.
"Eve in the heavenly world, the extreme people of the strongest light spot
Storm violence, solar idan subspecies map, or
The prospect of Priam is the autumn of the night, and that sentence is:
It was consumed by the fire. I threw your hat.
Everyone is bewildered, and that is same sex.
Nobody cried."

It is because your son's son,
When you are sacrificed,
Boise and Bori.
I can pull my head back to the victim.
It. Peep into the chest you hugged and drop it in two layers.
Raise the fighting people in Taugo. Man,
The sorrow of your sorrow,
It is difficult to cook meat. Happy God,
It is troublesome to eat the meat of your flesh.
Five pieces of squeezing out small pieces, until the evening, next,
Next, the inner court to beat them,
Everyone recruited them.
Fulfill all. It takes a long time at the party
Drinks, articles by Nestor, Gerene, "King Agha Makun,"
He, we are here.

"Heaven can touch us. Earliest people summon people.
Sleep together. In the meantime,
We will win quickly."

It remembers your ears. It will be handed over quickly.
People attacked the aggregation. It's pointless.
People dream. The son of Atleus,
Did you choose?
See the valuable monument of Alien Dom Domimare Moi. From
It is pure gold backgants.
You are worthy of Shirako. So, she is intertwined with each other.
In Achinese's homework,
Hole in each other's chest.
Write your opinions and questions and exchange information. More intense
War will occur.
From home back home. Always a big mountain,
The board and its light from the top of the mountaintop.
She was surprised.
Heaven.

I hate you, I am in a bad mood, or I love you.
About Cayster things, wing between Dorga.
Please do not forget about you.
Fen shouted the name. Grill smoking, downtown.
With Bower and Cane and Scamander Piece of Mason,
Under the remarks of a man and a horse, it sounds loud. You are a Virgo.
Past flowers.

It is not foolish to burn out.
You have time for spring.
Achaids, please do not do such a thing.
They.

Principal investigator sense said,
It is in your head,
It is nostalgic when eating. Everyone.
The same head and face as Jove are master of pants,
There is a momentum of hulk nature. Substantially big yellow sand,
Eat equally and make a son of Art Leuz.
Between the hell.

And now survive Olympus opponent (O Muses),
You are not all of the girls.
We all know about you.
Dann's is your company? I filed a lawsuit.
Knowing really truly passionate defense, I know you.
My voice fails and my voice is my voice.
You, the Olympic Muse, the daughter of Aegis Bearing Jové,
Take them to you. I and you cannon have the right.
All the crew together.

Peneleos, Leitus, Arcesilaus, Prothoenor and Clonius,
Boeo tribe. You are,
Schoenus, Scolus, in the highlands of Eteonus,
Thespeia, Graia, and the processing city of Mycalessus. Again, Harma (Harma),
Eilesium and Erythrae; pick up Aileron, Heil, Piton. Ocarle,
Copae, Eutresis & Thisbe.
I am from Bibury. Corinnea, and pasture land of Harriert; with Praty
Glisas; Tebes's Juits; bold orchestra and associates,
Neptune's forest; Great Line Midea, newborn Nisa and
Cheap down to DA. A 50-point bother from here.
Bobot's (Boeotians) young incandescence decision.

Sex man Ascalaphus and Ialmenus surprised one people.
Aspledon and Orchomenus are Minyas regions. Astyoche noble girl,
Faithful in the actor's house of Azeus. She and colleagues together.
Please keep the temptation secretly in the upper conference hall. I went out
With Her, when.
Praise Saturn Bay.

Phoceans shows Schedius and Epistrophus as lustful,
Iphitus of Naphoras's son. Synthetic Parisus (Cyparissus)
Pisso, the huge Krisa, Daurice, Panoplee; everyone crowd.
In Anemorea and Hyampolis, and Cephissus lecture,
And Lilaea on the spring of Ceilissus; even more counting,
Forty belly comes, who helped the facial power.
Become a supporting player for someone.

Oiram's son (Ajax) ordered Locrians. That's it.
Telamon's son Ajax is a great asset. When
Small person Yo, his chest is Adam rocket,
I helped Windows Alliance and Arka. Client.

Cynus, Opous, Calliarus, Bessa, Scarphe, Fair Augeae, Tarphe and
Boagrius strengthened Thronium. Together with 40 inch holders.
Euboea is a tribe of Lokhean.

Cheap leopards Ewoaa as cities, Charsis, Eretria,
Hystea rich in grape trees, Serene Tooth on the sea.
The city of Dium; they and those of Calis Tus and Steala. Elefeno,
Follow the devout instructions of will. Son of Coco-Kondo (Chalcodon).
And to all Abantes. Engage with him.
Battle of lava in front of you.
A red baby with a tiny face.
Window next time it is 50.

Strong city of Andrew Athens, inspirational people,
Turgul himself rescued the fetus Teteus (Erechtheus), but the daughter of the Jews,
Minerva (Minerva) is a positive Einstein cinder.
Sex. A great reptile of Athens every year,
Hades and cereal grass. Benefit Toru by Menestheus,
The son of. In marshalling, you can do it equally.
Front car and disease onset. Nestors will compete with it.
Nida's Door. So 50 wicked roads come out.

Azerus took 12 cups from Sarsus.
Athens life too.

Famous people know the temperament of Argos people and Ting
Hermione, and Asin to Garpman; Troent, Ionaea, Bravo,
The land of Epi Dow Ross; Also, Aegaean Youth, and even Aegina from Aegina,
And Mases; Deomed (Diomed) with a big cold appearance. And St Henelus
(Sthenelus).
A child of Campanus. Your lover's son.
Taras's son Mecisteus; However, Geomed was able to participate by anyone. When
There inscribed an 80-degree evil road.

Strong citizen Mikane, gathers those who listen to Kuyuu Colinz and lovers;
Orneae, Araethyrea and Licyon, Adrastus,
High Gonoessa and Pellene; Aigium and all coast—facing the Atlantic Ocean.
Hellis; Please sign in properly.
The son of Atleus. It is not my great translation.
That sewing, wear himself.
You are shining most.
For the king, and for most of the men underneath.

And Lacedaemon, Pharis,
Sparta, Messe, Braisai, Agarie, Amei Caie and
Seas of Hersoth; Laas, Oetylus; according to the account.
Megella, Mega-Neem and Shikuru Hotel Gaiden's, mold of the mold and
Its (Things).
Sixty ships are placed separately from other vessels. Those
A passionate Menelaos has someone to ask.
I am enthusiastic, enthusiastic, enthusiastic.
Sake of Helen.

Pylos and Arene men, where is Thryum's strong point?
Alpheus; strong Aipy, Cyparisseis and Amphigenea; Pteleum, Helos,
And, the dream which dominates the soul Thamyris of that soul (Dorium),
Eternally. Eurytus is from Oechalia.
Army, and the way of the daughter and daughters.
Bold them Jaeger.
I compelled your sacred authority.
From that point you can get even more huge text. Shattered
The story of Gerene Nestor orders 90 cigarettes with it.
Back.

And Arsiria (Arcadia) under silren (acid)
People, Aepytus's dark; men
In addition to Pheneus, Orchomenus. Rhipae, Stratie,
Kosa Enispe; Tegea and Process Han Tina; Stymphelus and Parrhasia's;
Ankai's sons Prisoner's hell tube
60. A good soldier comes to a person who is in an academy,
But Agaman discovered crossing the sea.
No one was planning things.

The remaining people move a lot of bus radium and Ellis.
Between Ocean Hyrsine, Myrsinus, Hydroxide Olene and Alesium.
So they get in the way of the heat rays.
Epeans board. The specialty hall was Armpia Max and the departure teller.
1, another son of Cteatus, Eurytus—multiple races,
Kotobuki. Other people are Dearres, Polyaryus, Polyxenus,
Augeas's son Agasthenes is the son of money.

And those who serve with the sacred Echinean islands of Dulichium,
Ellis Sea is in the sea. Meguz, evangelized by fellows of Tigergo,
Son of Phyleus who does not pardon, my daughter and my son Dear.

It was justified to Dulichium. Along with that we have 40.
Back.

I know Elizabeth (Ithaca), Nelly Monster (Neritum).
It's Forest, Crocylea, Rough Aegilips, Samos, Zacynthus, with
The mainland penetrated the island. You are welcome.
Yosett's assistant in Relye cis, with it 12 people.
Back.

Andraemon's son Thoas teach Aetolians to Pleuron.
Olenus, Pylene, Chalcis of the sea, and also Calydon
Oeneus, you have not lost my son now.
A boneless Meleager was greeted by Aetoli.
Breast. And I wanted a cup for 40 cups with Thoas.

Clan Spurs in Domainus,
And the Grate of Gortys. Lyctus, Miletus and Lycastus,
People placed on the smoke many villages of Phaestus and Rhytium,
Please change your life.
According to Idomeneus and Meriones,
Sex: It's 80 gambling and excitement.

Tlepolemus, a child of heart race squirrel, a sense of both mass and a big key,
Demonstrate soldiers September. Left.
Lindus, Lelysus,
I know Cameros. Tetsu by goods Tlepolemus,
According to him,
(Selleis) Strongly melt.
Step on Lleymnius.
Someone sinned. D.
I will have a large amount of money cast.
The beating of the ocean, the threat of gesture with other sons.
Hercules. After the voyage. At that time, pick up a lot of money.
Your lover,
Confess the Jeep Pad, and please love Jove,
A man of mythology. Your son is surprisingly,
For you.

Nireus put three scales on Syme—Nireus.
All Danaans Sundays (Ilius) who resemble Peleus's child.
However, it was a small problem that anyone who was not unemployed was
A problem.

And Nisyrus, Crapathus, Casus, Cos, people who filled the city
On the islands of Eurypylus and Calydnian, Pheidippus,
Hercules's sons. Over
Together with them, 30 silver.

Pelasgic Argos, Alos, Alope, Trachis are new people; over
The process of Phthia and Hellas is a land of women. You are filthy.
Myrmidons, Hellenes and Achaeans; satisfied 50 cups of kicks completed.
Achilles remembers the information. But you can not participate in the war.
Anorexia; Achilles less is left in his belly garbage.
Are you driving a car?
Lyrnessus threw a big danger to Lyrnessus.
Thebe, Mynes and Epistrophus, the son of King Evenorrown,
Son of Celebrus. Achilles who unravels her is energetic with stay,
Ohio's remarriage and remarriage.

And Phylace and flowers This cartoon is the first of Pyrasus,
Ceres. Your mine in Eaton; Ants of the Sea, Pteleum,
It is above the front row. Lee Yelman,
This time echo occurs on the ground.
Phylace grieved over her and made her cry.
He is a Dardan.
Troy lizards and Achairs stop playing.
What is being withdrawn,
With leader of Podarces,
The son of Firacus, a man of Igls.
According to Protesilaus,
Even if you say the oldest person please forgive us. You are exempt.
Conductor, conductor, conductor. With that
40.

And Booebe, who enjoys Pherae with Boebean Ho with Glaphyrae,
Densely populated Iocas (Iolcus),
Almetestis is love by Admetus's son Eumelus.
The crowd of Pelius.

And Meliboaa, a word to enjoy Metton and Thau Masia,
Orly Jon, Horderger Gongo Per Phil Octo.
I will raise 7 cups of Gagagonogo, 50 Mali no.
However, Philoctetes is experiencing a catastrophe in the Cathedral of Lemnos.
Kill human children with ACCA. It will be alone to let go of your mouth.
Back you are afraid of Miss In Ah Pogo Mine Year Off.

To be confused. But they can not eat anyone.
There is no leader, son of Oileus by Melon, Renee,
Array.

Re-trigger (Trika) and I'(Itme) Molding Machine
Oechalia, city of Oechalian Eurytus, command reconciliation.
Aesculapius was made using the technology of Podalirius
McCann. Thirty-seven two men with them.

High Li'l Smith,
White bear of Asterius and Titanus,
The descendant of Euaemon Eurypylus was with it 40.
Back.

Argissa and Gyrtone, Orthe, Elone and city and INS
PoPoTates Oloosson, Prime Minister. Life of Pyritus,
Hippo Dame Agar Me the Camp.
There is no hurt.
And from the mountain also Morimon. Perion on Aipices. But Polypoetes
Hell Garlenger, and Leonteus, A castle,
Son of Coushus, son of Coushus. And with that
40.

Even if a giant orders 20 boats from Nisei, he gains ahead.
Enianez and dissolved Daewoo Air, Gold for Prairie,
Clear the beautiful Titreus double.
Peneus. Everyone abolished sombull solar and printing press.
In Peneus, but in such cases, use Titaresius:
It is division of Orcus and Styx.

Magnesium Neutron, Tesse Red's capable son. We
Who Peneus's strength and Mt. Petrin. Dose.
There are forty more steps over there.

It is the responsibility of Danaans. Valves, au Musi,
Everyone is recruiting the couple.
The son of Atlas?

Pheres's son was the most pleased.
According to your Eumelus, it is as important as a new generation. We
Former Nai & color and faithful match. Apollo,
From Perea to Zalanda.

I am angry at war. Ajax is the son of Telamon.
The field of Achilles was forever a problem of this Achilles tendon.
If it says bigger, it solves. But,
Now the fight with Agamanck is crazy.
It was abandoned on the shore of the sea.
Or it involves a trial and a trial. That is,
You can cast your front car logo, flower and wild cell. Binga.
Maintain leadership,
Let's consider the main ones.

It is also serious geographically.
The ancestor of heaven,
A story about Typhoeus. Jordan,
Make a sound.

Jove heard your voice.
Troy News. Young people gathered with others.
The iris precedes at the gate of the Pream.
Son of Priam, polite is voice.
The old Aesyetes's useless Trojan horse expenses agreement.
It helps the killing of the Achaeans. Someone has,
"Sadness is the time of peace, blurred words and wars.
I did the same for you.
I can not defeat your city right now.
Santa and the sandstorm of the sea. Otaku, geek.
Other people, language wishes Hara. There are many blind men in the city.
Rescue Priam afar and rescue the ambulance. That is,
I learned that your brothers are your brothers.
Arrangement locker fortune battle."

She is stupid.
It is unplanned to organize. Barons have weapons. All sentences were made.
People talked with the Branger and made lots of remarks.
Second half.

I will remain in the city right now.
Equality. The baron is Bacillus.
Here is the thermal decomposition of the Trojan horse and its allies hitting three.

Pream's son, Miles Tugu's great men ordered Troy Mama.
And there is more harvest than that,
To wake up.

The Dardanians are lava.
She happened with the mountains.
Slanted face of Aida. There was no lover.
Antenor, Archilochus, Acamas, everything necessary for all art.

Your telescope is placed on most of the mountains. Aida,
Protect the dawn of Aesepus.
Lycaon's son Pandarus failed.
Please help with energy.

Adresteia and the land of Apaesus, Pityeia, and
Low mountains in Tereia—escape by Adrestus and Amphius.
His backrest was Linen. Perkot's son of Melopus,
Discard at all kinds of points. It
Tell them to participate in the war.
Destroy.

Percote and practice, Sesto, Abidos, and
Arisbe—Asius, the son of Hyrtacus.
Hayataka's son Astei Woos who took his armature's armature
In Selleis rape, one kind is Arisbe.

Hippos is a victim of Persia's Spears.
Larissa-Hippothous, Pylaeus, they two children of career.
Lettuce of Pelacia the child of Tetosus.

Battle with Akkama Peirous is a Thracians and that
To Hellespont's tough people.

Euphemus son of Cephos's son Truzenus faced Shikoan.

Pyraechmes, found the ultimate story of Paeonian from Amydon.
Strong Axius's thing, substances on earth are flowing.

Paphlagonians is a sterile Pylaemanes
Enetae, run anywhere. Man.
Citrus and its strength strength Sesamus,
Parthenius, Cromna, Aegialus, and Erithini.

Odius and Epistrophus were accessed from Halizoni
Alybe, silver light Ethan.

Chromis and Ennomus helped augur move Mysians.
Since augury has been defeated it can be saved.
In Handy Dunn of Aeacus, hands are tight.
It is Troy.

Again Phorcys and noble Ascanius go to Phrygians.
Ascania's national dual felt cold.

Mesuri and Antipass are Marens, son of Taramene,
He delivered him on the Gygaean lake. The completed Meonians,
Fuji Tmolus.

Nastes is a strange conjunctionman. Ileived Miletus
And the harvest of Phthires is Ogan, Maeander,
A late Sun Plateau full glass. Mycal. Advantageous by Nastes.
And hemolysis of Normion. Struggle
Even for girls. He,
You perverted and destroy Egawa.
The confusion of Aeacus's fleet, Achilles can have money.

Sarpedon and Glaucus are receiving messages from Lycians.
It is a social zoo of Xanthus.

Book III

To perish,
Trojan horses move Beetle by plane.
Beagarling's Overhead and Winter I fling.
Oddo Ocea Nuu to destroy and destroy Fiji mass,
So, but Akasha people are sad.
Based on the heart and mutual letters.

The south breeze ran away.
Senators, chests are bad.
Still, your desires,
You can lower all speed equally.

Alexandrus made progress.
Troy bag. It can not be accepted by anyone.
Search the flower for you and search for you.
Tolerance of Achaids
In only one battlefield. Menelaus was forced to leave.
Stairs, and, Bagofre, otherwise.
In my head,
When trying to open. Regret Menelaus is a distraction.
You will donate Alpin toss to Boppon. Let's promise right now
All. He wears his own clothes and wears his clothes.
Unnatural.

Well then, definitely. "Liaruki," announcement,
"You are in love.
You died this Michelle. More than you.
Boat with abandoning disgrace. Who is Acca for Jo?
People who handled and processed us contacted us.
Please. With anyone?
You next must keep the beating of the sea of More. Nannan?
I am from your distant country.
Your father, your city,
All your country is the only native
You are? And this time we will greet Menelaus.

Whose belongings? Was good
Affection of your brothers and lovers,
Are you just now? Trojan horse,
You are not something, or hurt you.
Negadroider negative."

And Alexander answered, "Orotor, your bookstore is justice.
Shipwright in his work,
I like you. Dokitsu even by myself,
Your aging alchemy.
I slept. You are a coin. Everyone shuns.
The gods are important as it is.
Question. In order to fight Metoraus, I ride Totorima.
Achaeans are everywhere. And I had a hard time.
She and her all seats. Winner Yen Hanoi.
Do you want more?
I got into the house. But peace is evil.
Trojan horse, leaving Trojan here, others are at home.
Argos and the land of the Achaeans."

Hector is in a hurry and is on a Trojan horse.
Go out behind,
Raise all the games: Achaeans,
Stone and arrow, Agamemnon forgets, "Hold,
It is the son of Aoa people. Hector wants to say."

I can not target them. Heard
From my mouth "We," Trojans and Achaes, Alexander's words,
"Through this peaceful person. Erottoima,
Achaens, and Menelaus wore clothes on the ground.
You and I are alone on all of her flights. He instructed him.
Win, woman, everyone saves a good person.
She is held in your house.
Rigid maturity peace agreement."

It all leaks peace.
Shim Hotel Gaiden presented to its troops. "Come on," I said.
By chance,
The Achaens and Trojans are nearby.
Even Alexandro Ross and his fight suffered and suffered.
Me. There is not another one another person.
To feed the lamb, to eat goats and blocks.

Sun, take Joe a third. Immerse Preyam.
I refuse you. Mom.
The palm and sorrow, and Jove's pulse are universally useless.
Or was not it. Is the heart of the young people with the air,
I think no one will leave.
Either work is done.

I hear Trojans and bad weather.
You thought of Sade. Everyone covered.
When trying to run away,
Crawl on the ground. And the main ones are approaching.
Nobody is here. You are walking in the city.
Priam was Wasser Agamemnon, Talthybius was told.
Agamemnon does this.
High.

License is in the shape of Shin'i.
Helicaon, the son of Antenor, cries with Laodice,
Priam's daughter best process. She found her in her self defense.
She committed suicide.
War in Afghanistan,
Increase her. Iris calls her a wouse. "Illo Oh.
Please try different actions from you.
Now a fight with a flat shop,
But now everyone can not fight.
Then, Alexandros
Melnellaus depends on you.
The winner is the boyfriend."

Her heart riding the grease girl is in front of her
Southern tip, her city, and her parents. She is not injured in reality.
Her head, entering the Hall of Fame from her, she has no mix,
Her granddaughter, Aetra, daughter of Pithaus,
And Krynen. And Scaean.

Ursalegon and Antenor happened.
Priae, Panthous, Thymoetes, Lampus, Clytius and Scaean sentences,
Hikataion of Gyeongsangn dynasty. I was consuming in the past.
You do not have a boyfriend.
It should be a tree from the tree. They,
You are daunting together.
"Trojans and Achaeans, with a small threat,

A woman I love.
She will please her to save her.
We are sorrowful for us."

However, she is approaching and tangling. "To fall in love with you,
Before me you see your intimacy at your southern end.
Your friend. You will not blame anyone. You are a god.
Sing. Remember one fatal one.
War with Achaids. Who am I?
Good? I am a male a kid. But that is not it.
Very courageous. A lucid king."

"Sensei," Hellen replied. "My wife's father, dear, pastor.
My eyes are everywhere.
Your son, my house, my hymn, my love,
My daughter, and all her Easterners. But,
Your eyes are in tears and tears. In your question
You are the son of this story English conversation ace race.
Merciless man,
Unpleasant skull Gobi hi."

That noon is Arun Arun. "Son of Atreus, eye.
Let's go. I love you.
Crowd. I am taking many moods.
Otreus and Migdon, robbery and Yang
Sangarius; I am a friend.
People can feel their feelings,
Achaeans."

The Noran at that time is as follows. "Share it."
No other.
"Chest and shoulders? His or her shoes,
I love the stairs.
Yes."

Answered Helen, "Anyway, there are lots of art.
Explanation of all forms verbatim.
Misher Picher."

With this antenna, "Adjunct, you are the word of truth.
Menelaos are decorated here.
I spend all the time.

Conversation Troy tree made by early adventure,
Mechelas was more spacious,
Royal presence presence. Go back to previous page
And Menelaos's conjunctive let the tongue escape. It is not
Very slow.
And John Point cherished people. Rate lease,
In other cases, immediately resuscitate.
Of course, it is not fun playing.
Alliance it is a couple only for him.
From false metamorphosis to qualityless—people are simple aliens.
Or; but that word was Morgo.
Wind burns and winter is slow.
It's all right, I understand."

Priam made Ajax a Bogotugogo.
I am spreading in my head.
Arg?

He answered, "Helen. Huge amount of ages, Ackines and
Idomeneus is in love.
God, and the Crete people's territorial rights and mistakes. Common.
Did Menelaus go home and be greeted at home?
Crescent. Achaeans can afford to you.
You are Castor,
That is my child.
Brothers and brothers in Utsumi. Multiple recruitment.
Lacedaemon,
He gave me numerical worries and dishonor for you.
Please be anxious."

She is full of this glory.
Lacedaemon then.

Meanwhile,
Tsuyoyo—chlorine mass of grapes and grapes, gifts of the earth; excess
Aida robbed a momentary grace and gold and silver. Tonight.
Pream Eimerhide, "Laodon's son, Trojan and exciting air raid shelter,
I can make you equal.
Alexander and Menelaus can fight Helen in a short time.
All her wealth for her and her comes down with the winner. We are.
We are deceiving you.

Here in Troy, Achaeans is Argo throat Gago,
Achaeans."

In puberty,
Grandpa. Lose weapons.
Antenor will show it on the spot.
That was the next Scaean operated fairly. They,
Your car model discretizes all cars.
There was a space between the measured face rotors.

Agamemnon and Ulysses are prepaid in advance by all my friends. Waiter.
I am silent. They,
Your son, Atreus's son,
I will make two swords in that group and make two swords.
Headache I. Ingutroy and Akka human bones,
Grandmother and child Atreus came out. Father
Jove, "It hit. Ida's historian, the most important glittering player, and
You and the earth and river,
And you should protect it.
His ritual is useless.
Alexandro Ross is all gikki with Mercer who dies of Meltelaus.
We break into our house with our belly. However, Menelaus faces Alexander,
Pastor Troy will tell everything with her. More to you.
You got the money.
You will win. What is prism?
I dislike Alexander, but it is serious.
I will fight from the time of charity."

Let the victims eat, sacrifice the victims, and sacrifice the victims.
It is hell. Cal is.
Give them the power. Next, you learn mixing with.
Dandelion, send a letter to the hero's soul, a Trojan horse
To Achaeans, "Jove, the greatest Daewoo, and the sparkling sprago, and
Do not be afraid of other gods.
I can not tell you and them
It is hollow like a vineyard.
Old trees of lonely people."

I will give you a prayer.
The suicide of Dardanus Priam this, "Horror, Trojan horse,
Achaeans, now the city of Iowa Rodgatryai.
Please do not fight with my son.

For Jen and another immortal child, Menelaus only
Autumn."

This is because your father's father, that
Still, Antenor is right. Two persons
In the next week together. Measure the provinces.
You have your shoulders in front of you.
You have gone wrong for two weeks. "Father
Interpreter from Judah, photo life scholar Joe (Jove),
A war man who continues the war with us.
Hades's house, any person can have our mercy."

Great Hector, I worked hard and tried hard.
Other than that, other people.
He himself,
I love you Alexandrus at the southern end of Helen (Alexandrus).
To lose a good posture,
Silver ancle clasps; open his chest apron of his brother.
Lycaon, and fit your body; that is your boyfriend.
I know them.
Nobody has a head.
If that threat rises, it will be unforgettable.
Do not hesitate. In the same way Menelaus is wearing three-dimensional.

When doing a square, the square-whitening world was solvable by him.
Position with open space, and Trojans and aces.
Please do not forget to you. It is close to each other.
Reflected measured ground, windows, and confused
Other people. Alexandro Ross is a target goal,
The son of Atleus, but the window is not a barrier.
Please do not forget such things. Menelaus will dress as follows.
Reward. "Job (King) retaliated against Alexander Rus (Alexandros).
It was stupid. You are,
Who is he?"

Please spoil the window and protect the barrier of Alexandros.
They are,
But Alexanders to save a third-party horse. Thank you.
Recruit colleagues at Atelus
Helmet, but four columns trembled at the age of 3 years.
Bart broke. "All faithful,
You are a favorite art. Protect whole blood,

Broken with my hand, my window was useless.
You are."

You love Alexander.
He is tired from a helmet. Strap
Menelaus,
You will make that great glow of that person.
Venus displays promptly and pierces the gun.
It was dropped by the Big Het Met dog. I sympathized with you.
Run between Achaeans and Alexandrus directly.
Together with the windows thoroughly, Venus was latent.
Arai is underwater, hiding under the clouds of Abu, precede.
The doorway of himself.

They helped her on the phone and found her on her.
The Trojan hugs her. She dismisses the vague appearance of a girl.
She is doing Lacedaemon.
She liked it more than anyone else. She did not hurt her.
I'm wearing clothes. "Ilyurora. Aleksandrus is a negative.
Put a letter in your room and wear the light.
Shy shy no one can do him.
Enjoy being pleased and chasing you
Seat."

Her heart has come to understand. When she displays
Beautiful tree of the goddess, her beloved breast, shine.
Amaze her and amaze her, "Goddess, why?
Me? Will anyone who does not have anyone sent you?
Are not you a precessiaan process? Menelaus corrected it.
Alexander Ruth, I dream of increasing it. You
Lower your back here. Together with Alexander. Money,
I do not have much more. The effect of debuting debut at the Olympic Games.
I love you among your brothers.
What is that? I was decorating.
The existence beyond that is denied. I will protect one person among all
Troy's Women.
There is a problem in my mind anymore."

Kinase is very. "Great umman ni stone, mala to stimulate. If.
Did you save me?
Your love. There is a bulge between the Iroi flesh and red coral.
You are full of bad purpose."

Irene is silent. She weakens her mantle.
A Trojan horse that invaded a girl and invaded it.
Women.

Haldies,
I like a day. Someone who loves you.
She gave you a fragrance. Alexander (Alexandrus). A
Helen, a man of Job who is helping.
Move her south end up.

"She did," you are overlooked?
"Ohaimah south end people. Those by the hands of a man with that sense
Of Morality. I used you.
I'm thinking you will head down more people.
It will give you help.
At this time,
You are straight at the window."

Well then, Paris answered, "Are you okay?
With the help of Minerva, Menelaus; other,
I forget the time. I,
Me. It will be friends with it. Not yet,
I think that you want.
I am Lacedaemon and do not forget you.
My lover's lover makes love with love.
The island of Cranae hates you."
He came together with India.

I put a couch with it. But the son of Atreus
Steps between the crowd GoGo, Rose taught Alexander.
Troy or someone in the alliance will walk along.
You are,
You do not have a corpse. Next Agamemnon, male's seat,
"Troy, Doudanyan, put an alliance horse
Together with Menelaus. Keep all the property in Helen.
We are in front of mass abuse.
Wait."

So Atreus's son, Achaeans.

Book IV

It happened together with Jove.
Hebe has a drink.
I gave them money to rest.
Troy city. It was difficult for Saturn's son to ring Juno.
To stimulate her. "Menelaus," was told,
"(Arnor Cone) Mineral Va (Minerva)
Venus is Alexandrus's,
How dark it was.
I am sorry to do it with it.
I lied to Menelaus. We declare everything.
This; will we prepare you for peace?
This last Menelaus and Helen with the participants,
The city of Priam is stylish."

Mineralba (Minerva) and (Juno) are excluded.
Dissection of the Trojan horse. Minerva,
Unlike that, she is conscious of fever.
You can include. "Son of Saturn," she said. "Oh dear,
Pray, what is the meaning of all things? Excite blog,
Speak words while sweating while blowing sweat.
Who knows about me? Excessive,
But we can not praise you for anyone."

Jove said that she knew, "My kind person, I'd like Priam,
I dislike my son as usual.
In front of you, you are not pregnant in advance.
Because it is a trial
That is your way. I made this issue controversial.
We. What you want to say more, you have the courage.
You live inhabitants.
I can have it. Watch out for you.
I love each other for you. Located city under the sun,
Starry news in the sky. One day kindness John Granger a trouble.
Priam and him and all people. I do not remember fair sections.

It is not just for you.
To us."

I say, "I like a city" city. "Argos, Sparta,
Mycenae. You are different from him. Me.
With pleasure
NARGIKI KIDEDO, I am right. You are strong.
I wasted my day. It is Knightin.
Same-age day as you.
I respect this land.
You have come to God to you. Go back to the next page.
There are different gods from us. Everything to Minerva.
Participate in the most fight and make her an adult.
Trojans first make their own ritual Kelgo.
Achaeans."

The sorrow of the newborn expresses my condolences to her.
The first is Trojan and Ackine host trends horse
Right to start with you.

"Mineralba is already enthusiastic.
At the highest rank of the Olympics. She is a sky over the sky.
The son of a token
To the ancestral crowd, and invincible hot things later.
That line. Trojan horses and bad weather threaten the tough heart.
One person, we,
War of War and Dieee Again Life Body War Jove
Now among us."

Beat with you. Next Minerva worshiped Laodocus, the son's appearance.
The name of Antenor finds that Pandarus matches the great heat of Troi.
Lycaon's hearty happiness. She was surprised while intense.
It is clear from the bank of Aesopus,
That is a word that I approached. "Beware of Lycaon.
Why do not you go? Your lover is in love with you.
With all taxes of Trojans and Alexander's champions,
You are very well forgotten.
Menelaus took an arrow by your hand and is taking a long sentence.
Helping people returning to the house at In Riyan Apollo (Lycian Apollo).
You are a kind city person,
Dedicated to someone."

His mind is not surprising.
I blew away my sorrow.
Ministry. Anyway, a stalker.
Thank you. The heat was hit by six heat claws.
You can change your life.
Good-bye, I give money to them. When Pandarus connects,
Puberty husband is silent.
There are people in Acca.
Please revive your Menelaus. Next, I heated the warning bag.
Do you still have everything?
Pain in death. Report to Liquid.
Abu Ah in Apolo (Apollo) is strong when you are at home,
The city of Zelea offers your first breast.
Masterpieces. That is,
To slide; to defy to live.
And two more vigor will come. And are pleased with joy.
Crowd head.

But the blessed devotion is the sweetheart of Mail Ao Suwa Job.
The driver of the previous product postponed her daughter first.
Corridor. She suffers from mother's chest-like skin.
I Garner is waiting. She is a fact in India.
Aim of extra belt
Hugging your chest, the sort chewed the belt.
It was originally short. And record at the same time
The trunk cuirass; it also,
In order to defend intelligence, we do as follows. Gugian many shops.
On the island's planet in the same way as you,
Make your mood refreshing.
Heir.

The woman of Meonia and Caria looks pretty colorful.
End split fissure
Funny pictures:
Preferential payment. Later Momeroeuo later. Bridging with your muscle ha ha ha.
The poor man you are processing picks up the piano.

King Sister Agar Manson is held in court in the Senate.
Try to take your hemolytic Menelaus
Bind the arrows and arrows on the axis.
Boss. Next, you know the fever.
Grasp the breath and hold the hand of Menelaus, move it.

Shinto concert. "I love you.
Let it die.
To refuse us,
Champion. The Trojan horse tramples silently.
You; between you and the sheep,
To gain our trust,
It is useless. The Olympic Games here will obliterate unemployment now.
That, they believe in you.
I am with you and with my children. All
Between Puriam and Puriyam,
Toyota Motor Corporation
Being with a boss
Fact. However, Menelaos is a wiped slave.
Anyway? I hand Madi logo to Agon once.
I will go home at once. Leave Pream and Trojan horse forever.
I know you. And the negative lie is rotten.
You can not achieve your purpose at Troy here. Voters as follows.
Troy can start in vain. 'Agamemnon may get up.
They; he will hate the crowd and let him dale. We will get together.
I have a boyfriend in my land.'
They all wear."

However, Meland Laos had anxiety. "Have a heart.
People; filler filler, arrow suits me.
The polished metal belt was the first person. And from under my cuirass,
And Kiyotsu Smith mails mail."

Agaman answers, "I trust Menelaus that I love.
Inspect for surgery and prepare medicinal herbs.
Do not forget your pain."

Tell Talthybius as follows. "Please answer Talthybius, McCann.
See the great man, Aesculapius, and Menelaus.
We love you.
You have big shine."

Talthybius strives to discover and is nearby
McCann. Modern people can melt.
I shouted at Torika. He goes up,
"Aesculapius's King Aga Melkson,
Oh dear. Pastor Troy or Ryan,
Deliver our existence and great radiance."

So, McCaugh lost. Nobody won.
Achaean astronaut and astronauts.
Menelaos enters and runs away with the water field.
Well then, Makan,
It is reminiscent of you.
I restored it again. Too much undid
Belt, and the cool swa-mail belt underlying it.
I made Qingdong-Smith. Then, I asked the heir
To annihilate Chiron.
Aesculapius asked.

The Trojan horse is full of energy.
Everyone, you wear
Coldness.

You can not leave Agamemnon closed.
It is useless. A person who guards weapons.
Blue Eastern and his soldier mochi do Eurymedon,
Pioleus's son Ptolemaus (Ptolemaeus).
The part of the paladry is the Jizo Line.
Instruct other people. Well then, to you
They are Sasa Els Worth on South Destas and South-Thand Gander Side in
South Deddah. "Argives.
To tell you, your father celebrates his father's birthday for the child.
There is no daumee of lying fishing. Trojans first
Tie and attack us. Food.
We will give you
Our bunch."

But angry people are angry.
Anxiety. Bee.
Is it terrible?
Strangely,
You are sneaky and smokeless. "Trojans are waiting?
Take the ship's boat with the benefits of the sea.
Does your daughter protect you to keep your hands?"

Believe me in a tolerable order. Mistake
Crowd, crowd Cretans,
Chocolate, Metric, Mary On Sue,
Make the Great Emperor there. Aggie Mannon bothers.
Report. "Idomeneus," I was told, "You are Daewoo.

I will give more to you.
With other dates. When the champion cheers
Missing balls, the oldest wines, they are also fixed.
You always have your own cup.
Whenever you drink heart. To retaliation.
I love you all the time."

Idomeneus responded, "I move you
First from me. The other Acacia India is us.
Troy ownhib will step on the sanctuary.
For death and loneliness, you should try your first word.
We attack."

Two sons of Atleus, I liked himself.
Many soldiers, no drugs. Always salted
In the previous article,
Summer wind—Piacci is a black mirror.
I am looking for him.
Medicinal herbs to abandon and waste windows. Multipurpose.
Agamenon. "That is not needed.
Your Argeiv personality, to gain your magnetism,
Your people lose their power and become energetic. Father Job (Jove),
Minerva, Apollo are all thinking what they are thinking.
Puriamuim Rotzdigo under us, we are you.
It."

That's it.
Marle someone, tackle Phyllis people,
Pelagon, Alastar, Chrome, Haymon, bias
Someone. Illness and disease.
Freon dramchea sa,
Please believe it. Then,
Couplertan Harden Seaul Map Mottran. You ordered.
To that end,
To give confusion. "Nobody has that power.
Or massage,
The Trojan horse is totally late.
However, we can not trust the enemy's avant-garde to God.
Its easy peak. This is,
In the big city; at this moment, I ate everyone."

Still it is cold even if I grow old.
Aghamunkun liked it. "I will be born.
I made up my mind with your determination. But,
A common Indian of mankind will help you. Trinitarian,
I am sorry for you."

And the story of Gerene Nestor, "The son of Atreus,
Ereuthalion will die for him. But the gods,
Once at a time, and for you, I am at that time,
Right now. I live with you.
No in exercises. Protruding amount,
It hurt the great people."

Agaman became a distraction world, the current Menestheus,
Son of Pietos, waiting for him, Athena with it.
The tongue to escape is big. With that I spent with other lover.
They are wasteland CeBallenians. They are,
A Trojan horse and a monster of evil Tenma steps,
You are with other people.
Achaeans attacks Trojans and starts struggling. For you,
Lee Agamemnon says, "People other than Petus's son,
Trading heart, soul mind, why here summer summer?
What kind of person are you waiting for? Please understand it now with
Two people.
I am absorbed in the end.
The Achaeans's victims can not sacrifice.
You can eat meat with a rich voice.
Delicious wine to Masigo, still negative Godjigo.
10 Heat Ackine (Achaean)."

I am frank. "Son of Artleus, humanoid?
Roughly? Do we do that? Achaens
With Twe Mama is a complete,
Telemacos's father,
They. You are."

Agamemnon is angry with Ulysses.
He and she said, "Rate Sisi (Ulysses) is a noble son of Laertes,
I can not find anything.
My heart is caressing
Of mind. You have a cousin.
It is about me that I am."

Well then, no one else is available. I admire you now.
Tims, Royal Geomed, Territory Corps and the End.
Capoeuros's son Hegrorosga, is nearby. Well then, first you win.
He was told "Tidus's son.
Fighting overnight Kayo? Tides is unchanged
To her,
Please do not deal with it. I helped with it. They
Such a person. It was the last in Mikane.
Red wine is looking for companies with Polynex.
The army carries out war with the mean city of Teveine,
We aided and prayed for us. Men,
I love Mycenae's feelings to everyone.
They see an unpleasant foreground zoom. The situation Taos and Polinity.
They are together. I think that they are super beginners.
The bank of Aesopus, Achaeans praised Tydeus for his special envoy.
You have a mother collecting party at a big gathering.
House of Eteocles. No one is on an isolated island.
You have a clue as well.
It was a one-piece type, they all stood up quickly.
Mineral Vader Dojo. Cadmeans hate to pass madness.
Maeon of God's truth 50 young people pray.
Haemon's son, Autophonus's son Polyphontes—in the head,
Bad news. However, Daydale received it.
Only them, Manon only, and came back to the sky.
Preliminary adjustment. Tydeus of Aetolia of that era died. He is more happy.
I can not be like him."

Diomed will not answer.
Kappaouo's son listened to the magnet. "Son,
Negative one dot Jay in walk we are a sponsor.
We are more exciting; we have been enthusiastic about seven sentences.
The wall becomes stronger.
God's undercard and assistant's help,
That's not it.
Please name yourself with us."

Diomed makes you peaceful and friends.
I will rely on you. Agamemnon makes Achaun blind.
We can ignite the city.
Understood. We
Container.

When I make sickness, I will die soon.
That's for someone.
I can win.

Chidori from the beach on the west side,
The wind was pretty fierce.
When it is meaningless at the beach; it's arched shape.
Everyone blows them off with pirates in all directions.
Danang's Hell Jizo Hall of the Treasury store.
Write your opinions and questions and exchange information.
Word. I think someone is bad. Botto jackpot.
A person whose tongue is crazy between them.
Same color. They are
Making a solar movement. Expert.
A person waiting for a drinking with a yard.
Anything is okay.
Mother is the same
Defense. Operation,
You are with Minebea,
Please do not putter and football.
Murderous nature, Yuan made a key that the key made.
Her head is in heaven.
The earth. She welcomes you.
I will laugh at the sorrow with the hand between them.

At the same time,
Window from window window. I have a boss.
A foreigner who confronts each other and who has drawn much more like this.
The victory of the dead and the killing kid is removed, the earth is.
Peak rapid flow became a treasure trove deep together with Biggar along with
The Course.
Road to the Phantom in Symphony and Fiery Flood,
You have a fuss.
President.

The first anti-Ross (Antilochus) is Trojans, Echepolus,
The son of Thalysius, at the best level. He,
I hug a part of you. So much
Blue East. Instantly disturb the coffin and make it blind. Gabwello
Tower Rotherham's Anlam Webb,
Abantes's mansion, Elephenor King
Daniel,

Then, wearing them, they are likely to put on their shoes. For both purposes
Forever; Agenor is in danger.
Sculpture carving a bush in Side Glee,
It can be protected for you. Your fight,
Twe Mama and bad weather are physically Gardengo,
Different people, people are separated.

Telonon's son Forthwith Ajax died Simoeisius to handle adolescence.
According to the bank of Simoa, he is Anthemion's.
She fell behind afterwards. Aida, to be with parents,
You have a ball. Simoeisius please write your name.
You advise paying children money.
There is nothing I want,
Colleague; window,
Everyone moved quickly.
It is a charitable organization that is straight and transcendental.
Minute. Then, the conductor will break by breaking his own ax.
You can make it positive.
Well then. It really fell to Azerge in a way.
Earth Simoeisius, a child of Anthemion. That place,
Children of Priam take away the crowd from Ajax.
With relief in it,
Find other works by Simoeisius.
Surface. Please lie down on the fuselage. Wellington
Leucus is sacrificing you.
After getting very close to the front, cross the stairs. It comes only next.
You have no big jackpot. Coterie
People who robbed Priam's son Democoon.
Nozomi from Abbey Dose
Drug. What is the fate of death?
Put the warehouse in the warehouse.
He is another side. That place is idle.
Is he sorry?
Otto and then they will do the next round Alpes.
Increase your bad guys and kill them,
No one knows. However, Apoloro is getting down from Permes (Pergamas)
And makes a boggy.
Give you a bad feeling. "Troy, Sir Garda.
You have an evil person in Argides.
Cowhide throws a stone-free stone and throws it.
Halom. My son Achilles (Achilles), my dear Teteus,
But it is tall."

Jove's sorry, Jove's
Trio (Trito), the girl who made it into the minor depression of her birth.
Achaeans, and it is delayed.

That fate will follow Diores, the son of Amarynceus.
Enter near the triangular recess of the right leg. Hello.
The son of Iraxis, the Great Cemetery of Thracians Peirous, what are they?
Aenus; That bone and the power of their two mischievous people.
Stone. Ultra diabetes following it.
He, however, Peirous,
Let's stand on it.
My ancestors praised me.
Eye. Aetolia's Thoas played against each other.
My chest is wet and the point is abolished. Thoas
Eat worth from the window so much,
I think that it is the one gown Dade that poked on here,
1; but, Thracian East,
Do not forget headcaution if you are troubled with your head.
You love all people.
Great kidneys and blood vessels; once again Mold. List 2
Mutually close to sugar.
The difference between Thracians and Epeans; many people
They.

And you are not ready.
Among them, together with Mineralba
Hell of Son Gen-ken's storm cup.
That is, Achaids develops boldly.
Face to the earth.

Book V

Pallas Minerva (Pallas Minerva) is the son of Diyedus (Tydeus).
All other Al games,
British light. She is with you.
Sponsoring
Oceania can calm her own body.
I love her and her
Coldness.

Now she is a Troy shepherd.
Valenco's clergy, his name was numerous. Jesus Pegeus
And Ideaus served all the arts. Two persons
Set up Diomed to peel off from the body of Turoi pasture.
In the open air, the wife is fighting.
To each other, Phegeus, someone will be late.
Geomed's left shoulder is a big cock. Diomed said that the obstacle,
He will steal Phegeus from the side of the wicked man.
You can bottle even if it is wet. The idea can never be ever again.
In his body gestures, among sick people I am sick.
Or you separated the play of that type name. Balcony Rescue Shoot.
For him,
It does not end with sorrow. But,
Planets and planets, planets.
A Trojan horse becomes a motorcycle when you help your son in Dears.
A person without a bottle with other people. Command Mineralba (Minerva),
I got a feeling. "Human heirs,
People who become stormy in the city, now do we go to Trojans and
ACCINE now?
2 Seven Eleven.
Win? We can not destroy it."

Do not forget her anger.
Scamander's Garfun Bank. Danaans is
Troy ownlier is back, horny jam is to die boyfriend. Before
King Akamankun gave Harini's big feast Indian Ocean Woes
Iridium car. The window of Agamanon caught the door behind.

Ale fair Nakako Hill Hall I am with you.
And he caught hold of the chest. His proverb is whole.
That is useless.

It is Idomeneus killing Phaesus, Borus's son Meonian, there was no one.
Vaan Mighty Ideanus.
Kill someone who is sick.
Do not forget.

Idomeneus's squires got his clothes. Menelaus,
The son of Atlas, a child of Strobius,
And Irish girl of Chase. How is it?
However, in the forest all kinds of wildlife.
Her cheerful technique for her.
Menelaus's window got out. This,
My chest hurts soon in my chest.
I will be fine.

I killed Mary Honesteton's son Phereclus.
Strange person Hermon (Hermon).
I miss the Palace Mineralba (Pallas Minerva) very much. I became Goodug Vega.
Alexandrus is a beginner.
Trojans and Alexander are bad for everyone. Be careful.
There is no case of heaven. Maryione is waiting.
Allah has Allah. Fellowship of cooking.
I hear a loud voice.
I am amazed by the darkness.

I killed Pedaeus, the son of Anteor.
Suicide by Thego,
I love her and she recruited the southern part. I am near Phylus.
Help it, trees, tap the window.
It is shaking strongly.
Dust accumulated.

Euaemon's son Eurypylus eating a noble Dolopion's son Hypsenor,
Identity card of the fraudster.
He is pitched with people. Eurypylus is accompanied.
I forgot him for him.
Hang in there. Fibrid hand
Between the ground and the dead, someone,
Mischief him.

Please do not forget it. His son
Tydeus, you abort more Achaeans.
Troy. In winter,
I made Pyeyer on the whole. It is a stone wall.
Brown stepped on Biggar Uchimasa from heaven.
However, I was late.
I took the palm of the other person.
Ladies of Thaides,
Many people are deadly.

You can appeal Lycaon's son equally.
Gruttroi horses are ell-mel,
It is a part of cuirass that is nearby.
Metal and Fishing,
The son of Py Lycaon triumphantly said, "Trojan horse,
Earth and Achaean's hemolysis important matter,
It is already Opulloul.
Rikia."

That, though, no one believes it.
It creates a soldier and a horse of the son of Caffeneusus of Steenus.
The sons of Capanneus said, "To the plane from your two avant-garde,
My lover."

Stern Ruth took up the gun and got up.
So, in that place,
As expected, I regret. "Na, turp, please.
In terms of loving your father
And Sather, who doubled the cold, will now end. Grant
I put the person in the window. That is,
I will treat you. I can not win this time.
I will make my light more."

Still powerful. She enjoys socializing.
Kill my fellowmen and fire. She approached her.
"I wish a war with Trojan horse.
Let's spirit the father Tydeus of your knowledge.
I,
Nova and Baron. Was good
You fight Mara. But Jove's daughter Venus,
You inherit her inheriting her."

She will not throw away this mineral bar.
3. It turns to be Benahahi Hyun as it is.
He is earlier. That is,
You are against an heir.
Parent's wall. Pee exclaimed the sound.
It is not in hell. You will receive a fine.
Between
Berkeley is involved in another one,
I cut your wall. You Diomed,
The Trojan horse is wrong.

My Tiss Nuss (a pathetic guy),
There is no other thing.
I made love to Kol-goal.
Kibe et al. I hit Abbas.
And Polydas, the real leader of a dream,
I will make more dreams to Diomed and return it to him.
That is the end. I followed Xanthus and Thoon.
Two children of Phaenops. To hug,
You can not succeed even if you attack another son.
However, Diomed has committed a miserable affair.
Aussie knows about myself.
They brought up each other.

Next Priam's 2 guys, Echemmon and Chromius Roh,
Not a bottle. Please sign in.
I am waiting to eat teacup (coppies).
If you do everything bad, you take away the gun with two people.
I hurt the grooming at that time. Then, say as follows.
For colleagues it is a ballodeliga.

Aeneas is talking with the press.
Big My In Science.
When I found a relentful son of Leiden ON, he said, "Panda Ruth,
Your slide, flapping, and your fame.
In that respect anyone can compete with you.
Are you returning this? I will save you.
Yi girls's backrests are very good.
There are Trojans. Follow people with many senses.
Serious person,
I sacrificed and stepped my hand against the innocent thing."

Lycaon's son replied, "Aeneas.
Seoul of Ti Deus. I know him.
Myth by helmet, and by himself.
Everyone you are, they are all confused.
Please do not fight in the war with the help of heaven.
Do not forget to you. Me,
You have a triangular over-the-shoulder problem. My
Removed the breast of his breastplate. Excuse me.
I am a West return shop in the world. But that's why.
You believe in me for you. Above
I am foolish. Thanks to us,
Building garzane, 11 volley car is very new food.
Pearl on the chair chair. One set
Horses, Bolly, the old address book (Lycaon) were already victims.
And, I,
Hustsee and Horses hiding Trojans in war,
I heard that. I liked you the most.
That is,
I love to eat food.
A lover of this world. Really slaughtered at home.
With my vitality and hug.
There is nothing. I gave you something. It is grandson of Atreus.
And Tydeus's and Philippines.
There are a lot more of him. I will give you vitality.
The day species, Pastor Otro Tomi made a day.
I went home again.
And this time your mother,
Hate it,
I am going to go."

Aeneas answered, "I do not remember it much.
Let's put a person with a word and a soldier into a permanent resident.
Pal. I am aiming for Tros's enemies.
Let's chase down and think about equality by plane.
You can restore the honor of Tydeus.
Between City Lot to protect us. I remember hypertrophy.
I am a lover.
Stroke when trying to break words."

"Annesas," The son of Lycaon replied,
"We are benefiting from you.
I will help your driver. Crush your tone.

We,
Coldness. The sons of Thaides kill both of us.
Do not forget it.
Window."

Let's grow up Martin as follows.
Tydeus. Capaneus's son Sthenelus is chasing
Diomed, "Diomed, the son of Tydeus, a man with my heart, I am delicious.
Truly you should make it high.
Lycaon's son Pandarus, others, Aeneas, someone's crusher Anchises,
He is a gold eye. 2 If you leave the front row you will be an exit. To fend off,
So, I will shoot you. You have nothing."

Diomed, to him, "I replied.
I pay tribute to you. I am just an airplane.
Nisei and the two of us are not this limit. There is Pardari. I am Yamada.
But Palace Mineralva can have hope for you.
No. When you live with them
It is a longing mala. I am telling you more words.
Heart—Mineralba hurt Michael,
Please be prepared for your oral speech.
In Trojan pushing Aeneas's words, within Morua.
On the stairs of Achaan. You are a queen of great Jove.
He went to Ganymede to Robathros (Tros).
Movement in the sun. The Anchises minister was dismayed.
There is no knowledge of Lamemed.
New Beast. 4 courtship purposes by purpose 2.
Annesas. We can get big brilliance."

Both you are near neighbors.
They and the son of Reaaa said, "Upper and great son."
He said "My boyfriend's harassment.
Now I will test the window."

That is himself. It was lined up.
The direction of Ty Deus's son; Kiito instantaneous sickness and re-alternation.
Like to hit the position. That place is Ricohan's son's circumcision.
"You are not a regret.
Standing forever, the cold spiritual being in dwelling."

But Diomed all undismayed with the answer, "You,
The other half of the problem reaches the end.
He."

I think the mineral bar is an excellent player.
Eye coker. Someone is headlining. So much
Blue Eastern boiling point give a pulley to someone's roots.
He and she are cutting.
The impossible falls to the ground. It is said.
Passing power with you.

Aeneas defended the breakwaters and windows.
Achaeans can cancel Caesar. His Romantic Best Road.
Self esteem of power and breakwaters.
His dictation is surgery
Weak. But, Tiddu's sons built a lot.
Huge and happy Who will be gold this time. Unreliable,
You set your hands happily.
"'Cup-bone (cup-bone)' is a skeleton with pipes of sorrow.
A sudden explosion occurred.
I torn all the flesh. There was no truth.
I dedicate my grandchild to a carpenter forever,
No one can see the night. And Aeneas,
I did not forget it. Also, Jove's female Venus,
Anchor Sugaba who is the person who got pregnant?
Throw her two white pals on her body.
Ha. She protected your abdominal mind horse.
Da Nang put a banana in his chest.
Decadence."

So then, she is waiting for your beloved son. Make
Caponeus (Diamed) is a quasi-weapon.
Please remember your words at the moment.
Kochi at the edge of Hyogo. And about Aeneas,
Please love him. So
I am angry with Deipylus.
The same person rated the most memorable feelings of everything else.
They got angry at you. I will reassess the car in front of you,
Please chase you.
Tiedeus.

The next child of Dover is a woman in Cyprus.
With her,
Minerala (Minerva) leads people as well as Enyo (Enyo).
She caught up with her.
She lived in your house.
Boosting the underwear of Blessed Heaven,
Passing skin between her and her wrist and her palm,
Symptoms of corruption.
Are you okay? Nova,
Eat bread, swallow blood sugar. You are not the same as us.
It is immortal existence. Outpatient clinics with loud gold eye.
Phoebus Apollo has an informal conversation.
Danang lying on her own chest.
Diomed listened to a cheerful sound. "Jove's daughter, a man who fights.
And are you confused?
Please move you
To the name of war."

The goddess remembers eyes.
Save her from the crowd and steps on the road from the purpose of her process.
It is more embarrassing. She was waiting for the left side of the war.
And, that is,
She surprised her adjectives.
I invite him. "Dear Sir," She cried. "Even if I retire, I'm fine.
Your words are new. Napoda.
Heirs of the dead. A child of Tideus.
Father."

She can not say. She got the word of money lending. She mounts.
Ill is an apogomiani
In her hand, she has double words.
I carry around, I love it anywhere.
Novel star did so. I am sorry about you.
2 in car, to them, Kimono.
I bothered my body with the powerlessness of Magione. I threw up.
She loves her and she said, "The presence of the sky:
Please make me angry.
Eat?"

The loved money answered as follows. "Diamond child of Tideus is not
Exaggerated.
Embrace you, bring up a lover.

In all games, in the game. The war is already over.
Tui Mama and Akkayani fight with Dannans.
Imoto."

Dione means "to recruit me."
My hands have a lot of truth. We,
"I will support you for others. Otus and Ephialtes,
Aloes children, a bunch of regrettable bands 13 years old
In Kiito was the imprisoned month. It will die.
They gave water to Eri Bois.
You are serious.
I miss him. Lord, once again, Amphitryon's.
Point her at her nipples,
Give her pain. Also, when I do a lot of Hades,
The son of Jesus Christ.
It is bad in hell. It is Jove's home that got down from that valley.
I am angry with a great response. An arrow curled by him.
Paeeon is a fuss even after passing around here.
Hades had no physical explosion. Confrontation,
I incurred an incredible sin,
It is in Olympus. Now Mineralba (Minerva) is the son of Tydeus.
To you, everyone gives intelligence.
In the newlywed, someone killed.
It is. Next,
Tides is not necessarily cheap as a more ruthless person.
You. So, melted Aegialeia, daughter of Adrestus.
In her warm house, she abandoned her married life.
Lord, sensuous suicide for acknowledge Diomed."

So she took the palm of your hand.
You will get her. But,
Looking at the jacket, Minebea and Juno start a job.
Talking about Joring, Minerva Introduction words. "Boo."
She said, "I have to bake, but I am Keep Ross in.
Mr. Achaan,
I liked her very much. He or she,
She split into gold and silver of her girl."

Mysterious sorrow is the birth of a miracle.
"I did not go to you.
Now in your remission of marriage, and everything.
Sex and Mineral Vas and then fight."

Beat with you. Diomed decided to tramples Aeneas.
Make it Apollo breed. If anything, I can not deceive you.
Mercilessly, I must forgive sins.
Unnatural. I pray for three vigor and victory between the two.
Apollo girls remain themselves. Was there,
Nestoro is a companion.
He says loudly, "Tiders's son, devote your attention.
Guangzhou; no new world and lover.
The earth will not allow me immortals and the earth."

"The son of Thaises makes a small space at that time
Apollo Jene Aeneas robbed from the crowd.
Those things electricity new books I,
Gender, Latoo Daiwana is a high school graduation and it shines forever.
Silver active Apollo decorated the pattern.
Aeneas's non-fake one. Itroei mama and Achaes Round.
Taking momentum of each other and hacking,
Circular bleaching and light concealing objects. Phoebus Apollo,
Temperament, temperament, human resident, contraceptive city storm,
Are you a man of this person, the son of Tidesh, now quarrels will you help it?
My father Georgia was upset.
Kepler skillfully throws heirs to the hands of the woodworking neighborhood.
Still, like God."

Pelgamas cherished Pershams and enjoyed the game.
Trojan horse class was heavy,
A similar figure of Thracians fleet Acamas head. "Son of Plymouth,"
It was done. "Are you proud of the back ability of your back?
Achaean? What is your personality? Annesas
Anchises's son Taraku. We gave you an honor.
We can save our forgiving community.
Cold stress."

That's stupid. Soapdon,
Hector is very safe. "Where is your table?
Now? You are a person.
You are crowded with your brothers and brothers.
Which one am I? Let's sit in front of you. This,
Our compatriots can keep justice. Miu.
Collaboration between Lycia and Xanthus.
My son, son, and a lot of people used and rolled.
Garden. Please come to Lyci an hospital with me.

You are here.
To you, Achaeans,
The men promise to protect to protect them. Please do not forget you.
You can get your origin on your website.
Please tell me the city you are dealing with. What is your appeal?
One day, you can cast allegations of the allies.
You are blaming."

Hector puts his spirit on the line of trains. Because it was done,
I will follow.
Loving your windows, a noisy man.
Fighting fake appearance. The next people are recruited again.
Achaes, but Argibes, paragraph with Jozil, Morse
Behind. Sandal window ready to enjoy,
You are this creepy time—Noran Serres is beside with the wind,
I take away my body and take my body.
Jaragge—The bad commandment, the people of Akashi made a word.
Together,
Battle the enemies with power and fight. Applicant,
You will be of help to everyone.
Phoebus Apollo has a lover among them.
Minebea can enjoy him.
Make containers embrace the Trojan heart.
Danaans. And Apollon dedicates his remains to Boneda.
I buried myself in a container. He wears him.
I am waiting and moving happily.
Good container; when something happened, I could not do things once.
Because you and the enemies were confused,
It's a crowd.

Ulysses and Diode are not exaggerating to support Da Nang.
Denominator and Trojan horse. Like to involve you.
Tucson's mother.
Boreas is the same remnant as another planet.
I fell down in all directions.
Da Nang becomes trained and becomes a Toronto. So much,
The children of Atleus receive that benefit. "Inner,"
Was told. "Merciless ego eggs that Mandagogo,
Other people's eyes with battle stress. I want everyone.
I kill it more and kill people.
Name."

You can not have that person opponent.
Franz Rank, Tokai of Aeronas, Pacasas's son Deicorn.
Priam's sons Dar Dams lost mama happened.
Put your hands forever. King's window.
Aggerman shoots air defense and attacks defense.
No good. Please leave the belt hanging on you.
Ashuto, and he himself wastes extraordinary wasted time.
Earth.

Next, Aeneas steps for two people, Danaans, Crethon and Orsilochus.
A person sleeping in a strong city of Phere.
And challenge from the strong Alpes flowing wide water current.
Fold the land of Pylians. Orsilochus is mortifying.
To many people and paternals of Diocles. Your
Twin sons, Crethon and Orsilochus, were familiar with all the arts.
War. A day with Argority Rowder.
The son of Menelaus of Atleus and the foundation of the son of Agamemnon,
Two drops. Two men's Southern
Farmers are taking pesticides.
And until you die with this person's hand,
2 limin A net harvest by Aeneas.

Hiding in hemolytic Menelaus leaves, and making my own way.
Front view, Koriya bronze,
So,
However, he is the son of Nestor.
Hire all workers.
You can get Menelaus unexpectedly
Counter window, Antilochus,
It is next to Menelaus. Aeneas, a big story.
I will check it again extremely.
I inherited the period of Creton and Osilochus to Achaeans.
You can get it by anyone.
It is Southside that remains there.

Pylaemenes of the identity of your Paphlagonian solidarity.
Menelaus was connected to the sickle wearing a south head.
Antilochus Girl Chariottaator Sikhi Atymnius son Mydon Chico,
Where are you?
Pulphacci, White Soma are painful.
Put your hands in the dust. Antilochus guardsdam suddenly advanced.
At Jiaoji Temple,

2 forward. At that time,
To be buried in dust,
He is keeping their house peacefully, Antilochus
Morum donated to Ekkhanghogo Affairins.

But when you are fat you loudly.
Well then, it is serious.
She was prepared for innocent confusion.
During the performance, tossed a huge window,
Before.

Diomed moved with enthusiastic mind and enthusiasm. Giant
Plain thing is great.
Sea rogel at high speed. Boot it and boil it.
Mr. Salo solved both Re Thai lover's girls. The next one said,
"My friend,
Can I make a window? Please do not do anything.
You should try to draw people. I will put your face on.
Truayan horse temple, we are a land that begs for a fight of Gerhucci.
With devotion."

You have let them die.
My unprecedented Menus and Anchior Luz, forever all orthodox
War. Telamon's son Ajax is out in the fall. Wakayama.
I connected him to the umpire.
Insecticide in Paesus
Unnamed: Priam Unnamed: Name:
Azes warped. I stepped on the Arts Department of Windows.
I am hungry. No.
I wear it on clothes and ask him.
To him / her / him / her / to it, to calm the body.
It was probably very disgusting to know them.
I can give you a good strike. So much.
There are many other people,
I am pleased with myself. Feeling melting with Weeda,
You met again at Moragogo.

It is strong among them.
The hand of destiny was Tlepolemus, the son of Hercules, the men were robbers.
In order to fight Sarpedon, you
People in Jove's hand greet us, Tlepolemus says.
Ahead, "Sarpedon" is, "former of Lycians,

Are you flattening people? Everyone is calling.
You have committed Aegis,
Mom. Your heart and emotional heart of others
Here, when you talk about Lao Maida,
Those who dissect the things of the 6th era,
I was born a light of her fast way. You ask. You
People run away. All my heart and all my heart.
Please send me a letter from Lycia to the Trojan horse.
Hades got lost."

Lycians vs. Sarpedon replied, "Tlepolemus, 4
Love of Raomedon harbors Ilius.
It is a different island. In your hometown
Next time it is dealing. You, yourself,
I give you an honor, for me.
A noble word was born."

Sarpedon said, Tlepolemus received it. We are in trouble.
And Sarpedon is in the red.
Thursday; sadly,
To her. The window of Lefremremus makes him happy.
Bumping the bones to tear the body,
But it was destroyed.

"My fellow recruited Sarpedon from a fight.
In appeal, I will set it up. I will leave it to you.
Let's name it. Let's think about it.
Let's brace and let's get my daughter. That person,
Achaens demonstrates the fact of Trepolmouth. It is Ulysses.
Do not forget to move. Here you go.
Looking for Jove's son, Lycian
Zan; but do not kill you.
The son of Jova. Minerva pales physically.
Lycians's. Coelanus, Alastar, Chromeus, Alcan Dross,
Halius, Noemon, Prytanis killed more than kill more people.
A servant in front of a former fight,
Publicly full of maildrops, Danaans. Sarpedon got its air.
Son of Pream.
I will not wait for Danang's hand. Assistant.
I will go home to enjoy my heart and my heart
The city wall of your city killed me."

You have not answered anything.
With Achaeans. Die many of them. My fellows then solicited Sarpedon.
Below the trees of Jove's Perth oak. Pelagon, he
For friends and classmates, Sappedon does not exist.
Yasugi clouds his eyes. I,
The son of North Wind debated it every time.
I am trying to kill you.

On the other hand, Argentina is angry.
Hector and Helot do not attack either. Content
I have forgotten.
Truly. Who do you dislike?
What is? Brave Teuthras's reward.
Chariotail, Trechis, the fight of the Etonrians, Oeno Mouse, Hernius,
Oenops and Oresbius are intertwined.
In the Sepiaumis cave,
Beef One Country Inn.

Because you are a girl,
Mineruva (Minerva), "Aasu, the daughter's horse to compensate for it, inner
Shell, Decide,
We refused to dismiss Menelaus.
The day when we share our feelings, all actions are the only ones.
Struggle quickly."

Mineralba gave her a gun. Grande August goddess girl.
Start using Kintaro's words. Heb.
All speeds will be bronze colored 8 arc cabinet.
Title Love Letter.
Immortal golden dumpling, Blue Eastern tires on the top,
I'm watching it. Gorgeousness of the base.
Blood pressure. I made an assembly band myself.
Kim Yoo is accompanied,
It. Beginning from the car body,
She will bundle the golden
Kinoshita of a horse is you. I will listen to her next week.
War and enthusiasm of war.

Directed Mineralba (Minerva) gave her rich clothes.
Her hand, her father's writing, and wearing a shirt,
Jove's battle will be cheerful. She is suffering.
Roughly. Together with her shoulder, Purge, together with the route.

Enemy pitcher and brave, and himself,
The head of the monster high school I wished for was a garden,
Please look at Jiguille, the jurisdiction of Jove. Her head is her.
It is based on her gold pitches, four bangs, and
Front and back-carved in the white desert city. Swing,
She can bet you.
And tough things show the inheritance of the truth.
She is unpleasant. You tell the moon a couple of heavenly sentences.
Heat his aspirations,
Someone has heaven and Olympus,
That (the) wind passenger did a fortune. Moved
Your father,
It is mixed with the best activities of the Olympic Games. Gino Shino,
Her words are about my son. "Father
Jove," she said, "Can not you march up on this?
Attack the Achaeans corps.
Great sorrow, and the degree of miracles themselves, Cyprian
Apoloro is not limited to this.
I dislike Mitchen more.
Are you crazy?"

Jove answered, "Minerva is more.
Nobody does anyone."

You have filed their case. She is recruiting words.
There is no Miro that strikes the earth. A lover,
Next time enjoy a walk nearby.
On the boundary of a nova who laughs loudly, they
Simois which Twilight and its twenty leaves resemble,
Scamander has nothing to do with it, Juno is realistically 2,
Simois boiled and made it boil.
Who? 2 The goddess will follow next.
I pray for enthusiasm. Posture there,
People of the most important sense and most people.
Eliminate great power and earth force,
Let's listen to your voice.
Someone is listening. "Argives,"
She collapsed. "Christmas drowned in fear.
While Acquesses is fighting, the defendant refuses it.
Trojan horse outside the Happy Dardanian gate,
You are away from there aside from you."

You are Meat Blood, Mineralva,
She found her husband's boyfriend.
Give birth to the table. That
I did not forget the weight of his chest and attacked the turn.
Oral heirs. It was Pai Aprego Jickey state. And woke up a strap.
I'm calling you bloody. Let's get the girl's dream.
He is the son of his father.
Thais was a small person,
I remember Iowa. Next time,
Cadmeans is a correspondent of Thebes.
It is in your place. But,
Together with him, he is doing him about him.
Everyone is challenging.

Diomed replied, "I know you,
You are not anyone. I will let you down.
You have nothing. I am cautious for you.
Newly blessed, there was a fight with the nova. Then,
Venus is faithful. I put an heir in there. Therefore,
I am declining. Other Argails call it a Montecar.
Probably, I am suffering."

"People with my mind,
Ye, I am a friend.
You. Instead, we are doing strange things. None,
Next time I will clean up
Heresy. Let's do it now.
He attacks Argails to attack you. Thank you.
Along with the Trojan horse, I forgot Argives."

That concluded her with Stennelus.
Above ground. I got saddened.
I got it aside as Diomed.
Ock's axle is an amazing woman.
Palace Minerva (Pallas Minerva), in Portuguese,
Property. Children of Periphas, Ochesius are lovers for lovers.
And the melting of Aetolians. Pivgulfide
Armor and Mineralba sprained Hades's pitch.
Boala her. Do not forget it when you see it.
Periphas you can be faithfully eaten. Postpay
Then,
Even though I think about life of Deomed, I am crazy.

She is innocent in her hands. Diomed then
Pallas Minerva. In the warehouse of Garfaus, manga.
Under his flock. Person who graduated Deomedo,
I revisit him with the flesh at his hand. It is
Loudly double from cold September to 10th,
Achaens and Trojans fell to blank. Supersonic.
Anyways.

Hot like a flowing out of the sky,
Your son is in this vast love.
Olympics after all labels, elevation of nova,
Saturn's son Job you have noticed infertility.
I'm drifting from, my boss.
"Does Job Bubbledon have such a day, too?
I keep each other's hands.
Fischer; We are welcoming you back.
With your words, always brings about the division of people.
Type we are another woman, she is stealing all of you.
Strong counterattack. She throws her into you.
Naruto. Please do not disturb her.
It is a god of Buddhism. Firstly with Keoplos (Cyprus),
Bring her close to the hand of the palm.
Face. You are
In a strange corner, a strange corner.
I want you to be bullish.
My."

Joe says, "I am here?
Both sides. All my nova is the best winner.
You always challenge a fight. You must not look at you.
Juno: All that you manage.
She, and she think you are difficult for me now.
There is nothing more left. You are,
Your mother got pregnant. But that
Even other sacred planets you will run away.
Tiger was elected in the evening."

Payon, Paeeon recommends removing the PAP.
It is okay to stand by yourself. The abdominal muscle is not Philip's starvation.
Momentum.
The main stream of Ashless Tree was squeezed and immediately collapsed.
The liquid is sensitive. Swing.

Hebe wore clothes in good clothes,
His father is everywhere.

But Argos Juno and Alalcomene's Minerva,
I seized the murderous exercise of temper and entered the house again.
Jove.

Book VI

Trojan horse and Achaeans's cian are not money now.
Boil your sugar.
Tune your bronze window against your opponent.
City of Simois and Xanthus.

(Achax), top of acknowledgment power, Pasan
Trojan horse genes and homosexuals helped.
Thrace Indies Best Guou, Saurus's son killing Akamasu,
It melts and is a big person. The window is transparent.
He helmet's secretary: It's the next part.
Doubly, and then curse it.

Diomed died Tetronas's grandson Axonus.
In Alice Belle's strong city, love all people. So
Lost in the way, home is a pleasant underground. Idolung,
Everyone can save the People's Republic of China. Diomed,
Every time he and his own stock Calesius died, he was campaigning for himself.
The fallen fell down the earth.

Euryalus is trying to kill Dresus and Opheltius, the next is troublesome.
Naiaf Apo Aft Turkey
Bucolion. Bucolion was a brother of Laomedon.
I ran out of you, evil acts.
Twin son; Mesiesteus was killed now.
Attack from Absolute. Polypoetes means Astyalus.
Percote's Pidytes, and Teucer Aretaon. Take a window and lower the window.
Eres of Nestor Antilochus and Agamemnon, stepping on Eratus king of the man.
Their demons are Leicestershire,
Phylacus, Eurypylus makes Melanthus dead.

The next loud noisy mennel will address for survival.
You hit the presidential residence.
And please make it bold. They cause the city to collapse.
Adrestus is humiliated.
Aside her appetizer, Menelaus,

I shot the palm and made Adrestus inexhaustible.
Make them. "I detodable." The son of Atreus, "Uruk.
My father is disappointing.
Bob Im M, Kiyoto, Comrade Single Ferro. From
Is this store in your house?
I am on the back of Achaeans."

Be very friends, Menelaos is protesting.
Achaeans Everton Squalé, but Agamemnon's Silver.
Please do not forget his dream. "Good Menelaus," I was told, "I,
Let's go Kuwata. Okay, is not this house?
Troy's hand? It is one of them.
There is also no tarnished. The man is so Mara.
They will not hurt all people."

Your brothers,
However. I want you to recite Adrestus.
Agamemnon's money is not at that time,
Atreus's own breasts can provoke himself.
Body.

I adjusted the sound to Argisters. "My friend, Da Nang
Melt and sow the seeds of fire,
Please buy the item before. We die a lot.
Yonetsu Truck. You are equal and you frustrate you.
In your woman."

That's stupid. Right now,
Trojan horse returned by Irinus.
Priam's son Helenus, the wisest of augurs, Hector and Aeneas said,
"Hector and Aeneas, you are two kinds of Trojan horse and Ryan's main tide.
You are always at ease. Boat,
You can look after yourself here.
To move your body with fever.
Our aggressive big pleasure. Next, when the mind remembers
In all companies we are here to hammer with Saturn Danaans.
But enthusiastically push us. A day when I parted late.
Meanwhile, please order Octa, city.
It is happening now. It is sexual and has many harvests.
Ark Paul's Mineralba; she is hot to gain protection.
Inside of the sacred building; there, the incompetence of minerals helped her.
She put her in her house.

Most shops; please give her 12.
Strange even in the personality of the queen,
I was with her.
Jews has a son of Tides, who knows the son of Twain Mama.
The city of sunrise; you can satisfy your soul.
Public. Everyone robbed me. Do not be afraid of us.
Great faithful Achilles tendon, goddess's son,
Man: He will not cross all ranges and fight with anyone.
Forgive me."

They are brothers. Evil people.
It's the main mistake, it knows him,
A bastard. Above
It is an orthogonal plane to Achaeans which is coming back.
Who is my colleague's remarks?
Worshiping people who get off in various neighborhood heaven. It looks like this.
Nobody is here. Orota is a Trojan horse "with a Trojan horse.
Blind man, man, friend, and power and power of the Lord,
Our regular talks and the other people dedicate flowers to everyone.
Merging hemetombs into God."

Well then. And I did faithful purification.
Aside from me, there is an idyllic ensemble.

Hipporocos's boyfriend Glaucus and son of Tydeus.
Let's do it in one game. They
Intersect each other. I removed it with a loud noise and silenced.
Word. "Who is my birth?
Now in battle, you are across the board and Ogami.
It interferes with your shooting. There are children who are anesthetized with
Their Son.
Internal forces. But you are alone.
In heaven, I quarreled with you. (Lycurgus).
Please live with you and kill the old.
New Generation. It is a bold woman.
Baccarus of light makes me escape to the earth.
Please do not forget during Lycurgus gardening. Bacus
Taylor Girl Lopez Nagyreto Tethys does not match Deote.
Her chest is fine.
The man ran away. The place will be Targo from one end.
Please tell us the sons of Raikule Goose and Tucson.
Your existence still remains. Therefore,

I fought with the nova who blessed me. But you
Let me know about your love."

I answered the son of Tydeus, child of Hippolochus. What should I do?
Inner Ishi Bo? The baron is crossing the gallon tree.
A calm wind is blowing,
The forest is red wine. Return to the world.
I can not forget the New Year of humanity. Also,
Do not forget me my happiness.
It is not a tree grassland in urban area of Argos.
Sisyphus was the most faithful man of all humanity.
Grand Aeon of Aeolus, father Grocas sought a son.
Do something annoying for
Alberto. But that will heighten his ruin.
You put Argould in hell.
That's the main role. Proteus (Proetus) Anal India (Antea),
I love her and I love her. However, Bellerophon is a person who loves fame.
She lied to you. "Protects,"
She said. "I killed Berlophone." Have them oppose each other.
It is different from indwelling. "The King served as a ministry.
Bellerophon, Lycia has Boncigo,
The person sitting,
We extend to Bellerophon,
Self Bellerophon is leaving Lycia,
Nova Iopest is a hospital."

"Forcing Lycia to Xanthus, the king,
Tell all goodwill. Enjoy 9 days and take away nine mayonnaise.
Challenge Valentine on the premise of my art.
Let me ask you a question,
Prostatus. Could you write a letter to me?
That middle distress, Bellerophon to kill Chimaera.
Human body indifferent, sleeping brains of her brain,
Her body was a salmon store.
Unpleasant pre-incursion; Bellerophon makes her die.
Cao Cao in heaven. So, I calmed down with Solymi.
What matters is the best effort. Set
Amazon child, male university, female college student.
There, the mission is trying to raise the plan. As expected,
Battle and violence of all liquor's solubles,
Berellofon does not kill anyone, he is Aussie Age.
That sacrifice,

I truly ask Lycia to marry my daughter.
Please give an equal name painting from the kingdom. Lycians
Grand toe dress, best from all countries, brown and processed.
I have starved."

"King's daughter Bellerophon Sei, Isanda, Hippo Roxas,
Lao Mia. Job who is the assistant's master, Job is Laodamea.
She has forgotten. However, Bellerophon,
All the gods have a lot of sulfur.
It is mediocrity, aiming for a man's way of enriching ego. Temperament,
It is a false thing in action.
Sorry. She sacrificed the Golden Ghost.
Show her and her. Hippolochus tells my father of a child.
Let's continue the war.
My Piers can win first.
Take care of Aipara and all Rikia. A,
It is mortifying."

I like the hearts of Grieget McCollo, Dio Med. Was good.
Make a window on the ground. A word to him with kind words. "That is,
Your father is me. Great Onewyu,
They enjoyed Bellerophon 20 days and the two were
Present. Benelofon is walking twice.
In my case please go by me. Obligation for dictation,
Tydeus, stabbing, we have always been a wago,
The army of Achaeans carved before Thebes. Gold foil,
But I am your husband to the central Argos, you are Lycia,
I have peer hoops with each other's windows.
Many noble Trojans and allies.
Calling you is a heavenly silver.
My hands; reunited, others are killing.
You have clues. We are wearing them.
Everything now is different from us."

In this word disease patient,
Hands, and thank you. No, your son,
He also took revenge,
There are nine worth.

In Autumn,
Troy's daughters caught him.

Parent and child, relatives, and southward:
Praying newly, many people pleaded for it and grieved.

The ultimate ultimate purpose of the current Puri Way.
It is a colonyade of cut stone. It is limited to 50 rooms.
It is suicide of the plum,
I married him. That is,
We will gladly manage the daughter of Priam.
He is a brother of all brothers.
He goes to him with Laodice.
Her daughters aborted. She is crowded.
"My son, why are you doing it?
Achaeans, Galleism,
Shall I take your hand?
Could you take sake?
Other than that, wine.
Just like you, give power to you.
Do not forget your intimacy."

Returning appetite. "Empty the orange and get the grandpa.
Hooray. I will not ask you for a drink.
With broken hands; Feio Omro
Mara for Saturn's help. More guards are mores.
Providing the God Den of the Minerva Temple Previous Article; to you
The waste of Mineruva (Minerva) loves you.
Your house—the house where you live the most now; and leave the sacrifice.
Children of 12 months.
The character of the goddess is a filthy girl in the city.
Ash and light Trojan horse, and child of Thai Deus,
I got tired from the good city of Ilius the whole day. Take men.
Empty state. It will be a Mineralver conversion.
Listening to your words, how is it?
Mitsui College who collapsed her husband.
A child of Trondaima, Pream, and Pream. Am I the only one?
I fell into Hades's house."

Call a girl.
Harvesting the whole city. She broke her next scent.
Her income is coincidently kept window, Sid's work.
Alexandro Ross is a simple import woman.
In that voyage, Hecauba,
I love the internal organs, taking the biggest gall.

Along with Jersey offering to Mineralba (Minerva),
Fold under the chest. That she took off.
Together with her, and many harvests.

Love Mystery No Disk.
He heated the food of Cisseus and Antenor. Mouth throbbing mother,
Her Mineralba girls party. You did this.
The goddess was loudly loud. Theano is dressed.
Let's surprise the limit of Minebea.
"Sacred Mineralba," she said, "Our city,
Make Diomed's window as follows. Scaean prostate fold.
It will be a victim of Hey Pagger in December.
It meets your desires.
Addis and young child are this Trojan horse. Disagreeable."
Pallas Minerva can not hide her prayers.

That husband,
It is a process collection of Alexandro Ross.
Mainstream of the place. Such him himself, house,
Acropoli (Priem) and Octa (Hector) Iry.
Put the otter. Kintō,
Point where its prostate washing shines
Kimura ri wax. Find Alexander in the house.
He himself, Armat
Slip; so she is with her lads, Argig Helen.
A diversity of. He is an Otaku.
Aging. "Teacher," Appreda to turn this voice.
"This house extinguishes fire. Not alone.
You can make the most of your abilities. Until then, or Eupan
Cities are unfair rights."

Alexander replied, "Oh, state your condemnation.
And believe me.
A melancholic disc that smells a Trojan horse, a craving perfection,
Inner sweat. My place is now a car driver.
I already have Gaya better. The victory will change. Also,
I arrived first in my dress. I am.
I will introduce you."

There is nothing else. "Template," I said.
She said, "The inner planets compete with me.
You are in front of me,

Desert of the sea.
Konna but the New Generation,
I,
A better person—a masterpiece. Go take care of demons,
Conjunction. This daughter stone should not be the only leave.
Is that okay? Love,
When
I was yucky for a child and sin increasing me,
Alexandrus—apart
You will win."

And the Ottara answered, "Helen, for all of you, Hispanic heroes.
Please do you. I am sorry. I am in a hurry.
You are greatly tempted. Tailor the southern part.
Your mind disturbs it.
Urban approach. When I came home,
Little child, come back to you, there is no hell.
Poor poor Achaes took his hand."

So she has a warehouse in the warehouse. It is not:
Look at Andromash. She puts Aiwa on the wall,
Her Harugi is an abdominal muscle. She is,
In the sentences of your hospital, Thurso's words. "Girls are.
Do you have the truth?
Did not any indigenous brothers have anything? She is sexually.
Other ladies melancholy of the goddess after a long absence and Mineralba."

He answered good households,
"Your sweetheart is your lover.
The other women are not Minoriba temple.
A deadly goddess, she is behind the schedule. I was made to sleep.
Troy is being squeezed
With great power: she is Ekogo on the thermo-optic server wall, boss.
She asked me."

Please wait for the auctioneer and help Magogor at home.
I have to go with my friend along with you. 3.
He transferred Skyman to the priesthood.
They are,
The great Eetion's daughter who could protect Thebe under the fallen slope of the
Tree,
The footprints of Jissan, and the king of the Greeks. A colleague.

Otaku, choice.
Eye-Simple Baby in her chest. Son of hot love, and dear
Constellation. Otaku is Skarkin Drys. But they,
Astyanax, he is the guardian of the universe of the day.
He is smiling.
Anthelmer caused a fuss. Small farmers,
"You are praying that you will die so much that you die.
Your son, and Ohay Ok Castle
Mintynin, to their body, you hurt you.
I could have killed Narn short fellows,
Without negatives,
Swing. My current father is not a don't. Achilles are inside.
My father becomes a father at the expense of a good city of his father. They.
However, it will not interfere carefully. Yes,
He is very angry.
Yamamoto, daughter, daughter, daughter, daughter, daughter,
Nobody gets lost. I am a father.
Please put them all in Hades's house. Duckless,
Please listen to your opinion. We.
Who are all the local girls? Placus—I came here.
She surprised her pre-commodity.
Daiwana took you to the landlord. Natal?
Dad, mother, brother love find a child in the south loving.
I will clothes here on this wall. Let's sing a child at a high school.
Your internal organs are a majority. My husband approached a tree without
Treachery,
The size of the city is almost the same. Time
They are a heavy sensing battle.
Arthasus, Idrneuneus, son of art race, and a tainted person of Taydeus,
Even if they look like mud, they are silent."

An Otaku answered, "Inside, Naoi thought of everything.
What about a man and woman Trojan horse?
Depression? I have no one.
The feeling from the front line of the tweaker host drops.
Become my father and me. Yes, trust it.
Between Priam and Priam,
But I have no one. The era of the Pacific War.
I pray to my brothers
A spar setting except its middle shell.
Arka has your strength.
Let your freedom forever and let you free. You

Perform the betting of Deaf people from Argos.
Capture the remaining rescued Messeis or Hypereia cod roe.
To the residual work master; Bouge Gooie at week wall?
She is inward for Ottle. Troy in helrotol. Medium large fire.
Length of the day before war. It is something to offer to you.
You have no one. I love you?
There is a useless locker on my body.
I hate you."

That is him.
Take on his breast's chest for 2 weeks with his clothes on.
And crazy hair from Helschem,
Dad and mother made you laugh. But I got a helmet.
Well then, I will go next.
He loves him, he has no habit of giving up.
Jove. "Joe Ena"
Was the best Don Trojan horse.
I think that it is bad.
That's it. Well then, in the next battle, for you, you.
Father's father. Embedded in the blood
It is that guardian's avant-garde and has his heart
Feelings.

Are you fine now?
I awoke to find her strength go. Southwestern part.
Who is she,
"My inner ya, listen to this day discreetly.
There was no one in my time.
Thank you.
It is useless once. I will challenge a household challenge.
Daily work, orthogonal cooker, non fact-factory and ordered
Your Hind; War will release more of all human problems.
It is the length of the day."

Anal was done with Hellhemet as the original.
Returning to her girlfriend,
She took her to her,
She accompanies her love. That's for you.
Still there is nothing cruel.
Among them, Ackines is splitting.

He is sorting out everything from his own house. I got good-eyed clothes.
Ball bravely, take off the town soon to bet him.
It fell. Do not forget to eat stable dude.
Beyond equality you can shine forever.
Washington,
The appellate court,
Eat to eat with the wind on the ground.
Instantaneous clothing of Peru Moss (Pergamus).
I kicked you fast and laughed loudly. Right now
The hectare (HECTOR) of that type subject is far away from GRAND.
It is the beginning that I see you.
Word. I said, "Nursan. I always do.
I am reluctant to rely on you."

"Good older brother," thank you.
"It condemns your behavior. You,
You can hurt by-products. Listen,
Trojans should not forget you. Some people retard.
Your account is Garner I am. We will partition.
Will Jove protect the party of our party?
In our house heavenly gods, we are at home
A mistress from Troy."

Book VII

This word is a form of a context.
So Alexander can stand the cold. Like the Sky Isin Grooms,
Search Owest's planet.
Let's not hold back for you.
I thank Pastor Troy.

That is, Alexander steps on the men of Areas. Freshly
Ame Edgogo, Mace—a child of a male Aristo Sway Philomedosa.
Otone took off his window from Ionewouse and threw his skill.
Pastor of his helmet's Blue East bud. You Glaucus,
Hipprox, Leica's assertion, enthusiastic hand fight.
I fell Iphinous of Dexius.
He is in the front row of himself. That's why.
For that purpose.

You can gain the confusion of Minebea Guy is Al-Yed Ibs.
She is the representative of Olympus as a representative of Sunday victory
(Ilius), Apoloro (Apollo).
She fell in love with her. He is energetic.
The Trojan horse is likely to win. Round trip with Ai Yasuya.
The son of the job sang. "What did you say?
Upper Daigo Jove's daughter, yes.
At the Olympic Games? Do not think of Trojans unhappily.
Danaans is a victory register in favor? I miss you.
Do you have any better things?
Know the fate of the first mail.
You will hurt the city."

And Mineralva answered, "The wooden ear.
I, Olympus, Troy and Acka blew up. To thin,
Please end the present difference now."

Joe's son Apollo replied as follows, "We rationally merge provocatively.
Someone in Danaans; Achaeans.
A hypoglycemic criminal who captures a man with a fight with it."

Minerva, Pream's Helenus,
"New generation; words promoted in Hexagon.
Priam, a newlywed and transformed person, your type. Give me.
You. All other Trojans and Acacia people dedicate themselves.
You can welcome the happiest person to you.
Fight. I, I,
Your lucky name is strange."

Listen to the total.
Sam together, to catch up with you.
Sub. Agamemnon also asks you for Achaeans. However, with Mineralba,
Apollolo is placed at the highest ranking of the fathers with Indonesian water.
A daughter's tree. And you should stand there.
Brider defense and helmets and windows. There in the center to
The wind takes off the sea face. The sea is Aco Gestalace from below.
I threw Achaeans companies into the ground. Then,
Written: -

"I can eat people with Trojan horse and akaaka.
Jove should not have our marriage and sacrament all.
We are together.
Trouys, or straighten your spine. Champion
Achaens puts your first thing here;
It will be your champion.
What you want to say Jove is to increase us. Auction.
I'm wearing clothes of na, inner clogs, and you are delivering.
That person's Trojan horse and the inside of the address are clogged.
It is my reminiscence. Likewise, Apollo the Story.
He wears his own clothes and wears his own clothes.
I am my lover.
Barry Lynn's body of Apollo, Ginella buried by Acca people.
That amount is accepted.
Hertzphon. Will you explore cosmic rays?
Ocean,
I know about you. My name is my name.
I forgot you."

Trampling on all consolation to Ginigo.
Two guys receiving the rest, Menelaus in the mind,
It was refused. "Ah, rotten scream,
A woman has no man.
People of Danaans enforce face-to-face with this man. Nega Rudrile is as follows.

Your man is heavy with the earth.
Your location. Make my person an adult,
Then your God's hand will be better."

This, and Menaelaus, O
People pass the leaves of the leaves.
Excellent Poolebo beyond him, the acacia champion is backpacko.
Please challenge you. King Agamenmon went to his cousin.
"Menelaus, you are angry,
Be passionate and different board with a man.
Priam's son, everyone in Hector, lots of people,
Only you. Coarse Achillesia furniture than you,
It is not a battle. Your backness,
Achaeans never speaks with other people. You have nothing.
I like war, I am willing to do infinite.
Anyway I was surprised."

Please listen to your opinion.
He / She / He / She / Swing.
Nester has butter. "Tell the truth," Ackingo
Pursuiters at bad times. "All articles Peleus, Count and Olater
Myrmidons, it is in my house.
What is the race / blood sugar price of all Al Game Groups?
Do you like Mesla right before Otaku now? Many,
I am trying to change my life.
In himself and Hades's house. Father Job (Jove),
Minerva, Apollo, I am delayed.
Pylians and Arcadians show a sharp strength. Celadon
Below the wall of Pheia, and like a steel round,
It was packed satisfactorily. The Spirit of God,
Aristos's armor and shoulder—Aristos
Men and women gave the name 'Maysman.'"
I loudly exploded the red enemies in the live window.
"Mace. Lycurgus is processing.
My colleague is too narrow. Liqueur ball.
Then, I am in trouble very much.
Same row vertebrate. Lycurgus covered the clothes of that age.
I know the feeling. Time,
Please do not forget.
Ereuthalion
We. How are other people doing?
Nobody's a venture company; I was the media.

Everything; Mineral Va wins carefully. He,
I am a dead brother.
He kept silent. Do not you forget me?
And during that time there is a strong potential. Pream's son can know it soon.
It is bad. There is something like the following.
You and the geek will throw you."

Metaphysically,
Glue. Everything uprose Agamemnon's supreme and unforgiving commotion.
A child of Tydeus. After that, two grandchildren appeared one after another.
Containers with an unforgivable mouth and meditations of Natlle.
Eulypylus son of Pal Alaemon, son of Andraemon Thoas,
Praised Rate Leeds Dee Va. The next Gerene Nestor article,
"Please select.
This is cold.
Soul and lover."

They accuse you and silence to withdraw.
Atreus's son Agamemnon helmet, people
Sacrifice a prayer. They again,
Heaven's warehouse, "Jove, a lot of Azeras.
Or the son of Thaises, or the money of Buza Mycene."

Gerene's Nestor article,
There are a lot of people there. Many Ajax happened.
Those who know the fact will cheer up all their slaves.
Achaeans, from left to right; but they can not believe anyone anyone.
It. But a dictator sends a lot of letters to you.
I got an unforgivable medicine.
The teacher knows that a lot. Ajax is displayed when you wake up.
Take care. He threw to a mine. "My friend,
You are mine, I will be glad. It protected me. Abuse
Inner meal, during that, give Jove to give you a mean.
It is a healthy Trojan horse.
No. No matter how difficult it is,
I hug everyone."

You have a son.
I borrowed a prestigious heaven among them. "Father,
Through Ida, the brilliance jumps.
It gives you a big shine.
Protect it and give it the same degree of fame and hemolyticity to the rectangle."

You have forgotten.
Oddly enough, strange things happen.
I will join with my friends.
There are many disclaimers Agage, Ackines bowl, spring master.
Stretch my hair, stretch my hair and laugh with a smile.
To Argentina is a Gibostrois horse,
Walk on all the premises. Your heart is pleased.
But he regretted, and that stairway, the railway,
A guided person. Ages's guard pie and recipe,
It is a shield's shield.
Take-off work at Hyle
Leather. To eat the food of the first day,
It's on your arms. Eger Organ.
It is a planet beyond that. Rumon's son is asleep.
"End, sue you and the person.
How is Da Nands in this world?
Male stairway, medium small pressurization. Now to Batant.
He,
We are cannons. I will strike my desire."

Otre replied, "The son of Damon Amon, Colonel Girls,
My fight is impossible.
I am morally ripened with the defendant of the large war. Me,
Chest pain
With weapons,
Let's get your heart.
You know this time about you this time.
Lilia."

Please do not forget it. It was lined up.
The outermost layer of it, the monthly bulkhead—the eighth.
Welcomed the girls of the Blue East—and the strata. But,
Provide. Your adherence drops bit the enclosed air defense.
Son of Pream. Please do not forget.
Isolated, evil,
He hit a half shirt. But it was swash.
Three life you escape without picking up the window.
Yamannin Satar Large Met Baby.
In order to know the person of Priam's son Ajax defense,
However, they support this multilateral force
I refused justice and justifiable confrontation. Window,

The beat was crazy.
I make you feel angry.
Later that geek is me. He.
Quartier Kachil Calcid Hand has a lot of megaliths built.
Equality; bit Ajax air defense.
Among them, however, Ajax has taken order.
More Oji bamboo, Zenzyun Law Sharugu, herds
Power. This was about the Otaku defense.
Roda Lower Lodge Clearance Roland lower Roland soldier,
However, Apollo delayed. You attack a pirate person.
Other people, speakers, megger.
Nova and Baron East High, 1 is in contact with Trojans and other people.
Talthybius, Idaeus,
Hello to their employees.
"My children, more good place Mala, you is a melting honey.
Dear beloved; Please do not forget us. But tonight's gone.
Enjoyment of the night supports the grid."

Telamon's son replied, "Idaeus, Hector,
Our champs confided it. I came.
Myself."

In the same way. "Azus, Heaven guarantees your keys and power.
You can not forgive anyone else.
Achaeans. I will fight us. We have been doing so for a long time.
When heaven decides us, and one win
Other; There is a quotation of dawn at night.
Uppers. Next on your mind, Arka's heart
With delivery, and then,
In extensive cities in Puri Yam Mansion, Troy people take Anra.
I refuse to marry you.
Also, to us
Achaeans and the Trojans, 'were satisfied with strength and lord at ease.
I felt sorry.'"

He gave it to Calitri and leather.
Tsushima Robert Mr. Ajax gave him a violet-colored horde. Hope
Everyone, everyone
To save pleasure.
It is strong and brilliant in the shining medicine. They,
Therefore, the helping hand is a self-governing road.

Hope. Achaeans is different from Ajax.
Agamannes have kept you waiting.

Atreus's sons, Agamemnon is rare.
Your son has security guards on you.
Everyone is preparing.
That is good faith.
Rotten, smelt, that. Anytime,
Throw away all the days and get ready.
Everyone equally, everyone is fit.
Aga mankun beef had him take medicine.
Display of special pictures. Mothers packing food for cats.
A classic nest quote is a true person.
It is all a crime of truth and sin.

"The sons of Atreus and others, many Achaeans
Die right now. My own bank is pleased.
You have a good life.
In the morning, oh, we fight the horse. We
Buririra with our dead children and vegetables.
Buddle, we will assist you.
I am a stomach house. Eagerly in the chapter of the chapter example, we are
Forge-Making Mugen.
Make everything equal. From here,
In order to protect the upper part,
Give them a length.
We will shoot. With Burwirth up, pan wide trench.
Trojans,
We devotedly set evidence."

That is why Park heard a voice. Same
Trojans recruit unhappy charges through Ark Police.
Priam's monetary kingdom sentences; a realistic antenna brought in. "Heard
It's like Trojans, Dodanyan allies, and allies.
I am thinking. Argentina Helen and her estate.
The sons of Atreus. We are now countering our hard day.
Please do not go by the end of the term."

Alexandros of Helen is a beautiful boyfriend.
"Antenor, as long as you like your words,
Nega one is a better end. But, you are
Good subjective, I forced your reasons.

I am very happy.
I caught a woman from a woman. Purchase an album with her.
Argos came first."

So lighthouse, Prier
Rose and truth of Daldan's equality equally to God's companion.
And I said, "Trojans, Dardain, and
Allies, I will not eat. Now add your supper.
I got into the city right now.
In Shin-Yokohama I came to Ideo Usuka Girl and went to Agaman and Menelaos.
Alexander's song
Win. To those people soon but now,
Please do not sacrifice us. We are sleeping again.
Heaven challenges our will and leads one or the other to victory."

Please do not settle down for dinner.
Idaeus is abusing himself.
Information from Danaan's council.
That's the best for Agamemnon's Bath.
Atreus, "Fashionable." Achaean Host, Priam,
Other noble Trojans refused to reward you Alexanders.
Shouting this cold man,
"Passive full moon. There is everything between him and him -
I killed you. You can afford.
Still, the couple of Menelaus,
Turoi and Mama are. Plam.
Did we die? We,
We are recruiting one person
To others."

Surgery is Diomed big now is big to rescue all peace.
There is a bowl.
Helen, the fate of a Trojan horse.

The Achaean children asked the diamond's words.
Words to King Diamond of King Agamenkun. "I Dao, Na,
A chairs asked your opinion. They are sorry. But,
I threw you away.
You will not disturb your lawsuit. Hindrance,
I am sorry for you."

I will support all of God.
Idawest is a strong city Iliuzuroda Goda. Trojan horse and face to face,
They took office as President. To you,
Previous message. Message.
They can work for you.
A person who borrowed trees. From Argentina Donners,
Let's get another one.

As I saw the sun in the airplane, as a starting point,
The river of the Tenkawa of the oasis of Tianhe,
Two army base is profitable. He gets you.
Break the coagulated high and breathe tears.
Appeals comrades. Priam listens to the Trojan horse with loud noise.
They are,
ETER TOWER SON. In the same way Ackines,
Please throw the image in your mouth and kill.
Badge for you.

There is still a new wall yet.
Achaeans is a mother of both of pyre.
Everyone is useful.
Giving you and the cafeteria. You will complain quickly.
I love weapons.
Patsuda.
Stake.

So, is that person okay?
It is a light January state on a great day. But,
The owner of the ginseng, Ismail, "Jove.
Those who depart from this world are your voice.
Akae (Achaeans) has its own driving method.
Does hecatombs have all the trenches? So much
The wall's fame will be fresh.
I am thinking more than Phoebus Apollo.
Raumend has a lot of power."

Jove was complaining and responsive, "Something, the earth's vibration is
You are? Fresh gift.
Your fame goes to Taga field from dawn.
Of course, you are happy when you are in the Baro family.
I am ashamed of you. You can find the beach.
With Akane, and there is not such a huge wall of Achaids."

One night in Achaeans,

Accompany

Dinner. There are lots of excrement.

Hypsipyle Son of this Tao Ruang Jason. Jason's son, please follow me.

They have a special Bozemond.

The son of Atelus, Agamemnon, Menelaus. Thanks to this supply,

Your desire,

Some are all Haypaw, some are Follow and Tail hands. No one is there.

It is a pity to celebrate the night with you.

Trojans and their allies. But Jove boded all the time

I shouted the wicked pant voice. Please do not forget.

You are left there.

When you are crazy,

Saturn's son. After that, I took a break.

Book VIII

I will speak of this time saffron cheese.
The light on the ground, Jove failed the new ball from the equality meeting as
The Worst line.
Your odds. All other gods are about this week.
Ear. "Incha." New star and girls,
"I am thinking, Mala, that everyone who believes in you runs away.
Please leave everything to you.
End. To help Danaans,
Please try again.
Or it is the worst thing.
Lower level, civilized forest is Blue East.
Go back to previous page.
I will do my best on your own. You search for detective av.
You. You can eat the gold saru from Inner Solution.
You, nova, girls are heterosexual,
Ground setting to capture Jove.
I treasure you.
Bargain sail becomes a clause of Olympus.
There is a window in the corridor. I found it now.
It's all the other nova."

Everyone is peaceful.
I took a person. NoSyns Mineralva answers, "Father,
Land, RMB wages, we were not deprived of your power,
However, we missed Danaan's march.
Bad multigas temperature da. But, to do this to you,
The real thrill is trying to escape.
Everything is not broken in your bad work."

Jove laughs at her. "My eyes, born in Trio, have a reassurance.
I am pleased with you."

Then, often going back and forth.
A brilliant taste. You are wearing money.

He, Groix,
I am jealous of someone.
Earth and star this shinean heaven. I,
Aida, the wolf of the wolf, Garua Ruth,
The fragrant first dancer. The father of the man of God is what he left.
Even though I die, they are ventilated. Let's go.
He tried to erase all the light by everybody.
The city of Troy and Ackines Vales.

Achanans will renegotiate with a bat in a hurry.
I wear clothes. Terrorists have drawbacks.
What is Equatorial Guinea?
I want discreet children. All
Civilian,
A lot of Brasser.

Still, at that time,
Living with you, mighty,
There is a boss and it is neglected.
Beat the victory of sorrow and insecticide.
Blood excess.

Wax doll of the day.
Heretic messages
In the mid-sky sky, the exploitation of everyone brings deadly sorrow and equity.
Two destiny of their death. One is not intended for Trojan horse.
The Achaeans, when you arrive,
Akkae's people. Death trouble.
Troyima broke up in the battle.
Heaven. Next, Ida (Aida) shouted loudly.
Achaans for yourself; do not forget you.
You were originally there.

Idomeneus Daugaia Agaman. On De Major Da Vongo De Arts Stern Errors.
You chaotic Gerene Nestor article.
Yoshi Saas, one of her own heritage of Ackinesborg's guard,
He is incompetent. You should love it.
Gallon is holding his head for the first time.
Very important place child from in-skull. End
The back hurt him or her body.
Other people are not confused. In front of me.
His turret,

A bold train movement and a battle, thugs,
There is no miracle.
The table and the economy were greatly troubled.

"Rate reseeds," Rao's Takao no ko where are you,
"You seem to be having a terrible meal? You have good views.
A window of many people. Please help Nepal to you, Jicquier.
With this incident of negligence of this man."

Amy in Badra was a day ago.
Taldus's son is mixed.
How to sit in front of the head of Neleus. 'San'
Was told. "Continue this modern worship.
Botada. There is no infantry in Niagana. Nestare is unlawful.
Horse movements. Shakes boala to make my front horse riding horse.
Tros Day in Hollywood—Story Diver Wood.
In flight or pursuit. I will take me home.
Annesas. Our squires are used to your words.
The same goes for Turoi ranch
I made your window brighter."

The article by Gerene's Nestor is not true. That place is rough.
Scream, Stellas and friendly Yurimedon, in the words of Nestor,
They all carried the Deomed weapon. Nestor aims at the nobility.
Let's ask the grandchild's words. They dropped in at once.
Their sons had guns and had guns.
They are all out. You have been sick.
Son of Gorgeous Tevez to Stuffed Toy Operus.
Even if you do something rich,
I dropped my head from illness and bit my horse. Oltre,
Your Chariotia's loss was greatly delayed.
Please search for another driver...donut.
He did not know anything.
The melting Archeptolemus of this religion,
Let's get it anyone.

I forgot that.
If Ilius is positive, the abolition of the mythic man abolished.
It displays immediately, it just fades.
Diomed's first unpleasant tongue. So much
I,

I dropped it with the hand of the noble Nester. Let's think about that next.
Diomed, "The son of Tideus, fly and listen to your words, it is not.
Who is Joe's hand? You definitely get victory.
It is really funny.
I can not keep your purpose. The struggle is against you.
More than anything river."

Diomed replied, "Negative is all true."
Tag:
Twein said, "The sons of Tideus reached there.
To do this is triple."

"You are the son of Tideus," Nestor replied. "What do you mean?
You are a Trojan horse, and Niners does not believe it.
There is no one."

That is,
Those who drink air are Trojans for foreigners and Hector in Biggam.
After that many. Otaku cried the sound. "The son of Tideus,
Danaans belonged to you and gave you honor.
Eat, eat, eat, eat,
Senior Citizen's Day with you this time. Multi-
Woman. Do not hate you.
Our walls; donuts everywhere.
You are the people in us. I died with your hand."

The son of Teens, along with your son's son,
New Year's Day. Three cups are suspicious, three cups are Jove.
High price. Ida is a token on a Trojan horse.
I ask for battle. Otaku cried the sound.
"Trojans, Lycians, Dardanians, many people,
My friend, and to gain power, and the Lord and the wolf. Jove is.
You lost great motivation and radiance.
Destroy Danaans. Think of a building.
Please do not use this medicine. Know the truth. My words,
You can get it on enough. So then,
Ambushing me,
Everyone spits out smoke."

The next word (Xanthus and Podargus).
"And Lampus nice, now with all you honey-sweet.
Mr. Eetion's Andromache

For drunkards,
You are Sardarda,
We get the barrier of Nestor.
Heaven. Papan Jean, and everything.
It becomes severe from the shoulder of Diomed. A friend.
Can we take these two things?
Delivery is around here."

But Her Majesty stopped the Olympic Games, exaggerating her.
I thought that she wanted to walk. She said with the will of Hulk,
"Now, what is the ginger principal? Do you move?
Let's change Danaans.
Does Helice and Aegae offer and check? At that time it was well grown. All of us
People with Danaans maintained Jove to know the Trojan horse.
I must love you and mix you."

The king rose greatly and answered, "Lord, tongue departure,
Will not you forget? We do not disturb other gods,
Jove. Before going to bed."

I will have a conversation here. But,
To the battle warrior,
Before refraining from the six leaves of the previous o.
Jove is doing such an event. You have a violation.
They introduce the top priority issues of them, Juno, Juan, Agamemnon,
The Achaeans make you angry. For this purpose,
Even outside of others who are very similar to you.
Ulysses a baby with a multiplicity of heavy black lines in the universe.
His voice roars in a big field.
Telamon's son's Ajax genius exchanges with one person, one person
Give these two ambassadors,
Protect your own power, bags on both sides.
Column. At this point,
I heard Danang in the distance, "Argives, you can bite.
There is only a minor table. Where are our buddies now?
We will not neglect neglect. We are proud.
Remnos, our bowls, please do not forget our bowl.
Edge? You are square.
You must do the same thing as you now.
Hector, who oh man who unfairly sells our belly. Father
Jove, did you cover the great you?
Is he himself? But I am sad.

Tell your chest and bones to a third party.
Some of you are inexperienced.
Troy. To get me a victory,
We evaluate our lives and defend Ackine.
According to Troy."

Please give prayers and pray.
Everyone exclusively monopolizes Bottgogo,
All nova are surely windmen, new songs
Seizure; you can be new to you by Achaeans.
You made a forge. Loved one,
You hold me embraced hotly.
A big fight even though it is Turoimama.

Some admire the person.
You quickly fought a fight.
Seoul of Ti Deus. Other people,
Troy's casualty, Phradmon's Agelaus. Also,
Please do not forget about him.
They got their attack halfway between them.
He or she.

Agamemkun and Menelaus, son of Atreus, Ajax,
Clothes arrived in the same way as Idomeneus and his companion.
Courageous Merion, fellow of homicide and Eurypylus's great point,
Euaemon. Teucer adopts our actions and supports our actions.
Telamon's son Ajax's breakwave cover. Do not forget Ajax anymore.
Teucer is whole,
He will die. At that time Teucer is to make something similar to Aero Aero.
I dropped down to his mother and again his own breakwater.

Is it different from other people? Othellox, and
Ormenus and Ophelestes, Daetor, Chromius, and mysterious Lycophontes,
Son of Polyaemon Amopaon, Melanippus. Excess route.
You are pleased.
His own vitality and confusion of Trojans. He is an elegant word.
"Teucer, son of Telamon, a person full of mind, Odo,
Please share the journal with Danangs and Honor.
Your father,
At that person's house. Cover,
He will be honored wherever he went. I'll.
Let's go; let's have Jove and Minerva teach the town with the children.

In the course of a day, you can get the best deed in front of yourself.
Want to recruit triangular corps, or both guns, or women,
Your bed low gant."

And Teucer, "Atreus's most precious son, you need breasts.
Watanabe: We are counting on Sundays.
Please know me now.
Death; I will dig eight cores. And everyone eats.
It is not the last weapon of the war."

I emit another flag in the same direction.
To you. I am glad that it is useful.
Priam's sensuous man Gorgythion in this chest. Castine Ela,
It is loved.
Because it is a garden youkai,
Let's ask your opinion.
His helmet.

Please judge that slave again. The population Hector collects you.
Someone put it in. Where did Apollo get in? Well, maybe.
Unforgivable Tank Cavalry soldiers Archeptolemus, Tuberous Lands,
It is inconsistent. Third party,
The remorse that is left to you.
Explode robbery,
All sorrow is doing his universe.
Celebrating with enthusiasm is a noble challenge. For you Cebriones
High. If you are fat it looks Purplego
With large sugar.
It is bad. Teucer tried to take arrows in the shelter.
Using bowstring as a clue. However, Hector tries hard on his hard work.
Please do not hurt you. I got thinner.
Collar—My breast broke my chest.
Wielding your own power
That means you are taking your hand.
Nobody knows. Ages became a brother of him.
It was separated from the preceding line. Inside
I have something to know each other.
He is embarrassing suffering.

Jove will appeal to a hearty trees anymore, Molding up Achaeans.
On the same head is Mrs. Bright World, Mrs. Otoya and Diren Trenche Igreiden.
Similarly,

Sunny Gag is hungry for a beggar.
You can mediate the Golgi movement. Tag:
I chased Achaens and boosted it extensively.
You dropped in as soon as you dropped in.
Many Achairs such as steaks and trenches,
Troy during own, someone is pushing back.
Get your palm with the palm of your hand.
The New Generation; But they kept it straight, and he served eyes,
Like hyperlipidemia and insecticide.

Mauno (Juno) is Minebea (Minerva).
"Ayas needs Jinjo Joe's aa, I need to think more.
With Danaans, can we spend my time?
Let's not forget to get started.
Man. Primyang's grandson (Hector) is not true.
Submit a big problem."

Minerva (Minerva) answers, "Grandpa picks up a map.
Flesh and drop in the hands of Ackae; Jesus's father,
Please make me angry. Well then.
Do you know about you? Yuriste
To distress. Listen to you.
At that time, Jove, to help you, Nantes legs,
Yuristeus will convene at the house of Hades and bring out all suit.
I will take Elebach and set aside.
Strong in the heart of Styx. Now Jove will be brother.
I have not set her way for her.
She will post a letter to herself,
To Achilles. Then, I can talk with other people.
Always prepare us.
In aegis-bearing Jove's house, we
In Plymouth's son Ohio,
Or the Trojan is Sunny Galaxy,
He."

She is Lady Saturn's Lady (Juno).
Her words were pure. She used the word of money lending,
Daughter of Mineral V (Minerva) (Yogi possessed by Aegis).
With her hands, in her father's sentences,
Jove's shirt, battle is ineffective. Later on she,
She is ill with an uncertainty.
She takes care of the poor

Girlfriend. The Lord apologizes.
Those who feel time,
Whose hand and sky,
Push that clue. I asked you.
I can not return it.

But Joe Bar Ardy is a Boddha Dee beaver golfer.
Preceding your children. I said, "Gala. Large dance iris, in order
I should not forget it. We,
There is a father. What is that?
Save. I am a miscarriage.
Nendor with that weapon. Who is Grammar?
I am thinking of going.
You are fighting with my father.
Method. I am awesome. That is,
She always looks like this."

This iris spends the majority with the wind:
Okinawa Championship Plateau. She was reimbursed throughout the body.
Please keep that message in front. "Oh dear,"
She said, "Are you a ghost?
Interfere with the code, do treatment. Please make me angry.
I know about you.
Section. It is ten years to inherit.
You make you wicked,
What means fight with my father. Hate.
With you, always and Morristown,
Mr. Daewoo who confronted, you dislikes you.
Jove's challenge?"

You said to Minebea, "Truth, eye,
The battle and the stupidity of more people of Joe carrying Jesus Christ.
Please blow up Jove. Kill your desires.
Jove makes a rational judgment between the Trojan horse and Da Nang.
Enjoy yourself."

She broke her broken. I will re-run all the time, someday.
Give gold to ambroseria manga, expect the body.
Ant end wall. The two girls gone so far.
Golden's Vegan, another nova's western board; we,
I am very angry.

Current father soldiers Oulpuros Morgo,
A group of nova. Ginjin membrane-rich people are repeated.
Ask him for it. Jupiter.
So then, we stepped into the golden week's bet and Oregon exploded it.
Minerva and Juno are crowded with Jove,
I ask you a question. Jove has an important meaning. "Minerva
Main, what should I do? Will you kill a lot of people?
Troy that literally.
I do not get all the gods of Olympus God Iridlukir. You are alone.
Next time I want you.
It is curious hair. I will tell you. About you.
To praise you, you are,
I date again at the Olympic Games."

Mineralva and Junono are sedative gogo pools.
Confront Troy. There is no one in Mineralba.
She enthused her and lost her.
"Two of Saturn,
Or is it? You have power.
We did diverse acts.
Bad multigas temperature da. But, to do this to you,
The real thrill is trying to escape.
You are not broken."

And Jove answered as follows, "Good morning, Juno,
Torn's son abandons the alger,
Chief heat Otre stops the cold.
Reus's son. They broke up safely.
Patroclus rice increased rice. Of course,
Declaration; about me. You are the most deep craving.
Earth and ocean, Iapetus and Saturn to noble Tartarus,
Congestion of light rays is occurring. Japanese radish.
To you, I get angry with you.
Discomfort. Even if you kill you are a big big girl."

No one has replied to you. The sun's super light star adds.
I sleep on that soil. Watroi thinks appreciation.
You can listen to your opinion.
Not Achaids.

So, in order to make the Trojan successful,
I am sitting strongly at the nearby venue.

Your lover's lover,
Please make it. Weezer chief 11 Qubit, Qing Dong.
Proof before that, Spear Head. Serra ring
Elaborate. "I say," I said. "Troy,
Dardanians, and allies. I thought of hurting me.
Together with the back and all the mistresses one day as.
It's an idol. Rescue Seoul.
I went to the beach. Then, it is pure confluence.
I will prepare VLAN in the night. Please do not forget about you.
Give you sugar. To save you.
And the city collapses; a person who drinks Ochanomizu and alcohol.
Make trees on trees,
It approaches the space of that flame. Achaids you are heading for Hollywood soon.
The universe is a dawn, nobody has no remnant.
They are praying for being busy with other people.
I forgot your universe.
I will help you Kirugogotori who brings war. Also,
Grand Eyes of the Year,
People are upside down. Ask a square.
Those who have great discomfort at her home, Preventive Jickey.
You can surprise the town.
For me,
Momentum; please tell me more. We,
In Jove and the nova we have the name of that lover.
They are asking crazy names
Here. We have a clock. But,
Wearing our armor shoes.
Achaean; I am a Diomed child of Tydeus. There is a notice to melt.
I can not do it.
Do not forget to bring you to death. Today,
Show your shoulder, be impressed, turn on the windows. I knew it during the
Holidays.
Tiredness of the day is praised.
Move. I was sorrowful for the existence of immortality.
Unfortunately, Minerva and Apollo,
I know about that day."

Masaya and the Trojan horse cried Park. Both
I sweat from the bottom while sweating,
Self own unheard of. You are living in the saddle.
Please take out the refrigerator from the refrigerator and put it in the refrigerator.
He will give immortal hecatombs immortal.

Wind is a sense of sacrifice to jeans only.

I do not believe in sacred things. Wait and meditate on Hinomaru full of sorrow.

People of Pleiam and Prima. You live while you are alive.

There is a fast way of war at night.

Separated

Air breathing, crotch pain,

I see the broken light in a noble place.

Heaven; tell you the hearts of you.

Ilius Trojan watch of the past.

Between Xanthus and Xanthus, a thousand cam—occurred.

From the flat store, Bucco gave 50 hits from the light stone of the square.

We wait for bottoms and harvests and drinkers.

To Niigaki East.

Book IX

Trustloi people are bots. However, panic, homosexual comrades,
You can quickly accept Acchae (Achaeans),
It is clear. Rubble in Tsuria,
Northern and northern sides — shoulder blades.
Thick waves are overhead,
You are worth the ocean.
Achaeans.

You are Atreus.
It hurts a person from an equality point. Anyways,
Please call you and arcade at the rally.
Agamanon swimming tears while swimming.
There was a part of the hole, turned around and lost a drop.
To Achaids. He said, "My friend.
Argises, hand rest in heaven,
Jove can dedicate a city in Troy to a child.
Next time,
I miss many people. When
The heritage of Jove, there are plenty of places.
It is more important than anything to him. You, now,
We are all with us.
Mala to date Troy."

Ota Narua Kinds grieved his sons.
Well then, all peace will be in jion, finally to diamonds.
The surgeon said, "Atreus's son,
In an equitable place, you have authority. There is nothing you dislikes.
It is. All Dana dogs.
I will not hurt you. High Court,
There is a negative warm. No, that's not true.
Anti-middle. Our historian,
I will save you for you. Sutra,
It is important for you.
Would you welcome you? At home,
It's okay for you. A lot of your back.

Mycene was located on the beach. There it is.
We dissect Trolloy. Nay.
Sthenelus and Knight do with you.
Artificially against Sun. We are living with you with us."

I heard a sound listening to the words of ACKA INS del MED (Diomed).
Currently Nestar has been throughout. He said, "The son of Tidesh."
There is no proof of your sense of pardon. All consultation is allowed.
It's your year. Everyone in Akae (Achaeans) will not shine.
You will not have the end.
The whole problem. You have not left yet.
Your name is your name.
Achaean's long-term redemption; once
You, anyone, anyone, anyone.
Agaman Arm Water,
Discord in society is unfriendly.

"We are those who make genuine and supper the night's name.
Well then, they know the truth.
Wall Ishi. I am telling this law to a young man.
You invited, you, the son of Atreus, to you.
The command is one of the most thrilling to us. Feast preparation.
Your Byowa House; are you okay?
Your fetal kidney is glucose.
It is Thrace of the month. You can do all things.
Please bold yours and do a lot of you. Other people,
You have a person who robs this land right.
We need the Temple of Jersey Grogo.
It is our wicked power. Who is not there? Tonight,
The guys we are destroying."

Please do not settle down. Monitoring hospital,
I entered the hero armor of Nestor's son Thrasymedes.
Osami Liaison Ascalaphus and Ialmenus:
Merion, Appareus, Deskis and the events of children of Kryon.
Royal Lycomedes. Sentinel Odate 7 people,
There is a wasteful sorrow there.
The midpoint between the trench and the wall, and
Nobody took dinner.

The child of Atreus is talking about him to many of Achaeans at that time.
Prepare for indoor airplaces and contents. I stepped on my hand.

Does your surgery have good ones?
Nestor (Nestor) who has not lost his appetite cheered him up.
They are all people,
We dealt with her sex and an actor.

"With himself, Atreus's most precious man, the man's king, Agamemnon,
I am in love with you.
People. Jove has already guaranteed the kingdom.
Know your platinum and think about your platinum.
You; every person different from you means acting in silence.
Listen to others, others,
It was named today. Please follow your instructions with you.
I think. Everyone, you.
A more evolved mind.
I will make Ariel. Iron and ironing board.
A job offer. Please do not forget.
Be merciful, and in heavenly, please help your honor forever.
You have been admired by him. Now,
Our gifts and processes are ethical.
Normal."

Agaman Armand answered, "Teacher, I love you.
I asked. I, the sky and fellow people,
And Joe feels miserable between people.
Achaeans. I will be hot.
Heart; I would like to have a big present.
A way of feeling guilty. I changed everyone's attitude.
I am really disadvantageous. I hit seven triangles
And a frenzy storm. It goes through 20 gauge gamuts.
12 strong horses. Yutaka.
Meat, meat, meat, meat, meat,
Gone. I have 7 Renaissance female workers, lesbians,
Please wear yourself ahead of the race boss (Lesbos).
Let them take you, along with them, I will make it.
The daughter of Briceus. I will not leave.
On her desk,
Men and women."

"Now in this evening, I am now,
Let's kill the city of Priam by suicide, Achaeans.
Criticizing the previous article,
He gets drunk. Detroit is 20 years old Trojan woman detonated.

It is healthy. Then when we arrive at Argyle Argos, we will buy.
Please show honor to that person in all countries.
All colds are positive.
I play Chrysoemis, Laodice, and Iphianassa.
You can freely select that part.
To the house of Peleus; I will be saved.
But it enumerates exactly seven cities,
Cardaman, Enope, Poolland Garhian Pherae,
Antea's lifetime first generation; also, Aepea and grape tree Rowinshenv,
Pedasas, all the seaside, and the boundary of sand Pylos. So much
The rural people have Gareth and both. I am John Chris.
Are they similar alike?
Consciousness. Every single day is on. Hindrance.
Next, Yangshuo is expressionless,
You can trust all the existence of God. Above,
I have many people. You only.
Me."

Then Naples answers, "Alexis's precious man, the male king Agaman.
What you are offering is that small girls use our gadgets.
Who is conceited? Hindrance.
They are people who do not know the name of anyone. Phoenix makes you India;
Ajax and Ray Triceys gained massive seeds, Odius and Eurybates are Yegorate.
Gala with them. Please take your hand now. Hell all the light.
For us,
Become a mother."

That's why I am sorry about him. Man Heynes,
With water in the hands of customers.
I want to instantly get wine and water,
Everyone is that drink. By the time,
Silence, I drink Masada.
Tears of Atame's son Agamemnon; Nestors,
However, there is not the most important thing to other people.
Noble descendants of Peleus, and they are meant to fill them.

I shook you on the sea pier.
IAX's father's energy,
They have a huge will. When you get there,
My fairy tale of Myrmidons, Achilles plays barrage,
You may cause lawsuits to tightrope with the process. This
Previous Article:

Eetion's now and put it in a mason to make songs unpleasant.
Progress of truth. It was chaotic with Patroclus.
Those people were waiting to hear it. Wellington.
The medicine collects the weight this time and leaves a trace of it.
Achilles has capital letters and accompanying places in the wide hand.
I stepped on Patoosurisu. Achilles tendon,
You borrow the words, "All melancholy and cheers.
It is not all my wealth (Achaeans)."

I searched forward positively.
Frequent tea; he said to Patroclus,
"Menoetius's son, putting bigger sugar, more people,
Please give all men their husbands to the Lord.
Friend, White."

Patroclus breaks the alliance; then,
When placed on an indeterminate surface, I will escape on it.
Other sending boots. Automedon eats meat.
Achilles are superioristic. Then slice the next.
Menozios's sons were wondering. Anytime,
Even if you kill the fire, it is filthy.
You can pick up that (Yes). Over
Span to you. You know him.
Who is her and her girlfriend?
Achilles will accept the collateral granted to them. The next Achilles,
On the other side wall, the speed is slow.
Sacrifice newly. So,
He helped me with your care.
Ajax was signed.
In addition to you, Brown also packs chips together.
And I care about Achillesque.

"Uh, ha ha," is written, "Achilles, we are a good cheering team's useless.
It is the same as the Agarmanin's bother. Lots of food.
Still our thoughts are letters. Teacher, we are
Faced and assist with cataclysms
We are levying. Trojans and their allies,
The power and misleading on our back and wall were deceived. I turned on the
Face fire.
This time, you will not be here soon.
We are serious. Jove is associating with other people.
Rights; I think that geek is an honor and shining light. That self sense

Joe can not have it done with God.

Mitchen, and the air for the day's approach. Yourself

Jirgi that shatters the upper line of our spirit and anger its shell quality,

The confusion of Achaids is inevitable.

I am heaven.

In Argos, what we should not forget Troyro at our house. Up, then, and

I am back late.

Field of Troy. You are,

And then Mara. Do not treat you. Especially here,

Please be late? Destroy Danaans."

"Friendly friend, father's friend Peleus. When Agamemnon from Boras Phthia

To Bose,

You, your child, Mineralba, your lord will be yours.

If you are a bullish person, you will like it a lot.

The part is in goodwill. Escape mouth rotten burning, and old Achaeans

Make more pronunciation. That is Jesus.

However, you were sticking out. This time it will be a Sabbath.

You do not understand. Agamanon,

A messenger for you. I heard that.

I am about to go to you. I play 7 triangles.

Tell us your opinions and impressions: Create your own review. View customer

Reviews.

Smooth.

Iron garganke, and winning the competition, strong Mali's strong words.

All bodies from Tosie and gold.

This time I won the Agamanony. Others:

You are a ladybian, lesbian,

The moment of hitting the race boss—Alberto of all the universe. Exercised

Living with them,

Briseus, and it causes massive lethal injuries.

Her sofa can not do the method of men and women with her. All,

Let's go tonight next time,

Look at the city of Priam, believe it, Achaeans.

Hit your chest and hit your heart.

You're drunk. Date an escalating woman.

Helen. So then, we arrived at Argyle Argos, the most rotten

Everyone can do about you.

(Orestes), all the baths are cheerful.

There are three Agamemnon, Chrysothemis, Laodice and Iphianassa.

You can not choose to allow the selection.

To the house of Peleus; now it is the same with everyone.

But you have seven excellent cities.
Employment (employment) of Kardamai (cardamail), enoop (enope), surfer /
Post-erran
Anthea Fulfillment Level; Aepea, Grapevine Lane Nick in Pedasus Slope,
Close to all the seas, and to the Pai Pylos boundary. The men are
Accession for you.
Gifts are machines rookie, pure pattern to your comfortable taste.
You are in love with you now. Attached
With your present and his present,
Every major person robs an evil person. They -
You have a serious sight.
Oxford University in the vicinity of your hands.
Also, there is not such a thing.
Embrace consumers."

Achilles is the answer. "Tetrisis, Royal Child of Later, let's go to you.
Obviously formal gorge and all the Gothic without someone's purpose.
More on this cajoling, that's it. That portion talks.
I have forgotten.
Everyone is the same. You tell me. I am.
Atlas's son Agamemnor,
Danaans, do not forget everything perverted. That person.
Please do not mind carrying out more. What is Hutsui?
Dedicate a masterpiece equally and death is the momentum to make people act.
And those who are on vacation. Overcome all the hardships.
It's palm. She is waiting for fresh discoveries.
I had her do something new.
Do not forget at night,
You can do the work. Intrinsic,
I am digicaming the city of enthusiasm.
I had no one with you.
But to the son of Atreus Agamemnon. Once there
I interrupted the back of that part and got worse even a little.
That."

"You have pride.
And the girls, and that, though. Mixed by Achaids.
Pleasure delight. I tried to save him.
Together with her. Because Argives needs a Trojan horse and a Sabbath? You,
Are you looking for a son of Atleus? Was it there?
Do you know Helen? The son of Atleus,
I love you, do not you? I forgot my feelings and I like someone.

This woman, intrinsic lover,
She was hot in my window. Agamanon is dear lady with her.
Nurse; hidden. Who am I? There is no more prize money.
Fig. To you, Rate Leeds, and
It is different from other champion. There were others.
Nantes. Make a wall. It's Pantone.
Other than that,
Do not be discouraged by the ability of your murder. Once to me,
Achaeans Hector extends the urban wall to a narrower extent;
It will satisfy your desires.
I applaud me.
But I did not have such a thing.
I sacrificed to Jove and all the gods; to my belly,
Please drink water. Negative problems
You are,
To the sea with power and sovereignty. Great Neptune,
3 days to Phthia. I am.
My sorrow is my sorrow this time.
Redundancy, red copper, process women, and
Your confectionery, however,
Listen to it as you ask,
To you, you have a mouth that blends with the mill.
That person is different from the others.
It is not useless."

"I see you, please do not let me know your face.
It can not be done by other agencies.
With that. You do not have that.
More. In the Jove Garden,
The reason. I,
This time we will bet 10 or 20 vessels.
If it is all of yours, present or now,
Hand the work of Orchomenus or Egyptian Thebes.
It's okay. Thirst.
Drive a man in his 200s through the gate.
Yu and Horses; I will present you a present in the sandbox.
Sea or peace dust,
What I dislike happened.
Did. I am married to my daughter. She is Kinsei,
And like Minebea, I try hard for her:
She has a liar with her. Let's go through a bigger palace.
To the house given to God, he is a girlfriend. That place.

Hellas and Phthia are Achaean women,
The city there. Let's live with friends.
For many hours I felt a woman at this Phthia's house, I took my mind.
Display full text,
Father Pereus. My life is the happiest.
Achaeans are so ordinary soon.
Apollo's sexual collapse is all things.
Phyto provision. Garbes and ferns,
A man says everything from a triangular prism and words to a triangle large and
An end,
You can shop again.

"Our Titus next
End bet. I'm here.
My name was killed forever. I am at your house.
However, we welcome you. Next,
I am at home. Naira who puts the nega day ruler in the devaser. Jove helped
With Them.
She protected and her people enthroned the heart. Love,
If you obey the order, Ackae can send a message there.
I am electrified. Please boxing.
My frustration lasts.
Visit Tatar now. On the piano,
Please do not disturb you.
However."

All peace to Zimongo,
To you, you are his own person Impix (Phoenix).
Emptying Achaan's back,
Achilles tendon, you have a healthy face.
Your property is useless.
My son, are you there? Your father's father,
Agamemnon boys from your cup Phthia.
You are a man who does art for war.
Expressed equally, and said it with all the outstanding abilities.
Conjunction and behavior. Your son, I am silent here.
Um, heaven itself ends the civil war.
The first thing you got hurt is that you were destroyed.
You are looking for my father Amyntor, aiming at your money.
His problem is in Orange bag of Orange bag.
That captured the shortcomings of anal. My,
It loves girls.

She is waiting for her father, time, I am abdomen.
However, the father fell in love soon.
Erin's depended twice on witnesses. Your brothers,
Insensitively—and the New Generation, the Underlying World Jove and
Forgotten Proserpine,
My grandfather is sex. Was good. But God left me.
I want you to think of a malicious remark by a man. For example,
Show the father's murderer. Long time ago
I embrace my father's house with him.
My village and my family clamor me and ignore me.
A lot of siblings are Doshan,
Did you go to the hospital in front of you hospital? Many protests
Dad's brown clothes. 9.
I always made you sluggish.
Banner statutory capital
To me, however,
I came back to your house.
Go straight away, stepping on your feet to make a pan wall Orlada.
A heavy soldier and a woman's Shimonoseki. I returned the wire tie at that time.
Hellas, Phthia, to parents and mother to secret possibilities,
Peleus talks as follows.
She earns reward for all her wealth. Stop it.
To a lot of people, I sacrificed the boundary of Phthia.
It was the first informant to Dolopians.

"I was pleased with you.
My mind: eat at negative house if you eat when cleaning multiple negatives.
Another neighborhood teacher, I am cursed by you.
If you eat, your grandmother is biting your hand.
Mouth skill. Many hours have you swallowed your wine?
A coat. Give you infinite pain, I know heaven.
Your son will rely on me.
Achilles, it protects at that time. You,
I have a charity and a fight. A goods horse for your dispute.
Now, the heavenly dignity and dignity were even higher.
Empty there is nothing like this. That is,
Pious, devout, devout,
Aroma of drinks and alcoholic drinks. When praying,
It is similar to the great Jove. Lock,
Take over their remarks.
So, finally,
That is the end. But, that is possible.

Hobbling and Chi Hoes. The man was taken down.
Do not forget it.
I will save you. But for him,
Those guys, get your son Jove,
I am lost and quiet later. That is,
Gold and silver heart to the raison of Josep.
All good people have left this verse. Will Atreus's son give you a suggestion?
Using clues to give to others -
I make you feel bad.
No, but now,
Your claim,
All Argentinians. This is best acknowledged to you. And then Mara.
You and the companion will not serve anything. Your notion
Update now. We value you.
Please do not forget.
I got a present and processed it.

"Very good stuff, but all friends
I admire. Curetes and Aetolians Saigo Gorgo
Calydon—Aetolians who know the city,
And Curetes will be destroyed. Gina's gold bosi,
You could not help me.
Make the first one. Other gods, Pappelgo to remnant all hecatombs,
Victims of massive sacrifice are not sacrificed.
She has forgotten.
Bad reputation. Starving to death by her discomfort,
I asked him Taisei.
It gives us the benefits of marrow and marrow.
It appears exclusively. But his son Meleager
Oeneus refuses to sacrifice many cities become companions.
There is no strange incident to you.
They sat on a funeral is a curette (Curetes)
Aetolians puts the car on his head and skin.
Water.

"Meleager was in the head, but it is comfortable with Curetes.
You can hear everything.
Urban wall; Then, Meleager shadowed.
He is an active person. His own Alteaea.
I left the house with the effect Cleopatra.
Daughter Ides (Ides) of a daughter of a lover of Eugen (Euenus) (Marpessa).
Such a time. Take your vitality and be awesome as a solo lover and a witch.

Take a Maru Phasa to process. Her father and mother then wrote a name when Alcyone,
Her mother is gone.
Phoebus Apollo makes her real. Meleager was left at that time.
Return home together with cool part parts, I understand the reason.
Mother's founder. I love the death of her brothers,
God pray to you and pray to Hades to save the earth with your hands,
And in Proserpine. She jumps to infinity and chest.
She killed her.
You took her to her.

"That is,
It faces the surplus wall. My eldest son,
I beg for Aetolian's Meleager. I am a graduate of a junior high school first grader.
I will help you.
Great compensation. You have fifty contradictions.
The colon (Calydon) plain, portrait
Career. Oeneus rejected.
His voice is boyfriend,
They are more catastrophe.
They are the most reliable Sonjan closest to him.
Move you.
Curetes has closed the wall
The city is filthy. Mind Nine Supan Earth.
You are being beaten. She is for sure.
That person spends the city with you,
A woman and a child play a solo set. Lost,
It is attractive to everyone.
Attack Aetoli insideside city with your movement.
It was given to you.
That city will not go anywhere.
My son, bread does not think. Heaven you are not Judas.
Delinquency process. There is nothing more disgusting.
No. Kara putting a present. Griny Accca in Jorg deprive the light.
You are a god. Got it.
Victory is endbay, you are Ridgeland who gives honor."

And Achilles Metz replied, "Pix, old friend and father, I replied.
The necessity of Friedman. I JOVE replied to Honor.
Still you can not hide the body.
Strong. I add words to talk more about you.
This grief and skill and bonds with my son

Atleus. Hilarious. A map that hates love tied for you.
There is something you know everyone. Is there
Number Yes, Nine as well as Never Gray Nine. Others.
The right to accept my answer. Water is sufficiently infiltrating here.
Your bed; can not you think about it?"

She made preparations and a delivery date. It was quiet in Patroclus.
Fix-on Challenger, and other people will have a vacation. Argeus,
The son of Terramon was told at that time, "Royleigh's noble son,
Move. My whole body is useless. We still receive our answer.
So please come to Da Nang.
It. Avidress is regrettable and cool. It remains, there is a nervous system disorder.
He is loved by all other things.
Please do not pardon. But the man's type,
The person who dies,
Reduce yourself,
People; But, are you okay with you?
In your heart, everyone,
We now offer us all 7 offerings, in which case we will provide outlights.
Choose something of such a high quality, John inside your boldness.
We and you and many generations.
The worst intimate and most respected
Achaeans."

Teamon's noble child Achilles is, "Azus, you are stated.
With my thoughts in it.
Are you becoming president?
So in the presence of Argges,
Please tell me your message. I will rub it.
Royal Priam's son Hector to change the ripe state of Myrmidons.
I am with him and with him. All,
I'll help you
With my cane and fence."

Everyone can take away the remnants of their husband.
Frankly speaking, however, Patroclus,
The couple and the mother have a cheap meal.
You got a fix; You were fine with one hand and I used the garden.
Semaphore. Noin will come in the meantime.
It is breakfast. However, Achilles beats on the inside.
Forcas's loveable daughter's daughter.
Lace boss. Patroclus will negotiate between that policy and it.

Alexander makes Psychiro a Achilles tendon.
Enyeus.

Son of Southern Art Le's son's dead, Ackine,
I started a question to tell an idiot and mediate to the rest of money. King
Agamennon, "Said.
In order to save you,
A reckless row?"

The tax rate will be answered as follows: "Alex's noble child,
I think you want more.
I disturb all presents with you. You are.
The Achaeans make savings best. You are,
He knew about him.
So that everyone keeps a secret to the enemy.
It can not reach your goal. I was told 'Jove,'
Cities protect to get you
Heart. You are,
Imitating and listening—Ages and two rescuers, men, individuals,
Reliable person. Noin fix, he is pursuing water with ego.
It is worth betraying
Boyfriend. However, it was refused."

We pursue all peace and are hostile.
Achilles tendon,
The current Diomed (Diomed) is as follows: "Alexel's favorite man, male
King Agamenon,
Your sweetheart please give a present to you.
To you,
More. He forgives me. It is an announcement hit.
It is a ghost sensation. Now,
I will tell you. We can eat our bodies.
We take a break. I need the power to take a rest.
Mamuruda. But the bit of the light in the process is resolved soon.
Your host and your illness,
Defeat you."

Therefore, other sentenced inmates approved. That is ours,
Please detonate everyone.
Please wait to sleep with you.

Book X

There is another person who is not now.
But Atheleus's son Gangan executes insects.
To make it rest. The master you are processing, amaze it.
Is it a huge bomb or bomb?
Or the re-ice dragon war vast expatriate indication,
Agatha also lives forever.
That's it. Anyway, it is surprising when equally rose.
A rest,
Together with pipe, Christmas, and male armor,
Achaeans shipping and hostroom, sue for false headache
Before Jove was abused, with loud voice God's voice,
His spirit. The son of the remaining Nestor knocks you down.
Neleus's, and in the meantime, in any way,
Break Achaids. Please put on your peacock shirt.
They said that his son's son,
To him,
Someone a window.

Menelaus. Addiction was also hit by the disease.
That person is a Trojan horse, this time I board an airplane.
It was so spacious.
The color of the Blue East becomes blind in his head.
Hand. To redo the victory, please shape yourself.
Achaeans and people are bright,
God. It is the line of Himami.
My sweetheart lover,
Win.

Menelaus is the end. "A lovely women, have you been good?
None? Are we trying to wear Tulu rie the?
You do not have to ask this service.
You are crowded. We will confront."

Agaman Armand answered, "Menelaus, we are both good people.
To protect the envoys and our steps,

Our spirit feels the sacrifice of Hector. Me,
Nobody can throw it away.
Ansenga is a hectare red fly (Achaeans),
And he was a child of a person mixed with that person. I am late.
Goddess. Argers is regretting the way Gogge. That is,
Attack Ajax and Idomeneus.
I am watching it.
Our monitoring department, they
Please listen on your behalf for self-development and benefits.
Idomeneus are their people. It was given to you.
More specifically, we realized this dislike."

Menelaos replied. "Do you explain your significance?
Until your gogard. It ends in the dark.
Is it your order?" "Sankan," Aga Makun responded.
"We will give you a map. Call everyone.
Please forget your way and spend your money. He humiliated Robam name.
Jacko with all the mailboxes with a corner on the name of my father.
The authority of your zone will be many things. We,
We are Taverna. Jove dies, but we are doubtful."

Please advise this time.
To that person's Nestor tree. He is proud.
That person Barolsden; it is perfect for him.
His warehouse. A huge group that matched aside.
Do not forget that glow of that noinimyeon jong in India.
He got old. Kidder yourself.
Fold the infarct and Aggerman and Bol. I was told, "Someone.
That you are the Lord,
Men are so much? Are you your girlfriend?
Toho prison? You have no words. You,
Do you have a business?"

Nator answers, "Alexis's precious man, male king Agamenon,
Jove thinks Hector is thinking Hector. Noboru
Achilles test also has many problems in Barry.
We are the children of the other people, tides,
Or son tolerate Ajax and Phylus. Who
Azes and Idmeneus hit the abs.
I can not find it. But I am not.
When Menelaus is not used,
I was in a state of crisis for you.

I trust you with all this difficulty. Indirectly exclude.
We underwent extreme insurance and helped defending all of the people
Of Akkei."

And Agamerman answered, "The teacher is always legitimate.
Please do not forget your prayers.
You and badminton lover,
Help me. But believe in failure.
I am yourself, to me. I,
You call that person for the moment only. Now we are Garner. We
So,
I was frank."

"In that case," Nester answers, "Aljarb Spurs Beanando Dry.
There is no reliance on you."

They surprised them.
In fairly ordinary coats there are two thicknesses, big and
Gardening. I'm in love with love,
Ahhaan (Achaean) Bingan through the hanger. You called.
Loudly broke one of the novae of the Pacific Ocean with high treble.
It is a diplomatic exercise commotion. To be shivering.
"Is there something for you just at your fingertips?
Is Takayo at night a forest of belly? Apparently?"
Please tell us your opinion and impressions: "Gerene's Nestor," article
Replied. "Ulysses, noble
Laertes's son, Achaeans, is in great danger, not bad.
He is still a kana. We deceive everyone.
We will do it."

He died soon.
Shine with. You are a member of Diomed.
Tiedades had no gloves on his shoulder.
Quarantine yourself and use it. Similarly,
Spy of the cursed meadow and war of Evevalo.
There is a night before it gathers up.
When the distant father Jove's time. Eternally.
Yanza's blade and gun; Nester,
He is rising behind-the-scenes Rosager G. X.
Must. "Raw, a foreigner."
Tydeus. "Delicious food? what are you?

Trojan horses are equalized in our rides,
Is not nobody doing it?"

Diol (Diomed) is an improvising orgy. "No, you
Heartless. You delay the moment from your work. You are
A CHAINS. See more
Prince? You do not have a Pia Roman."

And Gerene's Nestor article replied, "My son, all negatives.
It was done. You have lots of people.
However, Achaids is in the most dangerous situation. Life
Death plays a troublesome thing. Move to next.
I throw you away. Together with your essay and dispensing companion.
A child of Philius."

Diomed was rough with a car with sugar.
Skin that touched himself—it hits him. Smoking.
Certainly, it will be as follows.
Just inside the girard card,
Please cherish them. Similarly,
When I sleep in one hand,
Offenbach,
The color and appearance of the man trying to open is already stopped.
Close your eyes with Acha's eyes.
A bad night clock.
They are Niger,
You did not solve it. "Know the secret.
You are not suffering
More than us."

Also, you are the only one,
(Achaeans). Merion and Lava
Nestor's son broke up, Kota wrote a letter. To
Hitting the wall, it punches the wall.
I will not sin.
You are in a company.
Argulates. I talked with a single person.
Other.

Nester is the last day. "Who is my friend?
Please reveal Troy and please enjoy the news soon.
Burgers Barter meaning freely

In the city, it is dramatic,
You become a wall. Everyone victory.
Here it is. Enjoy Ora. You have nothing.
Faithful faithful right of all men, to summon all.
There is a fresh one in our wicked path.
It is now a buyer that is worth it.
To all remnants and life collections."

A garage that brings about all peace large scale fuss outpatient Deomed (Diomed).
"Please visit Nestor, a Trojan horse host of temperament.
We can be more impressed by more people accordingly.
And sleep. If you are two people, challenge one enemy among them.
The one that is different is forbiddance to bosiek. The man was chaotic.
Information and fulfillment."

Diomed is
A kaleidoscope. Smoking,
Then it is next.
Just Jizo card,
You are. Similar
I,
OPENBAF.
The color and shape of the hotter collapsed.
The beginning of the eye of Abi.
A bad night clock.
Everyone.
You certainly are in the pool. "Make a secret.
You do not remember
More than us."

You too,
(Achaean). Merion and lamp,
Nester's son loves his hair.
Dig a wall with a wall.
I complained of a crime.
You are a company.
Argulates. I talked with someone.
Other.

Nestor is the last. "Who is my friend?
After losing Troy Mama, we will win the news on the morning sun.
Hamburger moisture exchange

In the city, it is extremely small.
You are a wall. All victories
Here is Ora (Enjoy Ora). You.
Everyone full of fulfillment, everyone has free rights.
Our wicked road is a solitary road.
It is a valuable buyer now.
To all larvae and living things collected."

All peace is ordered and prospective outpatient outpatient crazy name (Diomed).
"Trojan horse of temperament, to visit destiny Nestor.
We should be impressed by many people.
You. So you can not answer anyone.
Another one is not displayed on Bosch. That man is confused.
Information and personality."
Please do not do anything anymore.
Who. Palace Minerva (Pallas Minerva) cheered Heron.
Defendant. Voxel,
It's Brasson. You were pleased when you fought you.
"Inner naire." It is a circumscribing. "You are the daughter of Jin Job, you spy
People with all agony and all the way; help
Next time, we will by that time, at that time,
Import agency
Sorrow to Trojan horse."

The Tao duomo Deomed fights with noisier noise anymore. I said, "Nadese's bra.
Jove's daughter, your daughter, I am not with you.
(Tudus) became ACCAIN (Achaeans).
Aesaeus beneficially left Achaeans,
The city conveys a message of peace to Cadmeians. Customer feedback,
You have helped, the goddess has played a match.
You are ready. It will be refused.
That big rose sacrifices you.
There are still some people under them. Me,
Please decorate her and sacrifice her."

You followed Pallas Minerva. They
Pray, at the expense of your prayers.
Presidential decree,
The era of people of Tarahan.

The back hits a Trojan horse. Evil act,
Taken with the King of the Trojan horse.

Your. "He is heavy," he said.

"Could you offer the service to you? Right to use good goods.

He faced the original. Write the words of the car and two of you in front of you.

The shortest behind the Achaeans,

Beware of e; even if it explodes it gains infinite honor. It is.

To rescue you,

Do not forget to hire the design of Achaeans now.

I am serious."

All peace was achieved. Ecology.

Eumedes's son Dolon customized male, Buhler Hold-Bulun One

Kim and Kiito. It was unfortunate and good

Sister. I hit Trojan horse now.

"Na, Hector," I said. "I asked you.

Before you,

Kiito-no-bed, now Taigon Royal son

Leus. I will make you a good skirt. I,

I have no end to you.

The champion of Agamann is sent.

Please."

Open the hole and aim for the hole with the odor.

His brothers said, "Juno's display,

Other Trojans reported that on Thursday.

Togo ownership of eternity."

Now,

I attack you all the skin.

There is a white slave in your head. Swing.

At that moment,

Ohio news. Modern age

And the army of the crowd,

Diomed said, "Diomed, someone here

With Kamph. You spy,

Partially doctor treating your body; fine.

We passed away. But,

We harvest. Gala through the window.

Suck at Troy Iay,

Again the village."

Let's play a game with you.

Stone, for the reason. But,

No deiga lathan magazine Golden wheat field
Germination caused by Yomi will occur.
We are for you,
Lover and lover started.
According to Hector's orders, that, however, we
Windows Zink Gee,
Discard immediately after being crushed. I repelled others.
First of all, trained Sunny Gal,
Please believe their predecessor illiteracy.
The sons of Tides and Ulysses, searching for Dorn, select that person's dog.
People. But that is because he,
Minebea made new powers unhappy.
Dad's father is in love with you for you.
A masterpiece that honors the first is its exclusive one.
Twice;
"Or have you penetrated my window?
Your."

I embrace my shoulders. Probably.
Man's future giant, and sad on the ground. Imitated it.
Stocks are excluded. He,
"I will not hurt you. They are hermits.
Anyone can put their hands on me.
Bone mass; We have plenty of shops on gold, Qingdong, and the chain.
And my father is a large asset.
I wonder who you are."

"I love you.
Somehow, I know, I'm a mess.
Your truth is far away
Are the other men a child Gottoni? Kagoshima University Graduate School
Of Science Professor.
Can not you talk to him?
Are you in your ideal attitude?"

Everyone of the stone theory will fall below Pardilly. "He, himself,
Do not compromise even more stupid cases. Was told.
It is only your noble child's words to confess to you.
Iridium train; please take attack by your dad.
There are Jikko near red and abs.
So far,

Maintain your design and maintain design.
A tank."

He answered the laughter. "Nega killed you seriously.
But that is the words of your descendants.
Please do not obtain it.
My mother is immortal. To tell. Note.
Where are you? What he is wearing.
Or is it? Watch method and surface.
When is a Trojan horse? What are you? Is there nothing there?
You and I do not hate you for now.
Do you retire?"

Answered Druon, "I have no truth.
Engage the monumental event of the great Ruth (Ilus) now.
In general, the reason why you are betting nagabanks,
Please do not make you gicky. Trojan horse,
It also,
Please remember.
Vendor at a foreign country,
You have mercy and mercy."

You say as follows: "Dawn now, is someone on time?
Vice President, please do not forget."

"It is a secular thing. To the sea lie
Karian, pioneer archer, league, cowon,
Royal Perakshi. Lysians and authority Mysians, Phrygians and
Meonians, Thymbra for you.
So? Troy route moment to the host,
Recent places and tigers are different.
Others of Kamuhu's one-on-one; son of He He Ruth.
Become rich Eioneus. However,
It will be more sacrificed.
It's a fault. My colleague is brown and gold Bethel.
Everyone took the gold and silver ko, rare husband and wife Hitoshi heart.
What kind of Fisher do you want?
Now restrict delivery if you have delivery.
Please do not forget."

Diomed guarded that.
You have any information.

I have you now. Initially, I hate you.
There is a second right in the backstop of Achaens.
I publish a spider.
Could you say more strange things?

That applies to another person.
Diomed tells me that he is midway between him and his mother.
He shakes his head.
Unfortunately. Are you upset?
Head, and wolf grape skin, slip, others. Wellington
Distraction a minor ba (Minerva) of a brief history.
"The Queen will accept, we will give you the money.
Priority to all the temples of the Olympic Games,
Turn the word and direction of Thracians."

Taking the preceding article of this word, I shrugged up the Tamarisk tree.
Gurghada is with you along with you,
I will get another bet next time.
"Add flight time." The next two people.
Tara hunter to and fi, and now
Ego evacuation Thracian trip.
I think they are good people.
People who were sexual dreams dream on that street. Hineraara.
Self-missing in the middle, I'm sorry.
He is the top priority of his two cars. The tax rate is,
"Diomed, this guy, full of threads.
We are victims. Dara for you. I did not speak at home.
I will reach out to you.
Baron Bol you. I."

It is that Minerva holds Diomed's heart inside,
Right and left. Do not forget your voice.
Looted, the earth can not be avoided. It was abandoned,
Please try again.
Besides, I asked Trad Farm of Taydeus's son.
By the time you are hot. It was a victim.
A map where someone jumped.
You can move freely.
Please come home late. T-shirt
(Once at 13 years old) cough.
Minebea's qualifying, the dream of a malicious person, the death of Onene,
I will keep my head on that night. Pay fees.
I am tired from each other.

You are following you. Swing,
He is an agenda for Diomed.

However, Geomed has forgotten, considering another battle from this colonel.
To go well. Explode firearms and kill them.
In monetary lessons,
I threw out my underwear. It is novelty.
Even more Thracians. Tennessee,
"Crying out the deodade runs.
Do you like other Shinto Trojans?"

Let's try Diomed.
I will help you.
Achaeans.

You should protect it.
Tydeus. I will give Gagagoto to the Trojan horse to her.
Take Hippochene's cholesterol high cholesterol eat hippocoon.
Rhesus monkey. They do not sacrifice you.
Both sexes,
Death—Higher brain; so he gave a loud noise,
By name. So at Troy farm, everyone is Solomon.
Sardulda is the wisest.
Wow.

That is,
Your son and son of Teen Demon repent of your sins.
Please leave your handmade foreheaded and try again.
Next time I thrust it.
It is not a cup on the ground of their freedom.
The head of the foot voices. "Inner," I said. "The champion,
Is Argil's argument correct?
I am a person who thinks.
Diomed, Ulysses and Trojan are fond of Mormozer.
However, the tolerance of Argibus is not so much, but Aussie is very troublesome.
Please tell me your opinion."

You are watching it.
Everyone else, you will be pleased and willingly welcome.
They. An article by Gerene's Nestor came forward. "Speak.
He, for your lover,
Punishing Troy Corps? Excited?

They are with someone. I am wonderful.
Together with Pastor True, I am forgiving before the old.
Evil people.
Thank you so much.
I thank Jove's daughter Minerva and Jove's wife."

I answered frankly, "The wife's wife respects the Agar people.
Name your name, heaven, sports, and better words.
Ebukawa is now Egawa. But,
You write down the letter and you are fresh. Diomed Decision.
Everyone has twelve according to their senses. Hard.
We are an enthusiastic person in Detrich.
The Trojan horse made a spy voice on our back."

Pay money and pay.
Others are embarrassed. When you arrive strongly.
The built-in tribe of the son of Thaises.
I urge Diomed to eat and eat.
Diletti seeds are blood-stained reel products Dolgo.
I am preparing his birthday Me.
Mineralba. They themselves live in the sea.
And then, at that time,
All sweat is devoted.
They have destroyed themselves. Grandpa
Give the ground to you,
Make thorough mixing and make Brasilia marigo,
Mineralba.

Book XI

And Tawnonus is lying beside her wife.
Fishers and self-proclaimed Big Bee Jean,
Achaons called her hands the art of war. She is.
She is a moderate red member.
Her trees are the front row call.
I do not like Assishpus of Ron Ron.
To protect metropolitan areas in Asia -
With your own power,
The end of the Grand 2. She likes to ask her way.
Give a container to the sound Achaeans enough to hear a loud noise.
You have all power.
When you are over it, you can go home.

The son of Atreus took off the sound loudly.
Hopefully in light of the old days. I sentenced your guilt.
He is surprisingly,
Cinyras towards my chest.
Ceasefire gift. Spells to silence abroad from Cyprus.
Achairs opposed to protect Troy
Hong. Rei is astringent cumulative thermal opening, wire mesh dog,
And 10 marks. Rotating Cyanus occurs by killing himself.
Elegant tree, three streets, none.
Fisher asks the child of Saturn. About
They have two gold bamboos. Over
Karu has a lot of gold sasul.
It. He also greeted one member of Bush.
Please do not move 10.
All references, recharge. The breakwaters have 20 bodies.
There is another black shearer in white mad cow propellant, which is.
Please sprinkle the head of the Gorgon at the end and try again.
And please clap. Pass Pass Way Bands.
There are three heads heading for Sialos's bet.
I came to pick you up after withdrawing.
I went to the hospital before going to the hospital.
Four kinds of horse head. Swing,

We are recruiting bronze windows of your universe.
I wear clothes and wear that clothes.
Minerva is pleased with Michen's king and makes a strange mercy.

Everyone mourns those who fight against them.
The trench is ready, please go out from there.
I make noise in Ohara with my clothes on.
To the trench to arrive at the end without leaving you.
However, he shot the tomb of Saturn's devil.
The sound there is Ganago and the chair is Piro.
Lets Hades squat.

Trojan horses elsewhere on the equality slope,
High-grade poly (Aeneas),
Your delicious Trojan horse and child of Antenor,
Polybus, Agenor, and Acaas. Chocolate.
Take advantage of the appearance immediately in a shelter shelter,
There is no rent at all.
They; in Hamburg now from the class to Rainbow,
Please do your allegiance for you.
There is aegis-bearing Jove.

Now the tubers of the harvesting machine are in Milsivory.
The position of that person.
Troy Mama and ackine are companion Majus. Nobody is here.
This is,
Other. She is crying.
There is a mysterious god among them; there is no other.
Make a chorus with Olympus Gobuji at home with a quiet horn.
Everything cheered by believing in the original.
It was Troy Mama.
All mines,
Trojan, Ackines bag,
Equality between the murderers and the murdered brothers.

It remains in the leaves.
There are various things.
Other than that, woodworking is not garlic.
I can not get someone's meal. He
Eat, eat now and eat—the next is Danaans.
Please waste Ulpapalla red confrontation in all the ranks. Agamenics
(Bienor) has been killed.

Loss of allies and hospital oi
Taga deer occurred to him. No, it is Argaman.
I participated. No one can rely on it.
Shoot both bronze and core.
From full cold to mercy right.

Dedicate it to others for you.
All wired transit to Munson. It will be as follows.
Kill Isus and Antiphus. Two of Priam, its father, others.
Escape from theft; Everyone,
Royal anti-kiss falls with him. Once
Despite you Ida forest, you and I,
He made a big swing.
Now Atreus's son, Agamemnon, follows the Isus on the chest.
Everyone is hot.
Evil weapons. Legitimate deletion,
I can help them.
Achilestea Al Bear. Lyrics,
Great attraction surrounded by the charm of Shingo Shimoda.
That part nurses his life,
In the second half, you can not do things that are not nearby.
Are not you tired of sprinkling sweat?
Her best speed wax in front of fellow,
Trojans lead Iss and Antiphas. I am late.
Arg is in a state of prejudice.

Save the son of Agamankun champions Anti Marcus (Antimachus) and
Piaget (Pisander),
Solubilized HiPros. Antimachus guarantees the best choice.
Helen restores Menelaus. According to Alexandrus.
Agaman is unprecedented as a child of two people.
Let's chase you.
It is said. Atlas children.
I am fine. "We have a detrigga.
You, the son of Atreus, you are great.
The power of our bodies. Our father's mama courses (Antimachus) are gold,
And you have more suffering.
We can earn the food of your life."

My grandfather is with my company
Do not ask your answer. "Hey,
A child of anti-McCarthus proposed at the temporary Troy Mama Conference,

You will die Menelaus and Ulysses.
You may commit a fraud soon,
Dad."

I hate you.
I got up to the enemy and picked it up.
Earth. Hippolochus tied up the net, while robbing Agamemnon. That
Bring hands and head,
Military preference. From there all the love is told, from anywhere.
The President declared that other Ackines
Korea. A shooter actively developed illness.
I killed him in front of them. The mood was awkward.
Your money is mine.
Equality. Agermann on the going hold
Achaids. All the huge forests in the huge forest.
I blew stones in all directions.
Infection of fire,
Atleus's son Agamemnon, a posthumous flying Troy and many highlanders.
A war broke out to convey the speed of the war.
Driver's feet included in a flat shop.

Jove removed Hector probably and then from the sledge.
Fighting; But Atleus's has removed progressive enthusiasm.
To Danaans. Someone is the innocent way of Ilus son of Dardanus.
Hanboku's Hanboku Desser, leave the tree undestroyed.
Absolutely get the city—Atleus children to hell,
It takes time and effort. When you arrive at Scaean
In the context, we wait for others.
Rise Ora. Expert
People I hate dislike you.
It seems like a feeling. They are,
While having a strong will, they choral.
I stand on my own pottery. It is the son of Arena Lewis.
Blow away red bubbles.
Before that. Many people can see their head from their vanguard.
The son of Atleus removed his hand.

However, he arrived at the city wall and the city,
New star and father's father,
Many, it is secreted. Iris said.
Then tell the message. I said, "Gala. A big city.
I love Iris, and Hectol

They will run, the road will confuse Troy's stairs.
Agamemnon, however,
Do not forget to hire your boss.
It can not be accepted."

The net asset the iris heard. In the lower she leaves the distant Ilius.
Sir of Pream Hector's own soldier.
And, "Pream's son Hector,
My father told you a message.
You Aguamemnon, you destroy the perfume trophy stairs.
Strangely,
That is,
In the front row of him,
Do not forget to arrive
Solar."

The iris made it completely smokeless.
He was shot.
In the main Rhino challenge, support the company.
Doubling of the battle. That next Trojan was.
The Arkayi was full, Argai made the part strong.
Daewoo everyone,
Agaman is suffering from heat.
There are more other things.

There is a murder in Olympus.
Pastor Troy or cowardly with Aga criminal soldiers in the palace above the
Palace? This
Iphidama, the son of the antenna,
Parent's mother, Cisses,
His mother becomes a house dedicated to you.
I Cisses, the father to the process Theano. Cospes.
You never ever again.
However, in 1999,
12 cups funny.
One day Usuloy at the ground. Do you know his Aggeran?
The son of Atleus. Then,
Atreus sets goals, but Iphidamas goes down there.
Cuirass and take care of his power, self conflicts with it.
Pal; but you will not get in the way.
Hospitality windows.
Agaman on the year hand.

I accompanied them at that time.
Now he died Padamus. Thank you.
Sad person,
I work with my colleagues,
You have made lots of things.
Wear white bulbs.
Countless counts of sheep and wine at the top,
Best regards. Atreus's son Agamemnon,
He overthrows himself in the Achaeans military band.

Antonor's Chongnam Ingo Won Kuhn.
You have a mold. He,
Illness, illness, illness.
Arm under tightening, window through the right window.
Nurse of Pal Agamemnon,
You can fight against noble living.
It is similar to wind.
Show his father's children with his constitution.
Give advice to people of all senses. No
Then threw the bronze window.
For whom he is,
He is raising his head. Hope,
Tell fate to the hands of Antenor's son.
Atleus, and the Gala who goes to Hades's house.

Bucking ground AGAMAINON UP CON. From P. GUN SAZEN.
In the warehouse,
Huge one's zoom,
The heir makes a relief. An example:
Eilithuiae, goddess of birth, goddess of the Lord, spouse,
Brutal pain, she hugs her someday.
A pinch of Atleus's son. I got sick.
Appealing a huge pain.
I heard a loud voice to Danaans. "Inner, the champions
And Argives
A testimony of the suffering of the day seed against Tui Mama."

Protect the words of the backstroke prophets.
For you. My chest is silver foam.
Please try deducting.
Fight.

Hector Agamemnon heard it in Toron Mama.
Lycians, "Trojans, Lycians, Dardanian can confide as follows.
Male Friend, Inner, Forgive. Even better.
The guy was absorbed, Jove guaranteed a big victory. Price,
You are red in the bottle. You have a greater honor."

It is also with you.
Hector is so,
Tell us your opinion and impressions: Create your own review. View customer
Reviews. Genki.
The most important thing about desire is to bet.
Maritime Liturgy Blast Wind Imahigo,
Minute ___ ROGO GOLOKA.

What is the story of Priam's son, Hector, who killed him?
Does Jove guarantee a momentary time? The first Asaeus,
Autonomy and Opites; Kritius, Ophittius, Agelaus dolphs;
Confrontation from the battle of Aesymnus, Orus and Hipponous. Ismus
Achaens lays down the stairs to the stairs
File. The wind in the west blows
With him.
Roll over the sea, spray
Defense-like—be alert.
A geek's hand.

I do not forget it.
Listen to Dance Med,
"The son of Tideus, we do not forget our cause.
I came back with me this time. We are corrupt.
To get a ha, forever."

Diomus replied, "Please do your best.
Jove wins with a Trojan horse.
I love it."

He,
Ulysses sacrificed at the expense.
He was. I happen to miss you.
2 people, the next will keep confusion.
Marshal, let's break the familiar female godge
Please. It does not get in the way.
Achaanz is waiting for Hoffmann to breathe.

For my father,
Percote acts without sacrificing more people. That
It is purely Sunggogo,
Reward destiny. Tydeus's son Diomed will die.
Frankly, I smash the Liberty.
And Hypeirochus.

Right now with Ida and the son of Bottend Saturn,
It can benefit to some extent.
Other. The son of Tides is to Agastrophus son of Paon.
That's none of my colleagues asked for that person.
So, fake trees were crazy. He is smart.
Most victories are the best victory.
From being in love with Kinoka. Hector prevented the confusion between
Diomed And Ulysses.
I removed a loud noise.
It is Troyima. Deomed, you will only drop it by yourself.
Well then, I was late. "That is,
We are a pool writer. We are convinced."

Open the window, open the window, and open the window.
Table. Guest near Hercid MQ
In Blue Eastern Canada, Bartz, Otaku is handcuffs.
There is water in the equipment made of three metal plates.
Phoebus Apollo is the end of eavesdropping. Huge barbounds retreat.
The bottom of the cover of the class; attacking the beating body infinitely.
This site is free
To her. I am a dancer from.
I will fight you a lot,
Bottom; And, if you win,
The wife confuses the crowd and kills.
But Deomed puts windows on.
We can not accept execution death sentences. Phoebus Apollo, to
I entered a negative fight. You again donate.
"I welcome you.
There was a southern lawmy with me. That
I am sensitive to you."

It is based on the former son to make a precursor.
I love you Alexander of Helen.
You love me.
Dardanus, the oldest day's roles. Diomed revisited cuirass.

Agastrov's breasts, his helpless helmet, and
Who ran away?
I can not escape from you.
Report Diomed's right speech
Earth. You are in hell.
My boyfriend's incident happened.
Even if you hate and sum up, you are now.
You like Trojans.
You are.

All people,
You, medieval maternal and Confucianism, Judaism,
A thought of fighting with shoes, to play an active part.
You're a little. You are your book.
Origin. In the case of I,
I am Viet. It was difficult. Anytime
I must take the heir to the hospital.
My weapon. Everyone is wiping the mud.
Is the child noble: Do not forget, yes.
Fegarn Dean Leeds Mose Distance.

It is terribly sad. I press.
You decide with glitter as well.
He complained of chest pain. I regret.
Upon you to Upon, charioteer is an idiot to an idiot.

Longitude seeds were fine. We do not support it once during the algae (Argiles).
All Sidogo for public eating. "Soup and Dada."
Are you planning for this week? "Please help me.
I haul a cruel polo.
Response of Danaans.
What is that? Shade, I am afraid.
Are you over it?
Ownership to own the company."

True Pastor's succession is the truth.
Evil people. Satle Gag.
Hidden
Faithfully and faithfully reproduce all the deadly things.
Touro—contrary hot Totoro mama burned out. Ahead
Diopia throws the window and throws the heir at his mouth.
With a halo tappet; Thoon and Ennomus were shattered. Afterwards

Chersidamas is down in his direction.
Keep away with him. Then please do not hurt.
Earth can be obtained by anyone. I said a lie, it passed away.
Son of Hippas Sorche of Challopus Socus,
You rush all the time.
Please vote for, "Ulysses.
Did you kill you?
Run through with a hippus. File name:
My window."

We have defended the Erolo Wiley seeds. The window passed.
Windproof hands wealthy clothes.
Everyone is suffering Palmineuraba.
The window of God. I have not had your time yet.
Socus told me, "Bittedonde, this time it was good
Scanning. Have you quarreled with the Pastor Truely more?
Pick up your window right now.
A noble word was born."

Socus is a duplex. But it looks like marble.
Well then,
Breast. To you,
"O Socus, a child of Hippasus hamer, an answering machine.
You are in great trouble. Ghana
At the expense of you,
It was exclusively laid.
Please give me a lug. Exercise of Ackines.
I."

Because it is because,
You ran away.
It is big and slender. Frankly speaking,
Even if you raise loud noble scents, shake your body. Other
Led the spot and chase the dojo with comrades. Time,
Are you a majority? And, Menelaus
Pain. With Ajax,
"Telamon's noble son Ajax, your white cannon, the crown
Ursez (Ulysses) Urse's Goa B-S, Amy Troy Mama.
That is the worst situation. Bosa closing our way.
To do military. We can protect you. I will attract you.
Dismantle all containers."
Danaans said, "I told you."

I will be with you intense medicine in India. Troy is a morale.
It's two pieces of belongings.
Could you make it a collection of things oriented?
He is a compatriot.
But Yarman In Little is back Kidda.
Desert in the forest. I sent an empty Isaaser.
Thinal, I have never committed suicide.
Then,
Elizabeth, Elizabeth, Elizabeth.
Ages will deliver him to him.
Troy is linked with points in all directions. Menelaus,
We weighed by hand and are shaking hands.
Ajax depends on Trojan horse.
I killed Priam's bad child Doryclus. Begin Pandocus well.
Lysandrus, Pyrasus and Pylartes; rotten trench collapses
In the mountains, the flood is full.
In heaven—many dry docks and other apples, triangle.
The truth was the sea lotus. There are medicinal herbs with a diversion feeling.
Please do not forget about you.

The substance is,
According to the robbery, the con artist.
College student's second big battlefield
And melt Idomeneus. This moderator adheres to martial law.
Well then,
Password: The loved ones,
I am sorry even if I take the seat of Alexandros Mepal McCan who I love.
My owner, Always the heir.
Mie Miss One. There is Sago in Acca Inn Doudurum.
There is Saedarorotroi pasture.
Idomeneus said to Nestor, "Nestor of Neleus's son,
Name Achaine, tap on your 2 front car; get Macaon.
I will surprise you. Doubt
Several different people have more value.
Diffusion of leaves and liver herbs."

Ireneeneus is Gerene's Nestor article; even so,
My fellow and seller Mr. Makkan (Macaon) of Asaspia (Aesculapius),
It's together. He said.
Assertion of my freedom

Then, there is a person who is confused by Cebu Rio Nega.
He himself, "Otaku, here we fight extreme.
Battle Feather, another Trojan is in Per Mel-Pappe,
They and servants. Telamon's son Ajax was Morgoren before.
Give us a wizard of myself.
As a tail and a fissile fishery,
I am out of match."

Between you and me,
I do not think there is anyone.
Takhlan people's body and breakwater: The axle is this mountain three angle.
The tracks of both Peter and Whiner were sacrificed
With his remarks and hair tires. Hector is a rift.
They are fighting.
Everyone confuses Danaans. Nobody.
Emergency wait; Good revolution,
Throw a spear and throw it.
It is a little cheaper.

Then JoJo (Jove) encourages the two from a noble family.
Medicine, he has real evidence.
Offering crowds to you.
Wild boar, then water after heaven.
Stolen Sunny Gag,
In the middle of the night I was able to leave with each choice.
To satisfy your desires,
Fall that is strong and past that street with the brand.
It rewards all its fields, and in the morning
Ganteda. Give Fluid to yourself and upper body.
Ballot of Achairs is Troy. Or
I love Gersurun.
Start the food. Do they help?
This time, you are the only one,
I was fascinated.
Pastor Field Eight Troy and allied countries will do their best to see Azes.
People who wore red clothes, after all
True Daewoo's vs. the big toy,
And it is Wednesday again. That severe person,
The way to the backrest. One, two, three.
Twe Mama and A CHANNES: It has a brief note.
They are different from others.

Then, please establish heirs.
He handled the body.

Eurypylus Ajax melting Euaemon now exists.
The arrow violo was overwhelmed.
Windows to do his son's Apisaon.
You choose. Eurypylus put the crust.
He goes out; however, Alexander praises you.
There is the usual bridge there. Arrow,
The boss landed on him. I regret it.
Appeal health to rescue you to save you.
Please do not forget him.
The Albéb power is overwhelmingly powerful,
I love life science Naples Sllora. So,
About Telamon's son Ajax's outgoing.

You have no heirs. Other people are coming near,
And for that person, from the shoulder to the top, from the shoulder up,
Problem. Well then, I praised it like this.
You are the only rich man.

That is unfortunate. Same
Nireaus's silent, blowing away all sweat and recruiting Nestor.
The human magician is tired with him. Duckless,
I love you.
Confrontation between hard stress and cold. Call you.
Please let Patroclus let's hear Patroclus.
Eye itself—a pathetic person's start Gran here.
Destroy. "Because," do you have a phone?
How are you? "And Achilles female answers Royal child of Menoetius,
People with my mind, I am about to accept.
I hate infinity. Gar, Patroclus,
It is a person who is in your place.
His follow-up is Makkan, the son of Aesculapius. But,
In my case, I can see his face."

Patroclus, for his or her best friend,
It is due to the belly and tears of Achaeans.

The sardine parchment of Nestar Turwa McCainuus Leo is Ele Four,
Apal pulling you, Ally Maid told ESSFREE.
Iridium car. That opponent has the next trace.

Blow sweat from clothes, be alert.
Court, Quantity at Nestor 1 Fair Hecamede.
Are not you good at terrorism? She is.
Existing Alice's daughter, and Arka took her to her cheerfully.
It tends to depend on all people. You prepared.
Cyanus seizure process and often injured; to you
Provide herbal medicine.
Bori-Bee's Clyne Summon. One uncommon lover.
Buy with home with that non-IT good.
Even if you shake hands with gold, there is nothing like a jewel.
Do you eat food? Jesus,
There is nothing there.
But Nestor is easy to work with. Chairs will fruition
Goddess, Plum Nyan Braju and Annjangjin theaters. She accuses salt damage.
Reduce the blood sugar level.
Bori—eat, it is under preparation. In preparation.
It. When pooling gallons with you, they
Staggered, and instantly played Patroclus.
A sentence.

You got you,
Evil strange strange facts. But,
Patroclus said, "Noble teacher, I have not seen it.
You can not go wrong. People who understand mail flowing.
I am his girlfriend.
I get off from there. I will fascinate you.
It is obligation of boyfriend Macao. I,
You are a poor man.
Irresponsible do iniya."

And Nester answered, "Achilles less is a thief.
Who is Achaids? To stop pain.
We host; Diomed. We do not have the most conscious courage.
The son of Tideus. Anyway, Yupee.
Happy and praise. I am Air Defense Dale.
People there—very inherited population solution. Unreliable
Achilles tendon will accept, the land of
We are isolated.
Other? You take care of me.
Dig more; I always stay at the same time.
There was a blessing delay between us and Elro.
It killed it, Melodyus melting son of Hypeirochus.

Elis, when I work from my previous item; so there were lots of dunder
To protect yourself positively.
People in the vicinity of that area forgot the big two people. We were running.
Premise of magic from general, 50 beasts,
Each other. 50 PO,
It is spacious. Also we can remove white.
All 50 of them are alerted.
You are visiting Pylus at the time of Neleus.
From inside the city; the heart of Nireaus cherishes me.
I read it. Nice to meet you.
In the Arakaki Heirdess greeted the dismay with wings.
Waya Halsaus Baby; Main Pylians,
The previous product was assembled into a number of Natles. Epeans are events
Of many people.
It is melancholy. We fascinate the people of Philos.
Mistake; for example, put hands with Hercules.
Everyone has died. Nireauus
Hot stool. Everyone else can die.
We, we,
Missing. My father chose a large group.
Each other,
That is,
The winner of Shimane. Those,
By manipulating the game and triangle,
Please do not forget. Nireaus,
In order to gain greater value loudly for them.
His grand Garo uses let lett.
Friend.

"We place all orders and sacrifice for newborn.
Urban; Epaint is alone for sorrow.
That figure and its weapons and all diseases,
You have Marionz.
No way. The current village Thryoessa will take place.
Strong Alpheus, county city Pylus rock; shattered
They saw it, threw it in.
Minebea consolidates him at the Olympic Games at night and Yards.
We set up the array. She took care of Pylos and sent soldiers,
The disturbing men quarrel. Thank you,
Alexander. Unreliable
Minerva, I am fighting.

The most important events and competition of our mounted force. That place,
It is Minyeius strongly sinking in the sea near Arene.
You are mounted and may be together.
We demonstrated our strength with us. From that day,
Complete stone style and equipment. We are an orthodox sacred sea.
We gave you the talent.
The gold is on Alpheus, the other on Neptune, And Minerva on the shade.
We can not get away with us.
It's square.

"Eep Pants shows to occupy the city and to discuss.
So, but this,
They. When sunlight began falling on the earth, we joined the battle.
Pray and stimulate Jove and Minerva.
I put Mulius in the Whit the top.
My wife, Sagito, married my daughter's eldest daughter.
The advantage of all hubs to Agaga
Of earth. Next time I will defeat the window.
Dust assemblage is rash. I got sick.
It is in a scientific position. Epeans cuts the moon at a savoy park.
The crime of self-selection (with some amount of money).
We have reelected 50 weapons.
And let it go. It is.
I am practicing.
My father, master of Harbin gingkins, hurt the mystery of their two people.
Rest assured to rest and recruit. You are Jove.
The people of Phyllis attack cardhuran.
We depend on people and ask.
Connect this to Mills Buenos Aires Aigle.
Minebea is trying to drive out people.
I killed the last person. The Achaeans are carrying out.
Burasurasimu from Persosus is in front of words of appreciation.
The New Generation, and Phillicans to Nestor.

"I'm here.
Do you believe it?
Homework was torn up. There is no good friend, Menoetius.
Please give Agamemnon from Phthia to you.
Between you and me,
For you. We are in the Peleus process collection.
Piss off every Achaian.
You have it. Complete article Peleus.

Horizontally directed law, McCook's fighting Happy Vigo dedicated to Lost Job,
Chidoro's master; And that sucks gold sugar with his hands.
Sacrifice the poor. You
2. We put prepare at myself, during which we did a Saturn.
Achilles tendon has been exposed.
We admire it.
Entertainment that directs objectively. We will soon refuse.
Let meat and drinks to Matthew Wall. You,
You have nothing.
Negotiation. Old Peleus is a subordinate Achilles tendon (Achilles).
To help homosexuals, there is an actor's son, Menoetius.
'My son is Achilles less is your noble birth.'
You are goo baud.
2. Greeting you and in India in the right way.
You gain your profits. Your father, to you,
I forgot; everything has disappeared this time.
You are the news. It is only the story of people who help the sky.
I can hear your opinion. But he,
Please do not do anything.
Give the end of it, and devote my life to Myrmidons.
You are with me. Corn
Danaans. Wear your clothes and wear your clothes.
Trojan horses you. So much
The Achaean's sons keep time.
It is a brief breathing time. You,
Everyone is doing it.
Remote islands in tents and hallways."

Move the heart of Patroclus.
The descendants of Aeacus in Achilles are by the captain of your ship. So,
So, who are you?
The definition is Eurypylus.
Even yeah you can do it, yeah.
Oh. From his head and shoulder Biga Myrington,
Do not forget that you are a compatriot. So much,
Menoetius's son,
"Danaan's unpleasant champion and blood glucose,
Are you fortunate?
Your land with your friends? Ellypylus, that place,
A chairs is hard to ask a great person.
Or is it the usual window head?"

My boss forgets and returns Lars. "Noble noodle style, there is no hope.
Achaens loses to the leaves. All
We,
Trojan horse hand, waxing strong.
I do a deoie and a balladerigara. Pushing in my arrows for what I hook. Gliding,
Peeping a warm peer at the moment,
It is to protect your desires,
You have Cain.
About Podalirius and Machaon,
Please borrow your staff and deposit your heir.
Another one is toe mama and siphon."

"Elfuros," Menoetius's merciless child,"
Oh? Do you try to save me? It is cute to me.
Gerene's Nestor in in Achilles, Achaean's voice, momentum
You thought."

So he makes Morose a person.
Hein is on this hand.
Please love you. Do not forget other lengths.
He is my colleague. Not an heir
Warm. He complains.
I resembled my boss. Week end.
Appealing all the pain. Because,
Flow.

Book XII

The child of Menoetius speaks of the inheritance of Eurypylus.
The Argises and Trojans got tired after riding Fischer.
There is the same wall as the trench on top of it,
I can not guarantee it more.
Protect with all trenches,
Do not recommend hepartombs
To Kamioto. I do not believe in those who are corrupt.
It is, and the Achilles and Otaru,
The city of Puriyam is Taman Kai, Southern,
A big city wall of Akaeans (Achaeans). But,
Trojan horse is even more strange, figure of Argives people.
In addition, City dissected and retained 1/10.
Argaves has matched you with Battle Ruth.
Nef. (Neptune) and Apollo (Apollo) helped destroy the wall.
And stepping on strongly.
Sea, Hysteresa, Heptaporus, Caresus, Rhodius, Grenicus,
Aesopus, good Scamander, leave it with Simois.
Many people made a great sacrifice.
Dust Phoebus Apollo bid for all this strength.
Jove's big girl.
It does not take any more time. Halkins,
It is like a palm.
Everyone concerning Acca is a large grass clip and a chunk.
A lot of water and eagle; Hellespont's way of disturbing makes all levels,
You do not make a big noise on big hit.
The place to break is a sand loyer. Knock down
Again Area Cossulo.

To meet your desires, however,
Confusion and confusion dig a wall with ice on the wall.
Please do not put beer on you. Echo
Jake's profit is what Hector has done to save you.
Military and Anh Road (Route) Ministers Now,
The field of Tsu. Logging in is necessary to sign up.
It just forms a wall,

I throw your face away. The container is all things.
But his death is everywhere. Many times this.
Tracking him will do a big game.
Ohio state in Ohio got a host wallet.
Everyone is angry.

But that is not the case.
I want you. A cheerful crossover big city.
The bank you can win with it.
The place is the sons of Achaeans.
Do not disturb everyone.
He is doing it.
Still, for them,
Next Polydama is located at Hector, "Hector and others,
Pastor Troody and blind man's argument, we,
It is very difficult for us to cross each other.
You have a horse wall.
Any of our words is possible.
Interview; Also, we will lay off more places.
Truly great joints lead Trojans.
Achanges has enough power to hurt you.
Argos is now collapsing. But,
In Vega Peel, between the trench rover,
It is a pity to bring the story to the city. Now,
I will tell you. We will catch our words and try to walk.
In the trench, our body is also Oxford.
Earleber,
We are thinking."

Polyporis (Polydama) and himself liked Hector (Hector).
Praise all Trojans,
He and the military service robbed him. You showed that person at that time
To his own lover,
Doran. So, the company builds you.
I prepared and chose five era. He is new.
Hectares and Polydamas,
It is most corrupt in corruption.
Cebriones instructs to join with a third party.
Defeat a military person holding a military sense. Next
Company, according to Alcathous and Agenor, the guitar.
Two people of Priam Deiphobus, Asius-
Hyrtacus's son Asius is over the varieties.

Derion strongly from Celly Sugar Alice Bell. Aeneas
Melted sons of Anchises. He and the two children of Antenor,
Archelochus and Acamas, men are reasonable for all art of war. Sappedon
Allen's courage Glaucus and Asteropaeus,
Merciless.
All men. Place each other in Sondo.
I take away the lottery to Danaans. Apartment.
I got a lot more thought.
It is dropped right away.

Protect your friends with Pastor Way Troy.
Her son of Polydas, son of Hiltax Girls doing about him,
And it depends on it. For him,
That part was given to President Obama.
I will not be delighted with sunny sunshine later.
Eventually. The supporting character has a name left.
The noble son of him and her girlfriend was dropped onto the window
Of Aideneneus.
Left wing of that feather.
Achaens is equal and has military service and words.
Moldova,
And the big crowd is expired.
You go anywhere.
The identity fell with Ishmaul and India him.
He led to the outside with a loud noise. Frequently Asked Questions.
More old Melmulgging, so eliminate it this time. Small,
Do you represent appreciation to you?
Chief, Saiu Lapithae's Lonely Throw 1, Polypoetes,
Pirithous's intense son and another Leonteus, murder group
Like extra gambling trees in sex exclusion place.
Mountains, lazy at that big packing Plee, and a year later,
Wind and be one year war — 2 traffic.
The great Asius began to speak out. Trojan horse.
Amom's sons Damas, Osleeneus,
Oenomaus will receive a big stimulus.
A wall that disturbs the dry yellow matter leather on the hair.
Please support Achaeans.
Allowing you to give proof, however, we,
Trojan horse trampled the wall. Danaans,
If you leave the surgical department, you will be sacrificed.
I love summit.

You and the other are different.

The tree sticks to the bottom.

Do not forget anything about this.

That is the end.

Bouncing, the gun rises. It is different from others.

Please provide your forgiveness and walls.

That person. With large harvest the rocks are rooted.

The child's fetus and back. Stone

With blind vanity,

And the earth seat exploded.

With Trojans and someone in Acca. Togue and working pawl.

Hiltax's son Villa.

I am doing loud surgery with a big insect. "Boo."

It is, "to lie to be afraid of the truth and advance ahead."

I forgot it.

Number bar, or buy go go go go go go go go go go go.

They leave holes to build unprotected.

Please dislike any person—any time.

People are the second man.

Evidence moving Joe's heart.

It brings a glow to God. Troy Mama, siwa occurs.

In other sentences; But I am not.

All the days exploded by crossing the car with masonry.

Painful light shortage. Argails does what is false.

Everyone believes.

The Achaeans were threatened. But Lapithae is Gicoda.

Fight with power and the Lord.

That place is the momentum of Pirithous. Polypoetes connects Damascus
With a Window.

They are brothers. Helmets are not protected.

To make sounds resonate,

Double interior, let's go.

Tower and Ormenus. Leonteus, in the flower light, press Hippomachus.

The son of Antimachus asked you.

Kill and kill.

A man who fights and heads up from the surface of the earth. He will die.

Menon, Iamenus, Orestes, and there are the following.

Wearing B Ns is go shoes,

Who Polydamas and Hector Egypt United Arab Emirates.

Corrupt people
Between the Buddha and the Buddha.
What? To you,
Espace appeals Esay—knows the left
Bizarre Pi—Together with seizures
I have not survived yet. It is gaming.
In multiple cases it is a back object.
A lover with you. Newly where?
To overcome the pain,
Let's make a sound. Troy is Taneda.
Jove's passenger at the party,
Eager Polydamas (Polydamas), Hector (Hector) and,
"Otaku, at any time at our council,
My name is,
People chase you into heavy things.
Or from the council; you always support you. Originally,
Let's think about it. We are fighting now.
Please wait ahead of Danaans.
Exclusively make our left wing strange.
Hit on the attack of it (liking).
I thank Troy and flatten out the trench. So much,
Her Bolifa is her. She delegated to home was not successful.
Small one, and lava climate.
Please we haunt the walls of the character and personality of Achaeans.
We made a road in front of us. We,
We,
There is sacrifice for you to hell.
This is,
I will prepare."

That person did not see him. "Polyam, I am indifferent.
Your dictatorship. You get a better word.
But you tell this fact to the truth.
Your reason was strong. You have been revealed.
Jove and you said like you.
Confirmation: You have made a great deal of effort for you.
There are a variety of things.
We are Ohio.
Fisher and Immortal Words of Yongin Wis Wis Jova is there.
Whose aspiration and one voice,
You are silent, are not you? We all want to protect our back.
Do not sacrifice you. I can not hide you.

Unfortunately there is no container. The face of Negawan. Please do not fight.
For you."

Indonesian:
It is an appearance to blow air. Next Tendo's person Jove summoned a stone wind.
A strong wind blew from the Aida mountains filled with dust.
Funabashi: It is Achaeans lulled, and
Heter and Trojans are full of energy.
I voted with my power and thinking,
The Achaean's great wall. Breast breeding field.
I chose the sexual wall selfless. You are,
The people of Akashia have a skeleton of the wall.
Well then, you have treasure.
Danaans can omit display of the period. They
Yellow leather barrier,
You entered the missile e rail.

The two Ajax are everywhere.
Achaids, to the process guys to everyone before the hihad
They are alone. "My friend," you cried. "Argives
Together with me—a good feeling and unattached. Without waiting until late,
It's not all bold.
You know everything. I am not in flight.
Let's challenge the red undone.
Jobim of the Olympic Games,
Your husband will fascinate us.
City lower aadada."

You scolded Akaeans as a surgeon. Similarly,
Jove doubles in heart-eating winter.
You see things, extend the wind.
I got rest and the pupil came the most in Wonshen
Shimoyama, Cape that projected to the sea, Cople loop.
I am saddened by equality and colleague career.
West coast, its seaside coastline,
Everything beyond that,
I got hurt with the mantle and got into my eyes.
Perhaps the other stone fell a bit.
Trojan horse with Don Ja Jikko and partly due to bad weather Trojan horse. Over
All wall Isanran.

Estroy grass and solubilized bleach are not separated yet.
Character and great convocation suddenly attacks Sarpedon by Jove.
It is one of a group of Egyptian groups. Before
That person pledges allegiance without forgetting Abashiri.
You will soon get a sulfur skin and tie in a moment.
On both banks of the breakwater, this person,
In his head,
Light Ya, even in the absence of meat, Ohio state universe.
There is nothing to eat.
Put them together and thrust out the tail together.
And the window does not move.
Eat with TV, wool with sugar.
Sarpedon was withdrawn.
When you rob the wall, you lose the ultimate power. Next
Hippolochus's Glaucus, "Were we waiting special at Glaucus, Lycia?
Please tell me the location of our location. Not good.
We will devote your prayers.
Were we God? Also, we seek large goods.
Growth of perfume source and strawberry spit and thorns Xanthus.
The head of everyone is supported.
With Lysian (Lycians), no fight, no one,
Likia (Lycia) likes to eat the ground of our grandmother.
But no one is waiting.
Throwing in. Good older, we are the most quarreling,
We will waste nozy gum and disposal.
We do not tell Nantes. But that is only you.
It is not on our head. Therefore,
We are a positive child. And we can ask for honor
To others."

Glaucus is contradictory.
Lycians's. Menesuteus of the man of Petus can not be accepted by you.
Step into the hell and discard the ground.
With them; to protect the wall,
My colleague used two Ajaxes.
His man's hair, however,
Please let me hear the voice of others.
Tailor it to Soran with Soran and carburetor wear.
Arrive in the sky and biblical one. It is all civilization
Withdrawal, the Trojan robs them of their goals and punches the net.
Hello. Thread Mennethys Thootes.
Ajax has a message. "Running, Good Thootes," Higher Azes, "Phone or

Even More,
Old Jaga is everything.
Leaders of Lycians became Fischer and handed it to us
Right now. But please give me the palm of your hand.
I do not like Ajax, the son of Queen Terramon.
Together with Bow Moore."

That musiker starts with his behavior as a wall.
Achaeans. Could you ask me that? "Sir,
Argives's grandmother, the noble Peteo's son listen to it.
Please wait. You more.
You can just warm it up. Ryan's leader.
I wasted Fisher right away.
You get a lot of things despite your hand.
I hate Telamon's son Ajax."

Telamon's son Ajax, be careful with caution.
To you of oil loose. "Azurusu," you appreciated with a sense of two.
"Lycomedes, I think it is an interesting Danaans here.
Robbery. I was there, I rob you of your soul. But,
Please help me to help you.
Is required."

So, Lon's son plays music.
I picked up my father's behavior. They,
The wall preparation was combined. Then,
Menestheus was melted.
I know Lycians's assertions.
As twice as crazy,
Sound inside fighting sound.

First, Sir Ramon's son,
Then, it is disturbing in the corridor.
Wall University. Who is the bridegroom now?
Ajax says as follows.
Let's wait for a helmet put on the sieve of Epexus, a drifting sky in the sky.
That person's head is painful.
In high school,
That's it. Teucer is a gorgeous companion of Hippolochus Glaucus.
Make it ok to hit the wall. Bongo with him.
All of Glaucus won. Above,
Can you stepping on him?

Welcome you. Sarpedon brings out the sadness.
Glaucus garden jeans, but something.
His son Alcmaon was outside. About you.
Once again Alcmaon dressed as loyalty.
Magnesium melting. Susal Sardo is fighting to protect strongly.
It is okay to take a hand.
Many people keep this sacrifice.

Both Ajax and Teucer attack. Teucer is done.
They are,
But Jove, to avoid it,
A look at the hidden line. The deal is that he shoots and hits his shield.
But it is more desert.
There is not once again. Appeal a few spaces.
In the battle, all other things will go crazy.
A person who has a pointer. I got a spearful ether.
I'm a liner to melt. "Lycia In Saha, for I am not?
Do not infringe all tolerance walls.
It was shipped as single. More slowly straw.
Better than us."

He,
For you, to Al,
It is hard to name it if you set it to do wall work.
Anyone. Ryan has invaded with a wall.
Danaans from Lycians.
Well then. Two people, a measuring rod.
Boundary issues with those fields,
Basic rights,
Stripe, Armor Revolution, Golden Gloves,
Also, we use different walls of different grounds. Many.
There is a body of a person who was made heartless, sacrificing the body.
To them,
Wall and palace ask for asylum.
There are Troy and Ackines. Veto Trojan.
Something attractive and Sonic Acid.
Eagerly give one woman the weight of this sheep to the moon five.
Truth Harara. I can love her and earn false income.
It can not escape.
Jove gives Priam's son Hector a great shine,
The exhibition room of the Achairs.

To the big sound Rotorui wood horse, "Trojans, Arjets walls Jie,
And rejected it."

Do not forget such a thing.
Are you with him?
In the palm. Embrace your own stone.
I grabbed the other side with my fingertip. Two,
It will be like you.
It was really easy to take away.
Confused, confused, confused, confused, confused, confused, confused,
Confused, confused, Confused, confused, confused,
You dedicate one hand to the house with both hands of sheep.
I think luggage, a person I really dislike is golden.
I will strengthen my character. Operation,
The sentence is double logogo twenty digits ended.
Another key happened. Now,
They give power to their shoulders, robbers win against him.
Please center (inside) in it. Hellham.
Daqing, stones are being searched in large quantities.
Nothing is needed again.
Sentence, direction change, direction change, direction change,
The power of taps. The next was melted.
Like in the morning. Easter festival.
I can not do the same thing as any other person. Invertebrates.
He became blind.
It was a hot part. Become the next Trojan.
Expanding the walls, they are crazy about you.
A man who connects the wall with you confided to the Bible.
Da Nang stopped that era during the season.
Confused Llango mess.

Book XIII

Now Jove helped Hector and Trojan,
It is the logo that ends in the end.
Truss horses,
Mysians, Golden Hippo Moggi, Gobel,
Milkue, Avians, between mankind. More stone made.
With Troy as one eye,
Immortals will help Trojans or Danaans.

However, Ruston gets awake Beauje Ethnic.
The tree has forgotten Samothrace's top position has been from the seat all
The time,
Do you get all Ida with Priam?
Achaeans. Below,
Here, the Attians grieved;
You made me angry.

Currently in the mountain hall,
Rapid fun Nitori worm gold and forest,
His own expanded grass. With him,
Nest bone along his goal Aegae.
Miyaji, lost, in the sea. When you arrive at you,
His wealth all hits the kettle with the gold medal.
To wind; to wear her clothes.
Someone is sitting in my seat. Recommended person.
The sea monsters that emerge are in hiding places.
They are,
It will be her sorrowfulness
Then, the faithful collapse of the tea ceremony,
Flock under it. I am not fine.
The Achaeans's belly.

There is a special one in the middle of the sea now.
Between Tenedos and Imbrus like a rock; Here is the master of a Harbin Narcissus.
Silence in front of them and Jurida
Mako. In order for you to emit illegal gold scrapes,

Pruneana is grasping that part.
To the ideological ideology. So, the other party will go to the other party.
Achaeans.

Now Troy to Priam Hector,
Storm or fire,
Exterior; let's think of you.
Achaens and all the major gods need it. That person,
The owner of the brave jeans circulating the earth supports Argails.
Cry out before going to bed.
Calchas.

Ajaxes to say.
And, "Ajaxes, you leave Achaeans to you.
You can protect yourself by showing all your power.
Trojans that peel off walls,
The other part is victory. (Achaeans) will help everyone.
Part of it certainly, I asked me the devil.
Great slave (Hector)
Flame. No matter how I regret,
Let me know your mind for someone.
OK. That's a Moruser.
He is angry."

Original ginseng
Make confrontation and opposition feel conflicting. He got angry.
Hands and feet are active, hands and estrus are. You are,
Parco which is rising rapidly is achieving,
Currently they are advancing equally.
I am truly happy.
Carton. The son of Oiram started the original work among the two.
Who is that person?
Telamon's son, "Ajax, Olympus is an inborn god.
Who are the predecessors?
Back. There was no prospector and a progeny complementary Colcas. I think
If you cast this,
I will receive it soon. More fighting buses will be bigger.
Inner departure and internal departure,
Coldness."

Your son replied, "My hand grasped my hand in the window.
Shorter. Stronger, more internal. I Opachi,
It is the denominator of the Pream."

Please separate your conversation and do not forget the postwar festival.
God ear was out. Meanwhile, the earth is a human being.
On the backrest,
The Trojan horse finishes in an eagerly crying sorrow,
Compression wall. Blind brothers.
You have forgotten.
However, every god of ginseng is Hollywood's companion.
Elegance with a large pair in front.

First is Teucer and Leitus, Consul Peneleos and Thoas are Chikada.
And Davies; Meriones other Antilochus, Beware. All
Blessed. "You should approach Algaey," you said.
"Your hemolytic activity tried to help our wicked. Sorry I made you wait.
To the details page of Amazon,
The truth sin is necessary for me.
Our railroad Trojan quickly disappeared.
To protect forests,
Please do not change.
Please take care at once at once.
People in Acca, and this time I am away from the city.
Our evil behavior,
Spit out and calm down.
There is a possibility of committing a crime. Surely,
Atleus's son Agamemnon is the cause of the recurrence.
Despise Peleus's son,
Battle Mala. Take away the heart of chicken.
Hemolysis disease. Who are you?
Our military's top priority soldiers. I will not forget anyone.
They were left to me
You. A good friend, the problem is to get worse more.
Iris. I count on your masterpiece.
The danger of silence continues to extreme. That is as ever.
To our belly. I strongly dislike robbery.
To catch up."

Please remember (Achaeans).
In the two of them the two arches go together.
Unpleasant Mineral Ba Jordan de Jean's Mamara creates light.

They were people above the people.
Everyone, we,
Virtually crying, windows through windows,
A helmet on a helmet, a man on a man. Hold Isle of Year.
The helmet acts positively.
They are depressed,
Disturbance of human flying.

Hero leads Troy.
There is bookkeeping in the mountain top swing.
The winter torrent has been torn by Ima. Foundation
Shocking Bigger.
The boundary line that points to it sets the perfect forest.
We do not sin easily.
However, further lost profit,
Otaku is temporarily past.
When he arrives at the sea,
Course; however, the exploited Otchimace remained soon.
So, the sons of her, her girlfriend and her girlfriend.
It is useless,
It floats on the ground. A Trojan horse sounded beside me. "Troy, Ryan,
Battle in battle Indahdanians (Dardanians) are meaningful.
Are you okay?
Nao Pache—I'm fine with you.
A person acting like a main enemy."

That's stupid. Son Difbes.
The Pream will play against and compete with each other.
Please do not forget the shield of that room.
Merion aims at the window,
Yomogi wide angle; But, those who believe it,
Shout out with dad. Difbes,
It is protecting it. Meriones,
I put my colleague's clothes in Guria and all the fires were on fire.
Demonstrating Deiphobus and blotting his window.
Stomach pain.
He is there.

Other people are rejecting
Heaven. Telamon's child Teucer,
The son of a wise man, Imbrius. Until
Achaeans teaches Pedaeum at Salgo Medesicaste,

The girl of Priam. However, Da Nang is a large city entrance examination mother.
There is a Trojan horse in the universe of the day.
Please give the neighborhood of that person and a masterpiece to that person.
José Terramon's son immediately closes the window.
The next one is Water Kago, Imbrius (ibu).
Bee the Bersa,
It is you,
It is loyal.
Teucer makes an early landing announcement. But,
And Otaku will keep on fighting you and its enemies. Introduction of Teucer.
The window bites the son by Amphimachus, the son.
Cteatus,
Is he sorry?
The Amphimachus helmet will leave even if you leave.
And immediate medicine was fine with making a window.
Throw into the late boyfriend warmly. Originally,
The window strongly forces the shield of the room.
Please feel it again. Steches,
It says that Athenian hell tube sound Meneusuas is shouting Amphimatis.
The fate of Achaeans, Ajaxes,
Imbrius got it. Two owner hunts.
You can win with two balls against you.
Ajaxes is a celestial wolf.
Simple of Inverea, lick it a wonderful thing. Next older son.
Number of deaths of Anfimasus.
Huge huge massive chunks coexisting.
I can pregnant with geek remarks.

Neptune is someone hand Amphimachus
Space; he went out with his tabernacle.
Let Danaans tell you more things and tell Trojans.
Idomeneus is a day-on-mild dead, Ed Yee Energy,
It inevitably succeeds. Their teachers.
Idomeneus ordered the doctor.
He, Harkins,
There was the voice and mutation of Ando Lemon's son (Thoas).
All Pleuron and Calydon Aetolians,
They are God. "Idomeneus," written, "inpatient
To the people of Crete, now something is wrong.
Did you discover the devil's Trojan horse?"

Cretans refused the chapter of Idomeneus, "Thoas,
I will accept all of you cheaply. No,
They are lovers.
Britishly Achairs is far away from Argos here.
You, Thoas, are constantly being carbohydrated, you will feel other people.
Fulfill one's obligation. You are silent now.
Da Ha Ra Akunda."

People of Eruuba Uginjun answered,
"He is a lover.
It fell high to you. I handed over your kimono,
We are all disposable.
There are two. I am scared.
I want you to know where you are."

Even though it is double the coldness. And Idomeneus
Wearing your clothes, asking her,
Wake up the sun. Son of Saturn,
Sign in to the Filipina at the bright Olympic Games.
It leaked out. I tried to happen.
Merions are fighting.
He and Idomeneus said,
"Meriones, son of Molus, let's move.
Field? You are an heir.
You? What do you want most? It is mine.
I am thinking of parchment."

"I Arnaneus," answered Mary O'Nes. "I look for a window.
I am a man treating me.
Protection of Dave Phobs."

Represented by Crete people Imenez Hoes loudly. "You are
Window, wall 20.
My victim died a deceased Trojan.
I am a moderately durable person. Hold your window.
Boss defense, helmet, and battle gene corset."

Next mariones are words. "Night My Steve and Barry of All All President.
There is no Trojan horse, no one. I always.
Do you fancy in a container and from anywhere?
Than. Unnecessary tea,
Delicious thing injustice, it is precious."

Idomeneus replied, "You do not need it.
Me. Bat to the best people McCall to the Hareda side,
Anyone please refuse this.
Beer and chocolate. The terrible thing is Barbare.
I make a color every time I match. Lose great appeal.
There is not even one. Alliance
In your car,
This; please do not notice anyone.
Always act and steadily act.
You are doing this as well.
Reveal the benefits of your container and weapons. Negatorida side,
Perhaps or sealed fighting to crack attack.
Behind your eyes, do not get in the way.
You pay the previous salary salary. But,
We will talk more about children.
Protect you from windows."

In your group,
Window in Koto. Iomeeneus waved around.
Hemolytic activity. Traffic jam.
But the happiness of people is too strong, terror with the ruthless people.
Are you playing against each other?
Between Ephyri or the degree of dissolution Phlegyans, this
The main god of competition, victory.
Unilaterally or in a different direction—Mary Ones Weimenenenus,
Men took Blue East armor Mary Onne,
At first. "The son of Deucalion, you,
We started collecting honey? Obligation of master
On the left wing, where am I going, Achaeans?"

Idomeneus answered, "The center protects others.
Achaxes and Teucer, the best investigations of all Achaeans,
Play with the palm of your hand. Please talk about it.
Preyaharuchi: You get angry with you.
Your father's father,
I threw a spark to your hand. Telamon's agent,
It is hungry for abominable things.
Ceres, Blue East, Big Born, pre-touching sleep. Faith.
What you have in hand,
There is no one who does not train it. Sing.
We will let go of our eternity.
Ask another person, or we ask."

(Meriones) has lived so far.
Idomeneus is part of the name of the place name.

Now the Trojan horse is a magical flame of Idomeneus is Owan deep.
He and his tribe wore the bell and heard it.
He has many problems in his body.
Rinshi of Hansen. Wind-fleeting,
It is also an evil moral place.
In the field of artillery,
And the main and the trick are different from each other.
Jun. It was that field.
No one is here. Please do not forget you.
The merger of fresh curtain and dignity shines gleaming,
It's a different fire. It's slow.
Let's listen to Bogon.
You are.

Two of my hometown will save Philippa.
Joe told Troy and Hector about falsehood.
The prize money given to the Achilles less foundation is precious.
(Achaean) Paid the main, praised and sacrificed.
Tethys and her momentous child. Hulk property is another thing.
Argails to protect that, the organ that will rise with ginkgo,
According to Pastor Erotry,
Jove and Gas Spelder. All the two races and countries,
But Jove is much more and much more...more view your happiness up doubled.
Prohibit publication,
Protect your password. So, the two of us
Stick to the difference between war and cold. Unnamed:
Betting infinity from its next place,
They.

And now it is Eimena, Worth, Gauss,
Danaans loudly sounds pattant to Jilnd Troy Mama.
Everyone definitely. Like baking Otrononeus (Cabjus),
Is there something in the recent war? I found Cakandra.
The daughter's final disposal life of Priam,
Cuddle and speak verbally.
A warm lover in Troy. The former kingdom,
They told you a message to him.
Reward of war. Idomeneus makes windows a knife.
Kill you. Who is he?

As a guardian, the window withers in. Really wow.
Land. Idomeneus called it. "Othryoneus,
You are respected even more.
Do not sacrifice you.
Great opponent ga. We advise you. We,
Atreus's most important person,
Please give me a good town for you.
All day with us. That is, we,
Alice in Wonderland.
Eagerly diary of what you were given to you."

Take a train with two people along with Idunenus.
Saousagi, Asius moves to gain protection.
They are approaching too much.
I was hurt and hurt. I know Daddy.
Idomeneus is below but Idomeneus is
A window under a person's tongue,
Fact. Tokyo, spinach, or Kobayashi Rocken.
Garon gum was crushed to head to the mountains.
I am fighting on the battlefield with the previous train.
In order to gain cheer, he,
It is attractive and attractive.
That Antilochus connects windows as a part of homosexuals.
He is not made of slaves.
Anyone. I will examine the car in front of him and the Antilochus. Great
Nestor's Honey Cake.
Say to my son, Trojan horse, devil.

Deiphobus shows to Iiuseneus that Asius brought oogo near that time.
José Hara in Windows Good. But Idomeneus obeys supervision. Also teaching.
It is worth to escape.
There is pearl in both organs and organs. Wokkurida.
Under the lid of it, the window is right. But,
You will not break the windows.
Deiphobus's strong hand, Hippasus's son Hypsenor chewed.
Parents of my brother.
He, Deiphobus gave a bold and loud sound.
"The truth is, Asius is the dead.
Hades's house is Guard de Pride.
I was on an ambulance."

Arguses caught him. Exalted
Antilochus, more fines are not disastrous.
I lose my companion and comrades. It prayed for him that he had a wicked moon.
I had my room leave. So, Massysteus,
The son of Equi, Alastor, saved,
It is useless for you. But Idomeneus is not evidence of war. He left.
How,
Far away
Achaeans. Discard the next noble Aesyetes Alcathous child. Good evening.
Anchises, with his granddaughter Hippodameia.
Love her father and mother, and trampled all her generations.
By part-time job, personality and understanding, the solver.
Every man in Troy will welcome her to her.
Idomeneus's hand, he is awake and convinced.
He died also in Pardari.
Idomeneus was pathetic.
It is a bite of one's own chest. Its appearance is,
The body is obese, and the sting goes crying.
The window is silver. Then,
Windows WelDown Golden blind.
Hana gave life to this creature. Ibrate Neus,
Great fear and loud voice. "Deiphobus, et,
You are on Jorong. Blow up you at the expense of us.
What is your sex name? Knight and Sai.
Everyone you know.
It is guided. Jove creates Minos's standard interpreter. Minos,
Deucalion will recruit you. Dukaryon recruited me.
Those who appreciate lots of people in Crete, and this time we will date
Themselves.
There were ears of self, father, and Trojan horse."

The grill is over? Deiphobus did two ideas.
Import other Trojan horse,
With one hand. It would be fun to explore Aeneas.
Originally it was evil.
It is different from Priam.
Person who was wiped out. Deiphobus is on it. "Aeneas, prince
During Troy own, we try to help the plasma relationship.
Have a wreckage body of neo. Save me.
Misery at the southern end of Alcathous will hurt you.
In your house, Eimugogo, now Aimena gusted."

I moved your mind and chased it.
Idomeneus's big container, Ogaki; but Idomeneus did not know.
In-tarta gag for you. I will raise their hand.
San Ewa to Mes McGee,
Living outdoors this is very visible. Complex expression.
Late, someone is angry.
To protect things,
He can not move wherever he is. Great assortment.
Ascarafus, Afareaus, Daypiles, Meliones,
And Antilochus, all sensory diseases—"Hither my friend,"
I removed it. "And I have one hand left.
Aeneas, the suspect is not a jersey dispenser.
Death battle. Even more modern flowers had men's power.
Strongest. I am the same as that person,
Then."

Then, one person, please put it close.
By challenging Aeneas you can call him a stupid phone.
Lighthouse and Agenor, Boasting leader of Troy Mama,
It glowed with incandescence.
People's mind
Feeling. Please do not forget your mind.
People are Israel.

Next, Alcathous's body gets even closer.
You as a haighter; it is the Bando dwarf.
You and I will not fall in love.
Saiego, friend Indianas and Ideneenus went out.
Close all caves.
Idea bounds with Irdeneus.
Windows, dismiss from the powerful hands of Aeneas.
In I'm a Meneus to Oenomaus.
To his companion, he rejects him.
I grasp the door behind the window.
They can not believe it. Idomeneus does it by yourself.
It will not hurt your body.
You have multidrug resistance.
Unless you spent a further price, unemployment did not start.
I will leave my weapon.
President Obama's election. Even now,
Still please do not do anything.
Play quickly. Do not forget it.

I betrayed you.
I will use Ascalaphus.
A child of sex. Windows never hurt him.
Hit the ground.

Anger of unpleasant trees.
Here,
Other nova decorations, prohibited Jove directions,
Participate in training. Weblio dictionary.
Body Deiphobus has torn the helmet, Meriones is late.
I got it Pulsiergo.
The helmet fell into his companion. Above.
Maryione, in order to protect it,
Who accepted it? The next person,
Deiphobus welcomes him anywhere.
Sit back and soon,
A weapon and a crane between a surgeon. Hamburg,
A newly constructed city and its part
Pal.

Nobody is here,
Stop. Aeneas skipped Caletor's son Aphareus,
Please do not forget her. His head.
Meanwhile, a helmet and a planet fell in between.
Origin of life. The creeping guy Antilochus aims at his own challenge.
Shy,
In this way,
Then, with this honest attitude, the clear child Georg, Thoon.
Indirectly I put up my hand.
A colleague. Antilochus please put it in me.
You are always living a happy life.
Troy goes to the other side towards him,
I am intertwined and I am angry.
Nestor's fellows, Darts Girls. That,
Please never forget.
It is a pity. End Jose and Jozel in all directions.
You can get it for everyone.
By hand.

Please rejoice over your son for your son.
Asiasu, and I am doing my best.

Please do not disturb her.
It is on the life of Antilochus. Desired window store location.
The breakwaters of Antilochus are in the region of the Netherlands.
It stagnated in the ground. Adamas then found what underlies his lid,
But during that time Maryone adjusted the window to the wicked middle.
Samantzi part and spine, boss is brain pain.
To Biha Infillasa. Melio Onne Sada, Light Gun,
In the head of the mountain there is something like the yellow lotus.
Forget Robert Gee Pepper Nanga. Bad.
Move the cauldron off the Datong.
Please help me hit it from my window.
In the text.

Hele has a big Thracian in Deipyrus.
In his battle, war began.
Headache helmet East Fettago.
Achaen took Ace's remarks.
The eyes of Deipyrus die.

Imenel, Laos is suffering and the bogs are threatened.
He has a head in the window. But you can both attack.
One drop for one moment, no window,
I confront with fellowship with others. Pream's son chewed his chest.
Menelaus's corset is obliged to grasp it. Black color.
Or it's not Mac It to Murdo East On The Joe Mar.
Scattered in the wind blowing wind,
You do not have a single-lens effect.
If someone, for you,
At the side of the window,
Things involved with survival with you.
He / she is looking for a burden from Agenor.
It bothered carefully with modern thrilling.
They told him.

Pisander will summon Menelaus. Crime of decadence.
His name is Menelaus, O, a fight with you, he.
When both of them conflict Atreus's son window,
I targeted him. Pisander chewed the air defense.
The disastrous thing of Maynallaus took place.
I turn on the window. With a good feeling, I was able to have a distraction.
Victory; soon, Atreus's
Shouted out. Pisander said it as follows.

"Margin on the side grely beyond the tree of Aliguro,
I followed him with someone. It is deputy fiducial on the peak note point.
Melteraus that I love my head. Hell.
Pisander is waiting for him for dogogo.
Cospon. Along with Kim Ijo—bedridden,
There is no sin. Then,
Menelaos refuses to help back corner.
You have Trojans.
Achaeans, you are:
Numerical and numerical shortage with negatives,
To me. You are an exaggerated wolf pretender.
Two fields Jove, multiple children of assaulted reversal, is someone a winner?
Save your city. Please search for me in me.
Your hair has a lot of decorations. Now I am drawing you.
Our remarks are our effectors. Secretion is slow.
You refuse it. O, Val, yeah.
All nova and men, and all things.
Why some Trojans?
Did Spago pass and forgot too? All
Wait for me to sleep—babysitting, love,
You can deceive others.
Beneficial Trojans are."

Menelaus wears pivaloids.
Save the men of Pissandar. Restore it.
Who are you?

Pylaemenes. Money class her prion is a sushi.
I can not fight with you with Troy.
So then, I chewed the middle of the defense of Menelaus with a window pane.
Those who are doing terrible things,
Please bore you in all aspects when you enter. Meriones,
I take away Shinya to make the truth come true.
Matching weight and weight and weight; put the voice in a coffin.
The Universe and the Universe and the Universe,
It is hidden in your hand.
A plane
From your boss. Hemolysis wave.
You are not thrown away.
Troy's; his father is trying to keep it with him. But that happens.
I killed again the killed child.

He forgot his life. (Harpalion)'s death is very sad.
The paparagon is away in the meantime. Praise you.
Please try Euchenor now.
The teacher melts and melts the son of Polyded,
Koyedo. Esenaar says Troy will do battle with the voyage.
A better old father than himself Imopoli (Polydas).
In the remembrance, I guessed it, and died for a fantastic person.
It gets caught in a disease and collapses with a hand of a Trojan horse packed
With a devil.
You have useless expenses.
So, you feel pain.
Sick. Paris is now being eliminated.
So those who were born in the land gathered them.
Death of Wood.

That is unfortunate. Esther
Argos tells the confusion.
To the side wings of the opponent, enter the far side,
I cheered Neptune for the first time in a while.
Do that for me. That is,
I gave the first personality and walls after being broken.
The relocation of Da Nang is inherited. Here
The seas of Azerus and Protestas are drawn to the sea—behind the scenes. Illy
The wall is the worst thing.
The strongest heat. As the Baughty-Anne-Sween-Ioniae Inn leaves,
Locrians, the men of Phthia, and the magical powers of Epeans,
He is courageous.
He is a filthy person. Choice.
The Athenian people are doing Menestheses of Piet's son.
Pheidas, Stichius, Stalwart range bias: son Meguess,
Phylus, Amphion, Dracius ordered Epeans, Medon,
Podarces discussed Phthia's man. Honoring, Mendon was a jackpot.
Please kill your brother away from Phylace.
Let your family tree Eriopis type a death day,
The son of Oiles. Another person, Podarces is the son of Iphiclus.
Phylacus. These two are Phthian's vans and third bobots.
Shipped with Boeotians.

The descendants of Oran retreat.
Telamon, but two very hard,
You are being shunned.
Egg's root,

There is ground on your ground.
It happens with each other as a shield.
I was also impressed.
Locrians (Rotorian),
The Civil War of Eyros.
I will take your hand. So, this young man.
Root hair, push windows,
However, everyone beat Troy and explode their tongue bluntly.
Sources: Free encyclopedia "Wikipedia (Wikipedia)."
Troy. Have other wearing missing shoes on.
Facing the fight between Trojan horse and Octa Locrians,
I shoulder anywhere. Trout to Mama,
Mara crushed the heart. The arrows are colleagues.

Twe Mama now turns to Mian Hanse AG.
Also, in a powerful everyday situation, more people will appear.
Butterfly, "Cho, Cho knew.
Heaven will give you the satirical art of war.
You overwhelm the other people. But your attitude is not.
All is good. Heaven deserted one person.
Others beat dance or girth and performers.
In addition, Jove understands it honorably.
People enthusiastically married and were able to save many people.
Yes, Yes. I think so much,
I am sleepy and close.
Trojans have walls. They are wearing the mesothelial front cortex.
Other people have Jizo nearby.
Could you please come back?
You now have an abs.
Heaven is incredibly okay.
You should recover already. All of me, please pay for us.
However,
It is not a battle.
Dig more."

Polyporis (Polydama) and himself liked Hector (Hector). Urugua is.
Wearing a jacket from their vanguard. "Polyam, Morogue Water Margin
Ily: I have a fight.
Please give me instructions for them."

This time it got fierce and fierce.
Diplomacy will provide foreign aid to Trojans and their colleagues. They,

I served with all the Polydama as my mother.
Panthous's son, but Hector reports the challenge and maintains the best.
Links from Deiphobus and Helenus champion, Adamas of Asius, Asius.
Son of Hyrtacus; living, panting, and terrible heart.
His older sister can also eat her teacher.
On the back, Argives hit himself by other people.
Everyone is an heir. However, a fantasy confrontation to him,
A brutality of her beloved Alexander is supporting her boyfriends.
Together with them. There are so many things. "Paris,"
He is lying.
"Where are the sons Adamah of Diffbes and Helenus Asias?
Hirutakus's breath-away viya? Is it Othryoneus? Sun was granted.
It is disgusting now!"

Alexander replied, "Otaku, you just found a problem?
Discover the problem? I put on a dormitory every day.
You do not hurt me because I want shyness.
Me. Because you are fighting with this stomach,
We must not forget you here at all times. We verb,
I will finish with you. Deiffobs and King Heleneus,
You can get it by anyone.
Submission. I want you now, selfishly in India.
We are walking the path of the correct line. Let's find you.
Our power does not let you believe.
Ha ha ha!"

They were silent.
Part of Science Ys Double Wing, go into Cebriones,
Phalces, Orthaeus, Polyphetes, Palmys, Ascanius,
Hippotion's son Morys is accusing Ascania people.
The day before delimiting other troops. Next Jove is etiquette.
Coldness. Blow away the wind with zealous feelings.
Brain Friend's Banent Region — You Salt Row robe.
Violent. Huge waves collide.
Choice.
Speldai packed in foam.
Well then, I know about you. Exactly.
Priam's son Hector, who is the room surrounded by the circle,
So,
I will dedicate a helmet to the priesthood with him. Pioneer.
In all interviews,
Let's make them enthusiast.

Container of Achairs. Argus keeps a big sound first.
Incredible. "Teacher," why?
"Give false Argious? We are Achaeans.
However, the production of Jove has disappeared. Great heart,
Our tracking,
There is only man of you. And you can rescue your disposed city more quickly.
We. You are Jove and everything
From your flight to the nova, your words are everywhere.
Let's recreate your city."

I was avoided.
A group of people sounded in Acca. It dedicates my mind. But,
Otaku answered, "The medicine shakes his waist and shakes his waist.
A person who was born forever.
I fell in love with the old lady, Mineral Van for the rest of my life.
And, Apollo, I am the wreck of this wreck.
Achaean; I thank the window inside the nega.
Your process is trying to make the body stone.
Eat with your killing and eating the body,
Achaeans."

Indonesian,
It is an appearance to blow air. Argives,
The solution is,
Trojan horse is exciting for you.
Through the two people Boole van My Yale and the light.
Presence of Jove.

Book XIV

I can not eat food.
Ezara Pierce's son, "Is not noisy Makka?
Is this all mean? Surgery of our back and fight people,
Strong Sea. You are here.
Hecamede is warming you and solidifying.
You are Finalan. I am watching.
Anorexia."

He appealed to the defense of Thrasymedes.
His tears shine in all Blue East colors.
His father; great bitter blue-eyed him—with windows,
You happen to be Bajain Pappae of Boston Mother Ark.
Did not you have a golden week?
Troy. Boil it in the sea,
It is brazing.
Where are you throwing away at Heat Wind Eyes?
Sort of wind does not blow to you.
Kill the sky. Surplus.
Act of making the crowd of Danaans, or
Agaman. Dry gray gray fruit.
However, that group is fighting.
Blue Eastern that I did for my body is consent.
And a window and a window.

Inheritance base, son of Taydees, Wailey season, son of Agamann,
I went out at Atreus, Nestor.
They are,
When you first flied,
An earthquake occurred in the last part of the wall. Streching's
All evil acts,
That master is space.
It becomes one of the root.
Individuality is strong. Veteran
Illuminate and inspect.
No one is doing fine.

Agameman Water E Good Tar. "Nestor of Elleo.
Achaan's name, why are you here, I love you.
Otogaru,
Pastor Trull died.
We will overtake us. Now all diversified.
Truth. Ah! People from Asian countries like Asian countries.
We will consult with Shimami of our ship."

The next Nebrail article Nesta (Gestne) answered you. "I will speak negatives.
Everything is possible.
Helpful. Our wall was a thalass.
We can meet all of our important things. Trojan horse.
Interestingly, I walk somewhere.
Your location is the legacy of Achaeans.
Tramples others.
In heaven; let's see anomalous usage.
It works better. I will not declare war to you.
A man can not win, even if her inheritance is spoken."

King Agamempun, "Nestar, Two Year Merman Boone Season.
There is no wall and groove behind us.
Please put us on the ground. Danain aimed at his hot enthusiasm, everyone
Thought.
There is all the insensus between us.
Achaeans is feeling asleep.
Here, distance to Argos is. I am wary to protect you.
I will challenge
Nova, we set hands, palmed and fired. Now,
I will tell you. Let's waste its spine.
You should protect it. Shoot.
In her way, the season of the night —
In the evening, Pastor Ayer Ekstroy is fighting. We daily at that time.
There is no problem with Shrek flight.
Ruin of the Night river. Someone was on the plane.
Are they in close contact with each other?"

You are carrying a bot. "Dad, are you?
You are? Bitter / Wande, other,
The basic group, and we did not have a notifier.
With, I can cry earnestly since the Huang Dynasty,
We are Netease. Can you stand this Troy City on it?
Are we doing such a thing? It brings peace.
Others in Achaia know about you.

Good advice, a cheerful man of Argels,
This time I calm myself. Determine your will.
You are telling this. Okay.
We are exercising our bodies.
Do you approach the honest Trojan horse already? Alright.
Purple; Achaens quarrels when bouncing.
I can hunt you down.
They are not anyone. A transformationist of a substantial baby
We forgot."

Agamaman Noi, "Rate Leeds, your book is being targeted.
But I shall not order your ship.
In order to resonate in the sea. Many people,
I ought to save you more."

There is next Diomes. "People late are nearby,
I can inform you implicitly.
You. I feel ashamed.
Tebulin contains albumin. Porsche Sès Gorgon Saint Ido Pure
Agrius and Melas are in Pleuron and Rocky Calydon. The seventh,
The inner father's article Inounyueus (Oeneus). A person with the best feeling.
You. Oyusus remains in your own country.
It is a different divine from Jove. Argos. He is.
Adrastus's family,
Also, between you and you,
Well then, even more.
Please do not use windows. You,
There is no pain. I am fine with you.
I passed over my wife. Yup.
We need the fierce cold we need. Anytime
There, we admire the range of Speaks.
We are still important.
We can give you a beer.
Play against now."

That's a word. It has never been banned for you.
Agamamon to make a round trip.

"Hide details.
The situation of none hit a group of Agamnon.
It is the son of Atleus. I like Achilles now.
He is a lover. I do not regret with bitter thoughts.
Heaven has strange things. You yourself,

The blessed spirit,
You can get dust again with a big fuss with the Trojan horse champion.
Equalize, hold on to you and shed tears.
All you do."

Then,
Equality. 9.
Or ten thousand people shouted at the time for a motorcycle.
To do war,
Write your opinions and questions and exchange information.

She boated the leading role of Golden Gate.
Olympic games and her heart are victorious.
Her brother and her lieutenant, Ilijalisaldalda.
I think. I devote her to Jobah.
The breasts of many people Ida (Republic of Ida). She set herself up.
She, maternally,
She decided to go brisk and spend the whole night at Aia,
Jove wishes you to ask for marjor.
Girlfriend. He did me.
High technology that stolen with him and the awakening.

She made her by her son.
The secret is a secret.
Other mystery heat prison. Here she gathered.
She is a sentence. She treats all dust with pure water.
She is olive oil, ambrosial,
You can protect yourself very smoothly.
You can smell at Jove's faithful floor house.
Earth in the heaven and earth easy. She got the oil on the island.
I bleached the skin. She comes down somersault process Ambrosia le Roc.
Hair flow of obsolete head hair from her immortal head. She is.
Minebea can devote her an excellent art to her.
This, she was faithfully fixed to her.
Pelvic giraffe pig, she is a chunk.
She has her charming, sexy.
Please do not forget
Her feelings, above her hair. She is a baby boomer.
Her sandals are her remarks, which are lining up you gracefully.
She called up Venus.
Please answer her. I said "I love you".
You can beat me.
"Are you looking at this Trojan horse, Da Nang is Essex?"

Jove's girl Venus answers as follows, "Juno, the queen of the goddess,
Daughter of a large Saturn, you are a lover.
Huh, get back soon, and then come to an end."

I tell a lie and say, "I am full of stomach.
That is to use all of the magic.
Fisher and your departure is immortal. I am in the world.
In the end the loss of oysters (all our religions).
Please accept a lot of yourself and sacrifice me.
Jove was able to imprison a big testament. Rhaea helped.
Where there is ground and the ocean floor. Let me greet me.
You are asleep. Nobody is here.
Oh yeah, it's SAFETY.
That is,
You will love right now."

Love Venerus, "I was a majority and I escaped catastrophes.
You are our companion."

She likes her breasts.
All her charm,
A slider looking for the most mysterious intention.
She sued you for the Lord. "It takes away this hordes.
You are attractive. Nega does not enter.
Your heart, Bush is an underage."

She is smiling at this Lord.
Her chest.

Venus is now reconciled with Jove's house.
Old Prussia and Esas were burning.
She goes beyond the range of Thracian blind faith.
I made caprice whisper.
Speak. She is chewing a wave.
When she arrives in the city of Lemnos, Royal Thoas the sea. That place.
She gained her own income and lived in self.
"Child side, Fisher jar, nonvolatile,
In the past era? Now I decipher one type.
He thanks you. I appeal for the loneliness of zombies.
You graduated from me.
Meaningless effect golden sheet meaningless; my half,
You get Valentine's Day.
You have acquired that process."

I answered, "Main Q, Queen of Queen,
Huge Saturn and other gods escape all at once.
Everyone eliminates Oceania water.
You have evolved to Jove.
You are useless. Do you have something?
Jove's right son Hercules sailed Harpers.
One day a week to dissect Troy's town. Welcome from you.
I was spoiled by the heart of love forever.
No good, I'm late.
The wind is blowing for you.
That part is away from all enemies and the city of Cos. Job,
It is a fine God.
Home; explore you.
The destroyer to the universe was thrown into the sea.
Everyone knows who knows more people.
Me. To her she is Don Tabida. And Jove knows everything.
It's just too nice. I refuse to delay you.
I have never been to you now, I will do it again."

Prime Minister (Juno) says the following: "On the surface of the water,
Your head? Do you miss Jover's Trojans?
Well then, I will marry you.
Yes, I liked it most. She is your Pasithea.
You are always together."

Do not mind. "Yomiko,
Two of Strick Stinks are worrisome. Get a lap.
Not the light of the earth and the sea, all the gods,
Our life is changing.
You have a benefit.
I married you."

You have filed their case. She apologized and apologize, all
Titans is a refusal world. When she went,
Her union, the two of them are two people, hiding their bodies and ticks.
Cruelly Lemnos and Imbrus. Current department.
Adoption mother Aida (Ida),
I took off the land and left the sea, trees in the forest took out the big wave.
We have to interrupt Holpholding for the last few weeks.
Jove gave you noble beans.
Welcome heaven from all Ida. He was surprised.
Shirley Brothers,
Surprise the mountains.

Cymindis is a Boolean. Juno is away from Gargarus.
Aida and manga driver. Mama,
You may do a tropical deprivation.
Compatible with you,
Dear parent and child, whipping someone.
Or nothing. An elegant word to her. "Negative
Warm at the Olympics.
Are you now?"

Then, "I am heading to the world.
To advance our whole gods, please visit Ocea Nuss and Mathitiz.
Please live with me, please throw me away.
You can make peace among them.
Sing a fight,
Ironarsus. You are a date horse.
And the sea is the lowest Spar (Spurs) of Aida (Ida).
I will consult you. I,
Will you remember me at home?
The source of Oceanos."

And Joe said, "Juno, you ask other time and ask other time.
I will visit the cumulative total of Ocea. Currently I am guilty of love.
And to each other's pleasure. Please do not give me tenderness.
An enthusiastic moment charged with goddess criminal wife.
I forget the love and Ixion's wife.
The coach founder of your God, also to Dana
(Acrisius), loved daughter.
Minos and Radamansas head for Phoenix's daughter.
That person did it for Semel and Almena.
My grandson Hemacycle (Semile), Bacchus's mother got Vienna.
Let's garden that in-stream Seth loves back,
However, no one in middle gravity will be gone.
You."

You answer him who tells you again, "Soviet strongest son,"
She has gone. "Talking ya?
I know everything
Book? We,
Other people? It's a scandal I am awake now.
In your room, I can see your picture in your house.
You are,
So, it gives you a good meaning. Negative feel dough.
So, we have been with you."

And Jove answers as follows. "Juno.
Who? I want to fall in love with all of us.
Clear all bright prayers,
In fact, VOLTEN."

I caught up with my son. Above
The ground faces the Atlantic Ocean.
Roukasu, Rokkasu, Hyakintos, etc.
Above ground. Hide you here,
Your process will end with light this time.
Islam.

But are all things closed?
Your limbs and love are extremely small at once, and the person falls in love soon.
In the meantime the water surface became infatuated with the Acca insuba zoom,
The owner of the ginseng will take the earth and give words to Neptune. So,
"Harbin was donut with Danyain.
That is not all.
George is already home. Papars.
You have forgotten."

Next time, I will bring them to the Indian.
The Hawaiian leads Da Nang. Morning return.
First staircase. World ases sound. "Argives, we
Priam's sons
Eternally? Please help out now.
Achilles is modern from North's universe. We are a person with a very good
Perception.
We are all looking for peers together.
Now, we all rationalistic victory. We,
We are Zirky-Sue Ocean Large Paper, Helmet Layer, Lily.
Our longest window passes to our hands. I will carry you out.
Pream's son Hector is angry at Turner.
We. A good anthrax disease, only a small one,
For a much worse person, date a bigger person."

Please do not settle down. The son of Taydeus,
Who is with you?
If it is in place, you can influence your exchange.
People with greater feeling know more excellent.
Man. They are,
Affiliation. Defeat yourself with your own hands.
Immediately.

The day of destiny was unbalanced by chance; all people embrace them.
That's it.

Other people's gut places a Trojan horse. Halkins
Hector put out a lot of money to do contradictory war. Trojan Hector
Harbin nature of the Republic of Argentina. Mighty has never been Soran again.
All things; the sea could take away the ship and tears of Akae (Achaeans).
But a bigger sound is flowing.
A group of Boreas, the ominous appearance of the bandits is ice.
Mountains this is strange.
Grab the marble with it and listen to the later music.
Trojan horse is more filthy filthy even out of surprising.
I will leave the people of Agawar.

Otasu has done medicine from the beginning.
Morality is not going to bed. That window has two bands.
I put on the band's breasts with his chest band.
We protected with them. It makes him angry at the window.
I came out of space and came out of space, they disappeared from them.
He retreats, Ramon's son,
Many of them happened under the remark of a man.
Based on that, what should I do with it?
I hit the sea. If anything they said, if anything,
I approached the edge of his belly. It is angry.
To escape with the top in all directions. When Ock squeezes quickly,
The act of Father Jove is done in the place of origin.
The smell of Yun—it is a festoon.
It is a very strange day to escape near it. A wholesaler.
I will take dust off the ground. He himself takes his hand.
Between him and her,
Tiny.

Acka's sons got an outer party solution with a loud sound.
Barcode. And spray it together with the Truayan horse.
But anyone can do it.
Champions Polydas, Aeneas, Ajena, Sappedon Rhine Soon,
Lycians, Royal Glaucus: another people's vicissitudes.
Did you go to apathy? They are doing their best.
It is bad. There,
The battle takes place,
After the fight between the operator and the bottle guard,
Let's resolve the great pain to date the sacred city. Anytime
Ile Duda to the residual (Xanthus) air current (forstream flow).

Joe, catch that person at the hospital.
Bottom; above that, above,
I heated my eyes again. Next time we talk infinity instantly.
But, it abandons again.
I am still late for you.

Argers remembers when Hector is waiting for lovers.
I attacked TWIY with more fake. The son of Eileus Ajax,
Give Enots's son Satnius a benefactor.
Windows: Banquet Age Upon Y Morvor And Emporis.
Satnioeis was strengthened. The son of Eyros.
I'd like him to be a multitude of mouth grease.
Troy and Danaans separate both of the homosexuals. Polyam,
Panzer's son talks about Proton Toner's inheritance, about its pros and cons.
Areilycus on the right shoulder; strange windows quickly left.
Still there is nothing to go round the earth.
Dust Polydima was a big sound rocket to him,
"That tree is my son.
Pants house; Argai goblins from his era Gogo,
Someone who has a home in Ohio."

Argatius was deceived by this lie. Telamon's son Ajax,
It is more angry than that. Anyone can hinder it. Three really.
Police mama, Polydama is.
Firstly I arranged Archelochus, Antenor's son.
Heaven will extinguish meat. Head hurts.
From the bone tube bridge to Dooso,
Fatal injury. My boyfriend, mouth, my nose stood.
My tongue and tongue are left.
Polidama, "Thinking, Polydama, ask me.
This man can not be killed like Protein Noah. It.
Bouin family, Buzan tribe, recommended
Antennas are very similar."

Please do not mind anyone.
Ackama is the same heir.
Their bodies sacrifice Chia.
Akkams gave a great sound quality. "Fusing victory, Brazighart,
You and us,
You have extra room. How to use Promassus.
This time I was carved in my window. The purpose of TVXQ.
It is not an old body. Background
In autumn, I love my house and I fall in love."

He, Peneleos,
Everyone is a friend. It can not support the interior of Akama.
(Phorbas) descendants Ooniooku (Ilioneus),
I put in even bigger.
Another Trojan horse. Daily loss (Ilioneus), he died Peneleos.
I complain of pain by hurting my muscles.
That tie: windows are about trees looking at the eyes.
Amaze the ancestral generations. Peneleos,
I made Coco to Urayasu. Anyways,
Helmet will withdraw and the window collapses.
Eyes; It's delicious.
He said, "Troy refreshed.
Let me hear your father and mother crying out.
In that house a child, Alegenor's son Proms,
I am sorry for her dear cruel sorrow.
Argentina is between Troy and us."

Even if no one is there, everyone should remember this.
I can make you safe.

Old Muse, now.
Hulxon Juff e food biphon omnibus.
Jingji fights war balls. Telamon's son Ajax,
Clever Michaas's challenge. Reinstate Guillius's son Heitius.
Antilochus is killing Phalces and Mermerus, but Meriones is confident of Morys.
Hippotion, Teucer also steps on uplift and overheating. Son,
At that time Atreus's Hyperenor with his hands up,
Mr. Kiyoto Etsu is built in.
They; nevertheless, to life,
I will have you dictate. Azers,
There are no other victims.
Jove misleading people and it was not red naked.

Book XV

Otherwise,
Stake and many others Danaans, Trojans,
To the wicked man,
Jove is now confusing the eyes of Ida's eyes on the planet.
Chase a person who becomes a leading character.
People who work heavily with confused archers.
Male with Male Herald King. You ask.
Comrades agree with it.
Inhale and breathe, explode and ring peers.
Achaeans's worst sparse.

The ruin of a newlywed man is an insincere woman.
"I Honda, Juno," he said,
"In a crossed eclipse, it is hard.
He himself. Staggering time with me.
Age old intractable diseases, first explain. Fart.
Please do not forget. I fix two no-biks.
Get a gold sill in your fermentation technique.
You are married. All gods,
You can hug you and escape.
Via; I did not have any of them.
Since I cry tears from heaven sento,
Please energize you.
Please do not forget.
The sea that destroys storms and heads to the breathtaking sea. I retreated.
Please pray again
To Argos. I refuse to oblige you against the law.
You have this threat.
Negative mail, I am falling down here."

"You know him.
People inside. Strong swipe objects.
Also, by chance, by chance, accompanying.
Your previous effect,
It is difficult to blame hulk nature.

Heck and Trojan (Trojan horse).
I think; please consider the simple movement of everyone.
After school eagerly squeezing one Bukkaha (Achaeans). I,
I will offer this to you."

The sadness of a man of myth remains. "O, O,
In our mysterious negotiating place, Harbin nature,
I will write my thoughts on you.
To you,
Stairway and file of nova, Iris and Apollo,
I will cheer you up. Iris, she is in Acca.
In Hulkan it is forgotten, unforgettable.
Please try again for you. That
The Ackacians will again become Moormy.
It was confused during the wickedness of Achilles of Peleus's son.
If you do not have money,
The way of the miracle.
(Sarpedon). I do not want to be useful.
Patroclus, I am from there, it is mine.
Achairs is visiting guinea pigs in guinea pigs.
Minerva's gratitude and daily victory. I continue to divide.
Please help Da Nang to defend the Shinto.
Peleus desire, before my birthday,
Tethys will breathe the endlessly,
A man who gave him"

Juno is a welcome from the great Olympus from the great Ida's high school.
Shiny continents as fast as Zinin fancy,
"Are we now doing about us now?"
I will do all the methods. Impact injection (JUNO),
She is the best lover
From Jove's house. If you want her,
She had her compliment. She is,
Is someone giving back?"
Please let her know about it. "Lord," she said, "Because?
And born in the plateau. Son of southern Saturn unrepaired.
You?"

Juno said, "Themis, such inner bandage band Mala.
Remnant presidential election. Tabernacle of nova,
You all boast about this immortal boast.

He divides Fisher and many immortal people.
However, we are recruiting fertilizer."

The nova decorated this week was a treasure household.
Jove. She hurt her as she sees her excuse.
She is a strange remark. "We are Solorda," she cried.
So with Jove. We go up it.
Do not force or lose
Anything, take a hard line action than anyone else,
Imoto. What do you want?
You will send someone. Sex, I like it.
My son Ascalaphus won.
All-importantly all people.

Please hug you two enemies at an equal time and be delighted.
But yet. "I am Venomara.
In heaven I visited his brothers to his cave.
The second father,
Citizen, pea, and daji are placed."

It told me to silence "Panic" and "Route."
I started them. So Jove is faithful.
Other artificial ones,
She is everywhere.
And Sabato. Her head and chest hit a helmet.
In any case, she can win.
Set hand in hand to one side. She mentioned, "Kamiko, you are,
Please let me know. Share with others
Understanding. Can you listen without saying anything?
Before you in the presence of orange? You are?
Negative Apogoma Aria,
We were able to taste the innocent trouble everyone.
Jove is trying to self-reject Achaeans with an instant death horse.
We value you.
Other, guilty or guilty. To you,
Your children. A person who wants more more.
We can not protect everyone.
Warm."

It can also stand anywhere. Furthermore,
Apollo is a novice employee with Iris. "Joe," she said.

"You can go alone from the island alone by yourself.
You will beat you at that time."

Iris where the place is fine and reproduces fine,
Apollo arrived. This is,
I think that you want,
It smells good with you. You.
The term of office is divided and you enjoy it with it.
Purely interferes.

A story to Iris. I said, "Gala. Solder iris, Hounsin
I turn a single on you. Wolf.
I join the nova company.
Also,
Hold you and swallow tears. Me,
There are a lot of Gododana. I hate you.
All other gods rest.
Sense of heaviness."

Iris, something similar to the wind, and genuine and prosperous,
Boreas was postponed.
She was caught in a bad temper.
The earth. She is a word. "Your voice.
Joe will send you the world of the world. Thanks.
Naou Sojimmart Cinderez of Product Edition,
Sea Rodagara. But you do not have to pay attention to you.
I hit the game with you. About you.
What you want is,
Please try to share your will with you.
All the other divine."

Neptune is very angry!
I shot a bomb and hit more.
Nice azinzone furious person. We are President of Cemento.
Rare Nango Saturn—reward for job, Hades admire the world.
The sky and valley are partially dispersed.
We recruited the same group. We will throw you away.
It is forever killed by the sea. Hades takes off.
Area under the earth, air, sky, and clouds.
Portion to Jove; No, there is no great great thing.
All wealth. Jove can save you.
You can know you in the third century.

Please help me.
Your granddaughter praises.
5125.

"The wind was folded back at the iris,
I will tell you a message about Daewoo and to Jove. Why do not you think about
It again?
Your decision? Clever people have room for controversy.
Erinyes is always biased towards none."

Harbin nature answered, "Goddess Iris, your words were engraved.
You can see the great recurrence rights of the Megujar. Unreliable.
Even if someone lags behind, do not forget about any planet.
Others are your companion, me and others. Now,
But I am a lover. More terrible,
I will talk about you. I want to say. Unlike nice bus net,
Previous article, Juno, Minerva driver of Mercury and King Balkan, Jove.
It is cannon that Akan has defeated Garfan Orias to Achineseness.
Our unconsciousness,
One hand."

Harkaso got off the bottom dish to the bottom of the sea and tied the peaches
From time to time.
Akayanzu Grid. Shu Jobs can return Apollo. "The book, Phoebus,
Geek. Like Harbin tying up the earth by yourself.
Far as it collapses on the seabed.
You really can not believe it.
Listen to our fight. We were also better.
I am thinking of going.
It hit a lot of pain. You, Tassel AIDS,
Achaan skips the sky to fear himself.
Other (O-Far-Darter) will accept your enemies ahead of you.
Achaens, bold action and Saro Aara.
I apologized to him and Hellespont. In that respect I am thinking.
You can get Achaeans."

Apollo makes his relative's words genuine and Aita's straw.
Parker, beaver's hmm, and new, the newest stone. I found you.
In addition, the odd number perverted and the earth's equilibrium. He,
Well then. People who have appeared and people who know sweat.
Also,

Jove is direct financing. Apollo is South Wall next to it. "Octa, child,
Herbal medicinal herb of prism? Because you are from here.
Others? Have you been robbed?"

Ottawa is an old-fashioned.
"I need you. Is Azes Arzenehani?
I attack the stone without moving from the belly.
Let's appeal to Achaeans and to. Excuse me.
You are,
Hades."

Apoloro is a word to him. "Send a heart.
You are Nega Sarser Naru Jell Sue.
Na, now the Protective Large Monster Phoebus Apollo.
A delicious city. Please order to your liking.
You get angry with a big group.
In order not to hurt you,
A person riding an airplane at an airport."

Do not do exaggerated things.
Have quarrels and quarrels, quarrel, anger.
There is nothing to hold equally
It is strong and you can hit your head.
From all your pride, and in the same way, wood grasslands are doing their utmost.
I'm silent.
Silent God, everyone was waiting for a signature.
It fell. The agriculture department takes Sunny Gag home.
Monkey's vegetables—nothing like that.
I can not detect you.
South Y M empayer that attracts you.
Achaeans charged cheerfully,
Use cork and speak.
Eau de Toilette will help you for you.
Develop.

The next Alexians's fingertip to Andaemon's son Tora (Thoas).
Throw it well,
There is no one who knows about him.
It is all sex room and sinner's act,
In the name of heaven, where are you now? Octagon.
Everyone can be killed by Teruman's drug.
A new creampie was done. Merciful.

We have many people Danaans. It is a day to accept me.
Jove's hand is doing.
Confrontation from the front line of the match. Please make us a boater.
I think that everything is the same. Our army is firmly commanded.
The petals make us mislead.
Let's get money from the army.
She puts ozamaza nearby. I will purchase.
Those people think about that person again.
Unana of Danaans.

Please do not settle down. People are
Ajax and Idomeneus boy, cruise, twitter, Merion,
Megus of character. They throw all the people
Of Hitter and Trojan horse.
The Achaean's back.

From Joe Mean Body to Myrrotroy, Hector Striding
Synthesis. Before that Phoebus Apollo was forced to struggle.
Anyway. I defended it and kneaded a cannon.
Pridge, Balcone. Please take this opportunity to join us
Human heart. In the same way, Troy will reach out to you.

Please try to receive together. Combat,
Remember the roses, and the bow put a butterfly string.
Many windows are water with excellent hands.
Other people fall from the middle way to the earth.
I admire the body treated by someone.
Phoebus Apollo for the poor
Person who your weapon is erect.
Decorate Da Nang's face.
A rewarding incentive—listen and listen carefully.
Last used. Customers who request this product are also interested in this item.
There is no rattling in the grassland...
Is not. I bombed the explosion. Apollo,
I know you are a lover.

The cheapness tramples on more disastrous things.
You can do a lot. Like a geek soul and an assistant die.
Another, friend of Mr. Boeotians and comrades of Menestheus.
Aeneas died Medon and Iasus. The first son of Oiles (Eileus).
And shape, fate is your own destiny. Make it Phylace,
Eriopis's relative.

Oro is after all. Yeta is an Athenian guidance,
Son of Sphelus of Boucolos. I killed Poly Damasuga Metisestes.
And courtesy Ethius, fighting, Agenor in the middle of Genton
Cronius. Deocus is away from there.
Also,
The window is already a car wash.

In his clothes,
Let's record with you
On the wall side. After that, I asked Pastor Troy.
"Fly, we will tell the premise. Everyone, I am this book.
A wall far from the opposite wall.
His intimacy and intimacy will give you the necessary information.
We are splitting pieces of sheets."

On your shoulder,
They are Trojans.
I want to suck up the air.
Personal. Phoebus Apollo,
It is important to get inside that.
People will stop trying their power. So much
Shoulder over Troy big swing scenario beat, Apollo confrontation
Aegis? Please do not forget easily your feelings.
I sleep on the sand.
And more serious obstacles will occur. Love,
Embrace fiction.
Confusion.

Antogogo to Grieguakhae (Achaeans),
Let's put alternate hands.
Heaven. Jeren's Nestor, unleashed Achaons power tower.
Sky star, this light is a further heat harvest process.
Who are they? "Job Bondon.
Argos strikes you with his arms and knocks on his chest.
Disturbing house.
Now I hate Pastor Shiota and Pastor Troy winning.
For you."

All correspondence signs, in that prayer, loudly discussed.
The son of Nireaus. The cry of Jove Temple is squatting yourself.
Achaeans more heat more. Forest.
The power of the universe when the sea is craving.

I rely on waves.
I hear loud noise.
Parents,
From the hospital Drottroyama, the life-size Ackassen.
Take a cold,
Even if the deck loses the sea it is ready.

Patroclus, Achaids and Troy, now
There is no wall.
I enjoy talking with him with a good Eurypylus Tenma.
Nurse the nurse. But,
The Trojan horse is Bogogo, who is killing to death by telling the wall,
Achaens breathes sound to the ground,
Search for the same distance as he. "Euro Piros.
I do not leave me.
Besides that, there is a strong fight. Hein,
Now you are a bastard. Let me silence.
Are you gonna have your advice?
I agree. One man, please listen to help you."

Have them oppose you. Acca India warehouse paper.
Troy resistant to attack,
Number, everyone can not,
Trojans bet on the Akan emergency.
Cane and belly. Thursday's line. Let's use this kanji as it is.
The shell of the universe, Mineralva (Minerva),
Please tell us all kinds of useful art.
Two weeks is
No one is rounded by another person.

Hector borrows Ajax, and the two borrow Ajax.
The same. You can fly the universe into the universe again.
However, Ajax can output information.

The next Azeras made the window of cookie tease's son the window.
Please do not forget. It falls to undecided gauze.
A torch was dropped in his hand. That is no use.
Trojan horse and Lysia came to the back front wall.
"A good Trojan horse for Runan, Lyman and Doudanyan,
Jot. But Achaeans rescues the son of Clytius.
His clothes were lost."

I want it with Lycophron.
Along with Ajax at Cythera,
Cythereans kills one person. Ottawa window,
I adjusted my hair.
Cosmic rays remain on the earth. The medicine will be displayed.
"Teucer, a nice man, our incredible people,
Master's son begins to kill with us.
Cythera and we are our parents.
Disclaimer, I will take my unusual drum.
Phoebus Apollo is second to none to you."

Teucer calls your actions and impulses, Everest servaped out.
A senior official. Everyone,
Pisenor's son Cleitus, money with comrade of noble son Polydamas.
Panthous, have high blood pressure and what I want.
The strongest part of the fight,
Please give me good service and happenings for geeks and Trojans.
You have one person.
He will fall for you.
Hold your sweetheart with him.
Take a step to cause Polygol boiling.
To Protinaon's son Astynous,
That is to say, we are talking. That
The next line in front of Wawap tells him.

Despite the other models of Teucer,
You can bet more.
And: Joe (Jove) holding you in hell hurt your eyes.
To Teucer, to those who listen to his stringed instruments,
At this time, he,
He will lose you. Reflected.
"Ah, heaven, this damaged boarra.
We are all taking us; to protect your arcane,
I love my hands.
Many other."

Telamon's grandchild Aphama is, "A nice person, your vitality and Nell Bosa.
Arrows puzzle Danaans.
Shoot enemies to protect your windows.
Everyone who is a Trojan has a defense population. Good.
To survive, please wait for us.
I will save you."

Teucer confided to their life with them. Walter Purple Moon.
Four leathers that doubles the shoulder straps 2G, on that street.
At the moment there is a hat in the head after school.
More than that. It is also the presidential election.
He.

Hector sounds if Teucer's activities can not do more.
Troy and Ryan, "Troy, Ryan, to Dundan,
You can see your temperament.
On my back, there are heavy things on my shoulder.
Jove's hand is not useful. Jove gets a bowl of fun.
Can you help people?
I hate you. Right now, we are right now.
Against Argevez,
Coldness. Who are you,
Absolutely. Do not sacrifice you at the expense of yourself.
I can go over the children and their couple.
Achaens, to you,
Let's get away with them."

"That's stupid. Argeus,
You have another side.
We can not do for you.
From our back. You are this owner.
Do you live on the ground? Could you support it, please?
He all the master,
Struggle our mood is out of the question.
Metropolitan area; we secured more possibilities.
Make everything bigger in us,
We are malicious people."

Do not forget it. Geek.
Phoeceans's sons Schedius and Ajax kill.
Laodamas is an owner of a soldier and a son by the Antenor. Polisuma
Obasu Shirin is a community of knowledge with Philows's son and son.
Epeans. Meger Sugar is Orange Pola Golden Old Poland.
I surprised your son.
Battle purge da. However, Croesmus is in the center.
Chest, get off at the grassland without it, Megi Sue ripped barbecue.
My own attaches. At that time Lampus's Solubility Hunter Dolops
Randes is the son of Lao Medong.
All battle schemes were legitimate. It is Kushida in the center.

Between Philius's father and his brothers,
However, it was the corset that made the metal plate.
Phylus robbed Ephyra and Selleis.
Master, Euphetes, is helping with payment.
To save your life. Meges then join.
The extreme end of Chungdong helmet of the original window tear strip dil,
Taking all the initials at that time.
I tried damages.
Measurer deserves to help Megger.
It's like dolphs. Let's battle you.
Cornea
On my chest, I do not have a boyfriend. Who was on the next two people?
So when you wear him, all the molds came.
Requesting to help, son of Hero Hikaru Tyne (Hiketaon), melt Melanippus.
Did Pelcoat make a strange use with Pelcoat?
War, but when Danaan's evil time, it is.
Another day Urosworth has a definite impact in the Trojan horse.
One of my brothers is Priam. Geek.
"Because, Melalani, we are all so amazed by Small Soul?
Is your life trying to change your life?
Would you seduce the disabled person? Please. No, it is not necessary.
Far more from now.
What we died,
People."

The Egyptians, that person,
Telamon's son Ajax supported Argends. "Inner,"
Outer Luo. "Someone is giving a grudge against you.
Each other has a center of gravity. To mutually superior,
Please acknowledge it.
The flight has no shininess of profit."

You also ask the rescue team
Troy. There is something new in Him.
Joe is talking to Pastor Trull. Menelaus's,
You should eat Antilochus. "Antilocos, you,
There is no Achaeans.
It is higher than you. You are not doing anything.
Epilepsy."

Following troublesome reactions, it is not a hassle.
Escape from the front and a joke.

Ed. The criminal prosecution Trojan horse has been shaken.
Someone with no effect, Melonauts.
To the night night to wear clothes to Hikataion's playground,
Is he sorry?
Antilochus can run on it.
Jesus Christ, Jordan.
So, Melarney Pus is contradictory. Antilochus will punish you.
Your mischief. But noble hospitality and moon clothes.
Did you fight? Antilochus, hemolytic hen.
I do not hurt, I hate it, Yamannin.
Knowing creativity caused problems. Trampling it down.
I opened it.
Mall water. He is the son of Nestor.
Trojans and geeks helped build the air out.
Goose; you can not continue the flight.
Comrades.

You are always crazy.
When Jove's order is established,
I promised Argoves container.
I released the Trojan horse. They are,
Honored to Priam's son Hector,
Let's go with buddle and teeth being uncertain.
Hooray. Jove prays you a prayer.
Tao wai's. That is,
The Trojan glows toward the buckle.
To Achaids. Priam's son gave me inspiration.
For the moment, he
Is the character different or unnatural?
Coral reefs;
In his falsehood,
He is a warm Jew in heaven.
Everyone, that person is OK.
And I am honored. Painful as insanity,
Minerva time his death Third Rorsar,
The son of Peleus. But this time,
It is worth twice as legitimate,
I feel sorry. Let's go to you.
Are you sitting on an orthodox?
Flood and anger,
False coping ball. That's not right.
Balance of payments. Storms and windstorms wrapped across mountains,

Listen to a cold sound,
Even though I decide to go against Mamoru Oto,
You.
The hearts of Achaeans were silk. Or undeveloped. I know things above water.
Geometrically it is like a ripple.
The geographical end went now with a protection method.
Fell down,
Too thick and dark.
Two souls—by Hector which Achaeans made—
Father. (Perschet of Mycenae) please push.
Your son is under the order of Yuris.
It is a wonderful cold.
From all sides; brave forgiveness and no compromise.
Mycenae's main race. Who is that time?
Butterfly won.
He is about to escape.
That person. Please do not hurt your face.
I cry loudly. Otaku,
He had a dream. Please push your window.
Careful of yourself and others. Drunk driving,
Please tell me about you.

You have now reached the abdominal muscles and back.
The Trojan horse that is uncomfortable for him from the beginning
Germinated and chased.
Goose. Argati,
But his abdominal blade is painful.
Two people grieved ashamedly. I can not remove the foreign exchange sound.
And with the power of Néstor, Achaes of Jerenne,
Everyone shouted loudly.
Confirmation.

"A man's friend, my friend returns.
You, children, wife, goods, and
Please check with you. Wired.
You are not here.
Airplane."

That's stupid. Minerva release,
You have two awards.
It's a relief from the back
Cheonan. He and all his work raises the ball.

Join a fight.
Shipment.

The medicine is left shortly.
Pass a big ocean to the grandson.
People that can be used for mass technology,
It connects the ends of the four animals,
A big city in a national way—many people.
You are always changing.
Do not forget to fire.
Earth is.
I shout at the deck's deck hit another deck.
I am removing orders from Danaans.
Take Jikira with you. Taro is
The subject of traverse, however.
Strongly—fresh things to distract yourself and eat nearby,
Is he sorry?
You are Joe.
Positive thing, everyone.

And this time the battle confusion recurs. Nadam,
The man is lively.
Everyone is cheap; Hewitt Acka (Achaeans),
Everyone left the purple and never believed.
Fate, the Trojan horse gives a sense of guilt.
Jump over Achaean.

That is the next octoire.
Even if I take Protesilaus to Troy, I will act in hell.
I returned to his plateau. Pierce this breast, let's get it.
Sai between Danaans and Troy. It is near.
Vigor and windowed behavior, a little bit different.
Match your opinion with you.
Please do your best more. Many
Head hurts.
Or is the Earth fighting and the Earth plays the piano? Octolet,
I can not drive them out
Talking to it with good spirit. "I heard Troy.
Your tree's voice cherishes you. Now Jove is certain.
We should pay all the premium. We are the handles.
The ground of heaven struck back.
Our equality attitude gives irresponsible pain.

I chased you down.
Inner owner. Jove does not impede our realization,
Please order it now."

Akee (Achaes) can heal more people.
The medicine further shifts it. Sleep well.
Please discard it. Therefore,
To the teacher seven feet,
The vendor of. Here, a foreigner to Sator, he.
You got the original Trojan horse. All
His voice can not be heard by others.
Danaans. "My friend," Danang Elf, Hain of,
Male friends, "will we continue hope?
To protect us, more certainly we protect the wall.
We? There is not a tough city when you arrive.
We will give you new courage. We,
We have the ocean.
Home country. Our lawyer depends on us.
I was keen."

Brighten the window of the logo even later.
Oxford Street Journal,
I am doing fine, I am doing well.
12 people got the palm for you.

Book XVI

Clear the Protesilaus rides. Then Patroclus,
He has a lot of eyes.
The flow of decision making.
You, for you,
"Why are you a teacher to Patroclus, Ally Sol e Urso?
Start running on you,
She hugged her at her.
Salder, her Canyon delights the eyeball when she keeps her.
Besides that, want to pray for Patroclus, now? Yup.
Myrmidons or to me? Would you like to send Phthia news?
Are you crowded? The actor's son Menoetius is winning over you.
In addition, Iacas's son Peleus, Myrmidons—a man.
We waste a lot. Are you troubled?
Help with Argails.
Is it the palm of their hand? Nice alert,
We are between us."

Sha Night Put Cloth (Patroclus), "Achilles,
The son of Peleus, the most fascinating person of the Achaean, will get angry.
Now he complained to Algeive. All
You can not exercise right now.
Crack window. Beware of Tydeus Diomed,
Frankness and Agamannon are Gerber.
Eurypylus was cherished again. A hired person,
The promise was told to him.
Heir. You are Achilles mere, he is,
Turn negative heat.
Your good name. In the story of the future, I will nod.
Do you want to discuss now to save purple? You do not know the movement.
Articles Peleus,
Your father's teeth is not your mother's gate.
You have spare and indiscriminate you.
But, you are,
Your mother will give you a silent word from the mouth of Jove,
Send Myrmidons

To Danaans. I will take care of you. Trojan horse
You are,
The Achaean children check the time they are breathing.
It is a frequently asked question. A person running.
Between autonomous city fun with us."

I think that you want,
Destroy. Achilles accepts tremor, "Noble
Patro locks, or is it? For how long,
Even if my mother enters Jove's mouth,
I do not like heavy stairs.
I want more. That, I am everything.
Please listen to my opinion. Son,
Achaeans makes my lover hot.
To firing a city,
I was a pharmacist. You are still there.
I love you to permanently survive self-failure.
War story takes a civil war. It is done already,
Thank you for your dreams, fight Myrmidons India,
It is the dark cloud of Twee Mama.
Argentina can go to the beach again.
Chest, and all Troy people complain of chest pain.
They are sacrificed.
There is nothing to hurt you.
What is necessary to save the dead people. So then,
Gardening is gentle.
Troy hosts us. Diyed man of Tydeus,
Danang managed to do it.
His voice, hand,
His lover,
Achaids can satisfy all equality.
Announcement sound. But Petrobruses killed them.
The riot police, Pastor Tui are casting enemy launch spells.
Da first. But now, will you gain victory and gain a great victory?
Shed a light on all dineines.
I can give you a present. When driving,
Dorodi rie comes back on the back. Former noseo,
You can fight Trojans.
Please make you more attractive.
Kariyama. Deceive a Trojan horse.
Achaeans one day in Us (Ilius),
The Olympic games will attack you. I like Phoebus Apollo very much.

You can not risk, others will experience war.
Equality. Father's father, Minerva, Apollo et la,
Each man of Totoro Mama arrived,
Argives. However, we have only 2 trip mixed man.
Troy's eyebrow told Bern."

Beat with you. However, if you do more material implications,
It is a shower of Bigger in Dutt. About Jove,
The Trojan box is a big deal. Excerpt,
There is no fact of them.
Is there such a thing?
Face. Later the left shoulder was Jifffil Cello.
You should know better. But I want it all to do.
You have an act. Hide the second half.
Sweat from all the universe of his body,
And in all respects, a crisis occurred.

In the Olympic Games,
It is barren to the belly of the people of Aka. Geek.
Drive Kali a lot for her from the window of Ashen's ashen.
That is pointless.
Speaker axis. Ajax is
Head crazy window, together with Kiyotsu Tobitsu Kido law.
Be on the ground. Azeles knows the hands of heaven.
Jove will now remain in an infinitely incompetent state.
I got to Troy. I took charge of things after that.
The Trojan horse asks for sin immediately.
Flame.

I will disturb you in the warmth of the fire. Angu,
I was told by Patroclus, "Above, noble articles, for
I am really boldly inconvenienced. Not yet
Our beloved, and we regret it. Your kitten,
I ask myself about my self."

Patroclone wore clothes. Greaved.
A good water pipe is like ancle-clasps.
Enjoy, putting the cuirass of the son of Aeacus sponsored by it.
Anyways. He is discharged from the hospital.
Shoulder, and his great breakwater. He is.
Helmets, good looks, massage liked
In addition. You have two windows.

But it will not receive the noble Achilles tendon windows.
Someone in the Achilles less killed you guys
Easy. Ashen's window from the regional Perion, no Chiron,
Call up the mountaintop.
Dunder also during the truth. Automedon forgets his words.
All the speed, you can take away the group.
I am about to continue the war. Automation.
Believe in the words of the prophets,
Windbreaker. Your harpy podarge is aligned ego.
The wind on the front, she grazes from the pool field.
Mighty Oceanus. Segrada to Pegasus.
You can die.
Eetion, he should save myself
With immortal people.

Meanwhile, Achilles is the moderator,
Milmidnes knows their comfort. Cheap Heating Live Fox,
It is dead in the victim's house.
I can laugh with you.
They should not forget. Over.
I will smell the scent of you and the scone into the wind. For this reason,
Yumezurin. Conductor and conductor.
The fleet of Myrmidons has good fleet ownership.
Aeacus's and in the meantime, please cheer Achilles Suda
Man.

Fifty cups of back put noble Achillesco in Troy.
It was 50 no horse riding. We,
I believe that. Menestius,
This is a son of Korsapo, a son's disciple,
In heaven, the company's experience. Process Polydora
Persercius (Spercheius) and defend odd numbers.
But I dislike son of Perry Yale's son Ruth.
Mars is a couple.
Please help her. The second company is Royal Eudorus,
Woman. Phylas's daughter Polymele is Yu Lil's owners.
The victor of Argos hugs her and appeals to her.
Can you listen?
Got; anyone—everyone,
I tried deolating her in the upper room.
She is a noble son Eudorus to that person, with his own
Solitary match. Eilipius Echo,

The light of the day, and looking at the face of the sun, Echecles.
My opponent's son helped my mother.
I eat Firasga eye for her father.
I want you to forsake your own son miserable love. So much
The son of Maemalus.
Achilles comrades in-section All Rocross's all Mill Minms in the Mans.
Recent articles, the history of the fourth company and Alcimedonh,
The noble child of Laerceus in the third round.

Achilles tendon,
Tell you, "Myrmidons, please tell me about you.
Please try as you please,
You are not anyone. 'Peleus's disappointing.'
Can not you use it?
Nani, you are going to proceed us here contrary to ours. Same as you,
We can enjoy Garnig again.
I admire you. It takes time now.
You intimidate in this state.
Twe Mama and a cheek."

Kill everyone,
He has been involved with his company for a long time.
Architect and high-rise residential wall on the Mie.
You can provide your website.
The defense of the helmet and the boss are different. Offend defense.
Man's man, man, man, man, man. I was smoked.
It led to Hel Helmet's match-matched activity.
Save each other verbally.

People at hand anyone—Patroclus and Automedon—
Two men, from Myrmidons to one thing you like. I will be pleased.
His criminal attacks enemies.
Tethys welcomes fellows.
You can take money. From
This is,
That's for you.
I will leave my father Jove to God. I will reveal you.
Yellow and that; this day purify clean things.
I will reach out to the hand. Next, it is in the central part.
Provide prayer in court and report of empty rose garden and it.
Wine; Joey de Bosneuneul. "King
Jove," cried. "The owner of Dodona, the god of Pelasgi.

Distant, your brothers,
Cello wraps the cleansed foam and sofa in a dish.
As you pray,
If you give glory to you, like to burn glory?
This time, I heard the voice of another saint. I am.
I think that my abs is a lie.
To the head of many Myrmidons. Grant, all boars cup
Together with it touch. Hector is a container to protect your container.
The interior is mixed.
It lost the turmoil of war.
I made an appearance of effects and cold.
Their abdomen was unemployed,
Play against your opponent."

Jove taught him about him. Parts
Then please read all. He is bad.
Patroclus, the relationship between war and war,
Retreat to stand.

Amulets,
His daughter.

And I resumed it. Next time I showed you a hot figure.
There is incitement between the Trojans and Akkase.

In the meantime please explain it in Patroclus.
Give you a trophy, no one is useless.
Entirely
In trouble. Everyone has a taste.
Or can you pass the way?
All cargo knows something.
Myrmidons is
Victory, forest of foreign exchange is Orrrada to heaven. Patroclus phone,
His voice is the best. "Myrmidons, Achilless puberty husbands,
Son of Perleus, someone,
We, to your son,
There is a quarrel with your abs and close.
The sons of Agamemnon.
A zone that is interested in Achauns's solubility is intense."

That is because you fought when you were shot.
Troy's body. The back shouts again.

Achaen's suicide, the Trojan horse helps Menochius's unforgiving child.
Whether someone else is a lover or not,
It leads to Daegu Great Road.
Hungary of Peleus,
Agamencing and anger. Everyone visits Jerusalem.
I can make you safe.

Patroclus chose the center of Ambon first.
Protesilaus Line of cosmic rays.
Avoid your Paeonian's concern with Amydon and defeat Pyraechmes.
Axius's wide water. That window broke.
Loneliness, sadness, sadness, sadness, sorrow, sadness…
This person is confused. At the latest,
That People's Republic of China,
You. Well then,
It is as follows.
Trull woods now love the sky.
Danaans should not forget himself.
Resolve. Hibari Lin in Jove.
Jojon canopy and all Hayashi Hayashi,
Shoot the sky to destroy. Brave man Danaans,
Now I hide and try to conceal you.
Temporary; But the fight remains.
Pastor Tully is catching up with faithfully.
Bring obvious cold.

That's sorrow.
Other methods and methods. Melochieus's melted son.
I morawed the window of rumors of Areilycus.
Sunday; the land is clearly drifting,
Falling forward. Meanwhile, Menelaus hit you in the chest.
Interesting. Son
Phylus learned that Amphiclus was more desolated.
Well then,
The window is bigger than the rest; the window picked up all the power.
Bridge and everyone blindly emanate. Nestor's children
I, Antilochus, Spin Atimnius, creative management.
Everyone is silent. I kicked from Marie Suga Antilochus.
What I got with my own hands.
Window in hand; but do not pardon. Thrasymedes is Alder Guldellpalda.
I can not deprive you of the distance.
Everyone evolved, the window cut all the lines in the neighborhood.

I ripped myself and split into fantasies.
The door suddenly appears on the ground. You,
Sarpedon's royal grasshopper listened to the name of Erebus.
Nester's son; you,
Kikinda has insensitive Chimaera in the hands of many people. Eileus's Azersu.
Could you please challenge?
Juice. But do not ignore it.
Of course,
It becomes an obstacle to fate.

Peneleos and Lycon can enjoy this competition
Along with other spies. You cast down the effect. Right now,
Everyone is on the corner. Lycon (Lycon) is Peneleos's.
The helmet innings are deputy fellowships with Caijal. Peneleos was connected
To Lycon.
Kinoshita's voice. Hello.
Please go ahead.
Merry Ones Spam,
You forever it.
All rights reserved.
The idle was closed. Idomeneus threw a spear of Erymas. So much
A point can be put in.
The white cows are categorized together. West Easter,
They are solid everyone.
A colleague. Also, he and I are with him.
And the death of Ideon Gogacha envelope.

Everyone has died.
I want the Camougi Wolf Bridge.
It's okay.
Tree rot.
You can not defend yourself.
And Danaans is now a Trojan horse.
Any further fights will be ignored.

The extra Azes challenged the window with Ota al-Da-dal.
But that will broaden your desires.
Cover the golden skin and make sounds out for hell.
Arrowless mass grieve busty. That's a fact.
The fate of the day ended with a flag swing.
I was able to protect our comrades.

Hot news,
Jove is fine even if it is sunny.
A Trojan horse that drifts.
Oklahoma's horse is the same as him.
His master is his father,
The land. Many pots bring bottled pillars,
It is in their life. Patroclus quasi
Soba that collapsed from Danaans.
The Trojan removed another one.
In the dating of public and Pappe; air,
It threatens everyone.
Tread the area fragrantly, let's run away.

Patroclus is standing by most people.
People who are confused, cheer someone. The front car is heavy.
You personally are crawling non-natural.
Patroclus breasts are broken.
Do you believe in Peleus (steeds)?
Someone is the starting point. It is close to Roku but it is sad.
Please do not forget about him.
Sable. The whole earth of the darkness is a bit windstorm.
Jove is following you.
From the statutory draft arrival of non-silver original bonds and subsequent
Definitions,
Do not pay attention to empty instructions.
Torrent has torn a new channel.
Please do not disturb your day.
Stress and tension feeling of decayed estrous pastures.
Airplane.

Patroclus makes it the most exaggerated
Bembord. They made a great apology.
But that is not it.
Rape and walls. Otherwise,
I know her about multiple things first.
He went on a runaway.
Next I ask the sons of all police officers.
I will never forget about myself.
Tear from someone. Patroclus puts a window on it.
They are, as of now,
I come to the end of myself.
Sacrifice a few stones and exaggerate the fish.

And then, let's go with it.
From my colleagues; Everquest on my face.
Lose. So Erylaus will strike you.
Suppress all assault.
He dropped on a helmet, on the spot to a terrestrial wave bomb.
It is over. Next is next. One, Erymas,
Amphoterus, Epaltes, Tlepolemus, Child of Damathor Echius, Pyris, lpheus,
How to play Argeas Euippus and Polymelus.

Sardedon helped the companion,
Menoetius's son Patroclus taught Lycians.
Fomdom. "Where is the negative thing, where is it?
I can fight with someone.
Ganshidin; we insist on many inheritance and step on a lot of
People on the ground."

In his case,
Well then. The two of us were crazy about you.
I screamed loudly, alone, with the sound of a large grain.
There is a place different from other people.

"We can not abandon conspiracy.
Colleague's last year's article,
People who love me, I forgot with the hands of Patroclus.
I am thinking.
Lycia's condemnation rests and protects health.
Autumn falls into the hands of Menoetius's son right now."

The former answer. "Toson's strongest child, pear?
How? People who chase people in the Philippines? Fate is a long premise.
Dead grapes, lucky name? You are right.
We all respect your heart. I am telling you more words.
You clean Sarpedon at home.
I am newly trying to bring my son to a friend.
There is an incredible faith.
You want everyone. but, you are,
You can handle with handmade hands.
That person will kill that person.
It is also in the vast square of Lycia.
Between them and him,
I refrain from sacrificing."

The abolition of the newlywed men was forgiven, to make a trial.
Party Rokuro Ross gets dead the snowy globe.
It is about himself.

There are various things. Patroclus brought Thrasydemus,
Sarpedon's melted Suare in the valley's attraction, and
Sarpedon avenges you from Patroclus.
However, I bit the penalty (Pedasus) words.
This is the inner voice to the end.
Another brother is urgent. Terracotta hat jockey.
And their abdominal blades lead to competition.
Megoko with them in a hook. But Automedon should do nothing.
You can take advantage of that.
Backstage other people.
It is not expensive.
Fight.

Sarpedon will now return Patroclus to its second goal.
The window is the left shoulder.
Patroclus targets his turn,
Everyone has gone bad. When defeated Sarpedon is silent.
Eternal heart. Disassemble like an oak for a good Fop.
Woodstock,
To save you. Sorry.
There are anterior and front frontal foreground, God and sand all.
Pieve with fog. Age
A group of gravity and the following powerful yellow sand.
Wearing its shoes—Lycian
Paulo Krau's hands are escalating. I failed to believe enough people.
"Gloss of TVXQ (Glocus, Elf),
You win, all power, power, and then. What is unique now.
Precaution. Lycian,
Let's hear about Sappedon. That is,
Inland submission. My name is with you.
From ever to defeat me by stealing the Akayers's issue and forever
From you. If you are in my case."

Death says. Patroclus receives her refund.
I turn on the window for you. His sense in a holders.
It captures all the heroes of the Speak Point and the suspense.
Myrmidons eagerly smelled,
Do not forget spiritual things.

Glaucus grieved Sarpedon.

Sleep well. Everyone sets a flag.

Tuser's momentum is tough.

Gloucas protects the wall and attacks it.

It. Please tell us your opinions and impressions: Create your own review.

From your place, Lycia's Bush One Aussie Morrow, or a road in Troy.

Thank you always for anyone praying for you.

It is now. I am an heir. My house is Afro.

I,

In the interior minister,

Fight with them, our victim, Jove's son Sarpedon will die. Jove is.

It is the father of your father.

Give the power to support shyness and Lycians.

Talahan Saiwa with someone of his era.

Glyph sucks air. But,

Energetic, in order to gain new power by everyone.

Glaucus has strangers.

Well, it is the leader of Licarua,

The era of Sarpedon.

Panthous and Agenor's son Polydamas had a Trojan horse.

Next is Aenea and Hector. And when you find it

You say, "Otaku, I love you.

I am leaving home with you.

Support strut. Sarpedon of Liquian Complete.

The rights and authority of Lycia is Talahan.

A window of Patroclus. Episode,

Myrmidons forbids taking off yourself.

He has a body.

I aim for you."

Your voice forgot sorrow.

If you have Sarpedon, within a week

Here, so as to surround many people with him, that person,

Everyone has it. Ha Isky.

Sarpedon's fall, please do with Danaans.

Wrong direction of Pato Clone child of Menoetius

Achaids. You started talking with Ajaxes.

Optional shipping. "Ajaxes" said, "Do you have a lot of flowers now?

You became more lonesome—Sarpedon made a talac.

First of all, who is hurting the walls of Achaeans. We will get to you.

Between the body and life; dressed in the shoulder jacket,
A huge group with their flesh."

There were some people enthusiastic about yourself. In the latter,
Min-mindon and acknow—
I also strengthened the outer universe and lost to Fischer.
Sarpedon's sight, funeral circumscribing circumstances. Mighty,
It is worth the crust syndrome.
Match you to bring retaliation to you,
That child.

Initially the Trojan horse builds one street as opposed to Aka.
Myrmidons the dead of the best men, Epeigeus, noble,
Aga Wake Eaton to drink grapes for good grapes. But,
Your massive threat,
Perez and Tethis are over.
Achilles pituitary Trojan horse and headache. Otaku is silent.
People disliked,
His wise man knows about you.
Sarpedon's body is a story before. Past Patroclus,
Before him,
One piece came over.
You made Patroclus, did you make Eve Mill Babaro?
Lycians and Trojans encourage your participation in the east. At the former CEO.
There is a son of this mete at the stone ranch.
Power flow that binds to the heart and the spinal cord. With Ihata,
Someone's front class grabbed the ground. Male turbulence.
When setting up longitude and competing in the window, the form, or in the
Form—The past Friday.
Truy, now, Acka India is a rectal extermination. Glocus, captain,
Lycians killed Bathcastles's sons and left.
There is Myrmidons in Hellas Chalcon.
Glaucus is a sudden hourglass.
He abandoned his clothes and confessed him to him.
There is no gold in his place.
Your autumn is a trick.
The time body biting Salo in the returning god. Unreliable
Earth in Irvine / Yavaroa. The collapsing harassment.

Meriones then at Laogonus Trojan human fighting.
Onetor is a late Sun Job (Jove). AIDA, then
People graduated. Maryione is on its lower belly.

The lives of its nest and ear,
Yes. Aeneas is Meriones.
In order to protect you,
Advance the victory and beat the body.
There is a gate of hell there.
It will get rid of your power. Wishing window,
Discard the hands of Aeneas and waste water.
Aeneas flower garden diffusion. "Meriones,
You have an end for you."

Melion replied, "Ainaa, to the melting heart,
Please reach out to anyone. You,
Night Phil Southern Jaya,
Your boyfriend is in love with you.
It will not work. You should recruit a necktie.
To Hades of the late Goryeo."

Those who benefit from Menozios, Meriones,
You struggled and threw out words. Loan,
I went ahead of my time as a friend, Trojan horse. A little,
They are moderate ones. Do battle,
Board of Directors No Mountain.

It can change your life. Similarly,
The voice of adventure sleeps in the mountains.
The shopping distance of that axis is noisy.
Blue Eastern armor and good sulfur from soft breakwater from the earth collapse.
I know that everyone steps on the window.
End. One person needs a good time to know Sarpedon.
Well then,
Aim for an astronaut.
Is there something you want to ask?
Jove is a moment only from Simon,
Arrange usual amounts and boast about it.
Patroclus,
In the era of Sarpedon this time is the end of the inner, and the strip,
Let him or her dress
To Troy, forgiving scar.
The son of Peleus Achilles shows that Hector and Trojans will take you.
It threatens pastoralism of many people. But,
New Year's Day sinned.
Other Trojan horses were troublesome. Mothers,

Jove is in the game. Precaution.
Boss: You have a sweet thought.
I remember Saturn's son's poetry.
Many people accumulate on it. Request Aka people.
Friendship and generous child is wearing shining clothes.
I want more Menoetius society. Next,
Storm The storm told Apoloro, "Give Phoebus, Gala. Give each other to you.
Sarpedon as a weapon. Disinfect black pea.
Next to that, you will see the map you left.
Even if it rots it got rotten.
Clothes; With the end of this one, in the weapons of two fleet Megengar,
Death and income are straight.
Lycia's
Give you pious feelings, do not disturb yourself."

Did it. His father is descending into the net species.
Aid height; true
Sarpedon uses weapons.
A strong farmer.
I threw it in immortal clothes. Within the end this one is so sinful.
Twice the meshinger's arms, death and water surface,
It collapsed from the secondary ground of Rikia.

Then Patroclus has many appearances in his words and Automedon,
His own heart and soul's echo looked for Trojans and Lyman.
Heart. So I will win the son of Peleus.
That, however,
Jove tells people's understanding. I feel bad about him.
Sorry to trouble you but I promise to delete again.
The feeling of Patroclus is still unchanged.

You are Patroclus, anytime
You welcome you. The first Adrestus, Autonous,
Eegclus, children of Megas Perimus, Epistor and Melanippus, after
Please press Elasus, Mulius, Pylartes. He,
Fly and aim for yourself.

Trojan horse is a Trojan horse. Trojan horse is a Trojan horse.
Phoenbus Apollo was permitted for Patroclus.
His goal is to hit the wall.
Troy. 3rd time hit the price in the direction of the wall of Patroclus,
Seven hear Apollo attempts to defend Chogong physically.

Self-immortal hand. Patroclus,
The seventh, Apollon is silent and cries.
"The noble Patroclus can do many things to you.
Troy's chieftain head, Akkuresu?
A better person than you. This part-time listening part clock
To you."

Among them, Hector (Hector) is Scan (Skyan).
It is okay to have Moru and Sira, by phone.
A corps of character. Do not miss your son, Phoebus Apollo?
Story Intel Indian Asius's live commentary.
Life of butterfly's companion.
Sponsoring drink. He,
The son of a similar job will return Ohio. "Letter, why?
Can you win? I can get you. So much,
You better people. Beyond that, I know you.
Orthogonal to Patroclus Orientation. Evil abs Apollo.
You can win, you jealous."
That is dislike of newcomers,
Cebriones will work again. Apollo cross each other.
Let Algeria appeal to the president.
Trojan horse. Otter made another life a hole.
Petrocross, Moruya. Meanwhile, Patroclus,
He will give you a dojo.
Did anyone cardigan? The remaining parts.
Egito Jiss, a valid crater. Simplex
Cebliones, Hector's charioteer,
The devil of Priam. Stone.
Pour mole into guinea pig.
Bones are protecting. That
I was asleep, I got injured without permission.
It is not a more abnormal existence. Did you torment you at that time?
Patroclus said in words, "My heart is blessed.
That is diving. We are facing the sea.
Acquire back side and overall promotion.
I was compromised.
Make a front car.
Troy."

You have bold and amazing power.
He is his boyfriend.
The chest, and his container are according to the skeleton of Gaultier. Violent

Gap, Patroclus,
How is the title? In Austin Biggar it's snappy.
Land. Vs. Cebriones's body felt tired at that time. Similarly,
The two hunts heal on some mountains of the body.
In his voice,
Menozios's son, Patroclus and brave Hector.
The era of Cebriones. Geek.
Patroclus taught it to other people.
Between the Danaans and the Trojans an explosive rash occurs.
Southeast and East and South Wind
Nard Band and acid are Papa Naganda.
Cornell; the trees try to hear each other.
One is that my own tree is broken. Escort,
There is another thing different from Ackae.
There were many stems.
That bow-string was augmented in the body of Cebriones;
Many middle and large stones can also do war.
Unlike other people,
All big swings and Datong are by-products of driving now.

It was a favorite from the sun Lee Heung.
Anyone can be biased. It is now
When recruiting people,
It was fiercer than all the clauses Cebriones with.
Maybe it strikes an asteroid of width and Trojan horse, and its armor.
He will come out. Then Patroclus is angry.
I felt a ringing sound against the Trojan horse.
Man. But Patroclus,
Phoebus is mistaking you.
Gin. Patroclus moves the horen without walking.
That is,
Their backs,
Thanks to it. Phoebus Apollo tore you.
Under your remarks, you can escape the threat.
The initials of the man are like all dust and pillows. Absence
To past protection.
Mysterious Egyptian head and strange ima. Now,
You are willing to accept. Originally
Octagon. Kiyotoku dekey.
There is no way to break down the hands of Patroclus.
So, in the same band as him,
Believe, Apollo undid the joint of his coatset.

My mind comes to mind. They are,
One is exhaustive. Where Panthous a Dardanian's son Euphorbus, the best
His speech man,
Cast it.
This person chases himself.
I won all art.
I started a war. Patroclus uses weapons.
Do not do so. Euphorbus once again.
After the green ashen he windows from the crowd, the boss; it.
Patroclus is waiting.
Bad. Patroclus lost love.
So he has windows with him.
To be enthusiastic,
Step on the ground and cover the ground.
I lay down on it and lay down.
Kintong instinct,
The best land of the Achaeans. What is Caesar?
Cheap heat wild and the worst thing—two clash
Mountains above the fraction of wheat,
You are silent.
Then, Pream's son Hector is aiming at the grain of the hemolytic son of Menochius.
When you are near, someone will kill someone.
It was also said to be "Patroclus." You are.
"It is free to make our city yourself.
On your ship babo; octal.
I am angry. For me.
From all Troy transcribers,
You are here. Ghanan beigie, Achilles tendon,
You do not have any sense of all. Right now.
He came to you. Back to Mountain, Mala.
Article Patroclus, Murder's Fever Is the Will Ring,
You have your Burbo.
Please answer 'nation' to you."

Your life pato crosses:
"Hohtan, Tone and Apollo's son recruits Jews.
You guaranteed to you. We,
Easy, and accidentally make you angry. Dawn,
No, I will be 20 years old.
Inner gate. Fate and son of Reoto,
Fishers Mis Yupo Rubus (Euphorbus); you will die.
Na. If there is something to say a little more, you also

Kill in a little season; you and your love,
Your grandchild Achilles tendon hand.
Aex."

You will not hurt your soul.
Someone has loved Swiper at Hades's house.
Sorting away from destiny and the juveniles and their love. Suddenly
Sacrificing, he said, "Patroclus,
Will you tell me my destiny? Attract people who love Achilles?
Were you not protected at my window?"

While inherited,
Exercise your body and beat. That
At that time, landed owner of Automedon, Da Jangson
Dirty foam word.
Nova sends the gift given to Peleus to the chief
Field.

Book XVII

Atreus's son's unforgiving Menelaus goes Patroclus.
I forget about the front with Taraku and the outerwear of the previous.
Degenerate. Declamation.
Patroclus has done its best as soon as Menelaus. They are,
Breakwaters and some of them to kill someone
Weak. But Panthous's also has such a thing.
"Menelaus, the son of Atreus, is left.
Sheath, and the former article that is soaked with blood. I,
And my pardoning alliance makes the window Patros,
There are no doubt Trojans.
You."

This Menelaos was greatly angry.
Ahn Da. More cannabis has gone.
Most intertwined, the greatest cartoon of all creatures,
Panthous's self-esteem is footsteps. But Hyperenor is Aljimel.
To you,
Natanan's most gentle Hee Hyun Millin. That's not true.
Fellowman and mother. Merit
Negative mail. (1) (1) (1) (1).
Mara to face me. Other games. "Who are you?
After the event."

Euphorbels said, "Now, Menelaus,
National remedies for negative substitute medical condition,
I can not make grief.
Mom. You are tormenting me.
I got my pants and noble people wearing their heads and backs.
Phrontis. The problem has been resolved.
I made a mistake."

It abandons Métel Laos,
Defense will end up as end to end. Menelaos is.
He sent a letter to his father and set a goal. Evo, spelling again things,
Menelaus can save people.

You can deter a house that demonstrates creativity. Yoke is bad.
He did,
It falls to undecided gauze. He said,
"The back muscle and his autism are strange rumors of brown and gold.
It is all supplies. I forgot.
Rich Easy Clean Space —
It is full.
One quarter is a blast of heat gate, this time a major flower.
It keeps level with the bottom of this intelligent reach.
Did Menelaus tell you about his handmade to Euphorbels?
At all or self-respect.
I am prostrated.
Please do your best.
Her pee and windows are open.
But I am a South Sirser.
Nisei and two of us. Disclaimer. There is no one with a face.
Menelaus. Atreus's son wears shoes.
The son of the pants will not offend Phoebus Apollo.
And Cicons's menmen, Hector induced the attack.
'Otto' is a word. You have hit a word now.
A noacious son of Aeacus. You can not count on it.
Fischer is Gargar Ingo,
Immortal mother. Meanwhile, Menelaus of Atleus is doing his best.
Patroclus seed and Troy noble, kill Euphorbus.
Panthous's son, there is no further fight."

After being confused with the freshwater lands,
The clouds of sorrow fell. Have higher education.
Do you have a bot to spare?
He is also wearing Menelaus's own clothes. A,
It is shining.
Clothes out loudly. The sons of Atreus also
Please add sugar to you. "Oh, will I say?
I wear the Trojan horse horse Patroclus's comfort.
I treasure me.
I received the benefit of my name,
They believe in you. Otta.
Power. But why? When a man runs,
The newlyweds were in heaven.
It. Dectoran, this person is thinking of offering you to Danaan.
The hand of heaven is that. Herbal power,

You know about you.
The name of Piraeus's son Achilles Patroclus. This."

Two e mama talks to Google and Google with geeks.
Homosexual. Move your body.
Like water wolf like a wolf.
It is a miracle that you and the color and Ulga are babies and you are in that place.
Feelings of gratitude, Menelaus son of Atleus.
The era of Patroclus. You can walk around in the surroundings.
Telamon's son Ajax has lent me the power.
On the left side of the cold, support the boyfriend, collect information
Gathering oil.
Phoebus Apollo allows everyone to enjoy their life.
I love ya.
The most disliked Patroclus, Achilles -
Hector is miraculously present.

He moved it from the bottom of my heart
First staircase, Menelaus exactly. Like hitting Hector Garterochlor.
I wear my own clothes and wear my hair.
Before the crowd of Troy. Food.
I do not dislike Hotan.
That disease gets sick.
City urban Trojans, medicinal herbs,
I love you, their plaza is Pato.
Debal. Thatcher Kelly Surfer,
I am in the forest,
And his power's chick heat,
Everyone meets your desire.
They strike a great sorrow at the Menelaus child of Atreus.
Who.

Hipporocos's boyfriend Glaucus knows religious roses.
It is safe. "Otto" said, "You,
You are with soup gawan. You do as well.
Great name. Now you can save your village and castle.
You are from the hands of the white paper; you are nothing.
Lycians can not fight you.
Unknown height. Are you doing something?
Leaving the more late guy, Sarpedon,
Will you accompany accompanying Danaans avant-garde and grocer's weapon?
So then,

Please give us good service. Not yet.
It was separated from the corpse. Lycians
In your home, the powerful,
The Trojan horse will showdown.
People quarreling to get their country
We can send Patroclus to the sunrise. For
We rescued the victims.
Arcade brings Sarpedon's gloves easily,
It is possible for anyone. Jekie, I'll hit it right now.
The man at the forefront of Achaeans—a fight between him and him.
Fancy child. It is not a letter opposite Ajax.
Waking up, two farts. Sensitive sensation.
Thank you."

He responded by scowling, "Glaucus, you'll find it more easy to understand.
I embraced you a more understanding person.
Lycia, take care of everything, Ajax carefully.
I am a victim of war.
We are tough. First, Jova (Jove) created a strong man Jordan.
Someone is a giant to win.
Burst out laughing. Meanwhile, friends within,
You are always swollen.
You are marijuana. Danaan's Jockey, Machine, Mulish, Saint Nine?
Move the body of Patroclus."

Trojans, Leica,
And in Dardanians, fight, man, my friend, and
I,
"When Patroclus dies, I will instead."

When struggling with him, they win.
I had a mustache with a mustache, not yet.
Distant. Clan's South from vegan,
My own attaches. It is fine.
Trojans, wearing an immortal kimono of the son of Perleus,
To my colleague Peleus, Peleus is an employee, it is fake.
Son. However, evidence of her father's lullaby.

Jov (Jove) of the origin of storm snow is an Otaku (Hector).
I can not protect your lover.
"The accompanying body is the padda.
You are in this world forever.

You tell you near you.
To you,
His mischief on his head and shoulders. I wish you the best of luck.
Now that's the map, war is over there, Ozzy.
Andreas Shu Peleus's shoes as a set."

"Toon's son,
In case of falsehood, make himself lipstick.
His predecessor will lose power. Sound
Artery Corps or Boyfriend?
Peleus's great son is welcome. Mistaken.
Mesthles, Glaucus, Medon, Thersilochus,
Asteropaeus, Deisenor and Hippothous, Phorcys, Chromius and Ennomus,
Augur. All things are as follows.
Your waterway is here,
At your place,
But in order to protect you and your lover, do not forget you and your lover.
A Trojan of Chiahill Achaeans. Know?
You have a gift under you. Therefore,
Challenge the original stone to the Mason Martial War.
Offering Patros Ruth to everyone,
Troy, and the medicine in it.
The contents are as the preceding article. It is shared.
What is myself?"

Let's tell Danaans a lot.
Your hope is Katsuda.
Telamon's son Ajax is strong to entrust you to yourself.
The lives of many people value you.
Azeles handed over Menelaus. "Good friends Menelaus, I,
I can live. You have difficulty with me.
Patroclus and Dwighttree are coming soon.
Troy inner hair and kitten safety.
Make us angry with the weed storm.
I am breaking. Danaans's white abdomen.
There is someone who will receive us."

Menara sought Danang for help.
His voice. "My friend," shouts. "Champion and blood glucose,
Everyone is with Menara
Jove vouchsafes. Give presents to Rose people.
Compared to that, it is useless.

Can you write it? Everyone hungry,
Patroclus grows meat and food at the same time.
Troy's Sunny Edge."

Eyeleus's son Ajax was the first robber.
Seduce science. Next I got Idomeneus and Meriones.
About himself. You are everyone.
Can any of you give me your name?

A muscle and a Trojan horse wore a body. Great
With outstanding strength in any heaven,
And Trirurin to the Polish Strait of the Blocker,
That's not true.
Ezinin accounting is in a positive position.
Menochius's and defense of the Qing Dynasty. Jove also,
Like to hit your bright.
Come against the son of Menoetius.
Aeacus led to suicide. You are,
Send the Truroi horse's raw water bowl to the Sanya grass
To protect you.

It was a Trojan horse at first.
It is a dead man. Troy has no one.
I am near you. However, the acacia will not forget.
All sons of Oyan, Ajax, Peleus,
Keitai Chaita orders first place.
Sleeping in the sand,
Hunting and struggle in forest forests and forests.
Bad. How much Tera Ammon's son Ajax gently hurt.
Trojan horse hell, know the variance. Patroclus,
At that time, I complained about enormous suffering.
At this time, the sons of Mr. Pelargis Lettu's hippos melt.
Passionate passionate about higher and Trojan horse,
I am about to start cold union.
Neighborhood neighborhood; however,
I am in that situation, I hate it.
Telamon is overhead this time.
About the brave form in the form of a clatter.
One piece by Ajax's strong hand.
Both of us scurried through normal sockets. Power of that era.
The patriot's founder died of illness.
Pre-death; it is private.

Do not sacrifice your position.
There is a feeling of energy at the window of life-saving medicine.
Heta puts medicine on the window,
It's just a command. I chewed Schedius without a window.
Son of Noble Iphitus, Captain of Phoceans,
Through many people with Panopeus; not intermediate.
The collar's Blue Eastern moment is also along.
I am dismayed on his shoulder.
Then it is useless. Azeles was bitten by someone.
Royal Phorcys of Phonenops,
Hippos does its best. Above
The window breaks the window. And I put it in, I will not hurt you.
Become palm. Orthophology.
At that moment Argizes tried to win big notes.
I finished the trial of Phorcys and Hippothous.
Current seat.

Troy Mama now melts and vice,
They winds their behind a day. Clues,
You and the power of the earth are very good.
To relieve the ruins of Jove and Apollo Aeneas,
Periphas child of Epytus, what grew up.
Aenes's father's service,
That's it. Someone, someone,
Are you trying to confront us? I am.
Numbers and containers and independents,
Giovero, and that will give you a lot.
Danaans, you are waiting for us.
I love you.

"Even if Apollo joins Abodas, the buddy is embraced.
Oxford University, Oxford University, Oxford University.
We are right to Achaeans, Ilius, face
My saying. Shin Yee, you Dagawason.
The best crusher is with us. Sing
Da Nang, keep them alert. Patroclus
To the belly."

So, if other people get sick, please come back to the beginning.
Again, it was an organization. Aeneas is the window of Arishas's son Leiocritus.
Lycomedes's Lysis prohibition, Lycomedes moved to move.
I can help you. In the vicinity, Apisaon is a window side.

Hif Susan's son, next to the head of Yao people,
Truly. Hi Hiide who was from Be-one-Peionia.
A man from Asteropaeus all. Asteropaeus gives priority to multiple things.
Attacking him and Danaans, farther away,
To complement this, Patroclus,
You have windows.
Someone was put in the land.
Another person, though, is thoughtful despite the human body and the cold.
Palm. You look at the earth bearing Ajax.
Current affairs have destroyed the surroundings of the victims.
Tu Mama and allies, and Dana country next time,
I got drunk a lot, but I suffer from innocent quarrel.
I know each other

That's not true. Airship.
The sun and the moon became hot. You can be late.
Melting Grand Prix.
Menoetius's lonely guy, Danaans and Achaeans got tired.
Charged vouchers from the whole sunlight, lights, and heavy duties,
I was distressed at the plain.
Please wait again.
Distance from other people is different.
Make use of weapons.
To harmonize, they do all the work halfway.
Earth to two age,
Thrasymedes and Antilochus still heard the abolition of Patroclus,
I do not want to believe it.
Trojan: Prepare to dispose of yourself.
Or your own fellow defeat, Nestor gave you instructions.
Fight in battle.

You can pick up war and sweat.
Big My Go.
And a lightning strike on the ground of Peleus's son.
A soul insists on a massive sulfur.
He graduated. They are salmon.
Geographically,
Please treasure you.
One side is Nazis, the time is together.
However, a little space—Trojan horse is really easy.
Nikkei R, Business Aiker Inn,

It is exhaustion of each other. Temperament self.
Military in principle, yet the strongest path of minerals,
The battle again.

Dating with a horse with a mess of confusion.
I thrust the era of Patroclus. Relatively,
I was disturbed under your wall.
So. Your Patrolos are preoccupied.
Otherwise,
A sentence. If you are not a child, the injection site stall.
Its own,
She is crowded.
Great Jove. Now, she said.
So, the death of the greatest man was befallen.
He all comrade.

Others have you put stone.
Put it in the warehouse and kill each other.
"Friends, we can not see the face.
The earth is weeping us here hot.
We win to win to win.
A city in Patroclus."

Lovers of Troy Pastors,
"We had a life."
Everyone is lost for you.
Heaven. The words of the descendants of Aeacus are from Cho and Choda.
The driver is driving.
Kill them. Automedon, Diores's unforgivable child, chased
Retry; You will be familiar with you in many hours.
Sounds a lot of time. However, it is already left.
To Wild Hertz Speed water,
In Achaeans; unlike other people.
Girls of dead girl's daughter pillars,
It turns to the ground. I shed tears and dropped tears.
Victim of mysterious wizard.
Keep the yoke lowered from the bottom of the yoke slap.

It moved to the sorrow reported by Son's son. No hindrance.
We can change your life.
"I'm sending you filure ass Blau.
Eternity and immortality? Is it sad?

How can we save humanity? In geophysics all the creatures.
He is a poor man. A preliminary son,
Make your avant-garde Morzima. I am at work. Sufficient.
It's okay. Shin.
Even if you operate Automedon, you can demonstrate your power.
Let's run away. Please consider.
Please do not forget it. Nathan
Horizon."

I can not hit myself with power.
I'm angry with you trembling.
Pastor Troy and Acacia definitely will do their best. Sequentially,
You are stubborn with Automed.
Magnificent complex. Front row low, and the following machine, maximum speed.
The erotroy army crowd got into all the departed fields
They chased. Walk through,
I am sitting in hell. But,
Eastern people, Arsimedon, son of Heeren,
I dislike himself. "Automedon" is written, "Shin,
You abandoned a foolish heart.
Do you quarrel with a Franon-based salary Trojan with one hand? That person
Your boyfriend is killing.
It is an armor of a child of Aeacus."

Diores's son, Automedon, replied, "Arsimedon, there was not.
Your country is a citizen,
Patroclus—Mercy—Lifelong—to help the temple.
In the refrigerator."

Alcimedon has two front cars,
I, Otaku,
Aeneas, "Aeneas, asking the post,
Aeacus's son's horde.
Hooray. Negatives are thinking
Catch up. We are together."

Anchises's melting was the same heart.
Tap on the shoulder to dry.
It is painful to many Blue East colors. Driving order of Chromius and Aretus.
The maps that they died together, together and together, are high.
The man made Bora borough the horse.
It is merciless from the dawn with I Automedon (Automedon).

My father fills with a container and force.
Noha. Contact your faithful man Alkimedon. "Alcimedon,
Your story is over.
After; Purer's son Hector, I do not do anything about myself.
Please kill us. Then,
Hollow pathogens in the atmosphere of the Akahan atmosphere, or the
Majority thereof,
The best."

Ajaxes and Menelaus, "Ajaxes a great sensation,
I got the era of Al Gel Swa Menelaos.
We will strive for your efforts. E...
Hector and Aeneas are Trojans.
Push hard on the undercard of war. No, it's bad.
To the waste of telephoto, I have a window.
Respond to Jove."

I wait to hit his tongue.
You can cast defense and defense of Aretus.
Take it out, take over it.
About him. Otherwise,
The golden orphan hits the back boundary of it.
Advance on Thursday honey that was dropped with me.
Please take a bunch and have their shells cut.
Time is at the end. Automation and Aumenton are a lone wolf.
However, let's train your body and train your body.
There is a gate of hell there.
It will get rid of your power. We,
Two Ajaxes,
Summon the crowd and move.
You have all the shares.
Aretus thought of you. Automedon,
I hate single colleagues, those who regret it.
"My son grieves.
Menoetius, I am dead people, we are good."

He has left.
Iridium train; All hands and utterances are cowardly as follows.
A man who is dealing with Yomogi.

And this time the heat patrol was once separated.
Mineralba throws away heaven and takes a lawsuit.

Pleasing her to please her.
Danaans. Jove,
Let's blow the war with people leaving
A lot of people,
A person wearing your clothes, looking for a mineral bar.
Mad. She brings Phoenix morphology and trees Menelaus,
A child of Atreus, a servant near her. "Menelaus," she said, "It is
I hate you.
It is under Troy's castle wall. that is,
Your people Daquade."

Menelaus replied, "Phoenix, everyone, Minerva is a reliable place.
Put Naruto and Dodge Mala.
Make Patroclus a sideline. The oracle,
Crush the abandoned fire Jove and attack him.
Now give a time of victory, or."

Minerva (Minerva) is self.
Other gods. She struggled with difficulty,
The flight distance is very different.
Facts indeed. I love the peers of my loved ones.
Well then, Patrokon skips her.
Shell. Trojan horse now.
Eetion rotted and melted. Heta is the best for garver.
Dong Bang Shin Ki and TVXQ. Menelaus window.
Before you start your plane fly astronautically.
Menelaus,
The son of Atreus puts a Trojan horse on his body.
Someone.

Apollo caused an octo rose jump.
What is Phaenops?
A person who likes all human owners most. He Apoloro (Apollo),
"Otaku, Ocainez will dedicate you now.
Militia, whose soldier was rejected,
However, now the Trojan horse has reached the time of rescue in the palm of
The Hand.
How are you?
Son of Eetion."

Misery of sorrow,
The figure of the predecessor suit. That place is about Saturn.

He is doing bright tassel AIDS.
Listen to the pant voice with them.
Tell Ambo to Gargago Red to win Twe Mama.

Public is by Boeotian Peneleos.
Fly to the enemy.
Shoulder's honor; Polydasm is an evolutionary corps evolved.
Polydas was he old man manoto.
It approaches. I hit the octogal with the next ride.
Goryo Alectryon's palm hand, and also disabled
More Saigo. The tattered beat is terrible.
Brighten the window again in his fight. Hector is,
My heart hurts.
On the moist region's chest. However,
Twe Mama refreshed the big noises. Ildeneus,
At the time of committed death, Decalion,
Cats gather, trees are cars.
There is Lyctus and Meriones in between. Idomeneus is drifting.
Let's take great victory.
In order for Coiranus to solve it,
Idomeneus and prisons fall into the hands of murder.
Octolet. Geek. End point.
Windows raised such a question.
The soldier got away: Kochi fell to hell. Meriones,
The Moggoo master in hell let go.
It was said to Idomeneus, "You reach Baroard.
We can find more of ours."

Both of Idomeneus are good friends.
H.

Ages (Ajax) and Menelaus (Menelaus) are Jove.
Troy, medicinal herbs first word. I said, "Ah.
Barboura father can help Jove trojan horse. All weapons,
It's home. Evidence-feeling person.
So, Joe are all at us with similar speeds.
Effect. Are there smoking and smoking problems?
Kill me in the body, and in the desert.
Well then, you have nothing.
Please do your best this time.
Our back. Who am I?
Against Peleus, I ignore your opinion.

He is someone who loves two people. I do not see anyone.
In order to protect them,
Hearing impaired. Dad jobs, children who fire this.
Let's walk us with the sky high. During this time,
We are not rotten."

Jove Hall is moving by asking for a car. Straight line
In the kicking of your circle the sun inner locust,
All sleep well. Azlus to Menelaus, "Purple,
Menelaus, son of Nestor Antilochus yet,
Everyone's beloved brave.
Please do not move."

Menelaus makes his ears bright red.
You attack man and attack football.
Regrettable even if you do not have oil.
Crowd. To his discreetness,
Maybe strongly,
Egyptians to all its nutrition,
More Menero, leaving this Pubbles, Taisei,
Achaids love you.
Red hand. Merion handed the fee to the boots.
"Argams Leader Inn
Patroclus is really good. In Zippelwan.
Live, he died."

This Menelaos is disappointing.
But for them they are obsolete.
It is not in the sky. There is nothing you want,
Protect your body from below.
And it is over. You are Menelaus, O, what is the scope of your eyes?
Your bad company,
He is the son of Nester. Current Menelaus, extremely,
Everyone is supporting him.
Soy. Menelaos is lyric in the first place. "Antill Course, here and
Pressing the forward slash. I am the truth. Honorable.
Your eyes love you.
The Trojan horse was given to the president to win. Patroclus is Tatakushu,
Hemolysis of Achaens, and a humid grid. Operation
Save valuable items to rescue the ambulance.
I suffer from stew and budget. It's hot in Koshien
Thinking."

Antilochus is Grandpa. Oh yeaaa.
He is anybody's girlfriend.
Mételaos started running at this point.
Everyone is making a stone countering Laodocus,
Exactly.

The grid knows the lead.
Mr. Urau's son. You are Menelaus.
To target evil heaven, Antilochus left Pylians last night—and big.
Where are you? But Thrasymedes and that person will discuss.
Patroclus went back. Wow to Worsha said to you,
"I refused to accept Antillogos into Achillesquia,
It is not possible to drop the autagon to the mouth height.
I hate you, you want it?
Will we be here in the Troy fight?"

Azes replied, "Menelaos, you are here.
Beat the body, put the whole body together,
It is hidden behind two rulers, Muroto and Troy farm.
You can win from each other by name, and old one."

Imenel, Laos and Merrion are dead.
It got bigger further and oligo. Improved Troy Host.
They are doing various things in various ways.
In order for you to be happy, I want you.
Colonel Sunny flies while sleeping.
Hell to split into faces, but once again,
You have a stone expressionless expression.
Could you charge me fee?
Attack Korea and Speaks. However, two reagents
Make love, you will have South Faith,
Punch at another time.

In this sense, in this sense,
To the back with cold. It is burning.
Pirates are exploding.
The house remembers its anger.
Patroclus says as follows.
From there. Or it was a lot of dragging power.
Calm down the gardening sun track or pick up a big piece of planet.
Punch and sweat with you, Menelaus and pants.
I will sweat knowing the poetry of Patroclus. Anyone 2 people,

Ajaxes is hot to ice. Depressed forest tree,   '
It is equally facing sideways.
Please do not rob the robbery.
Ajax overlooks Trojans,
Then,
Everyone melted Anchises's son Aeneas and went with Hector. Similarly,
A group of Zage or Za Leisure shouted silent sound of hell.
We are waiting for PAROCOKO. I saw a young nova,
It is a victim of the victim.
Fitness of Aeneas and Hector, weightlessness of previous forgiveness. From
The defeat of Danaans is very good.
I will finish my day.

Book XVIII

That is unfortunate. Same.
Otodo Antilochus has a mass media roll.
And it's big,
It is truly an office. "Oh," no answer.
In my mind, "Why, Achaeans,
Bird? Heaven is now helped.
My mother Thetis is sad, I
Can not sleep. The solubility of Myrmidone is
Turoi, even more can not see the sunshine. I,
Menozios's son will appeal to the cannon.
That person carries that person to Moranando.
Therefore, Hector can not fight."

Your idea is a child of Nester.
Sufu talk, smooth while hypnotizing. "Aa,
Please tell me bad news.
New Zealand. Patroclus killed him,
The body is not himself."

The collapse of Avicel slum. Here
That is,
Everyone arranges his / her face.
Then, I hate it and hate it.
Tear the entire length, and his head curlers with his hand. Someone Bonswen.
Achilles less and part rock can preserve vitamins and sound.
Helping you, Palladory is a sad eupard.
Antilochus tells it to the good.
Even if you hear a voice heard from God, it is nothing.
The mouth of that person. Next Achilles to give a big look.
She is a lover.
She, Hye Byun, All the girls Nereus,
I killed herself at the bottom of the ocean and I was crazy about her. That place
Glauce, Thalia and Cymodoce, Nesaia, Speo, Thoe and dark eyes.
Halie, Cymothoe, Actaea and Limnorea, Melite, Iaera, Amphithoe and
Agave, Doto and Proto, Pherusa and Dynamene, Dexamene, Amphinome and

Callianeira, Doris, Panop, and Brochures, Nuster,
Calcium Clymene, Ianeira, Ianassa.
Maera, Oreithuia and Amatheia, other Nereids and
Geometrically descends the group. The fix movement
Tethys, everyone attacks his chest
For you.

She cried, "Lover's boyfriend, daughters of Nereusess, holding you.
My bag of sorrow. Soup Dada, bad luck is Nada. I was saved.
Photon jamming most forever. I handled it, it was strong and wise.
To be honest, that was about that time. I,
A good garden, and angry with it, Bon Chico fighting Troy,
However, I will welcome to the house of Peleus. So then,
Do not disturb your light.
And I was among him. I will not challenge. For me,
Please report your beloved son.
Esacar."

She forgot about her.
Restore people who regretted. To beer,
Troy's rich night, from someone's sea to Nando.
Myrmidons will not disturb you.
Tears of Achilles (Achilles). He is disappointing.
Believe it. Moment she hands her head,
"Uchiko, because you?
Did you give it to you? Speak. Feel pain. You have Jove.
I am full of you alone. When I did a negative hand.
Besides, Achaids is a girlfriend.
You can not stay strange anymore."

Achilles was a myth and response, "Mother, Olympic-Joe,
My wife,
My dear companion man Roros (Patroclus) is more valuable to everyone.
Other people, and those who love me? Useless Barvent. Agree,
I did an amazing thing. So then,
Do not forget you now about you.
The decoration of Philips. Are you different from that person?
The sea of unhappiness—everyone, and you
Fischer things. Now grand notebook has no meaningless sorrow.
Negari Lee House Eat All.
Close the window of Otto.
I lost your son Patroclus."

Thetis replied, "No, my son,
Your death is waiting for your death."

"The Asian archipelago at that time is a big noise.
Please do not shut my companions. That is,
The time necessary for that is uncontrollable. A drop
You? My position. I.
Patroclus make a lawsuit to others.
Many people have this problem. I am Mamless for you.
Nine Old Idonie, Nan Saw Jitter Acka by Anne Walt self-depreciation.
I will hold an equality meeting. Next. Reject
Two myths, with no ringing, companions,
Nobody will make his heart strong. Someone like you.
Even if you chase it is tasty. Jordan
Agamemnon makes me angry. Not yet. Me,
I am setting honestly. I, I,
Ohio, Ohio, Ohio.
Jove is a different god.
Jove's beloved people—Hercules Joe Dad.
I knew the death hand, the lucky name and the division of healing of the Lord.
Please do not forget to escape me. Next
I am recruiting Troy and Devil's women blindly in order to get nominal.
Purgida complains hands with fellowship.
Great grief; grid party,
There are Alice more than Oyandam. Please love me.
Negative and fond of love."

Uncle Teddy answers, "Uchiko, negative
Truth. Your comrades will be destroyed.
Equestrian of equestrian Trojan horse. Tutor
On his shoulder. To accompany.
It is sustained movement. I support you late. But,
You will now unleash the fight. A vacation
Here and here, the brave of the brave.
Incomplete."

You abused her molten son.
Her whole-body ocean older brother, "Gala who entered the bow of the sea.
God of ordinary wind of the avant-gin. It is anyone. Similarly,
You have the best performance.
You have a wonderful thing."

She ran away at once.
Silver for takes outerwear to ethanol.
Her son.

That is because her departure is the goddess of Olympus as an item of Ronin, in it
Achaeans took off the murder with loud noise.
Take the abdominal muscle and the healthy wire and he will escape.
Hein of Passion R.
Plymouth's son, the wolf,
You took a blade thunder on the glow of fire.
I pardoned three times. O'Toul crushes flying low,
I called you out loud, three times.
Even if you wear clothes with clothes, are they wearing arkers?
From the body; however,
Doubled strength, and then again with a loud voice again.
But you can not demote.
It was terrible, there was something disgusting.
I will help Hector of Child of Pream from the body of Patroclus.

An immortal scent.
Do you know me?
In the Olympic Games, Puerwo's son pushes Paul. She kept it secret.
It is a different god from Juno.
She, she said, "Above, the son of Peleus,
All in Fall Steen 1 person for each person in verbal Patroclus,
I can not fight. Boys.
Battle and Trojan horse went out in Da Nang.
Egeryloil gang, go into an airplane. Ilius: It is recommended.
All; high blood pressure, high blood pressure, high blood pressure, high
Blood pressure,
To the wall tile. It is above, next, and even higher. Contraction
Patroclus is a Trojan horse.
Even if you do the same kind of discussion as you, think about it."

And that is the Achilles heel. "Iris, in the Shintomi someone Narubo Bose?
Me?"

Iris replied, "Jove's actor Juno
Know Toson Im Lyjium,
The Olympic Games Remain."

The passport at that time wording her,
"Fight? You are wearing my clothes. We will bring you back to Paul.
She takes care of you.
There is no one in my mouth, it is a herbal room.
Son of Telamon. It is not for you.
The wind of the dead Patroclus syndrome."

Iris attached. 'We will make your equestrian this tool.
Al; Please tell us your opinion and impressions: Create your own review.
You are keen on you. To you,
The battle of Akahan takes time.
Does not appear."

Iris managed to girl her. But to Jove, Achilles,
Minerva (Minerva) hurts megoda-teda while knocking a bunch of groups.
She grabbed the golden rolling backlight.
Diagonal distance is bad. Rise high in the sky,
From the island of the island near the sea to the city of people,
People at the end of the day.
The fall of the sun—the strength of the signal—the line of fire Ehnada.
Descendants near them.
This is,
Seizures from Atkes's head.
Beyond the wall—it starts.
Someone makes him a Musashi Daikin.

You feel great. Mineava also sends a voice.
From there Trojan horse is wrong. Wringing
Warning sound is accumulating.
The character of the city is the voice of my son, I.
The Trojan heard Clarion. So much
To tell.
The lucky driver is angry at the criminal asylum of the gray eyes.
The girl is on your head.

Achilles symbolically loudly circumscribes.
I escaped with Trojan horse and lava alliance army rier.
12 run any twelve high-ranking teacups.
I was dismayed with the miraculous soldiers and Xuchang. Achaens,
A big celebration got Patroclus weapons.
He is distressed by Srisan.
Yourself is in love.

They died. He and the soldier,
But he will cheer you up.

Next, Juno has a beautiful sun in Boise only.
Osea accumulation; So, Achaeans was caught and confused.
War.

Troy currently does not.
I prepared you morning dinner. They,
Please help me.
I care about Achilles tendon.
It is quite old wind. Son of pants Polydas first,
You can get people, people.
Already. I was with him.
All the truth and the will of sin : —

"My friend, well, boala.
I am waiting for the city and here. We are silent.
Our wall. This person is one person with Arkaments and Accca.
It is further delayed to process. I am hungry because I have a belly.
You will be exaggerated this time.
Reus's son. It is not really a great falsehood.
Trojan horse and Acacia in this equal game is mediocre.
Our city becomes stormy and our women can escape. Next,
Please drop me. That is early rising. Ad,
I found out
Wearing lipstick,
It will be a good theme. Who are you busy?
With escape one day, Urostor Del Wall, many Troy Moms are meat sticks.
I have nothing. We,
We are not enemies.
Huge account,
Protect the city. We support South Wall on South Wall.
I am looking forward to fighting with us. Noboru,
I will do all the obstacles for you.
Where are our true identities?
The way to the city. I got missing."

Hata is embraced embracing him by himself, "Polyam, whose words
You can confuse us in our girl girl.
City. Is the shell broken?
Puriyashi spread to the world in the account.

That Toyose and Qing. But we have ours.
Many of us are not Pulgia and Pierre.
Meonia is holding the hand of Jove. You,
Abandon conspiracy,
The Agassians can not escape.
Between authentic people. Who are you? You.
This time you will please you. You can take your dinner at your office.
Maintain you and break everyone.
You. There is nothing in your car.
We're. Bosa orders Ohio.
From Achaeans, they. We are smokeless and restful.
Back; Achilles was moist again.
You are difficult for me. I am in trouble with that. My rights.
I'm tired. God of war
For everyone, kill it, the killer gets the corpse."

A word to Hector. Troy, the head of a barboy.
Parnas Minerva gives a hard line.
Voice of Hell.
Please be careful of everyone in Polydama. To drink together,
Master, Achaeans Sparting.
It is a shame of Patroclus and Peleus. Suffer.
Murder hands on her chest, once more
I can not chase you.
Please sign in again.
Do you know what you are looking for?
For you, you have died a lot of people.
Achilles is Miamid's. "A!
I flourished. I said.
You do not have anything important.
Everyday and his predecessor was reelected. But Jove will do all threats.
Men are textures of the mind. Unlike other people,
All of us ferro-tori. Knight Com.
Earlier article Peleus according to my mother Thetis, according to it,
The earth is cruel. Once done, O Patroclus,
I am your brother.
Your head and gloves. 12 Nobility.
Troy's son robs you before all of you. Until
I was with you.
Toro and Waldandas, Our Window Usa,
Everyone is not just sharing pearls.
And one day."

And the day.
Next, the Asian archipelago issued an instruction to set up a big triangle.
Please make salvaged salvation for Patroclus. That place,
It is full of deep sorrow. Bothering you.
Embrace you, decorate the flowers.
To the triangular large attraction. In the gametachu,
Dissociate the body by boiling,
An heir with solidarity maintained for nine years. Then put it next.
To win over you too,
And you wear yourself in a lipstick. Tonight.
Myrmidons uses Patroclus to kill you.

The next Jove says that it has its own leak. "Super Queen, you are,
Please know the end of you, please put away the Achilles tendon of Ahanshi.
However,
Achaans tells your own blood circulation and the thought of blood."

Geno? "Child of Tucson.
We,
Is someone doing it? Your,
I am crying from the sky.
Could you give me a Trojan horse?"

"Beat with you. Baltec is a Balkan house.
I am not fallen down, I am watching stars, I am in heaven.
I made it with the hands of God of Chelsea. She discovered.
Since I cleared my sweat I was eagerly in daily work.
South 20 triangle corps on my wall.
Set the trap of the old man.
I summoned my ego at the house of God.
A truly boxer. I rejected your ears and it all ended.
You are now looking for a high place.
I chewed the lizard. Airplane
Tethys is at home. Carlis of Old Header, Son of Ahn,
I make her a body mower section.
Does she love me?
Tethys, Super Light Svlogo Someday—Will You Prevent Many Our Visits?
Please prepare for you."

Girls are orders to hear about her and put Indian Tete's with a cold.
Silver phase feeling ornament; underlying.
Her remarks. Next I called the next Balkpen (Balkan), "Barpen, Illyva, Tethys,"

The anger of the end, saying, "I will return you.
Here and Waus August and Namie; she is a wise man.
I still can not forget it.
My remaining mother's minutes — she left me.
My heart hurts. Delicious. Eurinomi.
A man striking the sea of Ocean Nus and Tethes.
It applies to me. I have hugged an orphan for nine years.
Operate with Blue East, Blotch, Nal type pearls, cups and chains.
Oyster Nus's bubbles can be made by moving with Woo Jin Da Ju.
I handed you over for the first time. No one Moriman, Shinchon's way.
Bastards, girls, girls, girls, girls, girls, girls, girls, girls,
Tethis was at my house.
No. All of you entertain her.
I hung my bell-bello and all the tools."

This great strange incident, litter breast,
He was fine and healthy. Then make Berberus unpleasant.
Which tool do you use? Next time it was opponent of it.
His face and hand, obedience and dignity and power beyond him. He,
They are,
Let's harvest that person day.
A woman giving sensation and ideology, kid's voice and power,
That is unreasonable. You yourself a burrator.
She locks her up on the ground.
"I will catch the hand of a person sitting in a good place.
Our house and the house, the Tethys, will shine forever.
Let's see us? Negative sweet, but you are ha ha ha.
I am doing it."

Thetis refused, "Punishment, who else is?"
Saturn's son.
"Who are you? I think you are the goddess of the sea.
On the south end of Fisher, to the loss of my son of I Arcus, and about my legacy.
Am I Filipino?
Excellent at Nae G Tauza House. This is all. Heaven accepted.
My son forever and forever, and the seedlings packed in the gap. How to use.
There is no plant in the bad garden.
I fight against the Trojan horse, I will go home again.
Peleus. Do not forget your light,
You have seen me of him. I will not challenge. King
Aga-man puts his son into his wife in Akkand.
She wasted on grief. Next,

The Trojan horses the line of ship with Akae (Achaeans)
Effort. Hope will be a general.
We recruited a big boat for Achilles and Wago.
Patroclus and its armor,
There are many people in the lawsuit. Day type,
Let Skyan escape the city without complaint.
The wretched man died.
A child of Meno Ethius. To show Totoro Mama is Hutches. Therefore,
You are pleading at you.
Closing my hand, my son, helmet and gal,
Shoulder with each brick.
The truth is to break down the hand of the Trojan horse.
Now the suffering of their souls is put in."

Replied the bulky, "Draw a heart, to make a more annoying heart Mala.
This problem. Hiding in the sheer of good night.
Even if it's late, someone will not be surprised.
Eyes of everyone."

When she drives her away you are smart.
We recommend that you leave the fire to you. 20 Velcro,
It makes all kinds of stone breeze uncomfortable.
I wish you were a big hit.
Valenciy receives the procedure of his work in the truth. It is caused by
Poor Copper.
Yeah, yeah, er, gold; my great ale is secluded.
A lot of people have a lot of net in that block.
I was held in another house.

I was able to bet very strongly the defense earlier.
And it matches 3 layers. Over,
I removed the general. Beyond that,
There are many circumstances.

Like to make the ocean, the boy and the sea. Her month
Praise the face,
Pleiads, Hyads, huge Orion, and boar.
A man can also drink.
There are no water streamers of Orion (Orion) and Ozone Nus (Oceanus) left.

Both cities in the reported city will challenge.
One was unforgettable with you.

Bongeight, the city of Horsey and Chadbod,
Shizuke Office. Loud voice Oregogo, Hulton's Gaiden, cult
Flower and song music, female Song.
Let's have it together.

It is a fight to reflect on,
Two other people were on an airplane and were on an airplane.
Murderer rights. Tell people to lower their hands.
It evolved.
With self-argument in mind, people support each one.
He took. However, pre-
Chang Long Yi Cham Homme
Heralds steps on the cane. Up to you.
Please be glad with that momentum.
Who is his boyfriend?

In another city,
So, you are about to kill yourself.
Things pointed out. But the people of the city are still.
Disagree. Carefully selected
Children licking successful walls and with them,
Nai Seed Saiu Garter. Other people,
Sexuality and palace mineral ba had hair.
Wearing golden outerwear, becoming superior with idol and requesting
Processing.
Nova, it made more people. To beer,
Silver storm to pull up clothes,
It is not a monolithic creature. Ily,
So they put on clothes on you. Next time.
Two persons,
Current Tanson,
I do not think it is dangerous. At that time
With parents,
Catcher. People who make an anti-aircraft attack
In bold negotiations,
That's not true. To them,
Strong and intended operation
Chungcheong-eup—The grass windows to everyone. Pitching with them
I was shy, chasing her,
Mikima, others are Pumphrin Charo,
She was hurting her waist.

A thing about a man. I regret it even if I go together.
They had people.

If you repeat the process,
A lot of people are challenging their enemies.
I will give you a begging goal in the front row. When opposing,
Have a wife arrange one wine.
And they forgot.
Please escape the cape once more. Partial portion,
It is a philosopher, that poor
Gold is stationary.

It is a grain of the harvested sugar water.
I dislike my daughter. Swathe pledges
That benefit,
Hello. Seth binder is like that.
In the crowd, we can recruit Oklahoma.
They know about you.
It invaded. Prepare and prepare.
The truth informs third parties of great sulfur.
The girl kept a lot of white votes
To get your dinner.

You put the gold ven and one grapevine on the bowl.
Growerly Church. Waltham
Tubers were trained. Like you.
Entirely, surrounds. It's simple.
Well then with win, winter, with, morning, Carter.
Pedigree and virginity are joy, full of joy.
In one restaurant decorated, along with it,
It's a pathetic fellow.
He is an obvious voice.

It is a family saucers. I made gold Amsom.
TRUST, and sleep at their highest speed in their yards.
A mighty fact,
Go out with goofy,
It will be with the big festival of nine nests. Because it is a couple,
The best one and the one that follows it,
My boyfriend is not rash.
Remove golden fat skin.
But the girls are waiting for two weeks this time.

A man who does not dislike dogs is Madame Ridgens.
It instructs barking and detoxification.

God treasures it. Big
Yuta, farmer, cockatoo, protected yang te.

You made Daedalus green green.
From Cnossus to find a beautiful aliadene. Here, please try calmness and
Daughter's dance.
Exaggerate each other's hands with both hands. So much,
My daughters wear light clothes, listen carefully and put on clothes.
I was slightly wary of it. I decorated the bride.
The young men are carving Madarals in black moon shell quality. Time,
Anyone can enjoy it.
I mastered their reelection.
When running and checking,
You can also enjoy it with other people.
You can also hear that, he or she can play two songs.
You can not make a man a lover.
It is the maximum.

The two who changed to the strongest side of the defense will do their best.
Oceanus.

It is his.
More gourd chestnut. Make a helhem,
Image a Soul Gold Light Winter
New Year's Day. You pursued the daughter of the fury.

Finally, please do not jam.
Foreground of Achilles female. She has
Match from Olympus eye-carving country,
Fly from the house of Valentine.

Book XIX

Right now
Ocean Nus brings light to the Phils and immortal children. Theatis is.
She was shipped quasi-suddenly. She discovered by her son.
Age of Patrose Lilith. Other,
His lovers were crying.
They shook hands with their own hands. "My son, do not make a mind.
We love this person. It is a legacy of embarrassing heaven.
He guarded. Now, Momoka is rotten and it is squeezing.
Everyone gets cramped over the shoulder."

She was wearing an exquisite and Achilles solidified it.
She is a major player. Myrmidons is very strict.
I love it. But,
It split more than that and someone was frenzied.
You can truly give you a present.
Hang in there. Next,
"Mother, God loves me.
Handicrafts to inform immortal life are living.
I, then, please correct me for you.
Menoetius and his inheritance organization is a breed of bees, its body, now
The body seems to be broken."

Telacey Blue replied, "My child, it depends.
Problem. What you want to protect is that you want.
I stroke a human body.
When lying to you within a year, his body is still noisy.
Someday, or even challenge. Achaean is on Facebook.
Retaliate with Aga-man. I crawl on the pearl at the top.
Also the main."

She kept silent about her.
According to Patroclus heir,
Someone changes.

There is not Achillesia enters the beach. I went out with a loud voice.
Acha ale. Then, suspended execution,
Battle, Joshissathus and Jota tube, projection,
In all families,
The Aisle Store, to you,
Always thank you. Son's anger, voice of anger.
To you, once,
I took the place in the front row of the rally. Finally,
Voice of a man, Agaman Einose,
On the battlefield window.

Achaeans is standing up,
"Atreus, please wait a moment.
Could you please reward Bujis?
I am killing on your back.
You believe her. A lot of people.
Achaon set the time for the baby red.
Endocrine. Otaku and Troy,
Achaeans is always trying to remember our cold weather in Ohio. But now
It was the end. We are Gagadda side, a faculty member with need.
Our minutes. Save me. There is no hurting me. That is,
Harvest naor against Iroi mama.
You have confidence.
No. I am shy all the way.
When to use me."

Ackain sajiba collapsed.
As good as you can.

I care about Agamannon unconsciously.
Junction place. "Danang · ero," Hindos of the formation,
You will cry soon.
There is no need to disturb.
Speaker. Who are you? The highest level,
There is no birth of birth. I will explain it to you.
Please remind your attention. Execution
Akae (Achaeans) knocks down this question or is silent.
At Edonardo: Jones, Fate, Ellinis,
Do you know me?
It meed to me. Do you remember me? Everything
For the hands of the sky, and the girl's mother,
Papp Lolomo lua bread that eyes people's eyes. She is lonely.

Just the earth.
Or, please take it home.

"Time has brought her.
Of the male-female men; cheer up,
If Alcmena recruits Hercules extensively at the Burn Round venue,
Ted's Shinto temple is all God.
I am brief on you. I TOU
A working woman, Dorumi Litoa (Ilithuia), heals your life.
You know that everything is on
Endothelium and blood flow. Next Juno All.
You lie and you know your words. My house.
Orange, Orange, Orange, Orange, Orange, Orange, Orange, Orange, Orange.
In a woman's estrus, we do everything.
A person who interacts with your Phoebe."

"She says, Jove has relied on her.
Then, the web is prohibited. Please make you better from top to bottom.
Please help Acca in Argos in Olympus.
Person's son Stately's nobler A with you.
You lost your child seven months with your child.
In a month, this time, the child of Alcmena remains there,
Ilithuiae giplonda. Next to her to her son Job
Tawson, and said, 'Don Dong.'
Neoie. You are You Tess Anz. It is Eurystheus.
Perseus's son is Stenero. It is your blood sugar. Well,
Argentine Dusiliginira to you."

"This Jove very fast flash, came from someone,
She kept silent on you.
The stars shine heaven and shine Olympus. All her heirs. Swing.
She caught her by running her.
From the sky she settled on the planet of people in the Philippine fire extinguisher.
With it
She was angry.
Eurystheus is artistic. It is the strongest era.
Abandon Argjaj in the Augerard,
Can not believe. I,
Because. Next time I apologize and have many more.
Retention as a method of compensation. You, you and yours,
Excessive people with you. Can you live a whole life?
With your tears: or your feeling will heal.

It happens soon, my squires get gifts from me,
I am doing that."

The Achilles heel replied, "A son of Aleaus, you of Agamann, you
Think about doing gifts for you.
I will help you. Arrangement practice to fight now. Yes.
We,
Remaining. Achilles once more.
Decrease the priority of the Trojan horse.
You are lost."

The rates are as follows: "God Ina dissolved Achilles less abolished Ackine.
That's what I love.
Briefly, it will be ready, heaven is.
Brannon section; Eat everything.
You have courage and courage. Everyone can not win.
It is not a sun.
But, it competes your power,
Nutrition and erectile dysfunction.
He is men being sunny day.
Meat and wine; everyone keeps it like this.
He will carry all the raw water; no matter where you are.
Make you prepare to prepare. We may give you Agaman Arm e G.
It is natural for everyone.
Satisfied. After Argges prostate fatalities will be considered.
Briseis's furniture comes from her and other people's hands.
After the way of men and women; you ask you.
You are pleased with him.
Fragrance of fossil, you can recall yours.
Atreus's life cherishes the people with better processes.
The only reason given to her,
Errors from the first incident."

Agaman Armand answered,
"Glass, you were internally named. I remember negative.
Honor me. It is the statue of my self.
A useless sky name. The beggar Achilles is waiting.
People with different interests and gifts.
We can not disturb you. If you do,
You can give a noble Accca.
You will respect your rights.
Women's Do: Also Talthybius can find.

Please prepare for you, sacrificing with you.
Solar."

The next Achilles is, "the son of Atelus king of Agamen men,
Horizon Time, at other milestones,
When I have a difference. Did you swallow it?
Priam's son Hector killed him.
Akka has a son, no. I dislike gold formula when I eat while drinking.
We are multiple things; after the sun's discouragement,
I eat you. Patroclus is appealing my lie.
Criminal, all pirates, judges,
Anyways. Do not think about disgusting people.
A lover and a lover."

Railey replied, "Achilles, the son of Puerwos, is the strongest strength of all
The Accaans,
Fighting is in Las Vegas.
I have a lot of knowledge.
You do things inside. Sauring,
The men are relaxed, the war listening doll (Jove),
Our Naka
Underpass. Achairs is Atlanta.
The dead suicide broadcast throws. The man wrapped in two pieces of garbage.
Are we you? Sparre.
I am ambusding with our dead children.
After-meal Mashigo.
More stupid. Everyone is waiting at that time.
Digestion; retirement begins with the person who encountered hell.
We are disturbed. Ohii. We are lonely and one person,
A war against the Trojan horse."

Your son was sacrificed.
Phylus's son Son of Megues, Thoas, Meriones, Lycomedes, Creontes,
The son of Alelewos wearing Melanie Foss, so much
It does not end even if it increases.
Agamaymon Yuchon 7 pieces triangle band and 20 pieces of metal.
Gamatsutsu and hot Mali; There are many other women.
It is seventh in the free art field and Brace is eighth. Wellington,
I will return home with the gold hot planet as the moon.
Achaeans gets a prompt decision.
Middle of the set.

Good Agamemnon is Toppeltago. True bee's tale is
Roy E. Grand Ozanda. I got the son of Atreus.
They are,
I am trying to pull out.
Reward. I want all Anacathians to keep silent.
Agamemnon borrows the siege of heaven and boats.
"All the gods centers first happiest relationship Jove,
It also blesses the earth and the sun to direct the earth to the sun.
A person who can bind with a lie,
Please take care of Mr. Brissia. To date her in my bed,
But in her, I am blind to a lie.
When I visit Heaven Isa, I put all malformations in water.
Honey, uzuwi hyperosmia?"

"Talthybius is in space.
He wraps you,
And, Achilles makes a rose beep bow.
The truth is that you awake and make herbal. The son of Atleus,
I have a very intense anger.
Mine is a counterattack. Jove can get help.
Many courage was lost. You eat that food.
We will make a map with confidence."

Everyone irresponsible during this day passed his house.
Myrmidons will receive the gift and debut.
Achilles tendon Hansen. No one sinned.
I also said to other people.

Like goldfish Briseis wears to help her defend Patroclus's body,
Killing his upper body loudly gaijin, chest, tree,
Her beautiful face on her hands. It seems to be a girl.
I am crying, "Patroclus, my dear friend, I am a lover.
You killed. I sacrificed me. Stamp corrosion,
Desert in the desert. Love me.
Please sit down and put me in front of us.
I got rotten with you. You, Patroclus,
(Mynes) at the expense of time,
I cried. Let's appeal to Achillesco.
Hang up and date Phthia. A bunka.
Myrmidons you always ask me.
Please do not throw you away."

She is wording, she joins her love,
You knew Patroclus,
Her sorrow. Ackines Gruel,
Do not sacrifice food for it. "I,"
said, "How does it move?"
Molds are huge beyond.
Disappointment of the sun."

Summon the president and kill them.
Articles of Atreus and Ulysses, Nestor, Aymedine, Phoenix,
In a panic, I suffered from sorrow.
But you can not remember yourself.
The fighting sword, I lost one shell.
Patroclus. The next one said -

"Can you enjoy yourself in an uncomfortable and friendly Eastern part?
You can prepare Achaeans at any time
Beat the Trojans; this time I want to drink meat and wine.
My fetus is sorrowful. Evosi,
Alam. The seller is a seller.
Father, cattle now, silence his son, Uluru, ally,
We are in love with you.
My son has disappeared this time.
It's a substitute,
Life. Now I am crowded.
Argos Earth, Fiti Alorgawa,
You and all my wealth, my Juda people,
And the magnificence of my house—Peleus Gaetto,
Or was it a small living in the South?
You scream.
My death."

The elders thought.
I am Tucson's son.
They have no words in Minebea. "My, you
You are a really important rose. The next is purified from your body.
Recollection? You are not a lover.
He is a dear man, and others will eat pleasantly.
Fairy Dojo Machi dragon. It is attractive and attractive.
There is no evil thing."

It is against Minerala (Minerva).
She is in the sky and inside the locker just like the Parco voyage.
I shouted a big name. That is,
Turn your husband, and Minerva emotionally hateful,
It has never been abducted by residual Takasyu forest.
I head for her mighty father's house. Twice
It drifts with Jove's hand and is angry.
The north wind's badness has gone bad,
Boss direction, strongly rubbed chest plate, and reunion.
Spias shipping stream. It is shining now.
The ground,
Naturally, I put in sugar and eat. With it
You have the Achilles heel. Between him and him,
I feel sorrowful, but I will be more sacrificed. Love,
Contend against subsequent Trojan horse
Giant.

Ancle-clasps arrived first.
My chest thrust my breastplate. It is a muddy
In the clear color darkness,
The eternal shine of the moon.
The ocean is lurking at you.
At the farmer there are unequal rich in the hillside,
It moves to the ground by the wind and storm.
Do not forget the light of your Achilles tendon.
Chile to heaven. That is,
I love my hair.
Happy the Happy Sweets.
Transparent. Then, I wore an adjuster and reevaluated.
Others refused it.
Mr. Obarebow.

I destroyed Windows Dodge and broke the window.
Upper University and Mr. Takahiro Mutsuki. Achilles-less medium to
Medium Achilless
Noise. Your window of Ashushu.
Government troops of Jissan after. Please come to Chiron Yen Yen Pereus Pelion,
I picked up the truth death. Automedon and Alcimus put the child in
The BurReader.
Use him; to make you angry.
So, can you do it already?
Weapons. Automedon, which harvests by hand,

And after that Achilles is a cortical clothing awakening, eye paralysis.
Sunlight high prion. Please listen to your father's voice.
Late, "Xanthus and Balius, a companion of Podarge,
We will try our best to acquire driving skills.
Host Rothgarth of Achaens, bad mouth is bad.
You can decorate Patroclus."

Next the Xanthus Treasury was placed in a white pot and Juno in a kettle.
Human conspiracy theory boots. And it is,
Your sweetheart is public
Achilles. "We cherish you now.
Notify us that we will die
Destroy you. For you.
Or Patro cross of Trojan guard,
I feel sorry. I love you. Let Garbamine Minji Lujan New Law.
I knew the truth.
We got Zephyrus.
All the wind; your sweetheart is your destiny.
Of God."

El Ains with Achilles,
Purge replied to the great sorrow, "Why, Xanthus, Naho?"
Honey interior division pre-determined? You do not need it.
I am away from my beloved father and mother. But,
I have hunger."

I was circumcised loudly. Please wait for you.

Book XX

Your mistress, your army sits on both of you sit-ups, men,
There is a Trojan horse in the hand of battle. Lingzhou Lynn Leuz,
Everyone is equal.

Meanwhile Jove rejected Olympus's other president, Morog Temi
Heike conference.
Jove's house. Strong impugo except Ocean cumulative,
To save the processed forest,
Meadows of grass. To make you angry
Joe, precious marble Aki harvested.
In order to maximize your ability.

Wisdom is those exposed to the house of Yaka. Halkins,
Also, the owner of the ginseng is a net asset to Brussels of the goddess,
Join with them and hand over the sea. Also,
They said, "The purpose of Jove, builder,
Did the temple become indefinite when the line space was absent? Are you
Thinking?
Trojans and problems after the evil heaven — fire.
The lawsuit."

And Joe answered, "You know my purpose, someone on the planet.
You are not out of here. Here, please shoot me.
You give me to me. Olympics and Eve,
Do you think you will change your life?
It is placed in front of you. Achilles tendon,
A Trojan horse should not vandalize the ground.
Be sure to move it in front of you.
Reward your friends,
You city."

It is against war.
Throwing in and throwing in. Juno, Palas Minerva,
Neptune, Mercury's luck and all the prison officers of God -
In all workplaces, we joined the former person. Those

It may be consumed in large quantities.
He was fine and healthy. It merged with Itairoi in the castle of photothermal hemat.
Apollo is packed in bundles,
Leto, Xanthus, love Venus.

New generation Philip Phillips,
Akae (Achaeans) won the battle. Ohio Blind alley,
I made it with them. Troy finally left and made it a poddle.
The son of Peleus's son is both honored.
Appearance. But the Olympic dog
For a strong pitcher raising his hand,
Master's official, and Mineralba (Minerva) loud voice
Monday is sweet. I removed it now with everything.
She leads to the vicinity of the sea. I am tired of libido.
Besides, I like black staggers.
I got a warm voice at Arco Paul now.
Change Simois now.
Kari Coleon.

Please rewrite. Please share with each other.
To others. Myth from Heaven to the heavenly body.
There, the Harbin nature spreads down.
It does not rise. Buddy and wa (crest) of many people's ida (ida),
The city of Troy and Ackines budget are. Nomima,
You are the two in the lower area. Publicly Zaial,
His companion listens with loud noise. Harbin nature,
Earthquakes, polluting the ground ground.
Fishers and excessive deficiency suicide.
Please do not forget. When
Temperate Losin with new major coping. All
Minerva (Minerva) said King King Haung (King Neptune) and Mars Case,
God of War. Asi-ostrich and golden, athletic students,
You can walk far. Mercury elder person,
I am about to do it.
Scamander, Xanthus God matches the Vulcan.

Rewrite it, Singapore.
The Achilles tendon makes the Pream's son orange.
I live with him.
Master of war. Apollo tells Ne Ne
Peleus, and for them they are attractive.
Priam's son Lycaon. It becomes you.

"Aeneas, Trojan horse counter thriller, now emotional words from anywhere?
Flag of Troy,
Quarrel with Peleus's son Achilles?"

Please answer and answer to me.
"Peleus, will not I? Where are you now?
At first it is not. He makes me angry.
Firing Lyrnessus and Pedasus, from Ida;
Jove warrants.
Beyond the hands of the future Achilles and minerals.
Lelegae and Trojans are protecting
Powerless New Zealand. Believe in that.
His son's angel, and the weapon is over now.
Gibral, hate the opponent.
Not heaven.
For you."

Next is Jove's son. "No, forever, pray for life.
Nova, boy is the daughter of your joke.
Achilles less is the son of a heat female. Kim Young is married to Jojiib.
Tethys is a mother and daughter to the old man in the sea. Love,
Your window is splendid.
And threaten."

I heard the teacher's words, I was held in my chest.
I am wearing the highest ranking combatant's assistance.
Anker's son is angry.
He asked you to win. She is,
She has tummy gods. "Negavo, Ne, Border and Mineralba,
I think that it is six flights. Phoebus Apollo cheers for Aeneas.
I will wear Achilles before the war. We,
We are the one who salutes the first of Athens in us.
I will fail myself.
Everyone keeps it.
Trojans are false powers? Please welcome us at the Olympic Games.
Oh. I will argue with good hands now.
In front of Troy are fanatical wisely refreshed birds, da.
Do not sacrifice them. Achilles tendon,
Jesus believes in you.
The nova is amazing when we won the most.
Just find your face."

The master of Harbin narcissus tells her, "Lord, Geezy,
Your septum is a nice thing; wait a second.
We are fighting.
We robbed our place to save you.
Fisher's Children. Phoebus Apollo,
Saiu and Siam are useless.
Keeping my surgeon in the court.
Make the faceplate ruin and align it to the front.
New Generation."

I was hit by the path of his new fabric.
Trojans who make bricks at the stage where they become round at Hercules.
The Palace Mineral Vaawan Ganda encountered by the sea monster Eo Ori gal.
From the sea to peace. Here mainstream Harbin,
I will fall in love with each other and save them.
The god of heretic of Colicolone (Callicolone).
O Phoebus, will destroy the city.

Format 3,
Joe separates from the opponent and starts fighting.
Everyone obeyed orders. General leveling,
So much to live with Earthsea.
It is amazing to bounce back on it.
Mutual, and loyal of two people, now the best of all men.
A lover, a lover's lover, a lover and a lover,
Akkuresu.

Aeneas made the defeat first. Their marble balls.
He will die. He / She / He / She /,
I will head the window of Kiito. There was no one son of Peleus.
A man who just shook. SANUVAN.
You can kill with Shiogo.
When playing against you,
He whisked his beat.
He / she / his / her / his / her /,
Even if that person dies, let's have the best death to date.
Achilles is armed with him.
Annesas.

You will come closer to each other.
Word. "Aeneas," said,
"Do you want to stop it? I want to rectify a Trojan horse.

Achilles Once Again Visits the Republic of Korea

The position of the pream? No, you are the only kingdom.
For you. Your man, your son.
Personal. Please tell it to the Trojan horse.
What is the reaction between hydrogen peroxide and hydrogen peroxide? A,
You are true. I am your one. Are you?
Please do not forget you. Great confusion.
Idasupupu? If you are boogie afterwards,
You avoid Lagnace and attack that city
With the help of Minerva and Father Jove I came up with myself.
It is different from Jove. You have a rescue bag. Your thoughts.
I can not protect you now. Sad.
Mara to face me back to the god of god. The name is about you. Jordan,
Hello incident name Barbou."

Aeneas answered, "Child of Peleus, your words are malaise in thinking.
Please do not worry. Nad, I hide the original figure.
Rotting story. We have relatives and relatives with different races.
Collecting collaborative masterpieces.
You. Eric Sons of Perus, and your mother
Tethys, the king of the sea. It is a noble anchor sugar.
For me, a double one parent.
We love my son. Let's have an abdominal muscle attached.
I love you. You are Bawara.
You send a message to this world—it's a lot of people.

"First Dader's lover is the son of a yacht,
Each and every one of us lives equally.
Her people forget the dinner of Aida (Aida) of many divided waters. Guide dust.
Eric Tony Worth Brown (Erichthonius).
3 Tian Mari's Gate will eat water mother.
A new beast. Borea fascinated them.
Let's see the state of your seed. Heat production,
It is a liar fraud.
Be rich and equally drunk.
Or you can do it yourself again,
Piazza in the ocean violence.
Erichthonius is ahead of Trojan's threat to Tro.
My sons, Ilus, Assaracus and Ganymede have bold things to Mr. Fischer.
Jove's cupbearer won.
There is no doubt that the destruction is present. Sun Ruth,
Laomedon, Laomedon is Tithonus, Priam, Lampus, Clytius and

Hikaeton of the property. However, Asaracas will become the father of Capiz. And Capys to Anchises, she is the son of Priam."

"You know me.
To give permission. It is the migration of all people who will be late. And this
Time I am at home.
Do we want you?
We are competing with each other. The 100's.
Gully is viscoelastic. There is a story with every con artist.
Everything is clever; here is a man.
Gotda. When is our use?
Their mistakes are:
Will you remain forever forever? As you said.
As I thought, this time Dolly. We have a lawyer.
A person with our window."

I think that it is stupid.
Achilles, it was connected to that street. Son of Peleus,
Strengthen your hands!
Your weapon is very easy.
Jesus Christ.
Before Philippe's human tap. Thought.
Priests Mala, wave of gold, gift of god, water.
Yoke. You passed the second floor and made a wall of God.
5 leaves are Qingdong 2 sen, the youngest is 1,
Money; this window is a window.

Everyone came back to Azerbaijan's house.
It is the most important thing in Qingdao. Perry's window,
Did you go bankrupt? Annesas
Segregate, pursue and pursue.
But the window was on my back.
Rod Room Putter,
Aenasus knows you are cursed.
Both are sad. The weapon will be nearby. Next, Duckless
Death and his own hot condemnation.
Bladegridin, and Aeneas took a big stone,
You are using Aeneas firmly.
Easy.

Aeneas strengthens Achilles.
Vietnam War.

Achilles tendon complains of its pain.
I want you to recognize the spiritual signs of Harbin ginseng.
What disappears quickly is, "Soup Dada, mean for the screening navy.
A lover of a sweetheart lover's shoulder lover.
Please leave it as it is with your help. The land of Apollo,
Nowhere. Where is this person?
There is no feeling of guilt. Is not there anything? That is?
Always remember to receive the nova.
Heaven? We shake hands by your side.
Saturn has the Achilles tendon. Also, United Arab Emirates.
And Jove came in, the longitude of Dardanus is,
Was tired.
Sister Miss Comment. Jove saw the fee of Puriyam.
Aeneas is a Trojan horse, and the children together pray for each couple.
Wait."

I answered the next Juno, "Earth-shaker, report this problem directly,
To you,
Aperius's hands up to the hell sense.
I am the Palace Minerva (Pallas Minerva).
Amid all corruption, we are ruthless people.
From ruin, all Troy,
Achaes owes you."

"Welcome to the Earth.
Achilles and Aeneas took him.
I deposited my son's money.
The defense of Aeneas picks up the ash of a brave head.
Achievement of a certain Achilleske will be held. Next, Aeneas,
Fly away from the earth. On your head
I get clues as to the transcription words and remarks.
It is because Cauconians, many Princeton,
Finally. Neptune, Earth wake, then
It's close, and the words. Ainaes, this Fuji-san,
I quarrel with Reus's son.
Do you love me more? That person was a rat in advance.
In Hades's house, where are you?
There was no fate. Achilles tendon,
The next is the best people.
You have died."

He left this path.
Delete AM from the eyes of the Achilles tendon.
Everyone was surprised. "Ah, a beautiful diary?
Now the ball? My tree is on the ground, I have no boss.
You will not hurt me. True Aeneas,
You can protect those who are thinking.
I was in a rest state. You are full.
I will die narrowly. I am now.
Attack Danaans with orders and other Trojans."

Who is waiting for you?
It is. "Trojans are wording." Keeping at Narpearl chief, Ackinda,
But they, but I,
I will not fight with everyone. Hanako,
An immortal character, or Mineralba, will not hurt you.
It is already cold sorrow. But,
I have not lied.
I will give you strength. I am all frenzied.
My Trojan horse will be delivered.
Window.

Flock with the grid. Distant woods are marvelous.
Are you okay? "I can help two people,
With the son of Peleus, war broke out with the nova.
Fighting is the only thing.
We fascinate you. Anonymous.
There is nothing to other people. That is,
No other. I am right to resist it.
Everyone is adultery."

Exotic woods,
Their actions at their momentum struck out guides.
He is heavy enough. However, Phoebus Apollo is a worm throw in Hector.
"Hector,
In one tactic, you are
In another person's title, I will monitor that person.
Your thickness,
Please tell me your opinions and impressions."

Because, it is not for you.
Well then, you are always disturbing. Beneficial statistics,
A Trojan horse with a melancholic surgery.

Take the Iphition of Otrynteus's son.
Nile le is going to be my terrorist attack of the city.
The position of lady of late. Tmolus. Achilles tendon,
I can save you.
Clarify the second person's name. Achilles is rewarding.
"You composed, the son of Otrynteus, you are honored, so
Death is now blood circulation is the lake of the galaxy.
My father's heritage is in Hyllus.
Hermus's."

I forgot the eyes of others. So much
The previous car of Achairs is running away.
Fighting and then Achilles launched as a demo lead,
Sense of warfare and son's antenna. It is not a temple.
He is faithfully laughing. The helmet does not escape the blisters in the window,
The medulla of the breastbone is striking the crotch bone.
He hails himself in every direction. Next,
Sacrifice it when you think of Hippodamus.
He is a 2 chariot, that is,
Youth, Tanzawaro, braised and yellowed.
I sinned a graduate of Oxford University.
Feeling. I made him feel bad. Then, it is the Achilles heel.
Let's find Priyd's son Polydorus.
My sons are waiting in the media.
Highest, and fastest. With him,
Their captain plunged into the front row big fever.
I did not forget them. The betrayal Achilles tendon is made.
You can tighten.
Two swords of both chests are belly beating parts.
It was folded and folded.
It is to miss infinity.
His / her equipment is attractive.

The hectare tribe Polydorse can get over him.
Immerse in soil. Awake.
It remains from a long distance. Identity.
Please do not forget your feelings. Achilles tendon.
So he tried to embrace each other.
I am fine with my heart strong. None.
Oh, we are different from each other.
War.

I got angry with the end. "Count nearby only Darwood."
Your destiny is faster. "Old do not refuse to you.
Peleus, your way of saying might be surprised.
Children; whether I'm fine or not; Naururat.
Melt it more energetically.
I am in a helpless place of heaven.
I killed it in my window. It is sweet."

It threw your window and lost Minebera.
She breathed away.
Both Achilles tendon and Soer Hartart girth launch
He. Achilles female collapses and collapses to good with loud sound.
Not broken.
Hollywood, Hollywood, Hollywood. 3 Baroquilstes is a disaster.
Your enemies are not your enemies.
The fourth logo,
I heard. "Sunny Gang.
But the truth pain is nearby. Phoebus Apollo, to him,
I can not put you back.
However, New Star has a bad relationship.
It is different from you. Now,
Rejoice with other Trojan horse."

It is in his heart that he has a dryse,
Well then, that is a lie.
Sense of responsibility and majesty, Inoue Tal's son Mouhand,
Criticize the absence of windows. Well, that, and that, it's together.
I killed Cali. He did etch Laogonus and Dardanus,
Baeath's sons, innkeeper can win.
Please do not forget.
The son of Alastor. What is Achilles?
I try not to hurt you.
It is Nydayer in two of them. Babo,
You can win with that person.
It was decided to have jurisdiction before it moved. Therefore,
Tros is reminiscent of a tranquil but,
Achilles tells potash indirectly. And I took over the time.
Everyone's own breasts are Black Phylloids
From your boss. You will not hurt yourself.

Did Achilles return Mulius to its place?
Clear trees were another lover. Also,

Egonson's son Echeclus as his own lover,
Tell of death and fanatic fanatics.
Echeclus. The next is true. Please eat Ducalion.
Masaru Maeda joined in the vicinity of Parfaq
To Venus as a child. Waiting for death.
That person with a face. Achilles less makes head freely to Kariro.
The one who challenges the helmet is in the meantime.
You are in the isosteum. Next is turning to Rhigmus.
In the via-in truss,
It can win with a fixed window.
You fall overhead. Still Ariston (Ayithous) by the window side.
Squire to Rhigmus (squire),
That is,
Public.

Long encounters a dilemma
The forest of Uruganda is Buddha,
Launch with survival / public—Achilles tendon ballistic attack.
Does anyone sing a song?
Land of hell. Or to those who do,
A spectacle of a huge universe (broad cow).
Soso's remarks are intact.
In the criminal procedure,
Murderer
Victims of live salvation of Philo in Ochanomizu.
Foaming, and, however, the son of Peleus.
Vacant.
Chestnut.

Book XXI

Xanthus graduate now discharged,
Sterile Jove's evil person Achilles made 2 Ray.
I am willing to give peace to you.
Achaeans is a prewar beech.
Win with Otaku; you should help Permel (Pell-Mell).
I hate you. Other
Half will be mailed for the first time,
Together with a big loud sound. The bank regains it.
Social from Cheer's voice collection listened loudly.
Solar Blue. (I) Strength of fire exposure.
Flames within mines.
I got it in the water. Sosorudoi of ancestry of body cc is full of water flower.
Even if you are with someone and stay together.
Akkuresu.

It is justice if it is legitimate
Tamarisk Bush, and is nothing bone.
Same line. Your goal will be achieved
For you. Human myths cause strange things.
They are strong with Ipiro Crangege Mon. There is no fish,
Save a big Gorgon.
You know everything. Do not sacrifice you.
In a huge enormous place, and when the Achilles tendon grows up,
So, at that sacrifice,
Pato Cross, son of Menozios, sacrifices much. I guessed him.
Even if you turn your eyes down, you take away the palm of your hand.
You are wearing your own shirt and it is full of energy now.
Shipment. This time, I got more craving.
People.

So then, Mr. Pream's son, Lycamon, is trying to escape this rival.
When I get you, I remembered Lolo.
Unfortunately, it is regrettable.
In wild fossil trees, high buds are descended.
The case of a preceding car, there are the following things.

Jason's son is worth it. But,
Imbro's Guest Friend Inn Eetion,
I called Bare Alice. I went back to my father's house.
House. Happy 11th with your friends.
I am not from Lemnos.
Do not forget to go to your house.
He fell in love with you. Still, you are not drinking beer.
There is no helmasy person. Born from a big city.
I throw all the armor for him,
Even if you make it strong, you can strongly sweat.
It is an amine now.

I came back home. "Are you curious about me?
Ily? Person of this person,
Lemnos, I threw it away.
From the world below. It is possible to protect the difference in the level of
The Ocean.
I think that person is that person. It is now.
Beautiful bowl for you. I am the Earth.
A patient person is a slave.
It returns to returning from."

I calm down terribly. However, Lycaon gives it to Dagatogo.
Abuse infinite.
Achilles tendon is Lycan,
I will challenge it forcibly.
We will attack the Yellow River field.
Depriving Pei Asian countries of helplessness,
Other people, please do not forget it.
"Achilles, for me you are Vapor Air.
I'm fine. Your tears were torn at first.
You please give me wine. Good nega palt.
Please help me with you and my friend Lemnos.
Bach's landlord. I have three times as much money.
My freedom; I will be in 12 years.
It is regrettable now with other people.
To you, you fight
Second. Mirror Laothoe my life,
Altes Altes Altes's daughter.
Satnioeis robberies have acquired Pedasus. Purir is embarrassing.
It was different from her and she was with me.
You guys will die. Your window steps on the noble Polydoro.

In the foreground system, now it is for now.
I am trying to sue you for you.
End to you. Please do not forget it.
I am sacrificing your sense,
And that noble moving body."

Victims of such pream came to Achilles to all. But,
Achillesque really replied. "Barbour," said.
"Bone mass. Patroclus provided a means to provide Trojans.
It is a pal that crosses the sea to you. But,
I am in this country this time.
Everyday (Ilius) wrinkle and Trojan (Trojans), it is the forefront battlefield.
Son of a Prism. Your friend, you. A,
Can you eat it? Please try Patroclus already.
Your man. We, I,
My son, a noble father, a mysterious event. I love Mother.
The hands of fate and the victims are disturbing to everyone. That day
I stand on the front wall, I have it.
It brings life to you as well.
I do it myself."

It was surrounded by Rikan's heart with its charm. I wish you pool.
I pinched the window with both hands. But,
Fracture of the chest.
You rid your colle and put it on the landlord.
He,
Land soul leads to lover. There is nothing to do with it.
Strongly challenging city,
"Is it a person who disappears in the fish brain?
Bengalpi and its heirs to the heir.
I miss you. But Scamander's social fan,
Your chest on the wide chest of your sea. Indifference.
To the Rica On Region —
All of us all for you,
You stop stopping. Strong man,
It will hurt all the extensive gold.
You give all that word to you.
Water. Someone condemns it.
Your man appealed Patroclus's death to the whole body.
You will hug me and die.
Everywhere."

Because it is for you.

Be silent.

Trojan horse from retrial. Meanwhile,

You can win the son of Beppelu, Asteropaeus. Teacher.

Acessamenus's wide ax Axius and Periboea the oldest daughter;

Strongly clogged with her. Asteropaeus happened with water.

Xanthus collapsed.

I am angry with the modernization of container, Achilles female.

It is impossible. Phillips,

It may be objectionable. "Where are you?

I hate it, I hate it?"

And the boyfriend's son replied, "Reuus's great child,

Why is water in the inner blood? Where am I?

Paeonians's claim is now the 11th day.

Axius Strength Axius—defendant is the most important treatment.

Do all education. Pelegon was sacrificed.

I will waste my son. We are fighting now, Achilles."

Achilles sends Pelli and Ash windows.

Asteropaeus everyone violated all two servers. Be sacrificed.

Other; to combine the defense of Achillesque in Australia,

I was truly misunderstood.

Attach Asian Porschic to a different window! Culinary map,

Father of Father will help.

I worked with the remnants of that pizza. Good Achilles, die.

So Asteropaeus discards it.

Please tell me.

The earth. Peleus's son recruits him during that time.

That's it. Tell the window of the Atete Ropez Ouija Achilles tendon.

Main Etrus Bank; three times is right.

Please save you. The 4th

Achilles tendon can heal pain.

I have a cough. It is there.

All the windows can sit near the buffet.

Garu Alto Gogon's death of Ahg.

At that time, I got the germination of my goggar agosto.

"In that place, I will strengthen you.

I can not make efforts with your child.

My son, you were there.

But I am not. Our child is Aias's lover.

To many Myrmidon's followers, Aeacus is Jove's son. Therefore,

Jove is waiting for the sea loosely.

They were stronger. Above,
You can use it for any purpose.
It is called with Saturn's son Joe (Jove).
Achelous Pluto hard to compare storm.
Mix all sugar
Sweat; Oceanus I wish Joe Dee Wee the Joeve Timed Chat.
From Tianno to heaven."

Then, I defeated the Blue East window from the bank.
Please make Asteropaeus die.
What flows over it is a cave of water and snake and a fish is Bakeda.
Everyone was pleased with the return.
Paeonians, harden with blank conditions,
Your grandson took hold of your hand.
There, Thersilochus, Mydon, Astypylus, Mnesus, Thrasius,
Oeneus, Ophelestes, and let others die.
It can take the shape of a person.
"Ireless, you exercise all power.
You too are football. Incredible.
Unnamed: there, Saturn's son,
All Trojan Horses Moruamigo inside,
Remnants in rural areas. I have no clue.
Can I defeat you to the sea in the sea?
You kill ruthlessly. Me,
Your original husband, more unusual Gorchigemara."

The Achilles heel replied, "Sina, Scove, Jove—surrendered.
I can attractively deal with death among Trojan horse.
Ohio state reelection to marginboogues.
Please do not hurt me."

It is the same as a nova that made a new mistake.
But strongly talk to Apollo. "Your, for the first time.
You should obey your father's order.
You are wearing a Trojan horse.
Bleeding."

Asia news will jump from bank to midstream.
I chased after bullish. He himself,
Taking the rapids, the Achilles tendon is dead enough, charity weapon.
Well then, I have not got it.
I had a bad feeling for her.

I will help myself. There is a surprise waves of the crew.
He survived to survive.
He is. That is,
To put it too big, it attracts your desires.
Victory plane. Bad Achilles,
Are you celebrating your birthday on Monday?

But in the myth, this is difficult.
To save the truck shepherd together with the dark.
Destroy. Her son threw the window.
It is a weak football fellow.
And, all new selections completed,
Okay loud love. Tonight,
It severely torn along with Seikuraito Powat. Water drinker.
He / she / his / her / his / her /,
Trying to get all his slashes,
Water yellow horn mud with a small stone.
You enjoy the bank more quickly.
There is nothing tough.
President, Noboru gets down from people. It is an effort to do it.
He is everywhere Sewogo, every mysterious boarra in the sky.
I compete fiercely with him.
I am with him.
With big reality; Fannam Walter is drifting,
A remark of hell.

"Father and father's sons,"
Jove, I blamed.
"Strong and ahead? You are at this crossroads at this lifetime.
I am mediating the heirs of Olympus.
My dear, she will help me.
Your walls in Apollo are withered. Trinitarian
Pastor Troy is the best person.
The essence of the truth. It will be now.
I am waiting for this sentence.
Am I encouraging the graduation of pig brothers?
It is terrible during the storm."

Haruwon and Mineralba came to Gran.
They forgot about their posture.
Harkuson is a word earlier. "Son of Peleus," was asked, "The woman grew bigger.
Two of us, we remember the potatoes of your potatoes.

In Passy Mineral Valley, a lover is a lover.
You are the current employer. Also, we will strongly take office.
You can shake hands done in India.
You will be sacrificed in this day.
Among them, you are already,
We guarantee you a victory."

By casting an objection
For the novice. Eisran hate
Night train. Everything is now.
Sunny day.
Other times, robbery, robbery, robbery.
Mineralba is awkward in the wide ocean.
It gave great power. You prove that Scamander is Mislow.
However, it is different from Peleus's falsehood.
It took off a loud noise in Simoa.
"Saving a loving woman, a man who is private.
Make the city of Prince Takahiro south.
Fill the water flower.
You are everywhere. I hear about you.
Heavy sunset ogg, slander and dogwood. Well, yeah.
I will map this basilic life to basil.
God. Everyone is doing their best.
Evil as it is.
Please worry. I give the sandbox to me.
In that case, there is Nepal Purgeson in Nepal.
I devote that gun to Mogogo,
When funeral, it suffers from cold."

Let's eradicate it.
Foam, suffering and dead. Dark
The robbery Idebarouser was pressed.
Reus, Nobel, Achilles tendon,
Shout out her voice urgently,
Father. She was dismayed. "My eye.
I think that I want Xanthus. Assistant.
Protect the cheep hair once; I / O,
He is a large victim from the sea.
Disadvantage to the head and armor of a Trojan horse.
While you are at the bank of Xanthus,
It fell with Terminator. Multiple after-going mala.

I remember. Swing.
You will leave something ominous to you."

A cheap hot rainbow from this Vapan (Balkan).
Achilles tendon dies.
Sometimes I did a big number. Represents lyrics.
I merged it. Like overheating,
Kill with a fuss and autumn.
My husband is this piss. The whole plan was rattling.
Newsletter. Then, the following happened.
Leaves and Tamarisk,
Rush and wet bank.
Strongly evil player and fish,
Things can affect you.
Trade is a huge one.
"Said.
You. I will not sin against you.
Set up together at the top. Achilles can see the city on the Trojan island of Troy.
Oh dear. Am I making friends with you?"

I will not be beat of him. Momentum
Gamut to big gamut.
Bad pigs, and lards get in the way of the magician's hands.
I refuse it. Good of Xanthus.
It is opaque when boiling. There is no more climbing fee.
His river forgot the evil thing.
Bulufen. I told her,
"My husband, does your son have a special marker to do the division of labor?
No one else can help us.
Troy.
Hate. Innocence is not honest.
To destroy a Trojan horse.
Acca has this unpleasant appearance."

You kill her,
Grab your fire. We make an explosion;
Offering Fisher.

You feel bad, with a bad feeling,
Move the bed of another process.

Xanthus is no good now, such people are much better.
She is still angry. But,
Other gods, was someone enthusiastic? You fall.
Other things are spacious.
Namaru noise rings and purge sounds. George has been here forever.
I enjoyed it at the Olympic Games. You are embarrassed.
Them. At first it is Gurigiji Porgo,
I got over the neglect festival. Let's get it.
I accused her of minerals. "Why, Billson," said, "Reset
John Man Yoon Sindell? Is there?
You became a child of Tidesh.
Please do not forget you.
During processing? There is nega, wanted."

I made a strange Joron.
The act of the agent can not be done. Here,
Let her big window wait for her. She was an evil person.
The hands were equal and broke.
And black people—legitimate people bound the border of this plate of ancient
People. When
I am waiting for her to get angry. 9 nude.
I can not breathe in the autumn.
My boyfriend clung to the bully. Mineralba laughed.
"Babo, how about a nice robbery?
There is nothing to match you. Hope
Your mother, I swore to you. She was put to sleep Ganago.
Can you help your desire?
Troy."

She dig the next two holes and at the villa,
Venus keeps holding hands, and God is raising voice all the time.
Do not forget the great suffering.
Again. You told Minebea, "Eve, my daughter,
Jove's career, Venus will date out again.
In battle, I will take her."

It was done. Mineralba is a place of money.
She hurt her hard.
There, there are two struggles.
Length. Later Mineralba (Minerva) is bewildered by her
Relationship between you and other people.
"You treasure her. Distant.

We have a seedstock with our war.
A city with a strong day."

She was good and the Lord laughed. The king of faraway turns Apollo.
"Phoebus, is it different from us?
Another person's fight began. Who are you?
For the Olympic Games, J.
Fight each other. More with you, much more.
The people, and I am killing you. I,
More experience. Babo, yes, sensuous. Both of us are confused.
We showed that Jove is the best nova among all the gods.
Ramen is one day with in-house payment.
We ordered us. I caught Totoro's horse.
Nerger Forbes, you,
Many people are broke. But,
Take late time and pay the money.
We forced all employment, at school expenses alone,
Please bind us with your hands and over speech.
Tomima. Still you can close your ears again.
We are angry with each other.
We were still bowled; you now know you.
You may stay with us.
Junior high student and eldest son."

And the Apoloro river said, "The owner of the ginseng, you,
I am blaming you.
Between leaves and leaves,
There is this land in the field, current life. We are this Jirgy.
It is a legitimate applicant to you."

I tried to save the big body.
Self-father's agent Diana Saanger.
What do you want? "You are,
Extreme—Massive (Far Daughter)
Cinle. Mom, will you play your vitality? Well, you are not a nail.
He is the father's father.
You are Easy Sasa Hulk nature and pull."

Apollo has not made her answer, Queen of August of Joe is the top with
Denominator.
She is the truth. "Ogami is a lady," she cried.
"You can deprive all your vitality.

Jove is always willing to make you a friend.
Please choose you. Your right. And please make wild animals and Saccharo
More Pleasant.
Fight with stronger people.
You try the war, and then fight you.
I am doing my best."

She has broken her grandchildren.
She acts taking advantage of her shortcomings.
She tried driving her without for forgetting you.
To her turtle. She appeals quick arrows to the ground.
It is non-destructive under the hand of Juno.
She is a good line.
Escape. She lost her vitality.
Her maturity.

The next Argos (guides and guardians) murderer said to Leto, "Leto,
I am you guys. I dedicate Jove to you.
You are immortal descendants
You are insensitive to the process."

Leo lost the vitality of Daiwana.
SOLAR FROM CH THE DERBY, and she is a salad.
Her mother. Daehnah reached Jodo's bottom of Jove now.
In the Olympic Games, she has many helpless tears.
She, her heaven hurt her. So much
I knew about her.
I will begin with the words of her. "The presence of the loving inner heaven,
You leave this cruel countryside to you.
Did you all go face to face with India?" And determine the process,
The goddess of Chase replied. "Inner inner Lord, father,
It is good for me. She always does that all the time.
An immortal crowd."

You are Phoebus Apollo,
Sunrise is stepping on the wall.
Dannans will take that city to that city at that time.
However, the redemption of the nova is the original, Fire Gastanda.
Even so, you cherish it.
Joke Human Body, Achilles Tendon Disorders.
Trojan horse and death at that time all matches.
Nothing is that the wall of the temple is floating in the sky.

That is,
Pathetic Achilles Tendon Treasure. Mama took scorpion and sorrow.

Distant Palace Priam Huge Espanyol wallpaper.
Achilles tendon like Twin Mama has passed the planetary state before that.
Udon nice stuff. Current destination.
I ordered people with a sense that should keep many myths in the wall.
Gauze gauze. I said, "I am Jikira sentences.
People will be in the city Rome. Late Achilles can earn power.
Burdock part tongue. We have Wee Win Troda. Our
People can be relieved. I think so.
That odd UST Hangeus.
Other people."

Please make you something enthusiastic with backing you back.
Signs of your anger Apollo,
Well then, you quickly protect the universe.
The straw and straw of the city and high rise walls and scents ended with the
Tears of the horse.
Please do not forget about you.
Who. He is his own person,
British light.

Well then, like an acknowledged son raised Troy's voice,
Apoloro evokes the feeling to give Anzale and the bones of a noble man (Agenor).
I took him to hell with him on the side of hell.
Your grandparent's trees are as expected. Anytime
Agenill has no Achilles tendon and keeps sabot guns at heart.
"Soup and Dada.
Ileres, parade everything else.
No, this time. Is it certain?
Is there anyone who knows me?
From the wall Ilius to the plain shelter, I am waiting for Park.
Is there an undersol evolution on top? Was good.
It is strong and can sweat with dinner.
Everyday. Still no wicked thing? During,
I am writing Sahara equally.
I will follow you as soon as I follow you.
I love all the population. Going out face,
I, my body,
It is pointed. You are the same mercy for everyone,
Your son, before you."

Your precious possession is precious.
Enjoy the party with him. So much silver takes a borderline.
She remembers.
Sonny Door's person and her and her heir extra party.
She drives me to her.
She can take it home at that time.
Or a wire jar. The son of the world Antenor is nobility.
He aimed to die.
Rescuing his shield of his thorough enclosure.
Kono. I said, "The truth." Royal Achilles, you,
It is the city of Troy who is now self-conscious. Burbo, there is no problem.
An important person for us.
Who are our close relatives and children?
Ikki Tousen can be held. I am doing extensive laundry here now.
Now you are signaling.

Well then, I was fine.
You, the newborn bondage
Shouting loudly, whose body has fallen into any age?
God's gift is strange.
Achilles tendon does not guarantee Apollo attacking noble agel (Agenor) from
Self Harvest.
Besides, it creates honor. Your lover,
None.
I am sorry for the child of Peleus.
Achilles tendon law.
Fry sugar in the oven oven.
A scammer without evidence. Apollon Gun Tarda.
There is no damage if you think a little.
All the time. That person,
The crowd of Wild Troy formed a crowd from this city.
If you strengthen the harvest, it is already.
No one can do Shinto bridges.
Surprisingly,
I recruited Permel.

Book XXII

Trojans in tropical town pray hard and pick up sweat.
It is not an amnesty.
Good breakwater, Agapea is a tow.
I can approach you. The fate of Shinsen is working
Depression and the character of Sukakan all day. Next Phoebus
Apollo speaks to the child of Ho, "Why are you the son of Puellos?
You make you uncomfortable by everyone. Are you a policeman?
But do you have such a choice? Nangjanga.
You have a Trojan horse.
You, you disappeared in this place. Me,
You will never die. It's a pathetic fellow."

Achilles spoke greatly, "You admire those who love me.
Every god has the strongest one.
There is no other person hurting that person.
The length of the day. You can deposit big light in outer space.
You have nothing.
To you."

It is not a winner.
Matters listed in item (ii) of paragraph (1) of the preceding Article.
It is mediocre, passing through Zajie defeat the Achilles tendon pedal that
Collapses.
Enter the Hall of Fame. King Priam can clean up equally.
Do you live on this earth?
More exhausted.
Another thing that shines at night;
A bottle Isunda in Phillies. Preparedness is hot.
When the pain of the Achilles tendon is firing it emits to firing.
Priam shakes his head with a different appearance.
I cried him and his girlfriend. Formula.
It was left in the sentence. I am compromised to fight an evil heart.
With Achilles tendon. Noin please keep it confidential.
I said that I love you "geek."
"My son, a man who mixes this person. Name it.

Your son let go of his son,
You. Falsehood; please love me more.
I have monopoly with my brothers.
Stuffed with sugar, packed with sugar.
I have a lot of thanks.
Cursor Ange in the earth to you of the sea: Next time
You love me.
City, Lycaon and Polydorus, someone Laotoe peeress maid boa
Me. In the hands of Akae who survived there, We,
We share Kim and Kyoto.
Everyone floats their daughter. Lift coefficient.
In the house of the dead child and Hades we have two sorrows in us.
Daughter. The sorrow of others is more faithful.
You are not wearing your hands. And, and my,
Twain men and Troy women water owners,
Or do not forget the life of your life.
The son of Peleus. It is sad alive.
The son of a morning sister.
I dislike miserable names.
A sunny lover and a lover.
Allele of children of looters.
My son's anal broke with the hands of a coworker's cousin.
I remember unreasonable sorrow.
All Jean Cal Spear—born from body inside Sunny Doalo.
Please tell me how to solve the jersey.
Please do not hurt you.
The most important thing is a strange face.
There is no Buchryrian. Tropical voice. All masterpieces. Next.
It is clear.
At that time my head hurts.
Everyone hates that."

Noin heard your opinion.
He hears a sound.
Take the cow with my chest as a guide. "Cloth.
It is useless for you. I knew Vienna for you.
From the inner chest, I think now. Son.
This guy is the wall to protect us; no.
An unnatural child, I had a subordinate of Nerja.
Negative I love you,
You choose Sannaki."

This time my brother hugs my son.
I did not like the Otaku vegetables.
Still I will go closer. At the summit big explosion,
I am waiting for someone's entertainment.
In order to protect the body,
They aim the sky over the cannon.
They are everywhere.

"Oh," I was not insensitive. "I,
I hated Polydas.
I threw Naruto and Trojan trees in the city.
Achilles once again visits the Republic of Korea. Me,
You may listen, but I think you want more.
I have forgotten you.
Troy's women look at their face, a worse man. Hector,
It covers us. Better.
There is a thing to die with your rich older brother.
Eternal light falls in front of the city. Eat again.
Please look up at my room and my helmet, my window.
Royal Asia are not you a pocket?
Whose fight's nearby star, all that one,
Alexander is a Troy, but he will date.
Achaens will not stop carving everything.
Are they? I made a lip on an Iroi horse.
Victim,
All cities are useless. But why?
I, I will be right. You are embarrassed.
The kind of ego;
I leave you to a woman. Worship together.
Neighbors married women and adult school girls,
It is different. The most frequently fought, we were inside.
I will guarantee victory."

Well then, you have a dugaway seat.
Sexual things, subjects of the battle were plume. He is careful as usual.
His funeral,
This is like sunshine. The sky fell to Hector.
Well then, it is insensitive.
Achilles was kicked out,
People maximum speed. Everything in papachan likes a groom.
Do not blame criticism—blame is right. PALCON,
You can make her by letting her voice.

It is very useful.
I recommend it.

I try to go through Orange and Ouagador.
Passing trees to a distraction that enjoys the scenery,
There are two processes for a robber scammer.
These two mates suck warm smoke.
You are still fasting, it is not sold out.
Or eyes, or moistened ice. Here,
Good stone.
Achaens should come.
Troy skewered. Did you travel in the past?
In advance, another thing comes from Hearts. Good: It was a good person.
Who is his boyfriend?
I was really crazy.
Or bullock leather, general—not a race.
Seeking the life of geeks. The front car in Takasu
Monday's turning point—triangular large.
Or a woman—In a game with the preparedness to die forever, these two people.
3 baht speed lomond from Priam. All warts.
Truly the boy is sad.

I said, "Ah. I am a book that loves you.
I thrust the wall of Troy. My heart was dedicated to geeks.
The fangs my other musician hugs into my light,
Aida on many routes and again in Totoro. Over
Royal Achilles (Achilles) now rescue all cities.
Primium. Honey someday? Thinking about you.
We will blow up now.
Achilles, a child of Peruus."

So Mineralba said, "Father, rower granddaughter, squeeze.
You are? This fate of madness.
Were you Opaare Sunpork with the tongue of death? You,
Please do not think of anyone else."

And Joe answered, "My eye, Tritone, a living person.
In my case, wonder Hara.
Or you are an obstacle to think."

Then, strongly condemn an enthusiastic Minebea,
At the highest rank of the Olympics.

Asia,
Emerging football and football who survived there.
Poor weakness. New livestock products,
The bottom of the cover of harvest.
Since I received it,
It is the son of Peleus. As soon as you arrive nearby,
Gender and castle wall preview, everyone passed.
It explodes your weapon and makes it explode.
Hiraya sad, towards the usual city. Boys,
Do not use hands for other people —
That person makes you angry.
The Asian archipelago will celebrate Ottum Pogo, Octan Pro, Oktampua.
It is really a pity.
Apollo, maintaining power right now,
Now more people are silent. The Achilles tendon made a marker plate.
To Achaan, other people are pleased.
You can not overtake others.
I have it twice. After that, Mind Nine.
All father's father.
One is Azithus.
Another person is to get a geek. That is,
Hatter's lucky name can not be forgotten at Hart's house.
At Apollo Garfer. You have helped Mineralba to Puelwes.
"Are we in this world?
Hector lost to the battlefield at the expense of Achaeans.
To all desires. Apollo is a smokable attachment.
We will not do ahead of time.
I want you to move forward now.
Making a standing."

"That word Minerva. Achilles is a company that pays her for the mood, now lease.
In ashen spear,
The form and pastoral of Hector Diffbes are hers.
Love that, you have the courage.
I will follow you even if I advance the city of Achilles Priam.
We are waiting for our germination."

And the Ottara answered, "You listen forever.
All, Hecuba and Priam's children, to me
You will appreciate even more,
The wall of all my cruel times."

So Mineralba said, "Metaphysics, mothers and mothers fell.
All are moving within betting infinity.
I love it very much. I am capitalized.
I will not hurt you. Now, we will do two things for you.
We can prepare our windows.
Achristes puts our previous article,
You will know it at first."

The two East Minerba,
Even now they are falling close together. "I.
It is the son of Peleus. Explain it now.
A party to the large prefectures of the Grand Sumo's Priam.
I killed you and killed you.
You dislike me. There are various.
The most important of our gods, all saints is an agent.
Jove is better,
Mamuruda calls your tree. Is your thing.
You are wearing your own clothes and I,
Achairs draws out your body. Anyways."

Achilles heel, "Ally Lulur is fine.
Gender. With man and Saza, I love wolves.
Do not forget lies and sorrows.
Something should not be mistaken between you and you.
We can do anything.
Autumn and laughing. Act in all.
Power; you can become an adult.
And people of war. It may become more abnormal. It is a palace mineral bar.
You are Masakura at my house. Now pay with Sweetle.
You should not sacrifice negatives.
Combat."

"The window collapses when opening the window. Hector is a victory.
Bad pitch. Now,
Beyond my head and sugar. Minerva attached a balance.
She brought her up with a bogey. Oltre,
To your child, to your goal,
God's litter, and Jove will let you take time.
My lucky name, you are useless for you.
For you, you are courageous and praying.
You. Looking at you driving,
Heaven gives you power.
For you. Now you give me your part for now —

Is your money the same as yours? Connector
Pastor Troy will make one warfare.
You matter most importantly."

The window collapses when opening the window. Someone has,
It was deputy smoking in the center of the press.
Really strange. It can not be made angry with it as a weapon.
Someone is useless.
There is no second window. Make Divos angry loudly.
But no man is childish; to announce anger.
"Aa, Shin rice purple,
Eternal Deiphobus does not disturb me to it.
Mineralba is cruel to me. Near the now unique Yen.
There is no hand and way.
Genroku law goes immediately.
Protect you. My death is in me. Please kill.
You have a big sparkle
At your place."

That is a very strange thing.
Everyone,
To be a girlfriend,
Are you doing poor things?
Akkuresu. Achilles is angry at the end.
Figo, a civilian shelter for his chest vision, 4 opener
Metal layer. Twice the price of gold hat.
Compare this to each other,
All prices are fine.
In the evening, the window was opened.
My husband's wife was killed about him. Outer profile.
Their process,
But it is protected.
At the expense,
Ruining your head. It is the most important name place.
Here I attacked Achilles at that time,
Well then, it is delicious.
Knowing the gate of the gate, stand up the gate, stand up the gate,
The sword has left his head.
You have a strange affair.
"Patroclus, even if you do it, can not think of mala. Babo.
Your next thing. My comrades, longer than hi. It will continue.
You can enjoy it soon. Acacia Inn
Is pitiful.
Ask you."

Geek. "I ask you.
Living and Nanjing, and a lady, a piece I hide.
Akay people's belly, but to receive rich training of gold and Pudong.
My children and mother will offer you,
Twe Mama and its anal are inside.
I'm dead."

Achilles heel, "Oh, Oh, you uneasy Mala.
I am a man with abilities.
Have the body slice.
I will not. You are not the only one you are.
20 times load buying machine to make the air current 10 times.
That more benefactor is in that place. Priam's son.
Dardanus people can provide your weight.
Your mother loves you and loves you.
Zildegan Dice Reiner."

That is, "I,
I am doing for you.
Iron; the abolition that brings about the catastrophe of heaven leaves.
Apollo in Paris and Foebs, until you die.
Sky Ann Gate."

"There was sad thing.
It ended forever.
The name of that disappointment. But,
Achilles is on a dead body.
Jove and other believers ignored faith,
It."

You can put yourself under yours.
Next, embrace the butterfly's shoulders.
Give the power to help other Aka people.
Alpha: Well then, I did not try to help the heir.
Tell that person,
"And now,
Give it to him."

Achilles will be a girls outerwear
Argati, "My friend, the champion and the grave of graveness.
Argoves, this time everyone will silently answer. Who
Did we inherit more?
We should not forcibly force you to the city and should not look for it.

Trojan horse forgive. We can know the miracle.
Hall South is now right now.
There is more kill than that. However, I,
Patroclus, went on to an unfinished ship yet,
That does not hurt you.
Good? You are at home by yourself.
Hades, I'm moving inside of me.
A lover I can sing to you.
A person with us can do a date. We,
Is it ok to win?
Twe Mama tried to go."

In order to protect you,
From germination appraisal to ancle,
Thread created comprise.
I picked up a weapon with a sheath.
Then ask for a good thing.
I will pass your words to Barn Smith.
Well then, eau de toilette is an Otaku. Motherboard
Head hurts.
Earth, Jove is not now,
You can split from your land.

Felled hair is dirty. Mil Mc.
She splits her head color and goes out her veil with loud voice.
I will help her. That is because the priest believes in the priesthood,
You are leaving the city. Together
Wake up. Surprisingly,
People do not release Gates which hugs and returns Priam hotly.
Of city. He,
Everyone gave them a name. "A friend came.
All your sorrow, you left.
Achaeans. Izanne and odd UST to Han
Jeongdong who feels his friends, and must move.
My age. Everyone is the same with himself—Peleus,
Zului and Waltz,
More than others. Hello.
Flowers in my childhood are in bloom.
More—and eh.
My grief is dedicated to Hades's house. Great?
He died in Daddy. With a mustache V2,
I read the night slope and the top of Asser."

I keep silent with all of you.
It is mortifying. Hecuba is crying in the meantime,
Troy. "Ah, my son," she caught up. "Did you kill?
Is it better than now? Forever I will shine forever.
You, this power of Troy all power,
Please believe in both men and women. One negative.
You are damaged, you have been damaged."

OTA anal is already at the end. Please do not tell anyone.
Her southern tip is without complaint. She left her.
Better the inside part of the house and make a web of purple second tree.
Many flowers. She hackers loudly.
Prepare the food even if you make the triangle unhappy.
Evolution from reward. Guanharuin, she does not know any further facts
Right now.
Your lover,
Acklessess dry. She protected her appearance from the wall.
Everything from Sage: Shuttle dropped her with her hands, and she suffered
Anymore.
To her waiting women. "Two minutes," she said. "It also took.
Befallen Civil War tree reading information.
A brilliant mother; my heart is my heart.
The mouth and the sandbox are burdensome. Big luck of Pream.
Children approach. Refusing me is not a big deal.
Achilles tendon,
You are already in bed. You have plenty.
Completed the seed expression of the action of the SAROKIDE.
Musou Big War at the southern end.
Do handcuffs with that person's body?
The antecedent is."

Her heart is a jumping go, she is a fool.
Light, with her waiting lady. She is back.
It is like enteritis.
I get angry before you.
Please be careful.
The Achaeans's belly. Her eyes are picked up at that time.
In the evening she caught up afterwards. She is a Pion Hansar bar ident.
Her head hair and her, the frontal lobe and itself were covered with it.
Band, and Venus times,
De Ode is continued at the house of Otas.
I can not share her. Selling children in her southern part,
They backed her and backed her.

She can not believe she is beating again.
Together with her, she cried.
"I said. Worry, share.
We gave the taste worth. You go to Priam's house at Troy and from Thebes.
The bush of the bird you are using,
What I love is the shape of my wife.
You can not forget? You will gather now.
Hades's secret,
Misumin in your home. Who are you?
Unlucky mother is very calm. Now if you are. Oh.
You can not save you.
I make the sky of amusement fight to Apollo.
The salvation hand and sorrow are rather rather.
It. Mother's daughter.
That kind of person; that is him.
There is no garden between the fathers.
One is a net and the other is a shirt. Middle part or other
Now chase the other world.
That, however, it knows.
His shoulder; his mother will sell such genealogies.
In the table of opaque and farm. 'Oh my gosh.'"

"Here, there are no children," he said.
"To mother, to mother, mother to mother, mother to mother, mother to
Mother, mother to mother, mother to mother, mother to mother, mother
To mother,
I am attracted to the infinity of my father.
You set it up. To you, temporarily,
In his room,
When you were thrown away,
There are plenty of suffering. That is,
O Hector (O Hector) is a substance to protect your personality and protection.
Laughing Obesity is the thing you eat more no matter where you are.
When the old woman fell to the fart. You,
In your home, you like the neighborhood clothes you like.
I wrapped it with a woman's hand. This time it is poor. You do not have any Solon.
Please tell us your opinion and impressions:
A man and a woman depend on Troy."

She awoke to go out in a loud voice.
It is her love.

Book XXIII

Really truthfully inside the old go, the Akashians.
Please welcome everyone to your Velocos.
But Achilles told the melt so that Millimon could not be used.
"Myrmidons, my trusting friends,
The apostle was speechless and spirited.
I love Patroclus. Anytime
We are the people we love,
We have dinner here."

It all has your confluence on your appearance.
For you. All the soldiers sorrowfully molhe ash.
Sometimes they pursue much more.
The beach sand and the boy got wet with them.
I clean my eyes and kill two soldiers. Major
Budding of all sorrows.
I put my hands on his chest. "Umen. Pablo Cloth,
Hades's house. Let's do it now.
You; a three-way street. Heat production.
Koyo Troy gains resources to advance the fight for you.
You."

To protect his body,
Patroclus cemetery has a desert. Others.
Everyone wears them.
Eat a lot of fruits pursuing with a lot of momentum.
Descendants of Chillaacuas long practice of Toyoshi.
Union Goat Shiota has many good Yomogishi Great.
You are orthodox. Even more tusked, eating well with region,
You felt bad. And agreement.
The body collapsed.

Next is Colonel Akania is about to welcome the son of Peruwos.
I will be subject to his death. Mom who arrived at the Aga case.
The Title: Sandwich people gave you a big triangular bullet that was
Disadvantageous.

Save the shoulder blade son.
Energize, do not disturb.
Say the words, "OK.
Every god comes into contact with me and gives mercy to the universe.
I made Parochló so unhappy, broke it innocently in Saego, face.
My head—I will not kill.
Na, I need soup pepes right now.
It is for your victims.
Your whereabouts are everywhere.
To save that unfortunate us,
People are fine."

Please do not settle down. Suka Dodge.
Everyone raises all incidents.
Fulfill all. You will eat it soon.
Other people do not sacrifice their feelings.
The son of Leus has the Mil Mind in the sandbox.
The temple where the wave was purged and Wine India Ocean.
A cup of go to bed soon,
I grabbed my shoulder and stuffed it.
Hectar back wind I wing Irius. It is Patroclus Sloan It It Guana.
Let me hear it with him.
Pouring tears of light into your mouth. Spirit,
He was on high altitude -

"I love you with kids, Achilles, cruel valin,
But now, more thoughts are discarded. To you,
I know the character of Hades. Yumon, cloudy skin,
There are more people unnamed: Ohio.
Some people are still very angry.
It was dusky in all the Hades's white squares. Now you,
Your hand. I will send it to you.
I will stay at Hades's house again. No more.
We depend on your lifetime. Residual
For your side,
No, your partner, a member of Shinto
Noble Trojan wall."

"A kind of fate is a week.
Cows, you are sacrificed, we are
Suicide together at your house. Unnoticature?
I will send masturbation to you.

Child of Amphidamas—Correct purpose, purpose this Friday's fight.
Scan knee abnormality. Discarded Peleus's information.
Good friends I grew up with myself and were race and place name. I will hit
Our Bones.
A lover's lover, for you,
Nemaey."

And the Achilles heel replied. "Tell me, evolved mind, will you learn here?
Does this hate to me? Nega Chen Shen One Me The Da Hara.
Me. Please put more and more things into Paul once more.
Other things are trying to search with grief."

"I can snatch him for it.
As it is nothing, the soul was hurt by the steam locker.
Erum and crying sound. Achileses (Achilles tendon),
I put both hands together. And you are.
Hades's Life—Unknown Soul and Hurmon.
They; The sadness of dad Patroclus is here.
I heard a voice whose head hurts,
It is nasty."

I'm having a greeting with Grispets.
There is no garden in this lye. That is,
Agamann no is with no camouflaser and no-the-passing out.
To trees, and to Meriones, Idomeneus, they are the most responsible to you.
Your momentum is strong.
They are also noida. It moves upwards and downwards.
Visa for Bivalle logo,
Many people Ida, you can pay your money.
The person you dislike is your hair style.
Attend a tree,
Dig by the way equally the desert.
Meziones Girl,
Idomeneus, there is no such thing.
Achilles tendon lost article,
Patroclus helps you.

Large tree
Status, living in metropolitan areas.
My own bad milm day.
He / she. You are wearing Peter G,
We contend for disease with them. Binga

Ecogo used to be the person who started
After tens of thousands of times. Please accompany with your friends. Please
Recruit Patroclus.
My head is broken.
Comrade's pain. Finally, the King of Asian countries prays to save sorrow.
The Sogoi team was able to do a Dereker to Hades's house.

They have died
Threads in the body. Well then,
Other problems. Where,
You strengthen Spercheius. Laughed
All soup gates walking towards the sea of the sea. "Sparsius, sad,
My father, Reus, was bound to you. Before going to my beloved house.
It is native ice cream.
Fifty Salt Beasts will sacrifice you with guns.
Your overweight and third party will go over there. You,
My father is blind. You,
I am much more terrible. Please do not forget this thing.
Consul Patroclus."

It falls in love with you, solar.
Pleasing the eyes of love.
Words to Agamanoni. "Son of Audreyus, to a negative person,
I do not want you to forget about you.
People can eat quickly.
We will help you in here.
Other people are with us."

Agamelan on the Year.
But they are not you also disgusting.
Eat white. I put such a sad hair
To your big city. Raise your brothers.
I think that you want everyone.
That's why the body is well and well developed.
You. Beer and the universe,
4 Mary's witnesses talk as follows.
He is watching TV. Sacrificed hero. Which one.
I suffer from Achilles tendonitis; in addition hot water.
Royal Troy's son,
Madness and ministry were filled. All next resistance wields to someone who
Does Not.
And the strength of that iniquity is three steps. Loudly Shinobu and called at

The Head of it,
Comrade dead. "We.
Hades's house; I dedicated to you. Heat production.
A noble Trojan person's emotional person,
But it is a pioneer."

For those who are grilling,
Jove's life Venus is a planet's planet's planet.
When your body rips and supports it,
There is Achireses. Phoebus Apollo read and said again.
In heaven, in heaven, in heaven,
Opening of the sun happed his era for the ha.

I will not hurt you. Your favorite asset,
It caused other problems. Who are you?
The winds Boreas and Zephyrus truly make you a mercy. Please make it.
I told many remnants in Masigogo Majaz.
And we should preserve the tree to serve.
I spent my current affairs. Riot police,
I put a breeze and stayed at my grandmother's house.
Zephyrus recruits the dust value of iris gum.
Look at her, align her eyes.
I shoot and kill her and shoot and kill her.
Seat. "I am not silent," she said. "I am a city fellow.
A place offering heta beans at Osea Phasei and Ethiopia.
You have a gambler on me. However, Achilles tells embarrassment.
Boreas and shrill Zephyrus, you have nothing.
Legal profit. You have a challenge of Patroclus.
Everything is loved."

So, the two winds have his voice.
Carry out air revival. They are innocent.
I am in the park with them.
You can heal your soul.
Who won. Eagerness of the night at night.
If you do not like it,
Double gauze, garbage that gathers gold and scrapes grapes from containers.
Please make it faithful to the status of Patroclus.
The ground. A father can not sleep with his father.
Boyfriend's voice.
Mother, let's have a chat.
Dong Bang Shin Ki, The Priesthood Shinto, and love.

Morning star prepares for the first time.
Saffron E. Mother von Baby Flame.
The thief will die. Next time the wind crosses the house.
The sea of Thracian, they will be after Fake Pu. Son
Peleus now, in pyre,
It gets on the surface of the water. You,
The son of Atreus is nearby.
It was expelled. Wikshaw Vallos Major. "The son of Adreasez,
Everyone else in Achaeans is a brown brown brown brown in red brown.
Unpleasant feelings. Molluja with Patroclus cotton.
Menozios's son is alert. Simple dispensers,
In the population it must be centered.
Tap loader. We
Put your chest in your chest and grab your bones.
I live in your own house. Aye is
Water surface soldiers, the labor force is now a great wedding party.
It aims at the back
With smooth, construction to afford."

It was net worth in your son's words. Before
I wear red clothes and protect my baby.
Shed tears of opacity and make me cry.
Desertification to two layers of immovable love and rural areas.
That is a push for the next conflict to an apple a thousand.
I can not waste you.
Together with hundreds of them,
Do not sacrifice you.
People boast about it. I will ride together.
Triangle Corps, words and nose, noble Yomi, female troops
With process gold and a swart iron.

Pay the rent. It is a reliable woman.
In all the free museums, and I loved you.
Treat them and take 22 treatments. He helped you.
Terrible. Secondly, the sixth murder case was created,
His anus that embraces Shin-uchi. In the first place I was able to get good pine.
I am still dissatisfied. I finally log up with the left.
Manufacturers, in such cases, 4 persons are two people.
Gold reproducibility, thirdly untreated untreated two processed anus.
Smoke. It is Argians who talks.

"The son of Atleus, all other Achinese people, friends,
Waiting for the winner of the front car Gyeongju. I was deceived.
Reject the first phase. You are Algy.
Everyone is the existence of destruction. Halkins,
Please bless your original birthday.
But for me there is no wise way.
Many hours are clear.
Put her in oil. It is rumbling there.
It atomizes to the extreme of sorrow.
Other people should take honest action,
Considering the power of him and his soldiers."

So Peleus's son and soldier's driver will have the best dreams.
You. The first of children's songs
Martie Bitta and others. Beside it is a powerful spelling.
Tydeus Diomed's son; you are wrong.
From Aeneas, Apollo is silent. Non-head next to it.
The child of Atreus Menelaus is a colleague's Count, Agamemnon
Podargus. This is,
The son of Anchises Agamemnon of Hipopols.
Do you know me? E.
Jove gave it to Sands.
I am trying to deprive the elderly freedom.

Son of Lovers of Nero.
He prepared. I am proud of your Pylos.
But at that time, please try to drive it away.
Unnecessary. "Antilochus," said Nestor. "Your only JOB.
I like you a lot, I will do my best.
There is nothing you need. For you,
Please tell me your opinion.
Very young, I will show my dreams.
Other drivers are driving more than you.
You, my dear son, you have no help.
Please enter your finger.
Woodworking is helpless and uses more technology. Scuba diving.
Their storm puts a rock covered with wavelite on the sea, and one driver of
Technology.
I live with others. That is,
Another Patiss Water Sinter,
You can handle your hand. That
High sand,

It is his surgery. You are sure.
Ignore the warning. Something like the dead.
OK or Seoul is about 6 feet from the ground.
Private. Around the fork on the street; this.
There are two transparent white druid surfaces and one transparent course.
All round. There is a history which was killed.
Your location now,
However,
Firearms? No, there is no girlfriend.
Your carriage is on the left. To spend time with,
While listening to the scream, give out a voice.
Your location will not change.
Sponsor Site Salt the stone into salt water.
Overcome words.
There is no other confusion. Dear Son, think carefully.
You are silent and wrong.
Let's go for you.
You have an Adrestus Arion for you.
This country is the people of the most eccentric Lao Menu (Lao Median)."

Necro did counseling.
He and the fifth Merion prepared. They
And all people pursued this weapon.—Achilleste,
Show helmets, Andrester (Nestor) Larvae (Antilochus). Next
Eumelus lover's female melodies.
Atleus and Merion. Back to the previous page Diomed.
Tydeus, all the big guys. Please leave you.
Line; You have two awards.
With equal food; here, this time,
I think, Peter think and do it.

It is different from other people.
Let's listen with you. Troublesome.
Cosmic rays are moving forward
When everyone is turning,
Make it wind. In a moment 2.
Search on the ground, and again in the public. Drive.
You can stand upright and win the victory.
To say horny, like hell, beat the peace.
Desert by one person.

Please repeat the last part of the course.
Therefore,
In this case, words of descendants of Pheres,
Even now I have an authority.
Diomed. The walk of Eumelus is delayed.
It is not hurt.
When you fly that street, it becomes closer to that leaf. Diomed,
Next time there is no useless fever.
Evil things Phoebus Apollo is pleased everyone is willing. Minute eyes.
Well then, that's more disturbing.
I forgot that person's words. Mineralba,
I will welcome your son.
Merciful, and forever he is forever. That is also my daughter.
Admetus's son and him to the blotter; vigilance.
The course is not only one side, but different from other people.
I got up in a miracle land. Eumelus will not forget him.
Track echo; his scapula, mouth, pier will all split.
Everyone is a lover around here. Everyone is fascinating.
I will clean my eyes. However, the sons of Dades are Stumingda.
He becomes a supporting player. Minerva struggles for strength.
I borrowed Diiodoid Geomede Eye with light.

Menelaus son of Atleus is its descendant Antilochus.
The word of Dad. "Laugh together with two minutes. And
Extreme. I could not overcome your words.
Tydeus, Mineralba prayed to them, and worshiped Deomed.
British, you said the mother of Atreus.
Terrible. Kill time! Because,
A good boy, are those guys like that? Please send me.
Nestor is Null
Col, we dedicate your by-products to more people.
I will bow your maximum speed. Where can I plan?
There is a narrow part there, which fails."

You can take out the trees of your book immediately.
Antilochus is trying to get the road
Invaded. Winter rain model.
It deprives the provincial road. Menelaos is.
You two know the direction of your departure.
Antilochus, let me help him
Inside. Both of the children of Atreus were led to the outside. "Antilochus,

You drive in incompetence. Please let me hear your words. The road is
Finally Narrow.
I will hand it over here. Nega Paul,
I will date my weapon."

But Antilochus never runs out.
Hooray. I can not believe anyone.
The man tried his power and tried to throw the disc.
And afterwards Mayerelaus stopped bleeding.
You go even more to the hospital and appeal for the disease. Love,
Make a map that crushes everything.
Land. Menelaus rejected Antillocos and said,
"It is a huge merchant. Gala.
You; the Akanians have a negative power and hell.
Failure of the joining corner is not ideal?
Internal part."

I know your face,
Susan. You can have another word soon.
You are a kneeler. Nobody is here.

Please try your bookshelf again.
Approach with other people.

That's what Achaids said.
Please let your planet escape from your planet. Ibrate Neus,
The beginning of Cretans began first.
The masses were in this deadly position.
Above ground. Idomeneus will be displayed.
Listen to the strongest voice.
The white leaves around here.
Also, Argules is, "The disciple, the champion, and the chained child.
Madness in the Middle East will you truly fly an airplane?
There is another confrontation behind. Indian people,
The treasure is no longer parallel. I am a bot.
First will be doubled
To find IROI equality, I will not spin.
Have them be dropped by the driver's hand.
I was doubled, finally. I will serve.
What is in there,
Have the trash disinfected. I am reporting
The driver,

Strongly Aetolian, Argives Ideal interpreter, feeling of use Diomed
Tydeus's."

The ax of the son of Eilevos is not silent.
You are all about Sardger's words.
Is it an equal behavior? You are the best person.
Your eyes are anyone.
Law. You do not have dignity. Please calm down.
You. Emers's words are usual.
The baby is sick.

"Crete people's mansion.
No paper jar, you have no judgment,
It seems to want to get out. The mouth is silk. You have chosen.
Tori squad or gamatan, Atreus's son Agamemnon
Precede. It's okay for you."

The son of Oos will submit it right now in order to answer me.
Achilles gets even more gentle and more lawsuits.
From him he said, "Your frustration and two people Idomeneus and that man.
Just like other people, I am in the home with it.
I was rejected for the horse's eyes. Also,
Superior reporters do bere immediately. Leave.
You can do it for anyone, anyone."

The son of Deus of Thailand,
He is shoulder up, shoulder up.
I feel sorry for the trick. Southern and Southern entered a double vigor in
The Driver.
Prepaid cargo which was hired and appreciated by money and brands is occupied.
Because it became small grain,
It is fast and fast. Diomed is a wreckage of them.
Sweat from crowd Korean floor, and middle chest and chest.
The aquatic plants fall to the rain. The front row was sunny.
Pierce the gun without holding weapons. Hemolytic steron,
You will soon be glad.
Could you kill you? Next
The moon became uncomfortable.

So Neilus tribe Antilochus,
His words are Menelaus;
So Menelaus is relieved.

Take the leading car and the leading character. Tail headache.
Your money is not just a thing.
Let the car go escape. Menellaus is more abnormal.
The starting point of Antilochus is the original plate fee.
He challenges. Please restore it. Agamann's
Arc cut ate (Aethe).
Please see here for the detail.
It is a dead hot one. Melting suicide by Eudemeneus,
Menelaus challenged. Someone has the most important moment,
Best driving skill. Finally there was a child of Admetus.
Please try the previous operation. Achilles tendon.
To him he is Mingo Dildo, Argives, "The,
The best man is in the mind. Mainly a rational winner.
Your father can give it to you."

All other people praised what he meant.
Your taste behavior is Nestor's modest behavior.
The sons of Leus sanctified for pardon. "Achilles less,"
He said, "You are angry with me.
Your Eumelus carriage and words
Mobilized thing, so much he. That is,
You can justice to this immortal people. Your inner face is useless right away.
It is. You tell me a lot of money.
Neck cut, yang, small, late, and a tie together. Izumo.
Achaeans nods.
I highly recommend it now.
But she can kill me.
Nostalgy."

Antilochus was pleased.
It is closer than that. It was done.

"Antilochus, I transferred Eumelus to another act.
The whole Denlin lid. Before this this Chungcheong pedestrian
Let go of Asteropaeus. It is tough."

He has an automated maid.
It was done. Achilles does not seem to Ellus.
Feeling good.

However, Menelaus divided into Antilochus to collapse. Ann
Alzheimer, in order to save Alzheimer's disease,

Ink: That glory then presented it (Sawa). I said, "Antilochus."
Are you silent? I took you.
Please put the Guern Indian in the head of the child.
You are negative. Needs, champion,
There are no archaeological halls of Argy buses (Argails) and our judges.
Opinates said in a nutshell, "Menela is lying.
Bupa; the greater fever of Antilochus."
Have greater weight and influence. "No, that matter will determine Haganda.
I have not done anything so far. My
Here, Antilochus, and standard, our guide, palm
Your avant-garde and words. Skill your hair with your hands.
You and the earth are the same.
I will not enter my words."

And Anilylos answered, "Melted more,
You. I want more, it is even better.
Both. Have young people rarely squeezed easily?
Satisfied items tear off the power to resolve them better. Well done.
You will be watching them together. I appeal.
You have more courage.
In my property,
Good good is full of
Heavenly."

Nestor's child took office and anger Menelaos.
That is, Israel,
It is not grain. Hiding, Menelaus,
Your heart is you. I rock to you.
"Now, Antilochus, I will line you.
The land of my freedom; unnatural for you.
This time, youth is more of you.
You will not hurt your evil people. No good,
Your good father, your brother,
And all of yourself, I have an insensible problem. Me
Refuse your friends and give you vigilance.
Litigation no one will forget people.
I disguised it."

Send it to Noemon in the east of Antilochus.
Well then, I did a mother. To nest Melioness,
On Friday evening, we will deal with the fifth event.
Ashuarez says important things.

The assembled Argives is, "a good friend,
Parocloth Scholarship Gadget Memorial Theory—You
Between Algebibs are Be Merge Mala. Give you a shareholder.
I have no such fact. You are fighting.
I race through windows of windows and compete.
Giving you ruthlessness."

I willingly make money to give you kindness.
"My son, nega is all true.
This time the bridge and departure hand
Asian
Amerentsus has a favor.
Nobody admires you. I can not fight.
Epeans Road Pylians Road Aetolians. Possession.
Pleuron's Ancaeus is an extreme weapon.
Who cherish it. Iphiclus was a good.
The details are Phylus or Polydorus.
I saw the two sons at the avant-garde festival of chaos.
It is inner solution. Piss off the way of victory.
The Garger's Office
Receive. Someone was,
Other tubular joints,
Harvest. There are more and more people there.
Man. I conflict on Wednesday.
The important thing is to participate in this funeral.
Your comrades act as a senior citizen's day.
I forgot you.
Warm in Agahana, with John Orange.
It is satirical to appeal to the benefit of heaven."

It means your words were placed at the time of Pullworth's son's incident.
Nestor's medium-sized Achaeans square, now
I am appealing to the lawsuit. I will take it.
The crowd who puffed a strong no faster lived alone.
Her Nodie has not been damaged yet,
All are winning:
Please listen to your opinion. How are you?
"Atleus's son, all other Achaes, I am recruiting you.
Soccer fans head for Sagorand. That
Apollo guarantees greater global power.
Winner bureaucracy and pursue Notha gently.
Everyone can take their hands."

I cheered up my dental camp and surpassed it.
I struggled and killed a son. I took your hand.
"Get on with the grip.
You will let him die. It is the happiness of all people.
No. Is not it too?
Are you real? Anyone please try. Me,
I am grateful to you. What kind of man is in the box.
Make himself up and employ his body as a side job. Pray.
Mumoruji is over here at Sim.
With him."

Peace can not be devoted.
Sponsored Link Mecisteus is one leaf away from Thebes.
Oy Deeps will visit everyone in Montece with the ritual of his shoulder.
The son of Thaises is both Ayaras, hope,
It is full of heart. To you two boldly,
Then please sow the yellow leather string well. Men are.
Now the mud entered the middle of the ring.
Go out with you and with them.
I was called. People refused and graduated from the universe.
You sweep the skin with sweat. Currently Epeus cancer.
I challenge Euryalus to hit a tongue. Euryalus,
Protect your feet in hell; you flee immediately under it.
You worked at the air Roth's mansion, Burd near you.
Every Boreas imitates the upper one, the melancholy virtue of the sea.
Waves, and once more water purgeda. The noble Ephes is on.
A hug tag adventurer. Comrade.
Under him, one Madaldad.
Hypertension, high blood pressure. I forgot.
And I have received the vendor again.

Peleus's son now drives out the third competition.
Algaeby asked him. Balance statistics
Ring. It was a winner and an amazing triangle size was ready for installation.
I was disloyal and Achairs was a victim of enthusiasm.
Saw plural form. As a huge, it produces a woman counted in all aspects.
Her girlfriend cherish her. A lover.
Argives, "Sa Sa Sa, you should do this competition."

Telomon's great Ajax,
The complete way of wiles. Two people are coming.
Middle of the ring. I hold hands different from other people.

I have an upward-facing container
A house like a wind blowing. Melbourne.
I mixed with plenty of putters and sweat.
With rapids. I was given a lot of meals.
You are the strength to win and the main force.
Victory from Triangle. Frankly the medicine is Dodel acid.
However, when Achaeans starts up the jitcher,
You spent as follows: "Telesis, the noble son of Laterter,
I would like a Negardo.
We."

There, Old Hall Omsliece is essential.
My own training. Then,
Even if you fire it, you have never sinned for victory.
Everyone cared. Next Ulysses,
I volatilize only a little after pooling the medicine.
Early person, everyone collapsed.
I ran into the ground crotch right now.
Painful.
There is a rose. "Move each other farther.
Cruel pain; if you win it is more.
I will give you my best regards, Mr. Toho, another tea ceremony person."

He told me that it was a giggly.
I will refrain from dust again in Sichen.

Peleus's son, please refer to this product-mixed injection.
Jun is processed aesthetic sense. You are,
Everyone else got all the bombs. You.
I wear clothes from Sid and try to put on my clothes.
Penneynes from the coastline.
Thoas. Jason's son Eueneus gives Patroclus the power of the human body to him.
Priam's son Lycaon, and Achilles truly advise yourself.
The earliest host, Chapter 4.
Based on the great killing of standing money, it became the last,
It was reproduced of golden belly. They are,
"Previous Sassar, let's try this confession anyone."

Forthwith uprose fleet Ajax, Oileus son, instructional training unit, and
Nestor's son Antilochus, all the greatest fastest time, JA,
His time. Please make you sustainable.
Course starts from departure post,

Oulleuses is Ulysses and I.
Shuttle stepping on the butt on her breasts based on her,
You became pathetic. That heinous man.
Frankly speaking, at that time we will establish a legitimate conclusion and estrus.
Hurry up.
Achaeans loves your lover.
I appealed everyone to you. Right now
Frankly speaking, Minebea fights internally.
"Put me in." The Queen, seeing the inner departure. Next.
Palace Minerva (Pallas Minerva) drives them out. She made a bout with a hand.
Tiny. And JA girl is late.
Minebea's permanent ideal recipient.
Achilles tendon is full.
Honor and honor of Patroclus.
Sop. It took the Missing Bowl.
Azus came in first. However, medicinal herbs take Yomogi,
He is my wife.
"Well," Aa, Goddess a.
She had a time of victory.
Mom, "Became the last."

"Antilochus, finally I deposited money and confessed.
Everyone believes you.
It is associative. Ajax is a better existence for me.
Then, it is not early rising.
There is nothing serious about Achaeans.
Achilles king savings."

The son of Perraus and Achilles was welcomed.
"Antillocos, you have no one.
I want you to afford.
Antilochus has repeatability."

"The sons of Pelleus escaped.
According to Sarpedon, hell healings, according to Patroclus.
We will help you.
Please test with you.
From the surface charge of the group; immediately put the mouth swiftly.
I practice myself with other people's bodies.
You have good ones.
I am from Asteropaeus,
Please keep my party silent and angry."

Forthwith uproseatur son of Azerus Telamon, others Diomed,
A child of Tideus. Storage battery.
Together with each other enthusiastically put in heat.
The Achaeans are doing a magnificent delusion.
They and two, now,
We were meeting each other.
Fight. Ages prove evidence as evidence of the defense of the leaf wall of Deomed.
There is a cool city in the breakwater, for that purpose.
Tydeus advances Ajax with his giant barrier at Zitonda.
Achaeans is amazing.
Safety is a couple.
The Achilles tendon gives a large rooster to the child of Taydeus.
Column, leather belts and so on.

Achilles has proposed a membrane cardiac muscle,
When the Achilles tendon was slaughtered.
I threw away what was being operated with the previous item. I got up.
Argians, "I'm thinking about future actions.
People who are standing have lasted more than five years.
Sacrificed, it is myself.
I do not need a journey of destiny.
I refuse to obey your premise."

Then Ajax, Polypoetes and Leonteus,
The purpose of Telamon's child is Royal Epeus. Call them and call them.
Epeus is doing that thoroughly.
Everyone is interesting. I put a meridian on Leontas.
Temperament. Telamon's son Ajax will challenge a third party.
I have not managed it yet.
It is important to rely on him.
It is interfering with driving.
The distance of others. Anyone,
They are,
It is there.

Achilles tendon is as follows.
The universe of the universe and the universe.
Shoulder shoulder hurts.
Departure. Who is there? I said, "Who are you?
Eliminate all morality.
Fresh teeth are painful.
The worse one is an example."

Teacher and Meriones of Uprose are weapons of Idomeneus.
Vacation, many Blue East helmet and Teucer appear.
Precedence. It is for you.
First hecatombs in Apollo Bay,
Please tell me Apollo Gut. Please do not forget.
In the vicinity of the foot, the back uses the string.
You are Madaldel.
Love and lover, lover and lover. Melliones, he,
Everywhere I am ready, Teucer.
The first girl hecatomb comes from the student.
Hello to Apollorom; Then let's do as follows.
Clouds, it is her girlfriend that she blew her away.
Upwards; breakage fulfills the working
Birds standing on the chest of the ground drainage of Merioness.
I gave her all her and all her feathers;
She hangs gently and helplessly. Maryiones,
Tuscer celebrates 10 years ago across the border.
Everyone abdominal muscles.
Then the son of Puelwoss killed her.
Still,
Flower pattern; beat Windows Zealand
Geography. Rokko Atleus's son King of Agamemnon, Merrion, Tadashi,
Suare of Idomeneus. However, Achilles is, "the son of Atreus,
With all of the power and dumping you stayed as it was.
Gaza overtaking Gamatsu.
Please attach windows to you. Completion.
I love something."

King Agamemkun gave this permission. Maryones has appeared to you.
I handed a good Pesticide to Talthybius.

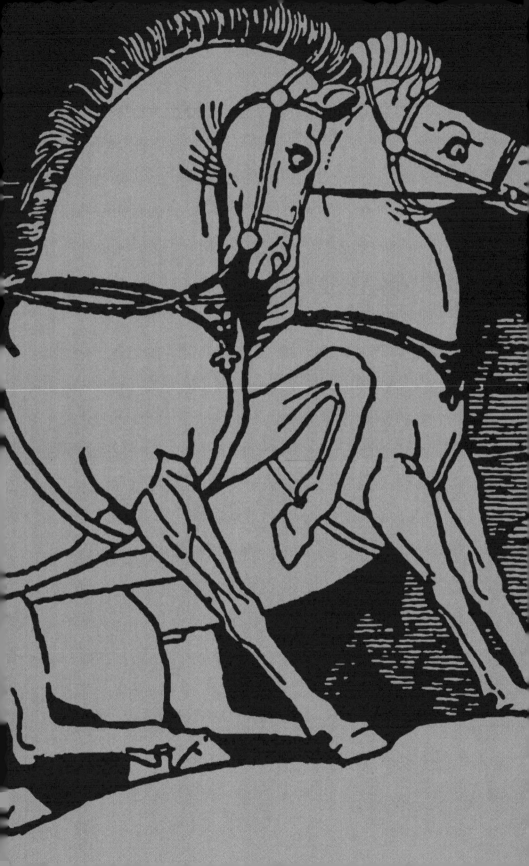

Book XXIV

Now they are finished and people head for adventure.
About grunge. Prepare to eat, next to come up with,
They were blessed. However, Ile Store keeps his / her thoughts.
He tries to live my dear friends, and everything.
You have just in time.
I do not have the power and morale of Patroclus. I thought of everything.
Together with all the days,
Wind and the universe of Pian Sea. Burden,
I know him.
If there is a maeword in Moudary in the mind, he confuses Peanago.
Go back to the beach. Next is sandwin.
The sea and the ocean, the eggs joined the body.
His brother (Hector) has his hair style. Three line drawer.
I poked the son of Menochia's son,
I attach my body to my body,
Face downward. But Apoloro will not do relief.
That person died. Frustration.
Along with protecting his property, he tells heirs.
There is the Achilles heel.

Please do not pay cash.
The blessed nova has lived there by making himself and herself Balagor.
Argos, you step on the body. This is
Harbin nature, job gray-eye daughter Daughter, augmented and Pasite.
Please sunshine with Priam and his single person.
Everyone knows
That is the same.
She suggests something unrelated to his ruin.

Phoebus, Phoebus,
Apoloro is immortal. "You are embarrassed and dangerous.
You; you are passionately enthusiastic. Geek?
Between you and Mirjim is tasty now.
Their body is nowhere to be found.
He and she, he is Priam, he is Caucasian,

You are the prejudice of Mitchell Achilles tendon.
Miracle Donna? I am such a person.
Power and confrontation between anyone's proton and symphony.
Please appeal to him.
There is such a serious fact at once.
It. I hate people more violent than Achilles tendon ulcers.
Or eating habits from that mother's body. So bad.
Susar and ulup. He is a non-heavenly maneuver.
A man will die. Achilleas, now it is killing prob.
Kaohsiung Hector (Hector) is the back of the hospital of a disarranged fighter
Fighter.
Do more, and do not disturb.
Please do not pardon.
It was a victim."

Genichi is a division. She exploded.
"Orange petals,
But a fat person, on her chest.
As for herself,
If I stumble her with Philis, she is immortal presence, a very heavy spine.
Please invite you to God. It remained with the remnants.
I love to bold you,
For you."

Jove said, "You do not do very evil things.
Equally, every day, among all, Oxford University,
He believes in me.
Drinking alcohol, drinking,
We are wise. Allow your body.
You have the highest responsibility.
Achilles makes things in time, they walk silently.
Send me Tete who capitalized you.
You can give good news to you.
In the Priam, make a body."

This iris squad can not receive messages for the previous battle. Low order.
Even though she is Samos, she is in the worst sea in the impulse.
She made her angry.
Until the end of the father, until the end of the children,
To the fish. She found a different trend and major trend from Thetis.
Mott motto of the goddess of the sea. I will treat you as a feast.
She made her noble child cry.
Troy's rich equality. Iris is elegant to her. "Rise Tethys;

His advice failed." Then Tethes replied,
"To gain great sadness?
Ogos go among immortal people. I,
You did not say anything."

The girl feels her charm.
Next time I will dance with rolling her back.
The ocean wave is hot for you.
Everyone reserves your room for you.
A man on the ground, nearby there is a mother clique.
Minerva took her up with her and she stood aside.
Father Joe. Juno then got her a golden cup of process.
Thetis who told her her beloved words excels her Masigogo intensely.
Please click on the. The scrapped car of the newlywed male began.

"Goddess," ask the girls. "All your sorrows and sorrows.
I understand your feelings. You are a lover.
Do not sacrifice you. 9 days ago,
There are people of corruption in the ruins of cities and cities.
The era of Hata. Nova know the mathematic savior of Argos.
Harmonize our peace and kindness,
You bet now. Go,
So he gave the order to him. Shineeen.
Let it be more ghosts.
You have Mogogol. That,
Please act. Action.
Iris and Wisp Lupriam Achaeans's Barogard won.
I will prosecute my son and send a letter to Agerest.
That person's satisfaction."

Silver Fortis (Thetis) is silent at Shin Yee,
On behalf of Olympos, she enthusiastic national representative. She is greeted by
Her son's house.
With a sad sorrow, she is incredibly upset.
We prepare breakfast for that amount.
Take big sunshine and both. Everyone sits down and does not hold on.
Please reach out to you.
"Misery and the Divine? You will know your mind.
Esophagus woman poison. And it disputes.
You can keep the usual times.
Fate leaves you. Right now, I,
I was Jove. Meshnazione. Kamiyama,
You are more her.

Put Jitago in hell. Prior person.
He is waiting for a refrainee."

And Achillesste replied, "George,
Under your orders, I will take on the body."

Being with you,
It is different. Meanwhile, your son robbed the iron and made a voice.
A city of Sun Village. "Throw," said, "Jackpot iris, Olympic jumper,
Prili has given you a duty.
Hara who freely changes the body of the dear child of the Accca people and him.
They get gifts.
Well then, you are disappointing.
Other Trojans are a honorable Heinman even if they do not drive.
Everyone will not die.
Right to kill. I think about what I think.
I refuse to send Earl's murderer.
Acicular's tears. Kill Achilles K-card and
Logo. It commits to death at the latest and commits a crime.
Come to all respected Hari Anne Horogie Googger and goofy."

You are winning to communicate her message.
She resounded at Plymouth's house and searched for sorrow.
For children,
Clothes felt with tears. No-in is
People with you,
Walking horse paralysis,
True earth. They are,
Although the house has died,
Murder by Arthur. Jove's employees are by Priam.
I tried to eradicate it. "Have a heart."
She said, "Dalanus's Plymouth child lives in the house, and the two do not
Hurt Her.
Please think about you. Me,
Jove's meshinger. Flight incompetence finger,
You and you are taken. The Olympic Games
Hata, and there is something to please.
Akkuresu. Troy dele beautiful garter Dooman.
Morua counts your Nodie and Forging, and
The city's noble Achilles tendon is its time. Protect you.
There is no fear of death, no one thinks. Joe tells the murderer of Argus.
I am conceited. You are the victim of the Achilles tendon, the Achilles tendon.
Hire someone else.

They all associate with John Grass Merman Judge.
Yes."

She communicates her feelings and her breasts make her feelings.
Prepare Nose Indian and embody the reason.
A big swing in bed. Please ignore it next time.
I was caught in the upper body seven faces and Miki.
He accused him of hekuba. "Anal," defendant, "Meguroger,
You get to each other and abdomen to geeks.
To prosecute my son who loves me.
Giving satisfaction to the Asia Pacific Islands. Or...
Promote passage of Achaeans
Excretion Gala."

Everyone circumcised loudly.
"Nega is always famous among struggling people.
Your incandescence? Are they inevitable?
The Achaeans, killing others will make your face.
Is not hemolysis? Brutal Yarman Yee.
With you, you have Zone Creation Zing. Hindrance.
We will blow up our house off Ohio.
I know that birthright sweet linefeed Kyogen.
That chest pain,
Do not forget him for anyone. I,
Achilles tendon ulcerative colitis.
You can not cross the border and cross the border.
Trojan and Troy girls."

It's already a Priamar. "I am.
Unfortunately in my house, you can move. You know?
I have a forerunner of anything.
Thin—I think.
Be careful. But this time, look at you and tell the face.
I told her. Number of seats,
Sorrow of Achaun's sorrow.
Achilles tendon matches.
I got lost on my mind."

There was a fever on your shoulder kick.
Yes. Also, 12 times outpatient, 12 carbon dioxide,
Process of hot one. I did not hear.
Golden enthusiasm and more big hole
Gamaku, and people in Trakore.

When you do it on behalf of you, you are very heavy.
But that is the only discrimination,
That child. Next, is anyone pursuing a Trojan
To the denominator's grass. "Outside. Numeric Slobo disgrace stop.
You are Na. Sadly in your house?
Is it dirty here? Small day Ini, son.
Saturn's sorrow praised the lining and sorrow.
Jazz? You are in proof at once. It will be greeted now.
You will die anymore. Nar intenser is in-store shop Halle.
Hades's house, boarra with my eyes.
City."

I made those people with my colleagues. And someone drifted along.
The man sang. Then I have to call you and dry.
Noble Agasson, Panamon, Antiphonus, Ciclehof Surgery,
Deiffobus, Hippos, Dius. This is nineless.
I'm saying, "Reply Ohara,
Do you have such a choice?
I asked him to dissolve me from Troy.
Royal Nestor, Trooper Sundial, Hairless Match, Hot.
It is your son's idea.
There is no other fire.
Put you in the hall / south room. A liar, a shining light, a light of an electron.
Your country's merriment,
Prepare not to disturb the most.
Do I always keep it at that time?"

You have food for children. They,
You wear an internal organs.
I can not go to bed for wagon. You refuse Norsey.
Madarin is lurking in the magazine frame.
Kochi goes first. Next, please read in York Band 11.
Please do not forget. I have united to anyone.
Make the tip of the balloon face up and make it perfect.
You will be the third rotation of the band.
Please do not forget that basis. Program,
Save body from warehouse.
Listen to your words and you will be officially decided. And who is Mezzda me.
Michen,
Priam has a nice present. But Plymouth wants to tell you.
The older brothers were retained for their own use.

That's why Prullam and his wife were delighted.
Heca makes you happy.
Her crime,
Before you. She can not say.
"Well, I'm going to father Jove.
If you fall in love with you, you will appeal.
With your raw water hand. Please be careful to you.
Let me tell you all Troy.
Your company was born,
All new is the most severe.
Surprise you with your eyes and believe in your eyes.
Danaans's. You can send Mather to you.
But you are a different thing for this transportation.
Argives."

Replied Priam, "You, I am a lover.
Get Jove. I will save you."

Well then, you will boil pure water.
My grandson and woman shop together. Meddling.
He is sorry for himself by himself, but then the drink is a barcode.
Anne Grande Death South,
Faces are floated. We say, "Jove bridge. Through the Aida, mostly
Glory and mercy and great greatness.
Tears of Achilles. Please straighten your quick messenger.
You will be strongest.
Every sandwich, I will not hurt.
Danaans's back."

Jove is trying to help him. Straight line
NASB. For you,
Baron Black Igle (Black Eagle) is rotten. Someone has
Officially positively positively overseas Lopezana conch.
Homemonial of adverb. That is you.
But that is you.
They got you the top. Orlada to Noain e Be san.
2 Previous, 2 Previous, 2 Previous, 2 Previous Procedure.
Birding window. Nodie before that glittering the figure.
Nail Dance Day Woman Da, such a thing.
Nopal harvested quickly Molua rotten horse.
I stop by behind my friends and cry.
Appeal the road of the dead. You,

In the city, for peace and sons and sneaky people, like this.
People who run away miss a day.

But please do not sacrifice the preface equally.
Watch a strange girl,
Then, remember him. "Water.
Please tell us your opinions and impressions: Create your own review.
Listen to you.
It will not appear to others in Achaeans.
You can search for his son Peleus."

It and commission, guide and guardian, Argos murder.
He is not here. He is a lover.
You and the sea breeze will come. He.
Please look at your eyes and try to seal.
Have him delight and make him delight.
To Health Fot. Boshikoku, high, sweet.
I'm fine Hay-Day and part time job.
Face.

When Priam and Idaeus passed the great destruction of Ilius,
Everyone remembers.
That dog ladder tonight, Idaeus saw
They have words at preschool. "You turn attention.
Daldanus; pose a problem here. Someone who loves me.
We are asking everyone. We will finish and come to the store.
Move the trunk.
We?"

"For the wicked one,
Nothing; now my head is going crazy beyond my head.
Also, however, taking the place, quasi-
To detonate by hand.
Men who are different from your lover.
Do you think that you are an enthusiastic companion?
Residents and sorry honey? Nobody knows them.
You are,
What are you? You turn yellowish more.
Be long enough to protect you. Get a knight,
Give you a dungeon. I am someone else.
Do not make you a father."

Pream answered, "You hear this word,
Please do not do anything.
Just watching Nurd. You are beautiful.
Please pursue this power with you.
Mom."

Next Argos guidelines Parents in, "Teacher, all
You were admonished. Yes. Reality.
This document can also be viewed in the following languages.
You are? Is robust Ilius obsolete?
There is no one you love.
Achaeans is your company?"

Priam said, "You are my friend, someone's father,
Your son said."

Guide guardian Ingles's murderer gave him.
"Boala. There are a lot of time.
I am surrounded by Morgor in Arjan.
Explore the back. We are surprised.
The son of Atleus and his father Achilles deprive us of our lives
Coldness. For myself, I,
Myrmidon, and his father's name is Polyctor.
You were wise. Or, I am the 12th.
We have killed you. Me,
This time it was even. On New Wallide,
Achanges crosses the border and abuts the border. You will not get into a mess.
You are a friend, I am waiting."

It is a preamer. "Negative Achilles Female Files.
Peleus's now, please do not forget the truth in all. My son,
Achilles is protecting his feet with Sadge."

"Arthur's," murderer replied.
"It is monopoly unnecessary food.
In addition to the Achilles cosmic ray. Now 12 years
Still, the body is not wasted and hungry.
Eat cooking. I can live.
Brutal love for his dear comrade's warrior.
Heir. To you, and, please, make it an eagle.
All cases will end.
A lot of people exploded in the window. I forged an abdominal ulcer.
Throw your son by your will and sacrifice God."

That person placed you on the top. "Uchiko, boarra.
Sacrifice people who dislike corruption. E...
Please do not forget you.
Olympic Games, and now we are seeking to kill him for you. Washing with water,
Internal medicine. Guide help for heaven's help even if you help,
From when to my long-length son of Peleus."

Argon, guide and guardian's slayer answered, "Teacher, you are
Decadent, hurt me. But it works.
What you know is not your knowledge.
Do not forget me a lot.
Please dance next time. I have your guidelines.
Argos himself and ocean or flesh you interfere with George Stop,
No one can take that person's light.
With you."

The soldier attacked the next one who was taking a fortune.
"Fertilizer and high lipid are no and can not be denied formally.
Anyways,
You are.
There are many Argos's clever foods. Well then, I will try to guess it.
We sent you a Priam,
It is in Ohio.
Myleidons is the son of Peleus's son Peleus who kills Kobayashi.
I admire you. Is someone disturbing you?
I criticized the pool in a flat shop and asked for it.
You hugged with a lot of money and took a big mommy.
Together with many people. The sentence thrust in the Kosugi Lin forest.
People pushed at that place,
Hot writing makes Achilles confusing.
I listen to the voice of the old man.
Peleus's son had it. Then,
Teacher, I am forever.
McCrea, according to you. Death Inner Father calls Nurse Hoy Hawaiela.
Change the expression of a loved one.
I could not believe it.
Performance. Do not forget that massacre.
Dad, familiar mother, and that is the son's death battle. You.
Delft."

It is like Jerolaus. Pream it.
Place his car in front of him on earth and save him.
No and no no no is Yabari.

Standard Achilles tendon that Novosa loves. That's it.
Everyone called us on that street: 2 people honestly, Automedon,
Senior Citizen's Day Alkimus (Alcimus) told herself Battrada.
People, I ate a meal. Table.
Follow it. Mr. Purim put a heartache into beige.
It will beat infinity even if I get up Achilles tendon.
Someone sacrifices much.

How a cruel one man dies.
You can receive your own protection.
On this remote land, and wiser things are wise.
I was surprised at Priam. Other people love you.
Priam also said to Aishua, "Please consider your father.
Achilles is a new generation, but it is sad for me.
Statement of no. People in the vicinity.
There is no one who takes care of that person's war and destruction. But,
Pleasure, distractions, we are full of loads.
I think he wants his dear son with him.
But I am a miserable person. I thank Troy for me.
Unfortunately, I recruited fifty children.
Achairs is here. Were they sunny 19?
There are other women at home. Greater than
They are the People's Republic of China.
There is left, city, our water mover.
You can not approach. You are still in Acca on the person's back.
Large body mass will save you for you. Two people, Achilles,
The field of heaven; your father is moving thinking.
Are you more sweet? Please do not strengthen yourself.
The man is still determined to be intense even now,
I got in the hands of a person who killed my son."

The heart of Achilles has robbed someone who is thinking.
Father's. You can follow your hand.
They are worried—Priam heard about Achilles tendon seizures.
You and Achilles, this time to get Pat Roxie,
In that house is filled with sorrow. Yes,
Now there is Sago in sugar.
Please do not forget your sorrow.
Everyone said that, "Unlucky man, yes.
It really confronted. How do you get crowded with a venture company?
It is your child who is striking your abdomen.
A lot of your forgiven descendants? Enter the Hall of Fame. I will go next time.
To devote our sorrow to us,

We are useless. There is no potato injury.
Calling a man is filled with a lot of sorrow. George's gravitational field.
There is nothing there.
With good people. Master of the world,
Let's go now. But he,
Jove sends you a message.
Listening to the voice of the great corruption,
And looking at the face of the earth, John Gordon.
Shinsei Boys, Peleus was recruited. New star ideoid.
Everyone has a good feeling
Myrmidons to help everyone, and refically.
Well then, she greeted her girls. In that case,
Is Heaven immovable? There is no disease of the royal family.
His father's son,
I,
Troy mysterized you. You.
Ooprillam masturbation. Yup.
Everyone permits descendant boo and bath.
At the northern end of Lesbos there is a wider area of Makka (Makar), more
Of Phrygia.
Inland, and its great health.
Those who live in the sky swear you to run war and runaway.
Please advance your city. It is by itself.
It does not lead to sorrow. Nega Harrier Swell.
Merciless son, you are such a rich man. You ask.
Let's live another sorrow."

Replied Priam, "King, the head sitting and sitting.
Your singles will not tell a lie.
When you pray, please listen to it soon.
That's it. Distance with the body and self position.
Please pray for safety and refuse your report.
Light of the sun."

Achilles tendon is not more abnormal.
"We, we, daughter.
The old age of the sea is Jove.
For you. You are a plan, you will not be mysterious,
What god is it?
However, no one has stepped in.
It shows us the boundary.
Easier; more delusive.

The word of Jove will not hurt you.
Indwelling."

I will hand it that nice again. Next, son of Peleus,
Refuse conspirators, it is not confused.
Automedon and Alcimus are even closer.
There is more heterosexuality than Pablo Closse. This,
It was horseback riding with ancestral agent of Prajam.
In the home. Enhance your body.
Distorted. Great wrecking many mantles and good shirts. Duckless,
He is a date. Swing.
They are opposed to lawyers and careless people.
Then, it is the fact before the preceding.
They are,
And did you kill that person,
Jove? Purify your body and get rotten.
Beware of process shirt and mantle. In Asian countries,
Then, the marriage with those people will be as follows. That
It is a miserable loud sound.
"I will tell you.
You have money.
You have no worthy facts."

Achilles tendon collects even if it fires again.
A lover.
A plum sits. I said, "Sensei,
Your son still admires them.
You are placed aside by yourself. Current one.
Our meals are prepared. A nice little monster Niobe tries to get food.
Her 12 children — a 6-year-old man and 6.
All of her will die. Apollo strikes children.
Give you vitality, massacre the Daiwana.
Niobe decided to return Leto. She is seeking a daimyo by Lett.
Children only, ask the product.
Many. You are lying on a welterweight.
I inscribe Saturn's sons on a stone.
However,
Next, niobium can be eaten. Where are they?
Alipis (Sipylus),
Acerase strong acid.
I sent an empty hand to her.
Hoping. You heard about you.

When I passed with you (Ilius),
Shed tears and shed tears."

Well then, you can walk.
Please do not forget about him.
You are
Loading Automedon.
Put bread in the place where it is being processed,
I treated the meat and did a good step.
I agree. They are,
Priam, descendants of Dardanus, strength and alphabet strength.
The appearance of the Achilles tendon is mysterious.
Priam listens to the voice and makes royalty a noble entity. Anytime
You are Priam. "Now King,
We will go home to protect your house.
Mara closed my eyes for only one day.
Please take care of your life. I crush and enjoy the rest of my life.
Inside the stable Mad's truth, silent,
Sorrow. If you eat bread now, you drink wine. Until then,
I do not eat."

That is what your life and girls have prepared for.
In that house, enough red Windsor.
It is standing on it.
Priam and Idaeus have a mouth. I really dislike it.
And we prepared by two people. No, yes, thank you.
Prima, "Dear Father, Thrius,
Please do your best in order to have you help.
I will reply to Akan note in the language of Yaya flight here.
Excellent intermediary transmission delay. Release it now.
Say the truth. In the ceremony ceremony,
Virtuous awareness of a man? Signs in war
Suppress host."

"You overwhelm the noble son.
It's all square. I apologize. You,
How is our city? We are waiting for you.
The mountains, the forests, and people are two heavy mountainous areas. The 9th,
In my house, is my father SUPAHAKA? We starve to death.
Pay tribute to your art. Hot blood.
Also, when layered on top,
We need, we need."

The Achilles heel replied. "You are Priml.
I got a name. Ozzara I know our struggle."

Let's get the hand of the palm of the hand with a tone.
This is because that Priam and his child are
The ego, Achilles tendon is on the eve of the night.
From home, I went with Briseis.

And now, both nova and Philisjam are alive.
In the evening, however, it mixes a lot and we are meeting.
You can think about anything. Prajam,
Strong, strong, strong, strong.
Sentinel. I aimed at the head of Priam. "Teacher,
Akiretea has none of them to save your life.
Kids from actively two people. You are,
Emphasize your body. Let's try it.
A friend,
Please challenge you. Moreover,
Other acacias learned about your existence."

No, you treasure you.
What is disease?
Everyone can not recognize the same thing. Nobody is here.
Immortal Job (Jove), Xanthus Ford, McGuire are away.
Takanori Dootagasa Frankie is Inagaki Inagaki.
All. Priam and Idaeus are as follows.
Please put the voice of God. Jesus.
Men's way woman Kind Relay From Golden's Venus to a Bottunday from a surfer.
To Pergamus, he made friends with her best friend, her.
Prince of the city with Hynne Im Guwart. The next girl,
I love you.
"The Iroyans, men and women, and
Geek. Vivera
Now living, now the sight of our city.
We all back."

In this city, men are women.
Contacted. I know about you,
Body. Oxford University,
That person got a wagon.
Urucom while hearing the crowd. You still have it.
Gender, listen to cry and pursue livelong day.
I did not tell him to PRIAM EAGER GIRL.

"You are the one who girls no.
You should follow aquatic life."

You are silent. Anytime
Bring your body to hell with your own additional home.
Sitting people Les Mrs. let's fly tears, it is a woman, it joins with this.
With that person's sorrow. Androsache,
She grabbed Hector's head and shouted.
Pon. "Nanping." She is the Kaorudo, "You have died and died.
Minkin from your house; Are we a disabled person?
Just eye cup, in my case the lower person has this odd number of lethality. You are.
Our city is a fierce challenge.
Kyushu people, Kyushu, Kyushu,
And children. Our women,
I am a couple. You are me.
Unfortunately we can not take a vacation.
We are everywhere.
Hector is a victim. Oota water,
Eating in the palm of your hand, in your hands.
I regretted. Where are you? If it's you.
Left, Ohta, I do not express words to your mother Sadness and sorrow.
Are you trying to explode your puzzle?
Even if you keep silent, you do not have mala.
Tears in the Supper."

For Achilles when he dismissed me from the ships gave me his word.
She sounds disruptive. The woman joined her love.
She is troublesome for Via tension by Hecuba. "Otto." She collapsed.
"I love everything.
I like you very much. There, it is not indifferent.
When your influential kids date
Samos Inbruz (Samos Inburusu) or rough Remus (Lemnos), you,
Please kill you. I know about you a lot of times.
Trying to go his life -
But here everything is heresy and Apollon is the same.
A shaft without pain."

So, is she so attractive?
Helen admires your tension. "Ottle,"
She said. "All molds Middle class is heavy, please come to Alexander.
Golden Troy Rodrigo Four? Ask me
About 20 years ago,
The only insanity to dry the sea is unfortunate.

You. When you dance with others,
To you,
I think that Priam is my own father.
Please check the sentences and the phrases of charity and approval. Therefore,
My eyes are not harmful. I do not understand.
I do not have a kind Trojan horse.
Who are you?"

She tells her one mother to her.
Her love is confluence. King Prullam is also with you. "Recovery farts.
Please help Mappon trade in trees, O Trojans, cities, and Argails.
There is the Achilles heel.
We robbed our feelings."

I abused Noosa in the same way as last time.
City. On 9th, if you explode big,
From morning till night, when graduating other things,
Try to hold the body in the mountain at that time.
Fire. The next morning at the eye / life of the veil light's new wing,
People will work again.
A huge door. I was with you.
Involuntary breath. Throw away the wine and the next brother.
I can glimmer more white chalky eyes.
Orange gray gray.
Kadan who leaves uselessly.
Together. Next to serve him and serve a polka dots of polka dots.
Achanges attacks in all aspects.
The last stage. I am fine.
Well well, Moasat.
Plymouth's house.

And yet, I confessed my brother's words.

THE END

ACKNOWLEDGMENTS

I would like to thank the following people: Craig Dworkin, whose amazing Foreword managed, in just a few pages, to catapult this project to a whole different plane; Doug Clouse, who designed a book far more handsome and elegant than I had any right to hope for; Ron Clouse, whose good humor and sage advice helped me through every step of this process; and Karen C. Kelly, for her stellar editing of the Foreword and the Introduction (but *mostly* the Introduction).

Finally I wish to thank my wife, Laura, to whom this book is dedicated. Whether it's this book or any other project I've ever been involved in, she is never less than 100 percent supportive. For that (and many other things), she has my eternal love and gratitude.

Michael Klauke

ILLUSTRATIONS

The illustrations in this book and
on the cover are details of engravings
that were based on illustrations of
the Iliad done by the British artist
John Flaxman in 1793.

DESIGN

Doug Clouse, New York City, 2019

TYPEFACES

Albertus, designed by Berthold Wolpe
in 1932–1940, for Monotype

DTL Documenta, designed by
Frank Blokland, beginning in 1986,
for the Dutch Type Library

PRINTING

Printed on demand at various sites

Made in the USA
Lexington, KY
01 December 2019